THE TROOP

"IT'S GRITTY, IT'S DARK... AN ENTERTAINING READ."
COMIC BASTARDS

"EVERY BEAT IS MASTERFULLY DONE... A VERY
STRONG FIRST ISSUE AND DEFINITELY WORTH
THE READ. "
SUPER HERO SPEAK

"ENGAGING AND HORRIFYING AND ENTERTAINING
ALL AT THE SAME TIME."
NEED TO CONSUME

"AN ABSOLUTE CLASS ACT."
THE BOOK, THE FILM, THE T-SHIRT

"ABSOLUTELY FANTASTIC... A HIGHLY INTRIGUING
TALE OF DANGER AND VIOLENCE."
GRAPHIC POLICY

"IF YOU LIKE YOUR COMICS A LITTLE ON THE ADULT
SIDE, WITH EXCEPTIONAL WRITING AND ART, YOU'VE
COME TO THE RIGHT PLACE."
NERDLY

THE TROOP

ISBN: 9781782761884

Published by Titan Comics
A division of Titan Publishing Group Ltd.
144 Southwark St.
London
SE1 0UP

A CIP catalogue record for this title is available from the British Library.

First edition: October 2016.

10 9 8 7 6 5 4 3 2 1

Printed in China.
Titan Comics. TC0426

TITAN COMICS

EDITOR STEVE WHITE
DESIGNER ROB FARMER

Senior Comics Editor Andrew James

Titan Comics Editorial
Lizzie Kaye, Tom Williams, Jessica Burton, Lauren McPhee, Amoona Saohin

Production Supervisors Jackie Flook, Maria Pearson

Production Assistant Peter James

Production Controller Obi Onuora

Art Director Oz Browne

Senior Sales Manager Steve Tothill

Press Officer Will O'Mullane

Senior Marketing & Press Officer Owen Johnson

Direct Sales / Marketing Manager Ricky Claydon

Commercial Manager Michelle Fairlamb

Publishing Manager Darryl Tothill

Publishing Director Chris Teather

Operations Director Leigh Baulch

Executive Director Vivian Cheung

Publisher Nick Landau

WWW.TITAN-COMICS.COM

Become a fan on **Facebook.com/comicstitan**

Follow us on Twitter
@ComicsTitan

THE TROOP

WRITER
NOEL CLARKE

ART
JOSHUA CASSARA

COLORS
LUIS GUERRERO

LETTERS
ROB STEEN

Titan
COMICS

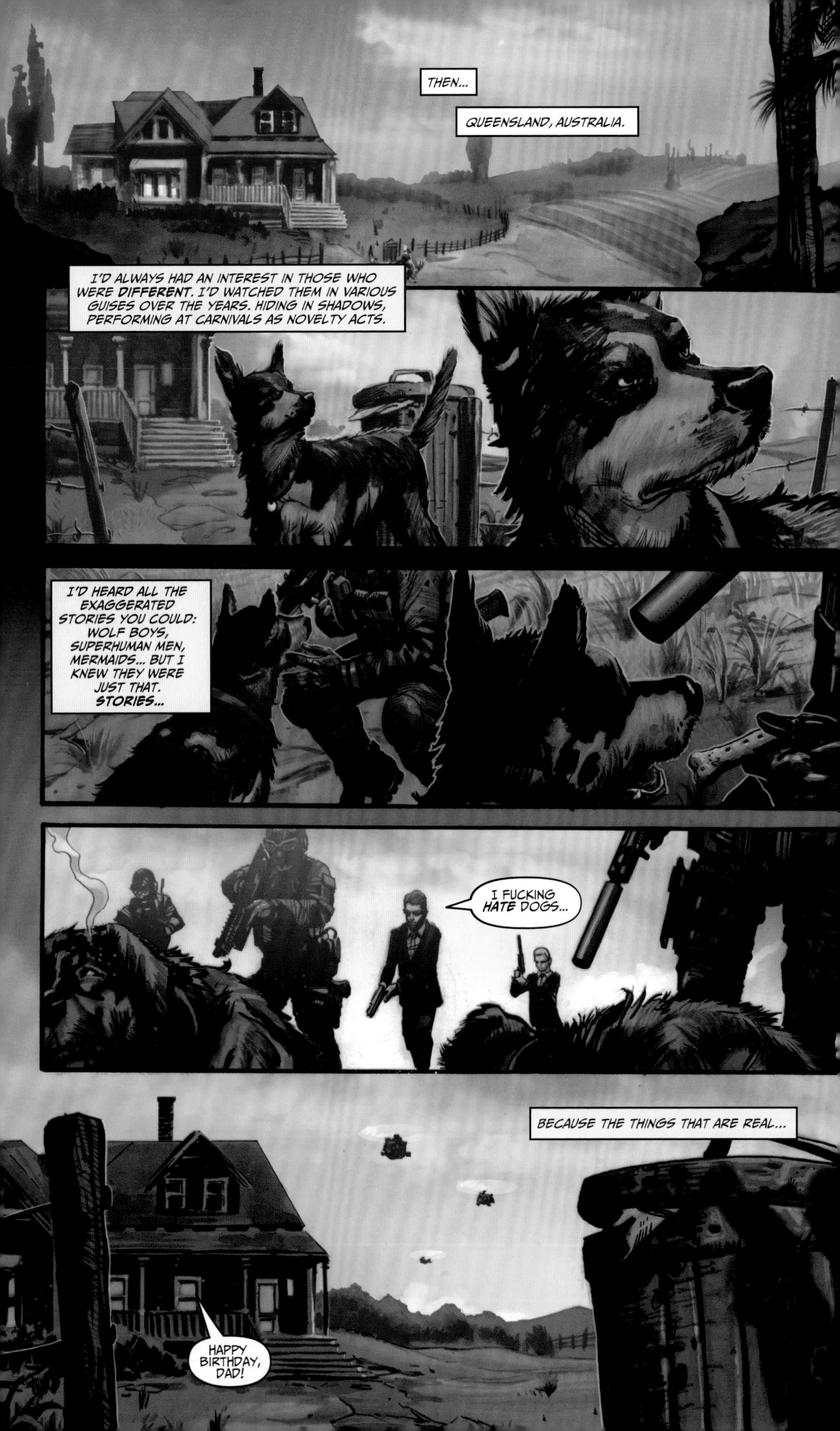
THEN...
QUEENSLAND, AUSTRALIA.
I'D ALWAYS HAD AN INTEREST IN THOSE WHO WERE DIFFERENT. I'D WATCHED THEM IN VARIOUS GUISES OVER THE YEARS. HIDING IN SHADOWS, PERFORMING AT CARNIVALS AS NOVELTY ACTS.
I'D HEARD ALL THE EXAGGERATED STORIES YOU COULD: WOLF BOYS, SUPERHUMAN MEN, MERMAIDS... BUT I KNEW THEY WERE JUST THAT. STORIES...
I FUCKING HATE DOGS...
BECAUSE THE THINGS THAT ARE REAL...
HAPPY BIRTHDAY, DAD!

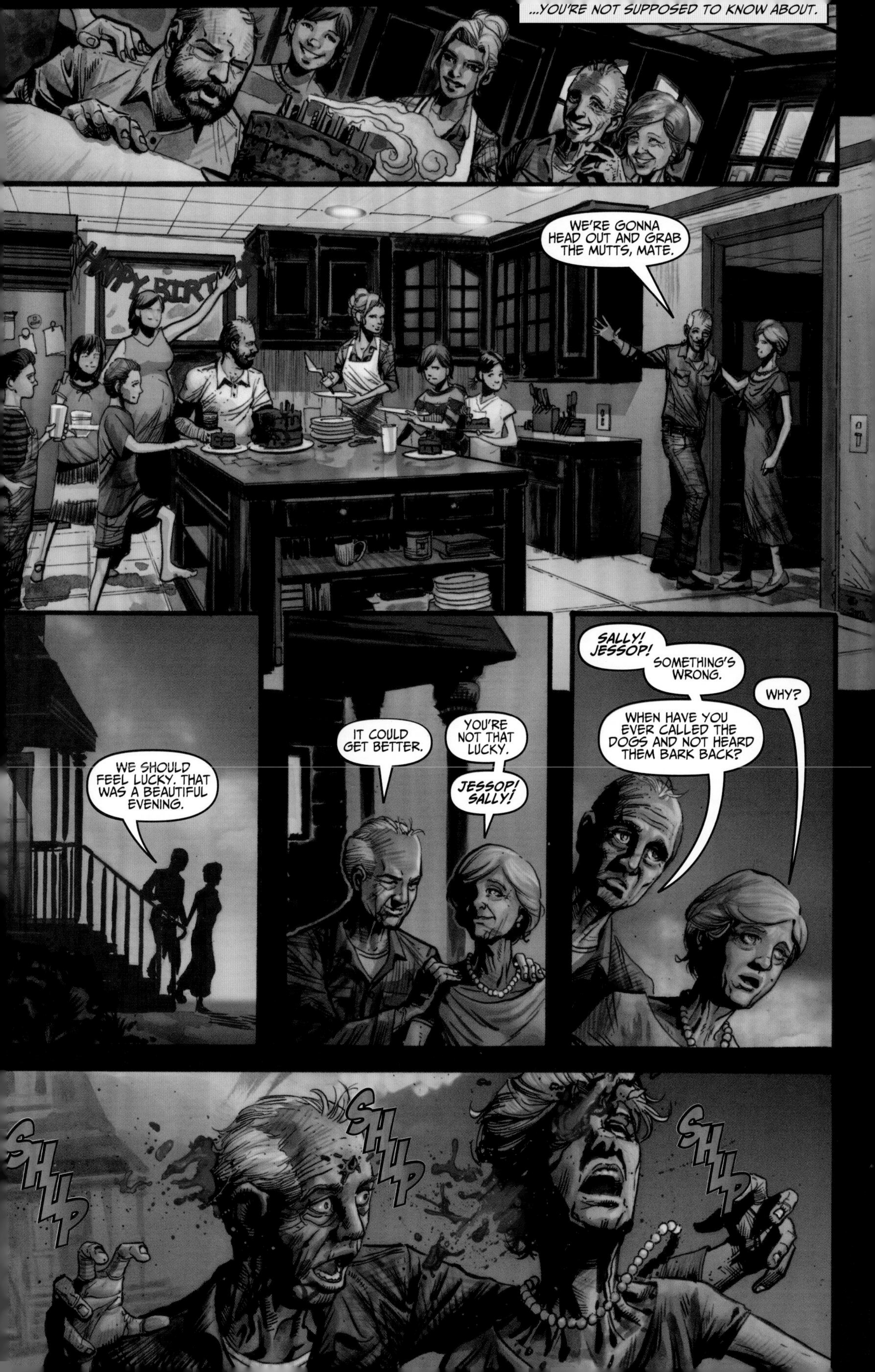
...YOU'RE NOT SUPPOSED TO KNOW ABOUT.
WE'RE GONNA HEAD OUT AND GRAB THE MUTTS, MATE.
WE SHOULD FEEL LUCKY. THAT WAS A BEAUTIFUL EVENING.
IT COULD GET BETTER.
YOU'RE NOT THAT LUCKY.
JESSOP! SALLY!
SALLY! JESSOP!
SOMETHING'S WRONG.
WHY?
WHEN HAVE YOU EVER CALLED THE DOGS AND NOT HEARD THEM BARK BACK?
SHUP
SHUP
SHUP

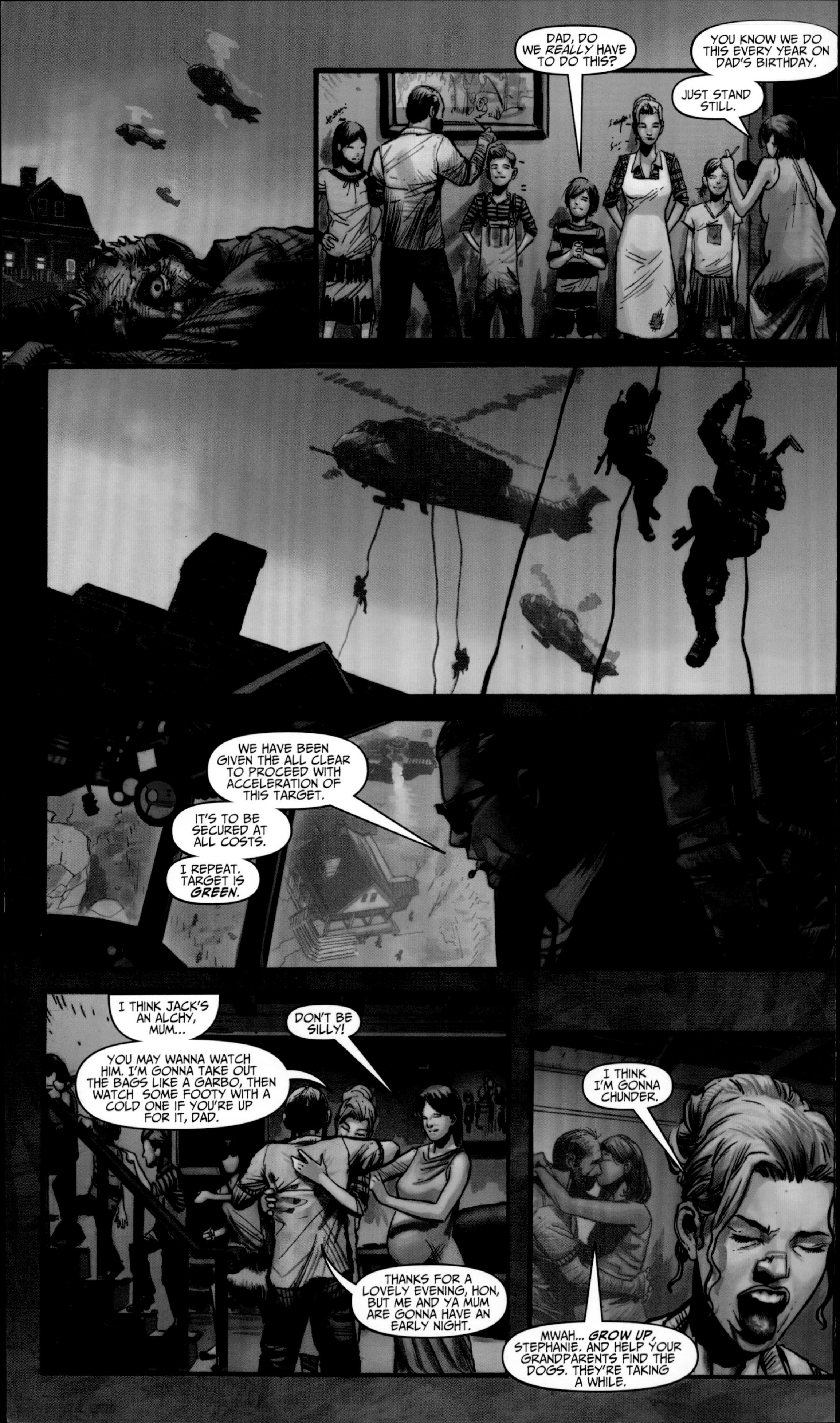

DAD, DO WE *REALLY* HAVE TO DO THIS?
YOU KNOW WE DO THIS EVERY YEAR ON DAD'S BIRTHDAY.
JUST STAND STILL.
WE HAVE BEEN GIVEN THE ALL CLEAR TO PROCEED WITH ACCELERATION OF THIS TARGET.
IT'S TO BE SECURED AT ALL COSTS.
I REPEAT. TARGET IS ***GREEN.***
I THINK JACK'S AN ALCHY, MUM...
DON'T BE SILLY!
YOU MAY WANNA WATCH HIM. I'M GONNA TAKE OUT THE BAGS LIKE A GARBO, THEN WATCH SOME FOOTY WITH A COLD ONE IF YOU'RE UP FOR IT, DAD.
THANKS FOR A LOVELY EVENING, HON, BUT ME AND YA MUM ARE GONNA HAVE AN EARLY NIGHT.
I THINK I'M GONNA CHUNDER.
MWAH... ***GROW UP,*** STEPHANIE. AND HELP YOUR GRANDPARENTS FIND THE DOGS. THEY'RE TAKING A WHILE.

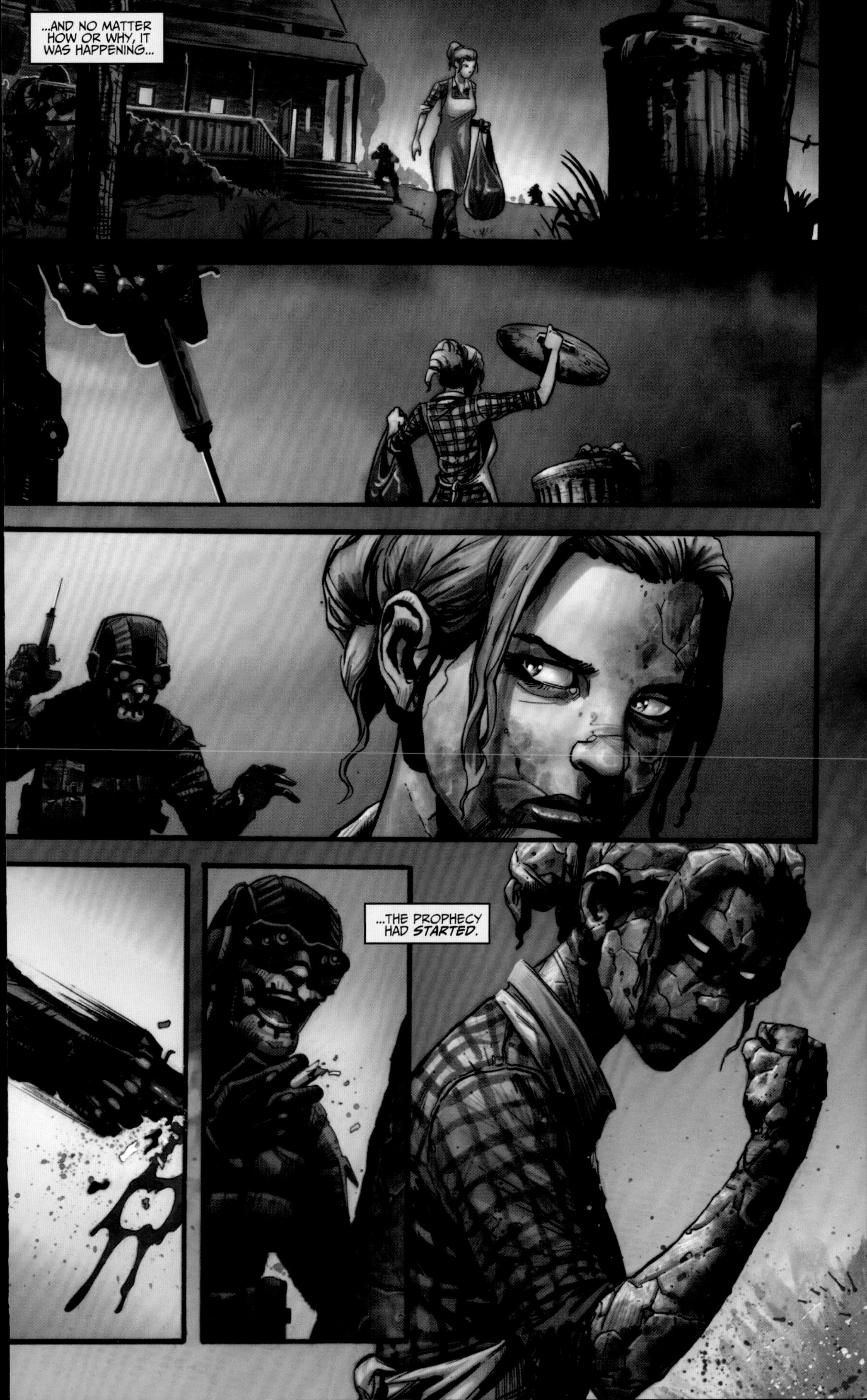
...AND NO MATTER HOW OR WHY, IT WAS HAPPENING...
...THE PROPHECY HAD *STARTED*.

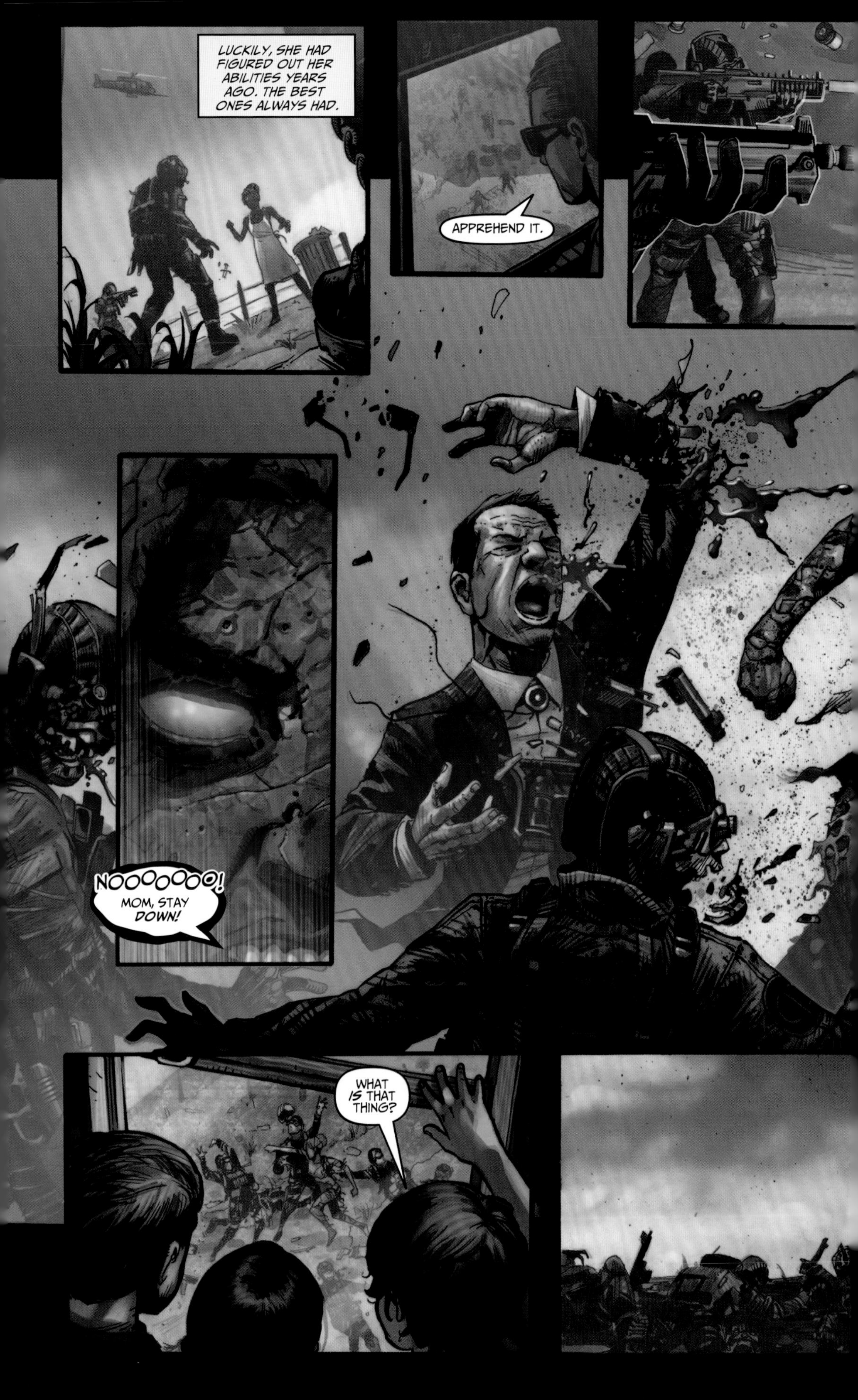
LUCKILY, SHE HAD FIGURED OUT HER ABILITIES YEARS AGO. THE BEST ONES ALWAYS HAD.
APPREHEND IT.
NOOOOOOOO! MOM, STAY DOWN!
WHAT IS THAT THING?

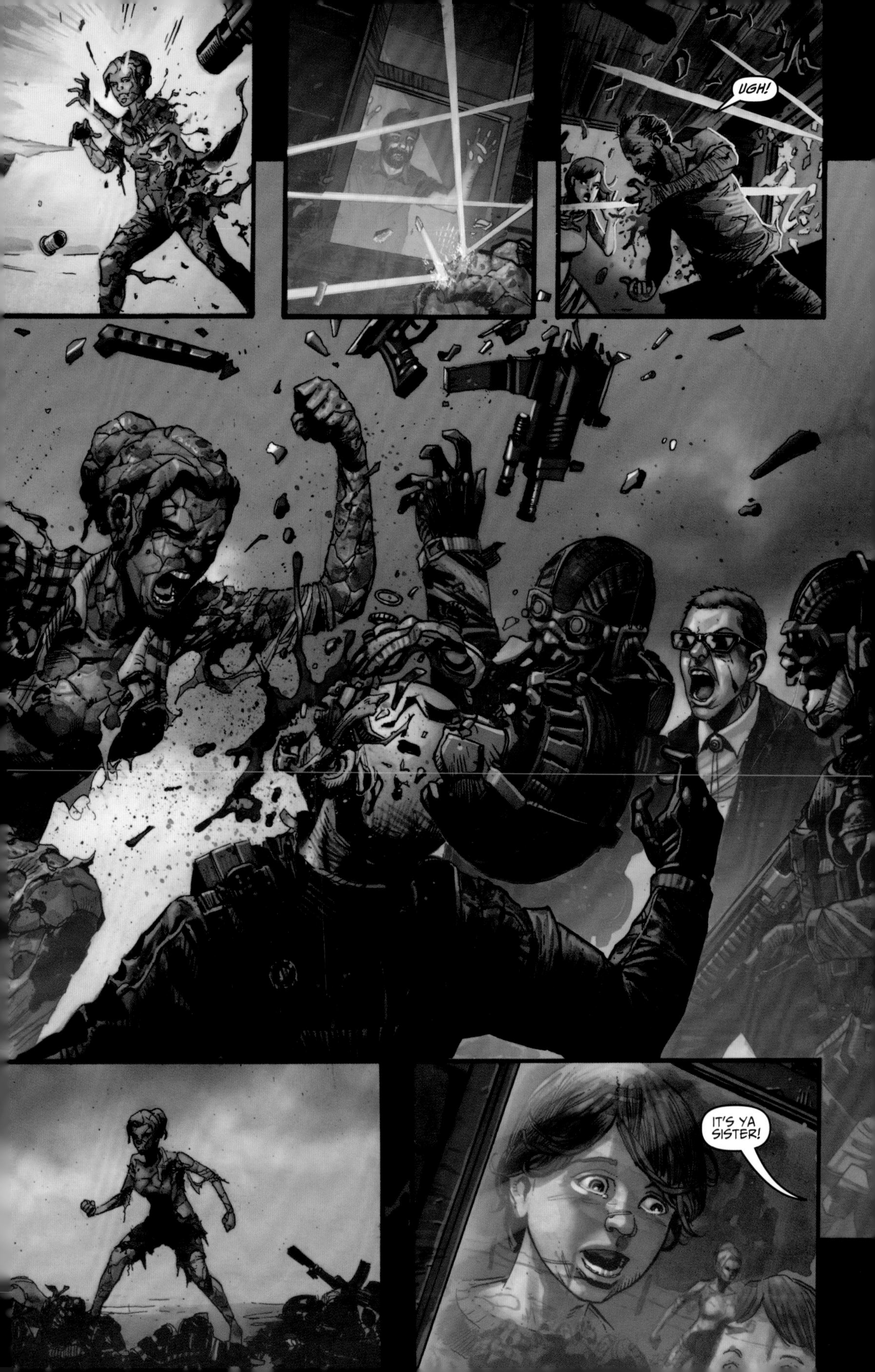
UGH!
IT'S YA SISTER!

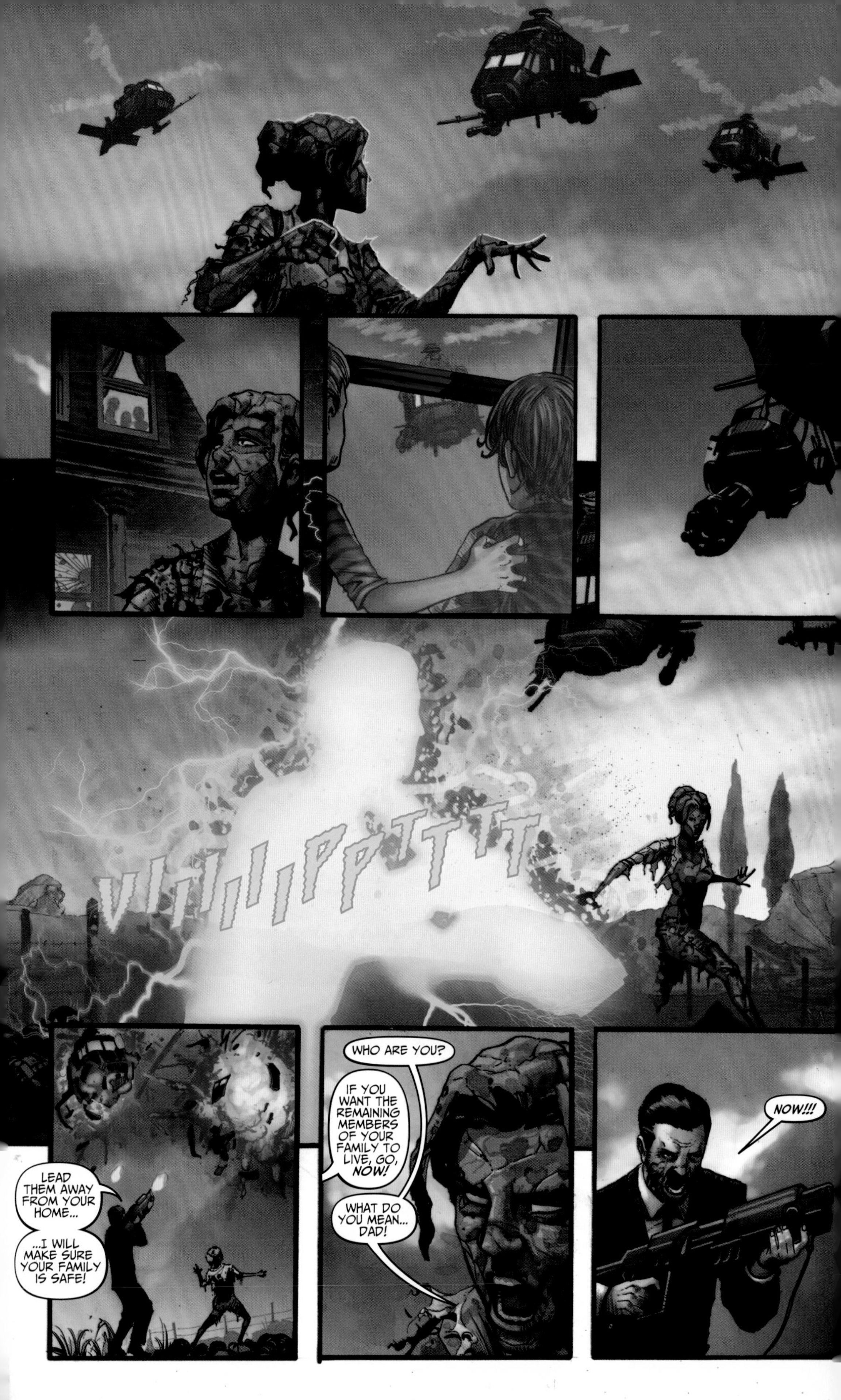
VIIIIIPPTTTT
LEAD THEM AWAY FROM YOUR HOME...
...I WILL MAKE SURE YOUR FAMILY IS SAFE!
WHO ARE YOU?
IF YOU WANT THE REMAINING MEMBERS OF YOUR FAMILY TO LIVE, GO, NOW!
WHAT DO YOU MEAN... DAD!
NOW!!!

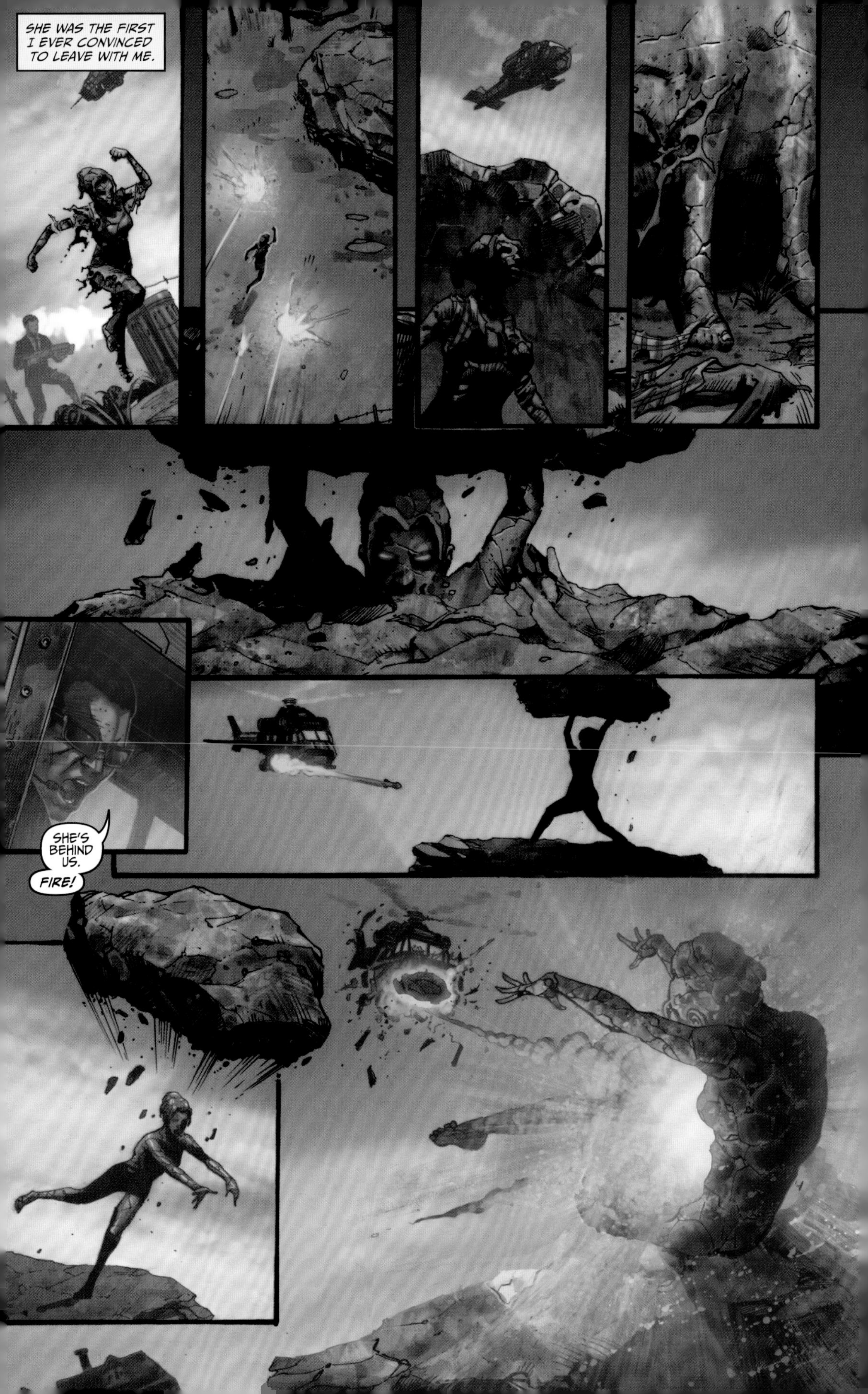
SHE WAS THE FIRST I EVER CONVINCED TO LEAVE WITH ME.
SHE'S BEHIND US. FIRE!

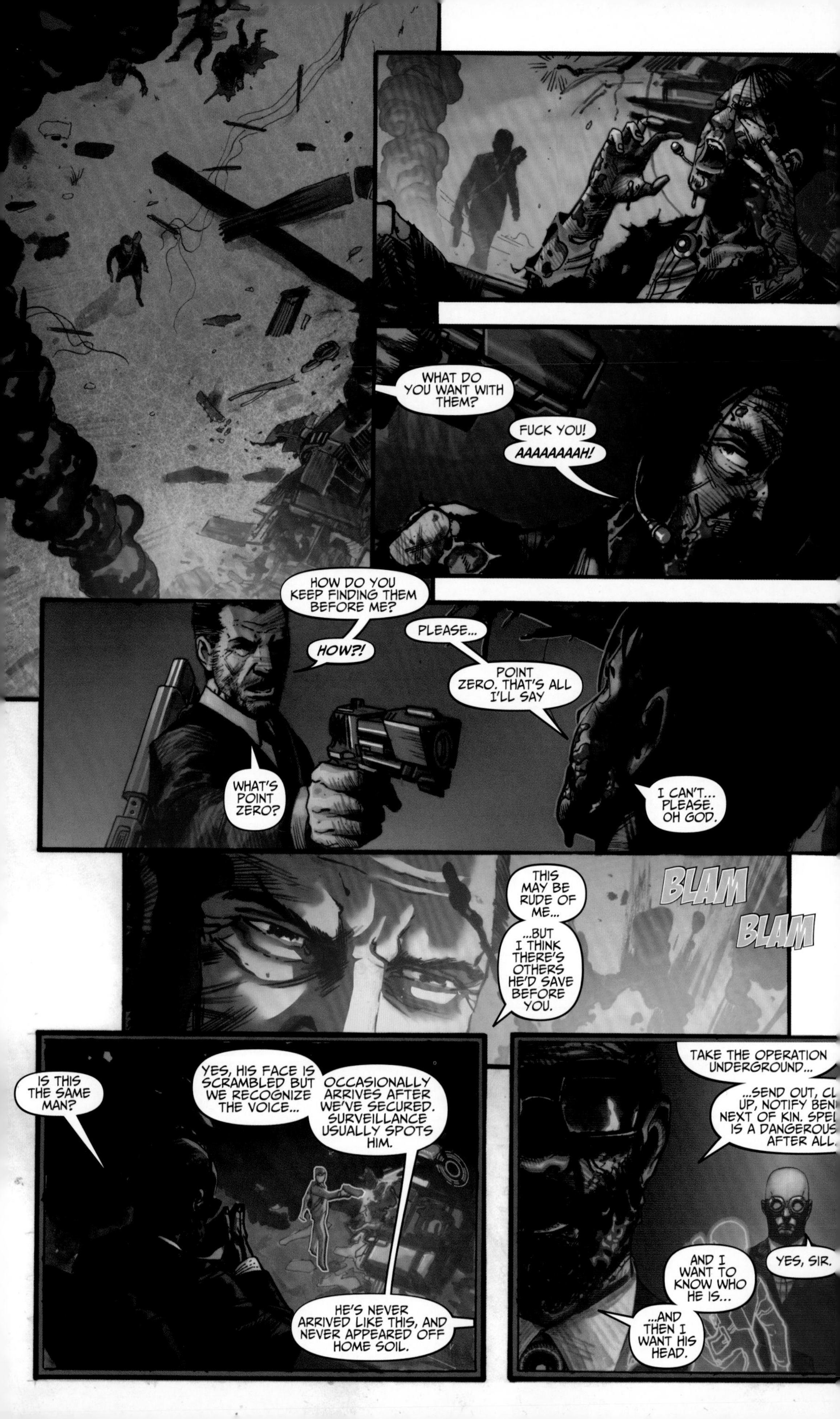
WHAT DO YOU WANT WITH THEM?
FUCK YOU!
AAAAAAAAH!
HOW DO YOU KEEP FINDING THEM BEFORE ME?
HOW?!
PLEASE...
POINT ZERO. THAT'S ALL I'LL SAY
WHAT'S POINT ZERO?
I CAN'T... PLEASE. OH GOD.
BLAM
BLAM
THIS MAY BE RUDE OF ME...
...BUT I THINK THERE'S OTHERS HE'D SAVE BEFORE YOU.
IS THIS THE SAME MAN?
YES, HIS FACE IS SCRAMBLED BUT WE RECOGNIZE THE VOICE...
OCCASIONALLY ARRIVES AFTER WE'VE SECURED. SURVEILLANCE USUALLY SPOTS HIM.
HE'S NEVER ARRIVED LIKE THIS, AND NEVER APPEARED OFF HOME SOIL.
TAKE THE OPERATION UNDERGROUND...
YES, SIR.
AND I WANT TO KNOW WHO HE IS...
...AND THEN I WANT HIS HEAD.

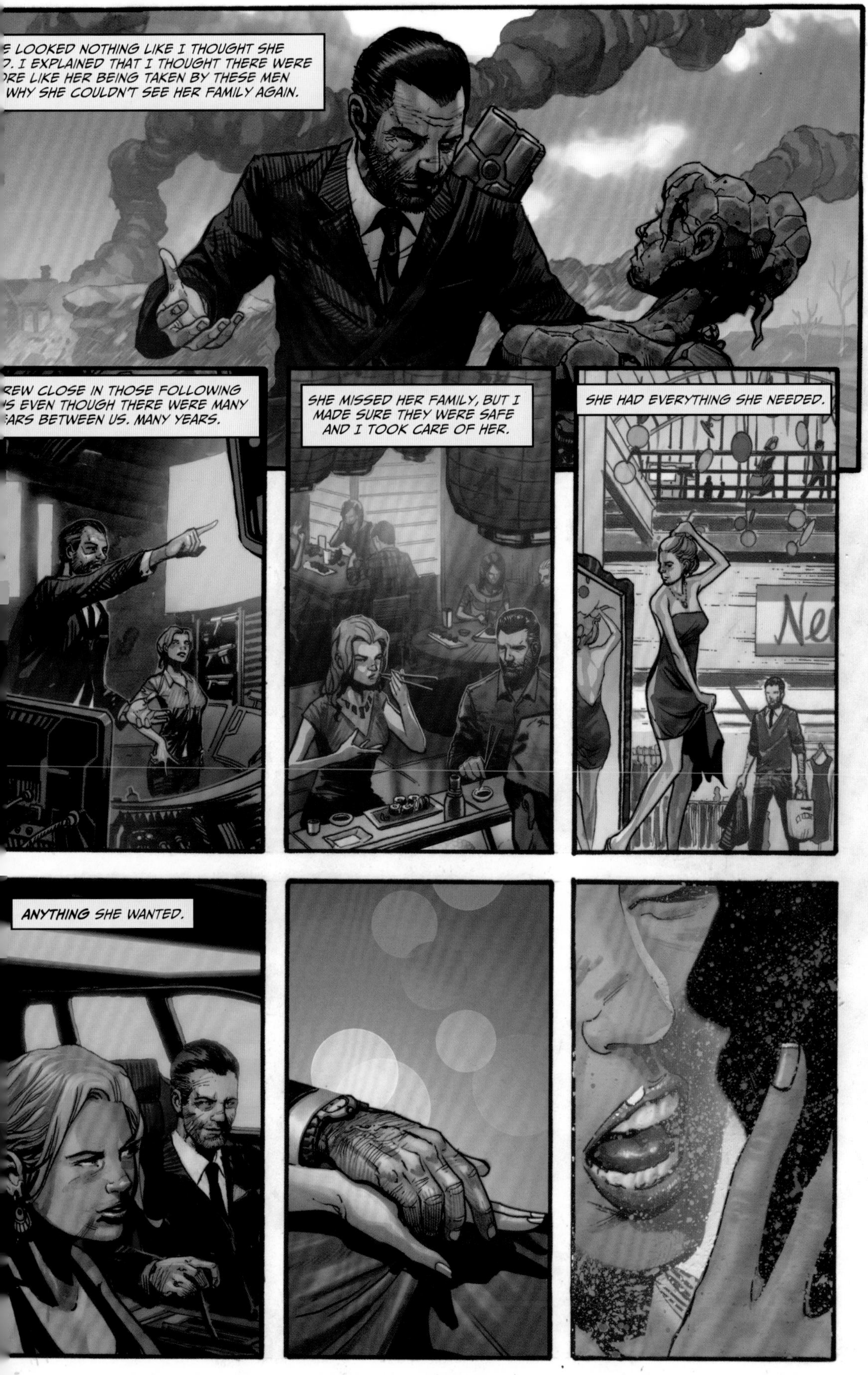
E LOOKED NOTHING LIKE I THOUGHT SHE
D. I EXPLAINED THAT I THOUGHT THERE WERE
ORE LIKE HER BEING TAKEN BY THESE MEN
WHY SHE COULDN'T SEE HER FAMILY AGAIN.
REW CLOSE IN THOSE FOLLOWING
S EVEN THOUGH THERE WERE MANY
EARS BETWEEN US. MANY YEARS.
SHE MISSED HER FAMILY, BUT I MADE SURE THEY WERE SAFE AND I TOOK CARE OF HER.
SHE HAD EVERYTHING SHE NEEDED.
ANYTHING SHE WANTED.

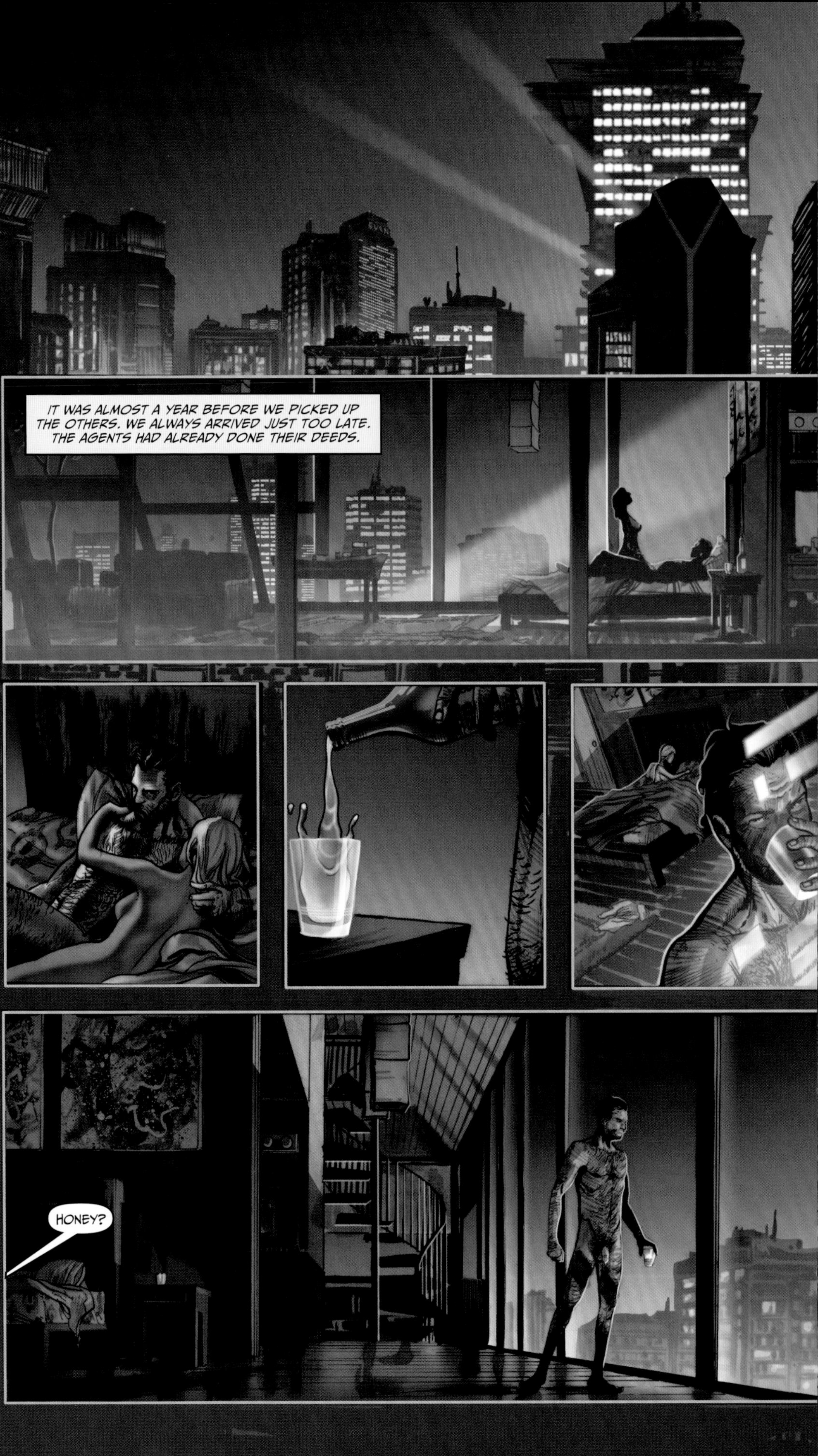
IT WAS ALMOST A YEAR BEFORE WE PICKED UP THE OTHERS. WE ALWAYS ARRIVED JUST TOO LATE. THE AGENTS HAD ALREADY DONE THEIR DEEDS.
HONEY?

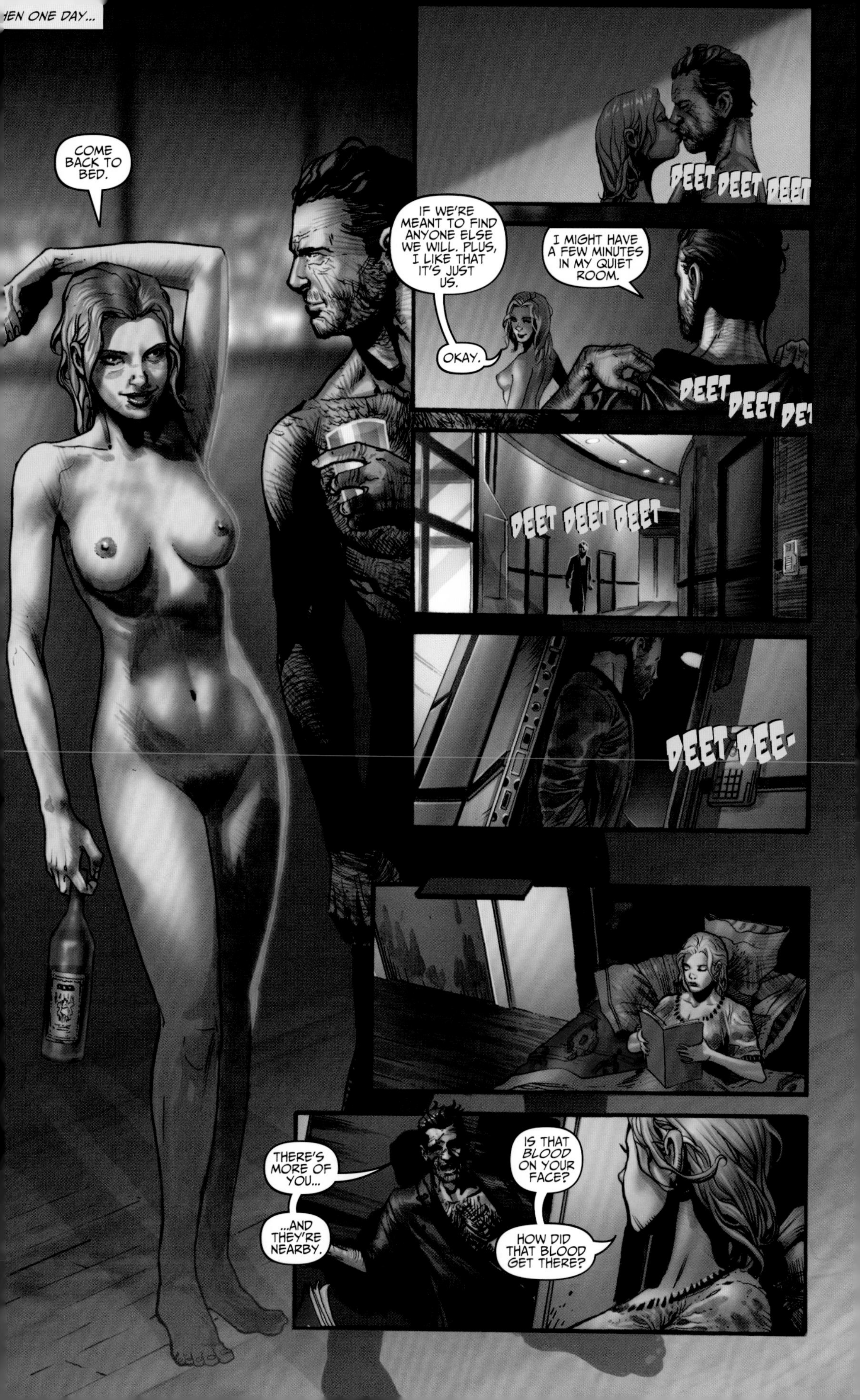

HEN ONE DAY...
COME BACK TO BED.
DEET DEET DEET
IF WE'RE MEANT TO FIND ANYONE ELSE WE WILL. PLUS, I LIKE THAT IT'S JUST US.
OKAY.
I MIGHT HAVE A FEW MINUTES IN MY QUIET ROOM.
DEET DEET DET
DEET DEET DEET
DEET DEE-
THERE'S MORE OF YOU...
...AND THEY'RE NEARBY.
IS THAT BLOOD ON YOUR FACE?
HOW DID THAT BLOOD GET THERE?

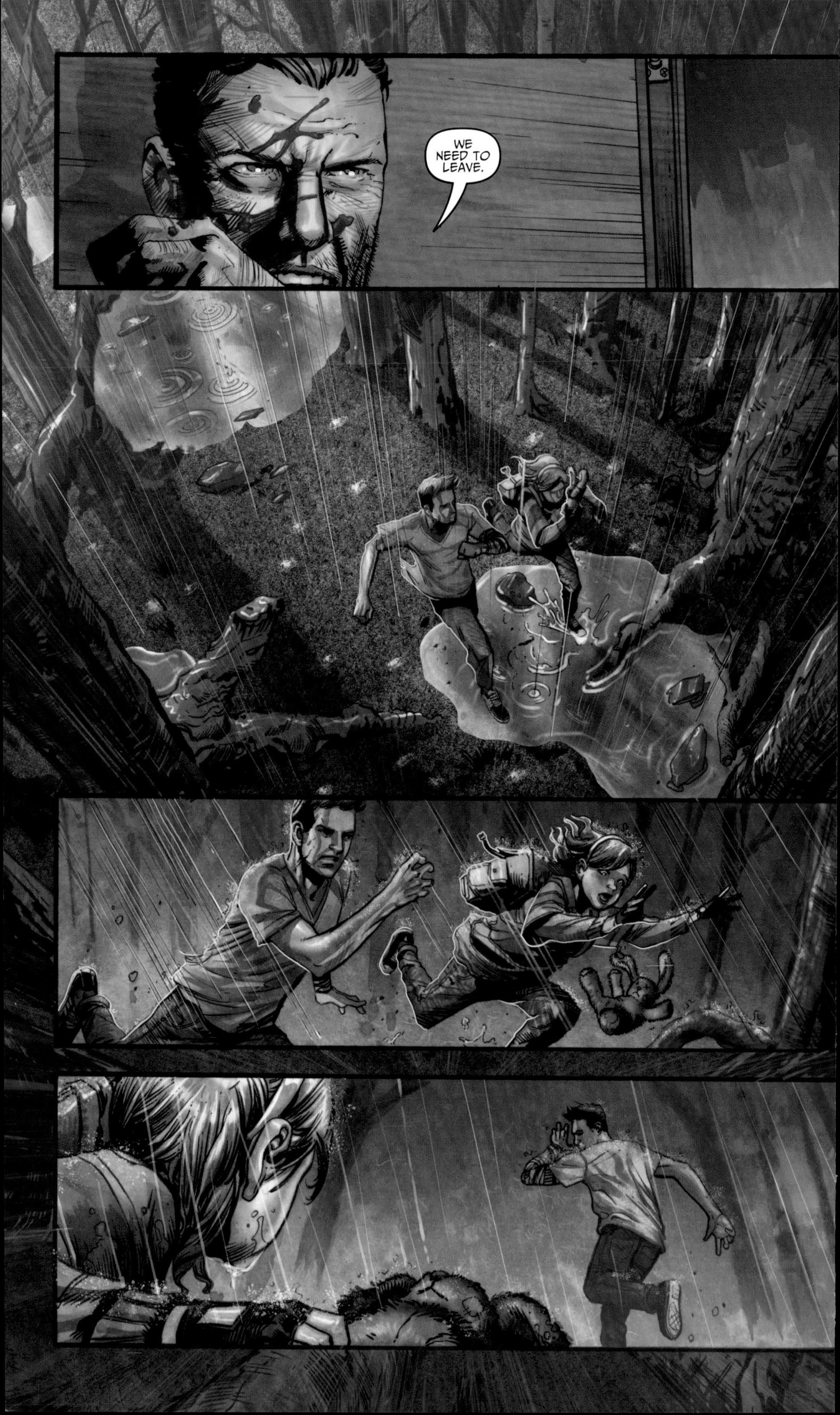
WE NEED TO LEAVE.

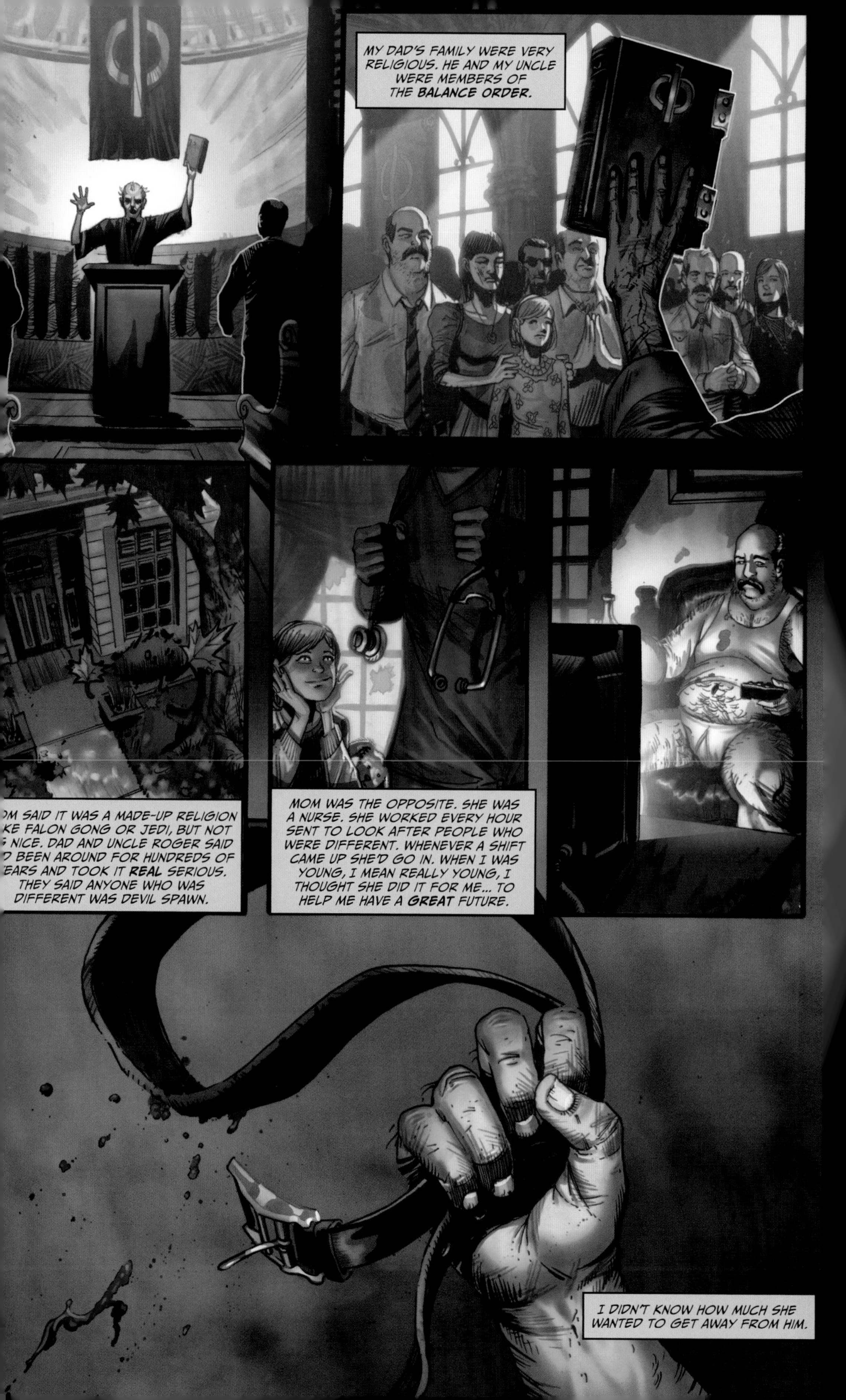
MY DAD'S FAMILY WERE VERY RELIGIOUS. HE AND MY UNCLE WERE MEMBERS OF THE BALANCE ORDER.
OM SAID IT WAS A MADE-UP RELIGION KE FALON GONG OR JEDI, BUT NOT NICE. DAD AND UNCLE ROGER SAID D BEEN AROUND FOR HUNDREDS OF EARS AND TOOK IT REAL SERIOUS. THEY SAID ANYONE WHO WAS DIFFERENT WAS DEVIL SPAWN.
MOM WAS THE OPPOSITE. SHE WAS A NURSE. SHE WORKED EVERY HOUR SENT TO LOOK AFTER PEOPLE WHO WERE DIFFERENT. WHENEVER A SHIFT CAME UP SHE'D GO IN. WHEN I WAS YOUNG, I MEAN REALLY YOUNG, I THOUGHT SHE DID IT FOR ME... TO HELP ME HAVE A GREAT FUTURE.
I DIDN'T KNOW HOW MUCH SHE WANTED TO GET AWAY FROM HIM.

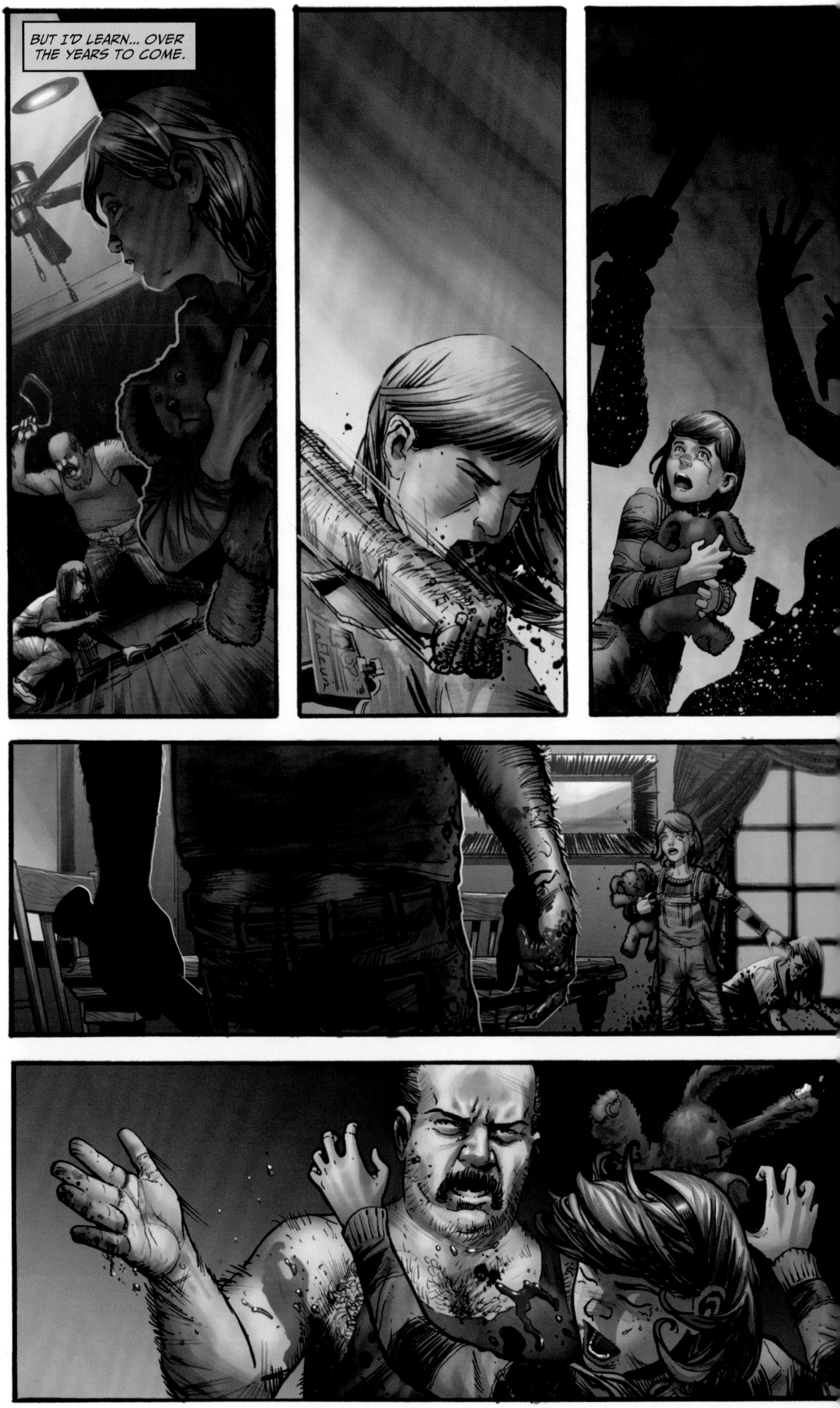
BUT I'D LEARN... OVER THE YEARS TO COME.

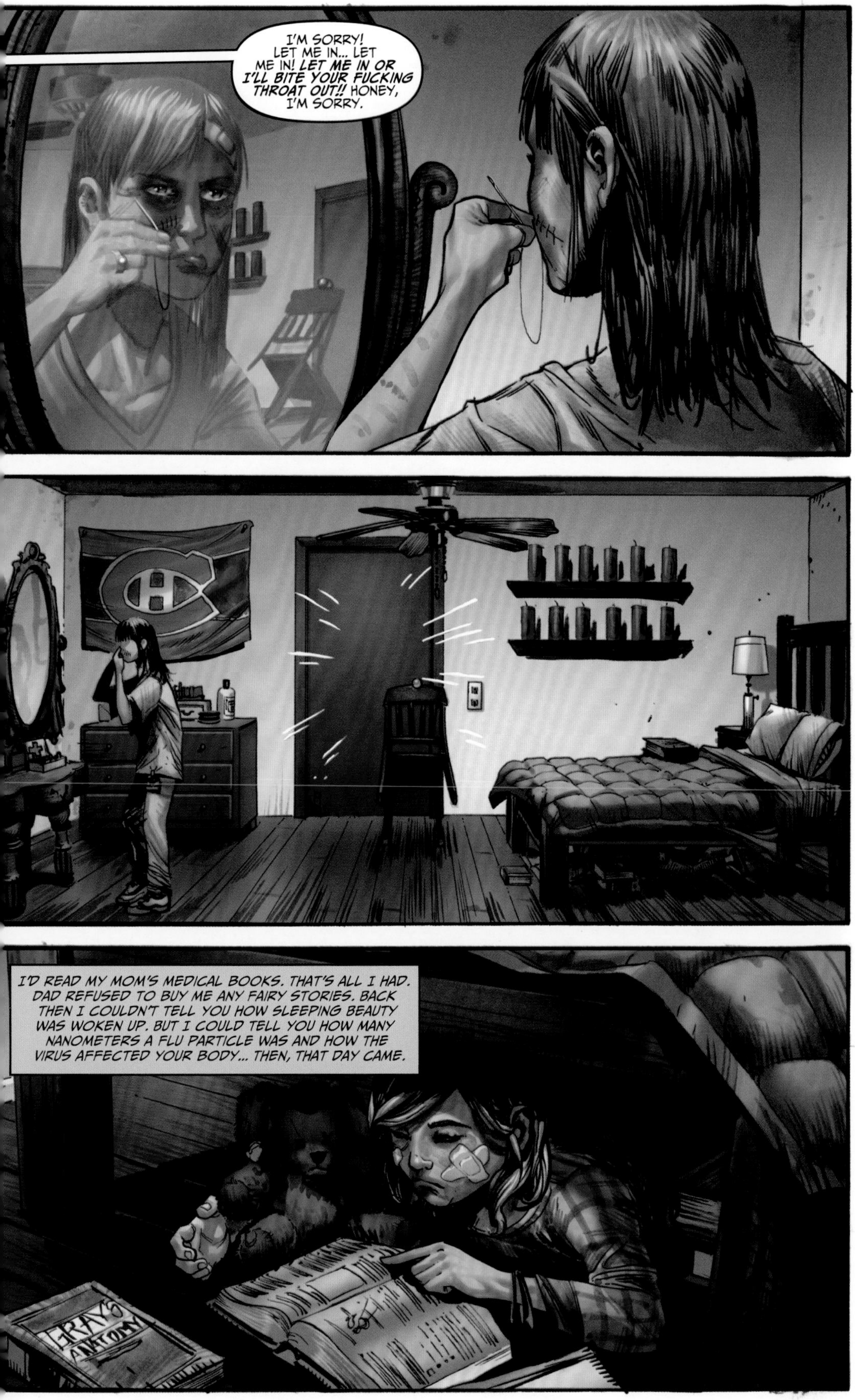
I'M SORRY! LET ME IN... LET ME IN! LET ME IN OR I'LL BITE YOUR FUCKING THROAT OUT!! HONEY, I'M SORRY.
I'D READ MY MOM'S MEDICAL BOOKS. THAT'S ALL I HAD. DAD REFUSED TO BUY ME ANY FAIRY STORIES. BACK THEN I COULDN'T TELL YOU HOW SLEEPING BEAUTY WAS WOKEN UP. BUT I COULD TELL YOU HOW MANY NANOMETERS A FLU PARTICLE WAS AND HOW THE VIRUS AFFECTED YOUR BODY... THEN, THAT DAY CAME.
GRAY'S ANATOMY

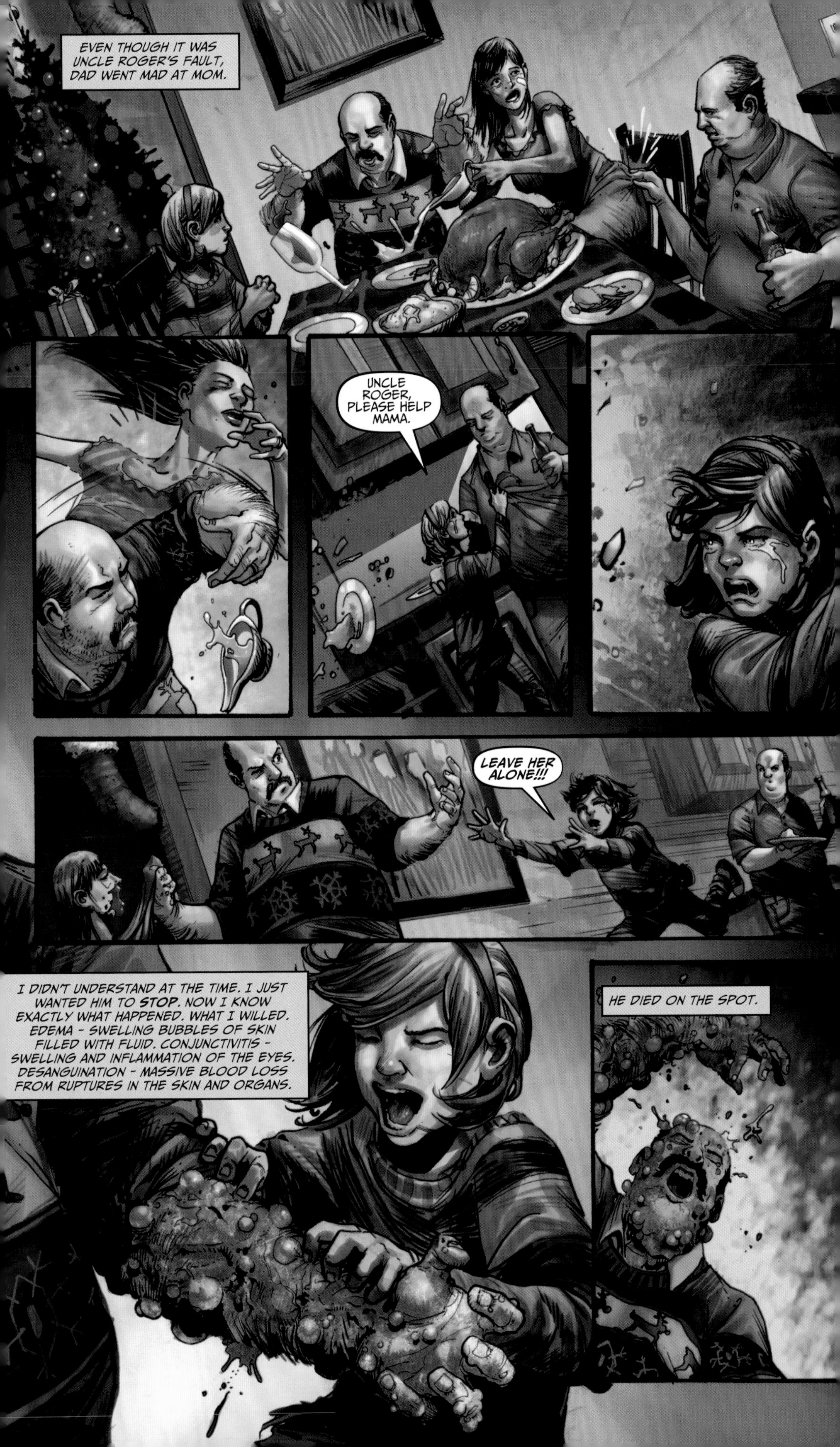
EVEN THOUGH IT WAS UNCLE ROGER'S FAULT, DAD WENT MAD AT MOM.
UNCLE ROGER, PLEASE HELP MAMA.
LEAVE HER ALONE!!!
I DIDN'T UNDERSTAND AT THE TIME. I JUST WANTED HIM TO STOP. NOW I KNOW EXACTLY WHAT HAPPENED. WHAT I WILLED. EDEMA - SWELLING BUBBLES OF SKIN FILLED WITH FLUID. CONJUNCTIVITIS - SWELLING AND INFLAMMATION OF THE EYES. DESANGUINATION - MASSIVE BLOOD LOSS FROM RUPTURES IN THE SKIN AND ORGANS.
HE DIED ON THE SPOT.

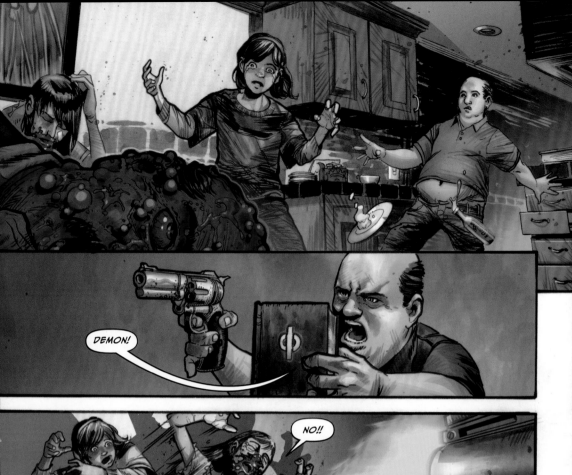

DEMON!

NO!!

Y BOTH DID.

RUN...

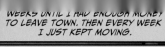

WEEKS UNTIL I HAD ENOUGH MONEY TO LEAVE TOWN. THEN EVERY WEEK I JUST KEPT MOVING.
MY UNCLE HAD TOLD THE POLICE THAT MUM INJECTED DAD WITH THE VIRUS THEN HE SHOT MY MOTHER. SO WHATEVER AUTHORITIES BELIEVED, THEY WANTED TO FIND ME.
E D'AUT
I'M SORRY, YOU'RE TOO YOUNG TO TRAVEL ALONE
HAVE YOU SEEN ME?
nette Lafleur
PLEASE CAL
514-562-9
THERE WERE OTHERS WHO WANTED ME AS WEL BUT I DIDN'T KNOW WHY.
15
TICKE
I NEED YOU TO COME WITH ME.
You've revealed yourself.
Now you must perish, Demon.
LUCKY FOR ME, SOMEONE WOULDN'T LET THAT HAPPEN.

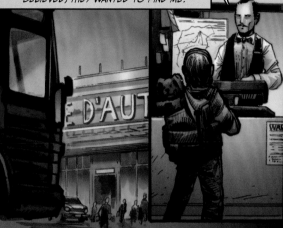

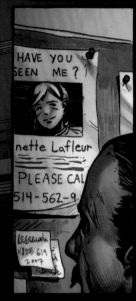

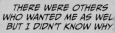

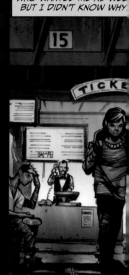

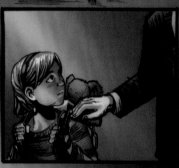

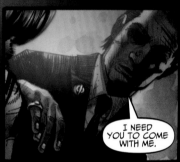

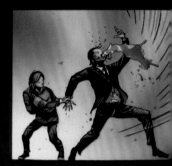

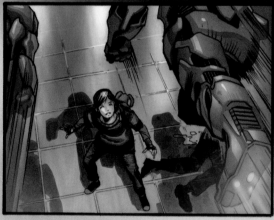

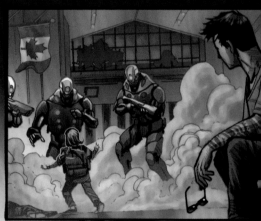

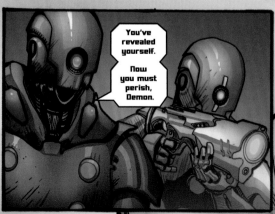

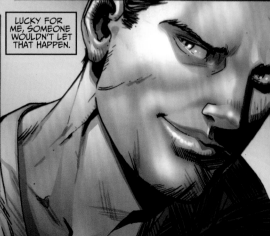

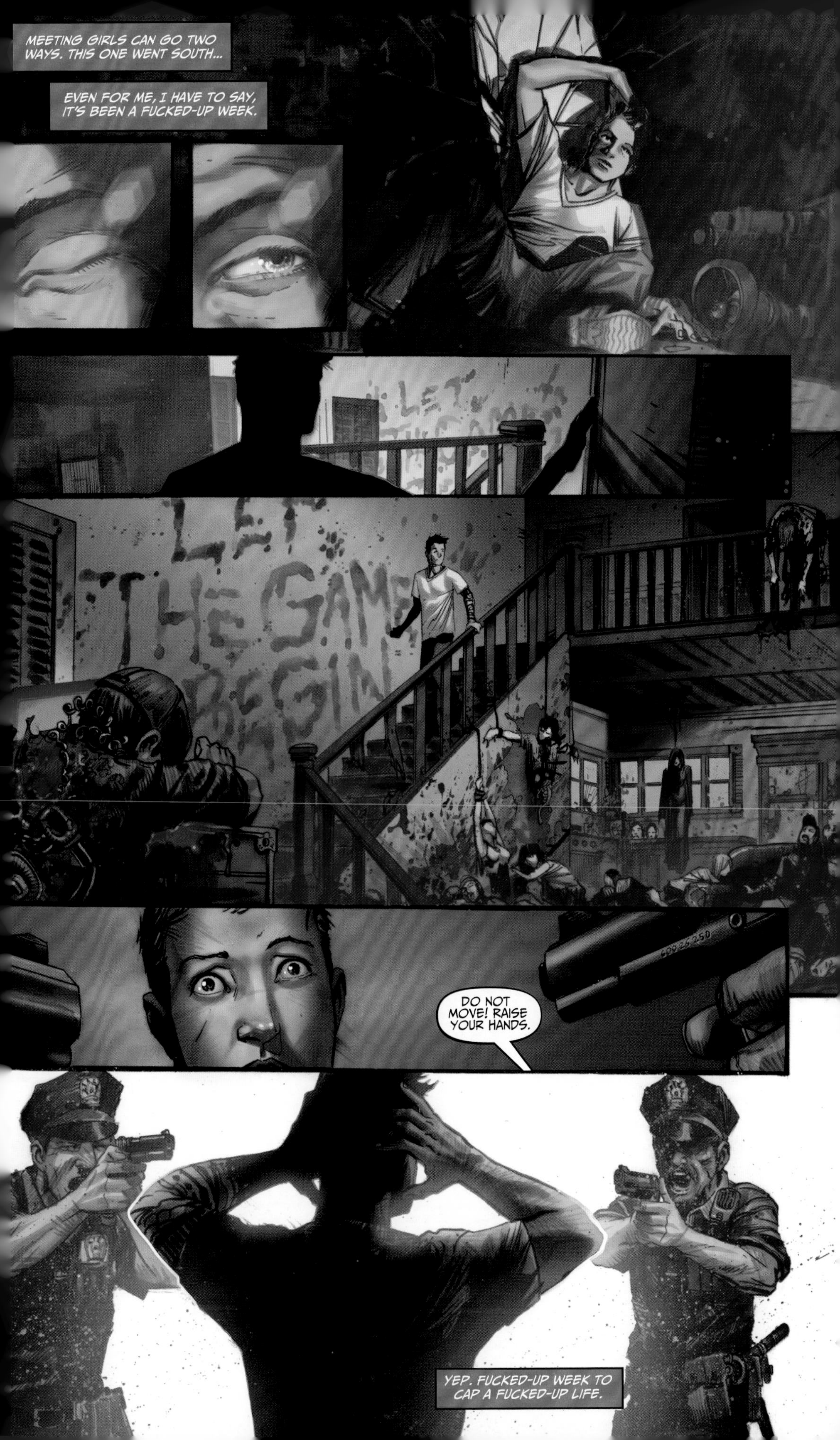
MEETING GIRLS CAN GO TWO WAYS. THIS ONE WENT SOUTH...
EVEN FOR ME, I HAVE TO SAY, IT'S BEEN A FUCKED-UP WEEK.
LET THE GAMES BEGIN
DO NOT MOVE! RAISE YOUR HANDS.
YEP. FUCKED-UP WEEK TO CAP A FUCKED-UP LIFE.

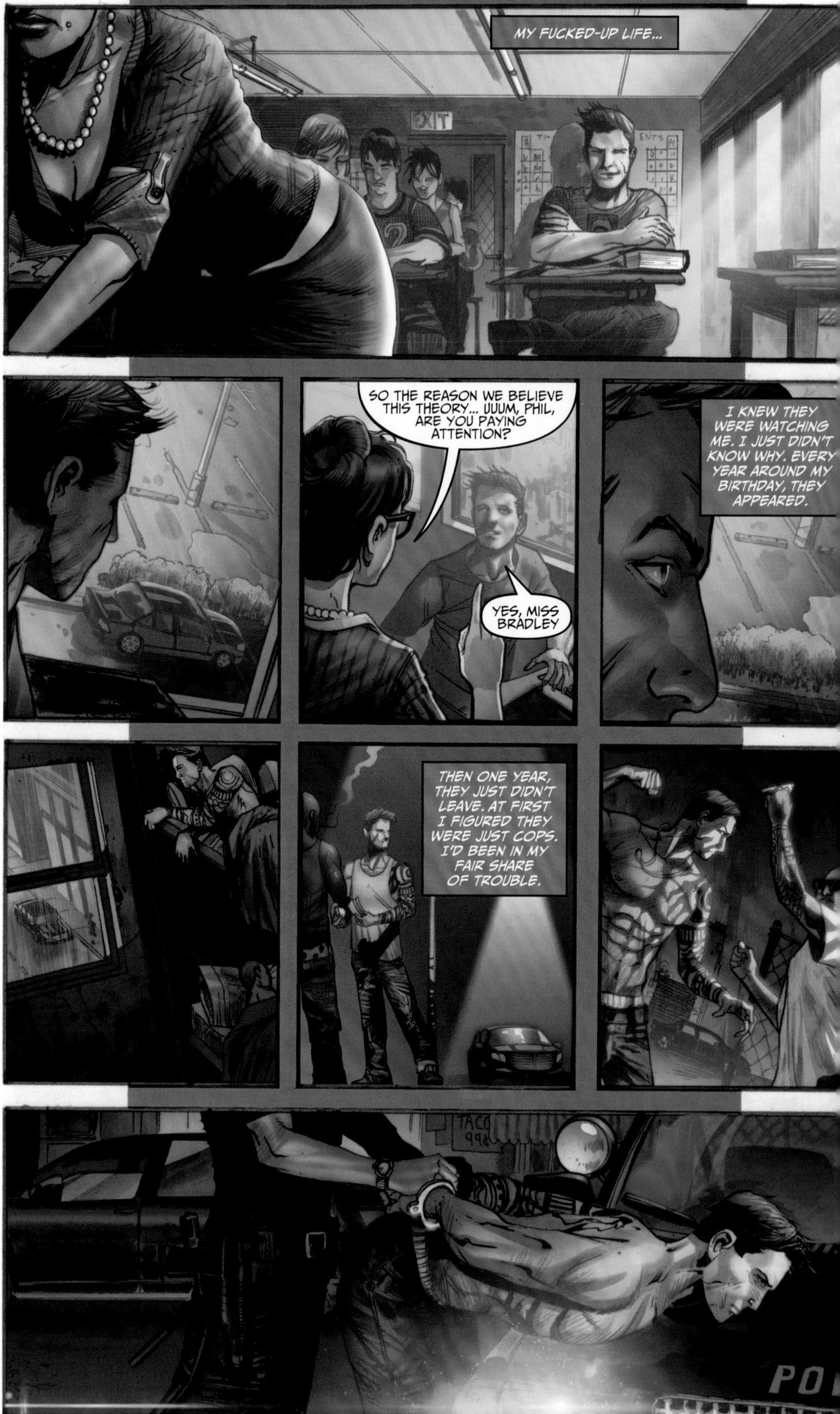
MY FUCKED-UP LIFE...
SO THE REASON WE BELIEVE THIS THEORY... UUUM, PHIL, ARE YOU PAYING ATTENTION?
YES, MISS BRADLEY
I KNEW THEY WERE WATCHING ME. I JUST DIDN'T KNOW WHY. EVERY YEAR AROUND MY BIRTHDAY, THEY APPEARED.
THEN ONE YEAR, THEY JUST DIDN'T LEAVE. AT FIRST I FIGURED THEY WERE JUST COPS. I'D BEEN IN MY FAIR SHARE OF TROUBLE.

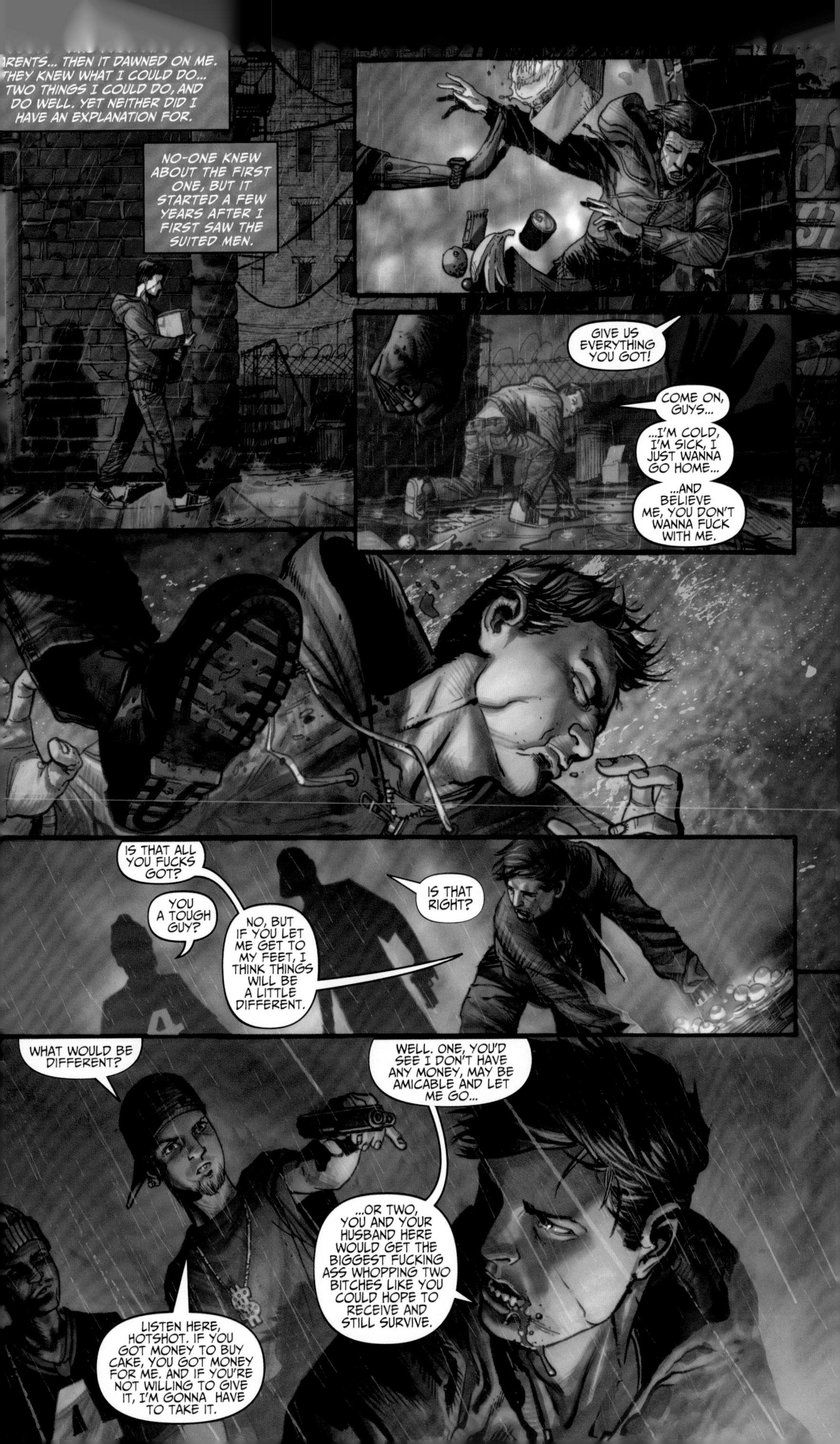
ARENTS... THEN IT DAWNED ON ME. THEY KNEW WHAT I COULD DO... TWO THINGS I COULD DO, AND DO WELL. YET NEITHER DID I HAVE AN EXPLANATION FOR.
NO-ONE KNEW ABOUT THE FIRST ONE, BUT IT STARTED A FEW YEARS AFTER I FIRST SAW THE SUITED MEN.
GIVE US EVERYTHING YOU GOT!
COME ON, GUYS...
...I'M COLD, I'M SICK, I JUST WANNA GO HOME...
...AND BELIEVE ME, YOU DON'T WANNA FUCK WITH ME.
IS THAT ALL YOU FUCKS GOT?
YOU A TOUGH GUY?
NO, BUT IF YOU LET ME GET TO MY FEET, I THINK THINGS WILL BE A LITTLE DIFFERENT.
IS THAT RIGHT?
WHAT WOULD BE DIFFERENT?
WELL. ONE, YOU'D SEE I DON'T HAVE ANY MONEY, MAY BE AMICABLE AND LET ME GO...
...OR TWO, YOU AND YOUR HUSBAND HERE WOULD GET THE BIGGEST FUCKING ASS WHOPPING TWO BITCHES LIKE YOU COULD HOPE TO RECEIVE AND STILL SURVIVE.
LISTEN HERE, HOTSHOT. IF YOU GOT MONEY TO BUY CAKE, YOU GOT MONEY FOR ME. AND IF YOU'RE NOT WILLING TO GIVE IT, I'M GONNA HAVE TO TAKE IT.

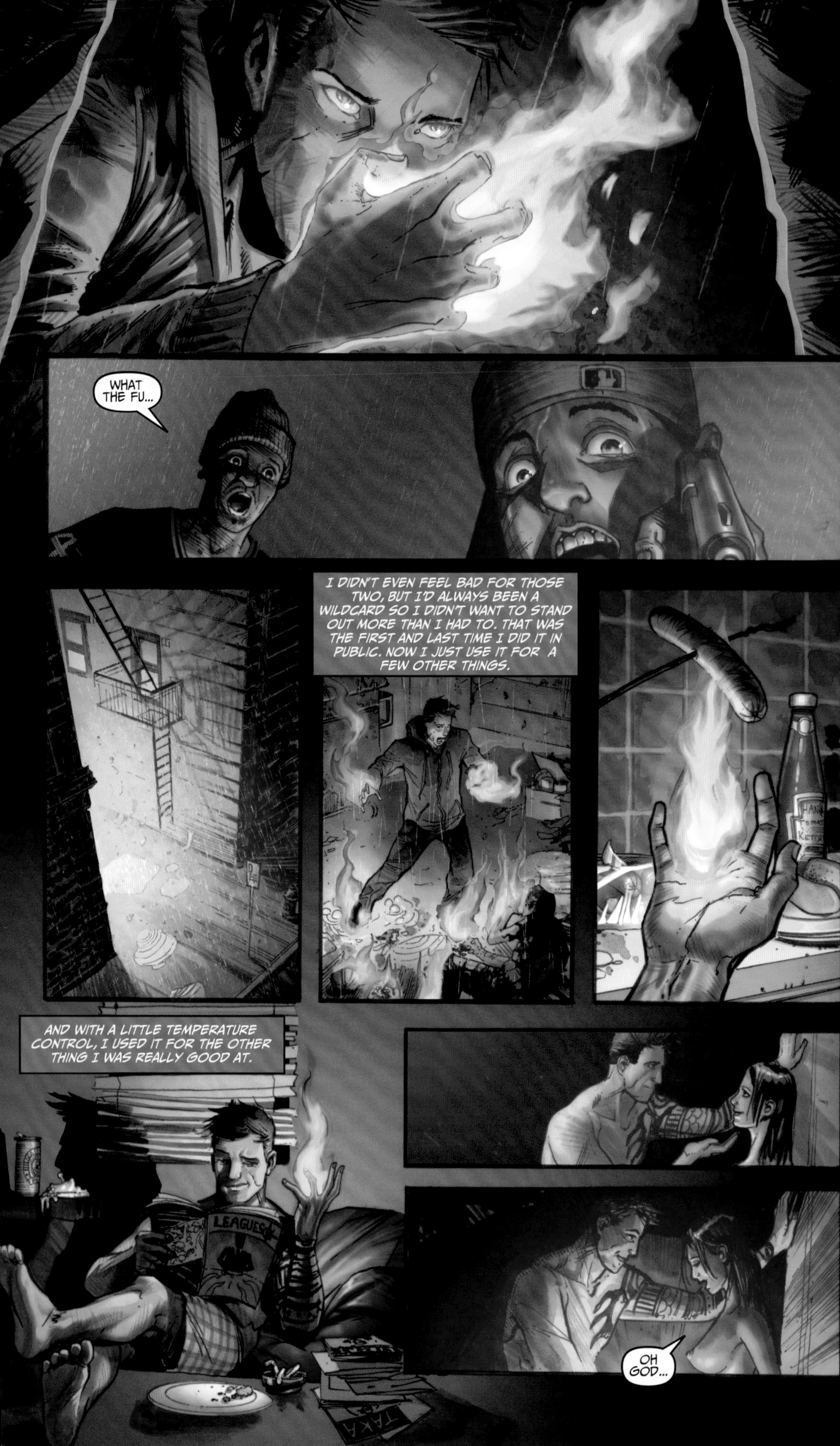
WHAT THE FU...
I DIDN'T EVEN FEEL BAD FOR THOSE TWO, BUT I'D ALWAYS BEEN A WILDCARD SO I DIDN'T WANT TO STAND OUT MORE THAN I HAD TO. THAT WAS THE FIRST AND LAST TIME I DID IT IN PUBLIC. NOW I JUST USE IT FOR A FEW OTHER THINGS.
AND WITH A LITTLE TEMPERATURE CONTROL, I USED IT FOR THE OTHER THING I WAS REALLY GOOD AT.
LEAGUES
OH GOD...

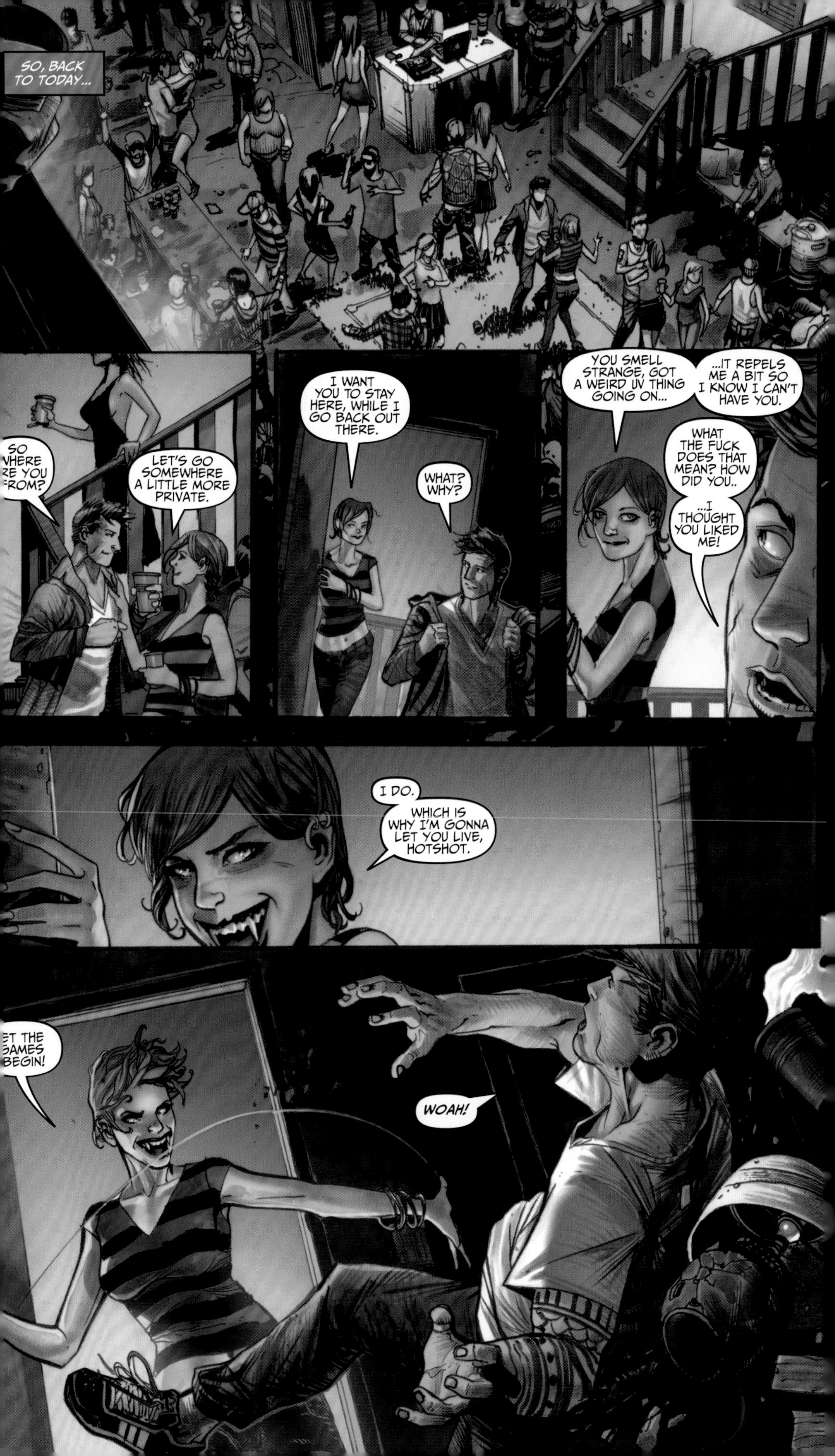
SO, BACK TO TODAY...
SO WHERE ARE YOU FROM?
LET'S GO SOMEWHERE A LITTLE MORE PRIVATE.
I WANT YOU TO STAY HERE, WHILE I GO BACK OUT THERE.
WHAT? WHY?
YOU SMELL STRANGE, GOT A WEIRD UV THING GOING ON...
...IT REPELS ME A BIT SO I KNOW I CAN'T HAVE YOU.
WHAT THE FUCK DOES THAT MEAN? HOW DID YOU..
...I THOUGHT YOU LIKED ME!
I DO.
WHICH IS WHY I'M GONNA LET YOU LIVE, HOTSHOT.
LET THE GAMES BEGIN!
WOAH!

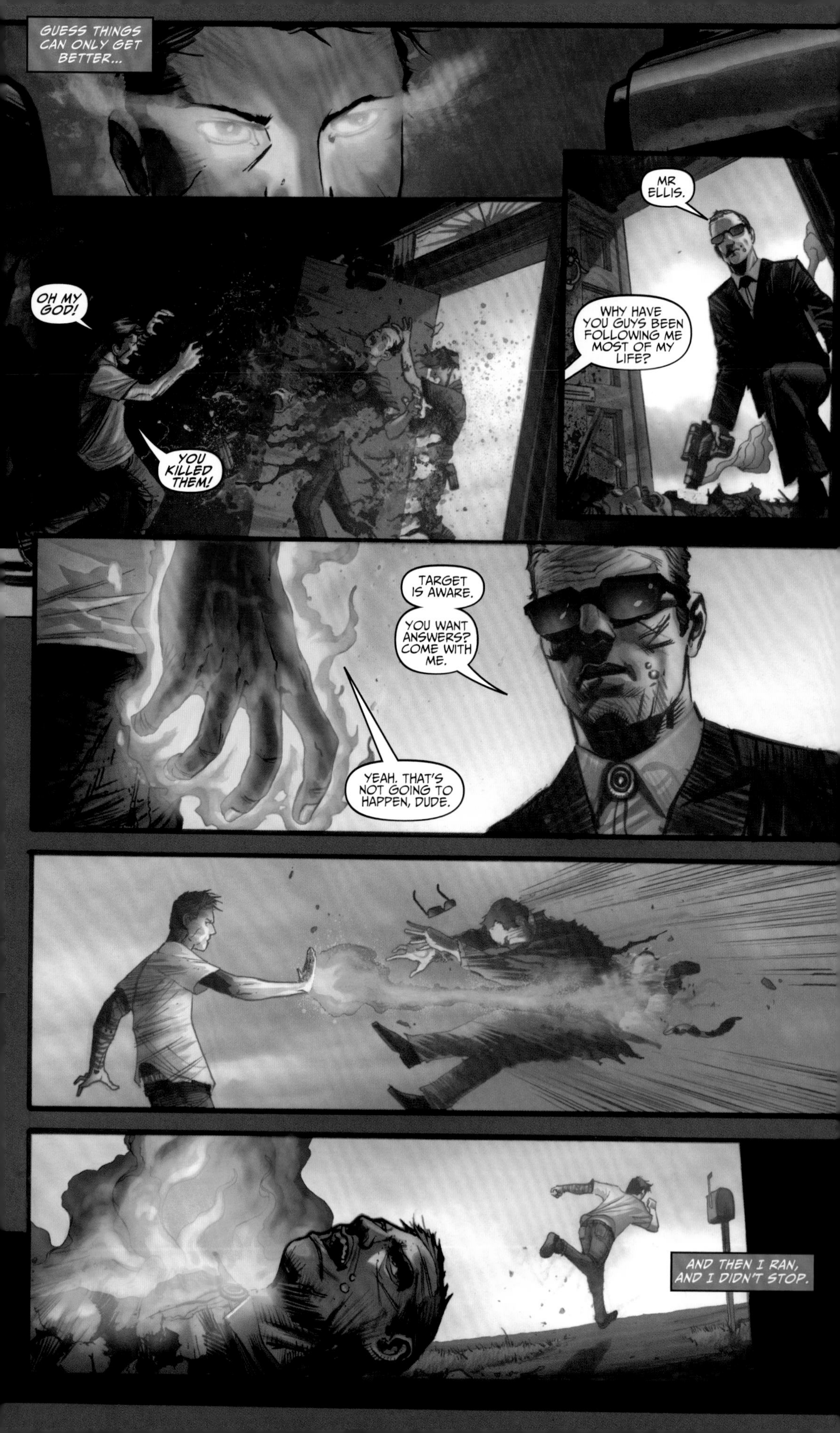
GUESS THINGS CAN ONLY GET BETTER...
MR ELLIS.
OH MY GOD!
YOU KILLED THEM!
WHY HAVE YOU GUYS BEEN FOLLOWING ME MOST OF MY LIFE?
TARGET IS AWARE.
YOU WANT ANSWERS? COME WITH ME.
YEAH. THAT'S NOT GOING TO HAPPEN, DUDE.
AND THEN I RAN, AND I DIDN'T STOP.

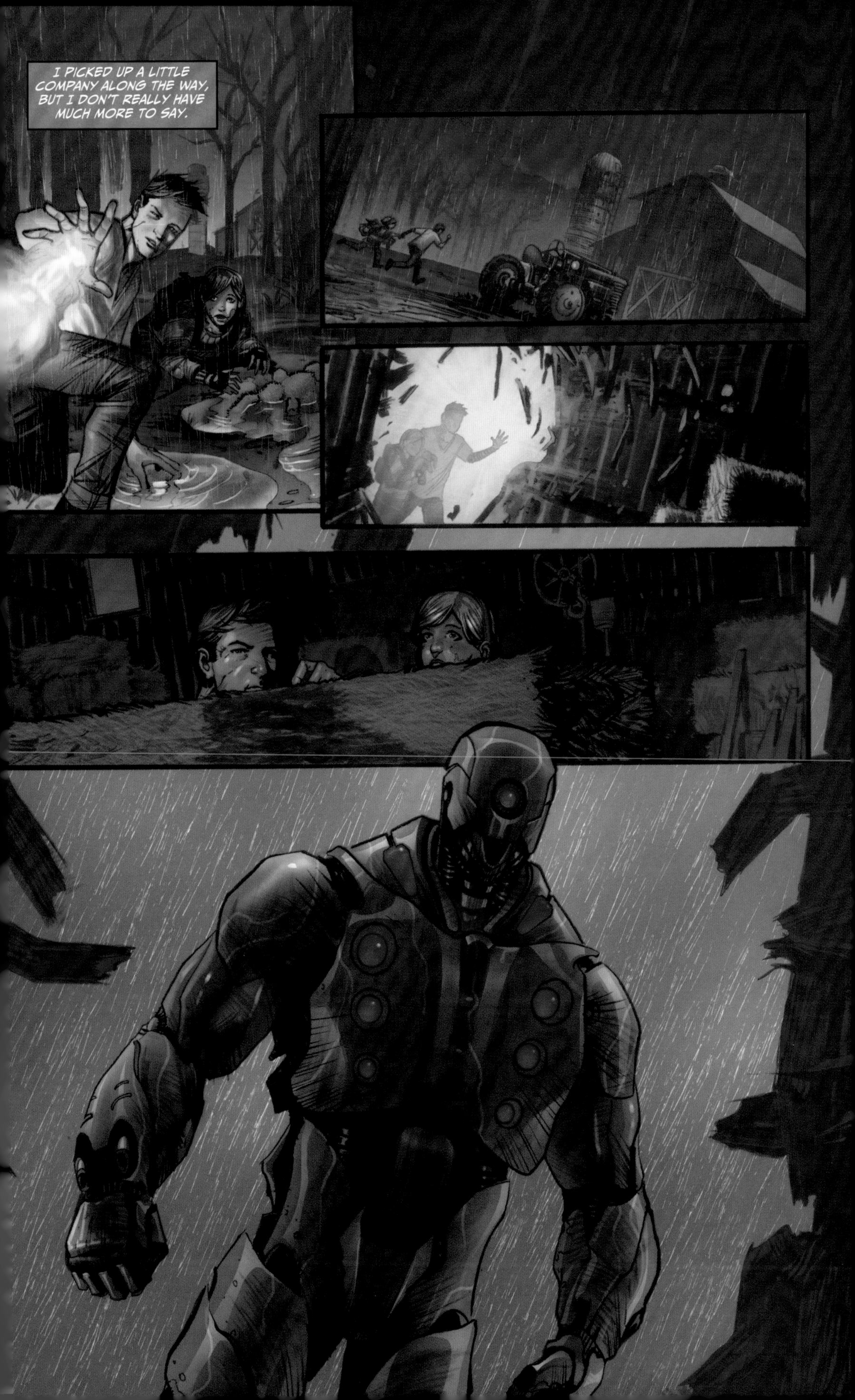
I PICKED UP A LITTLE COMPANY ALONG THE WAY, BUT I DON'T REALLY HAVE MUCH MORE TO SAY.

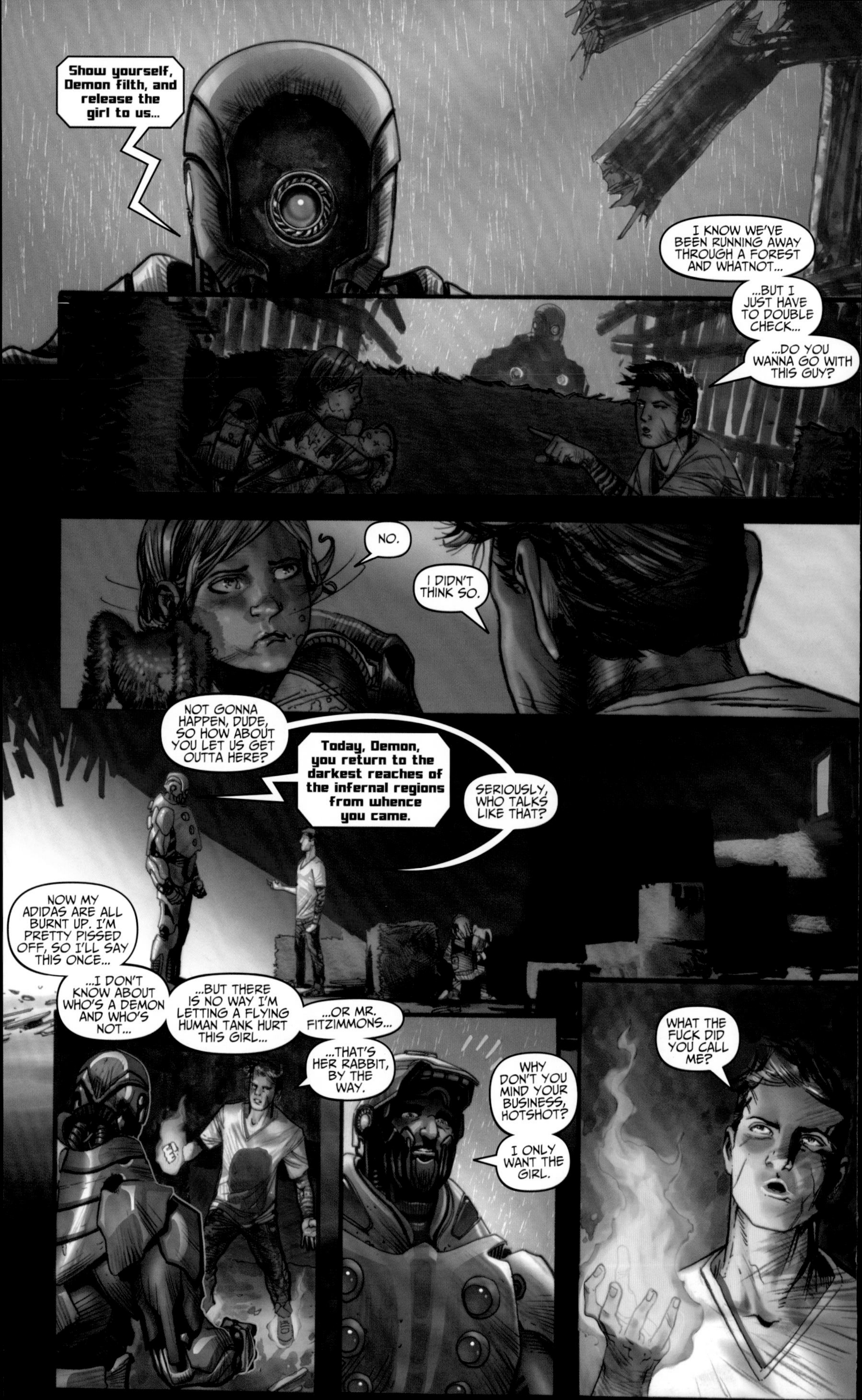
Show yourself, Demon filth, and release the girl to us...
I KNOW WE'VE BEEN RUNNING AWAY THROUGH A FOREST AND WHATNOT...
...BUT I JUST HAVE TO DOUBLE CHECK...
...DO YOU WANNA GO WITH THIS GUY?
NO.
I DIDN'T THINK SO.
NOT GONNA HAPPEN, DUDE, SO HOW ABOUT YOU LET US GET OUTTA HERE?
Today, Demon, you return to the darkest reaches of the infernal regions from whence you came.
SERIOUSLY, WHO TALKS LIKE THAT?
NOW MY ADIDAS ARE ALL BURNT UP. I'M PRETTY PISSED OFF, SO I'LL SAY THIS ONCE...
...I DON'T KNOW ABOUT WHO'S A DEMON AND WHO'S NOT...
...BUT THERE IS NO WAY I'M LETTING A FLYING HUMAN TANK HURT THIS GIRL...
...OR MR. FITZIMMONS...
...THAT'S HER RABBIT, BY THE WAY.
WHY DON'T YOU MIND YOUR BUSINESS, HOTSHOT?
I ONLY WANT THE GIRL.
WHAT THE FUCK DID YOU CALL ME?

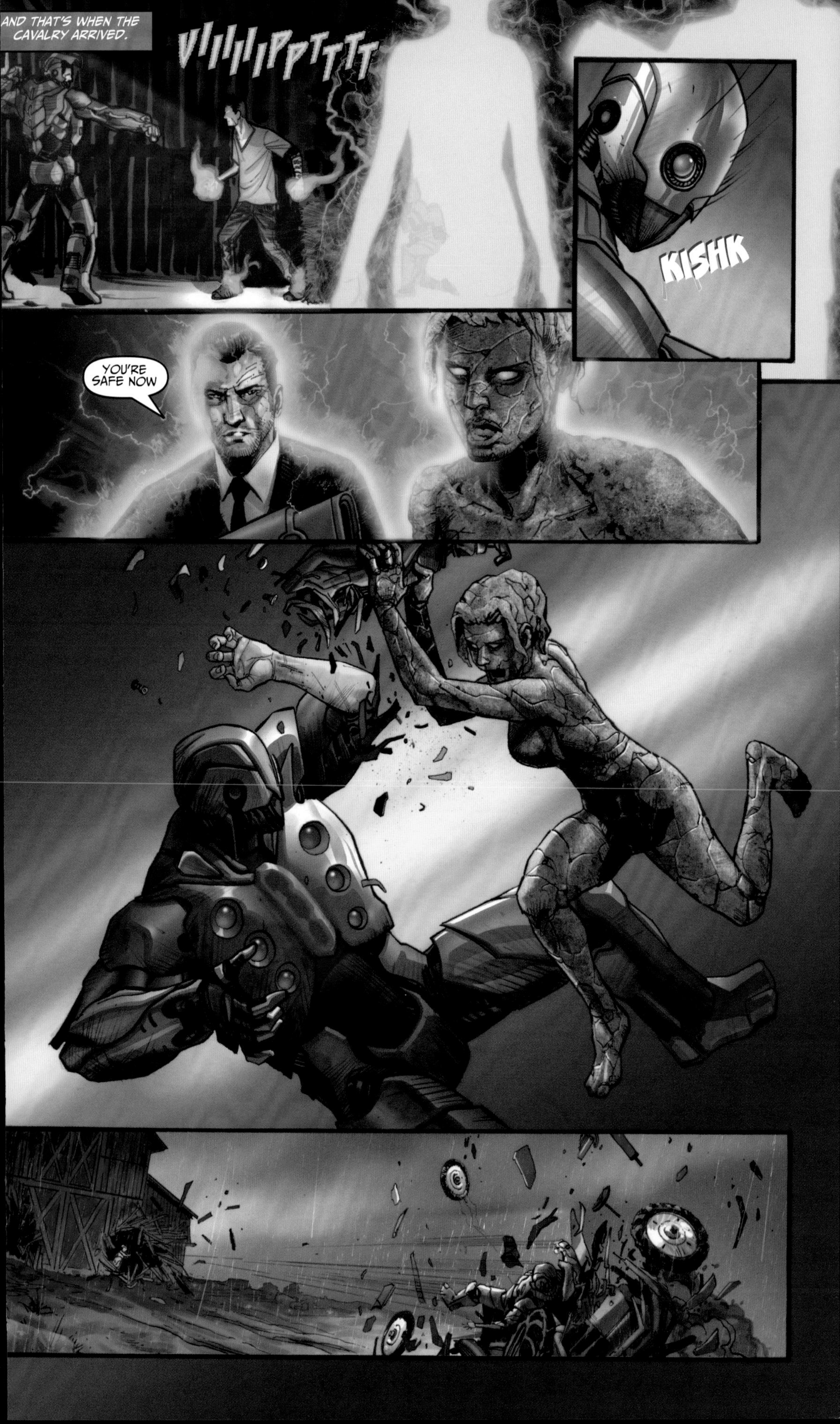
AND THAT'S WHEN THE CAVALRY ARRIVED.
VIIIIIPPTTTT
KISHK
YOU'RE SAFE NOW

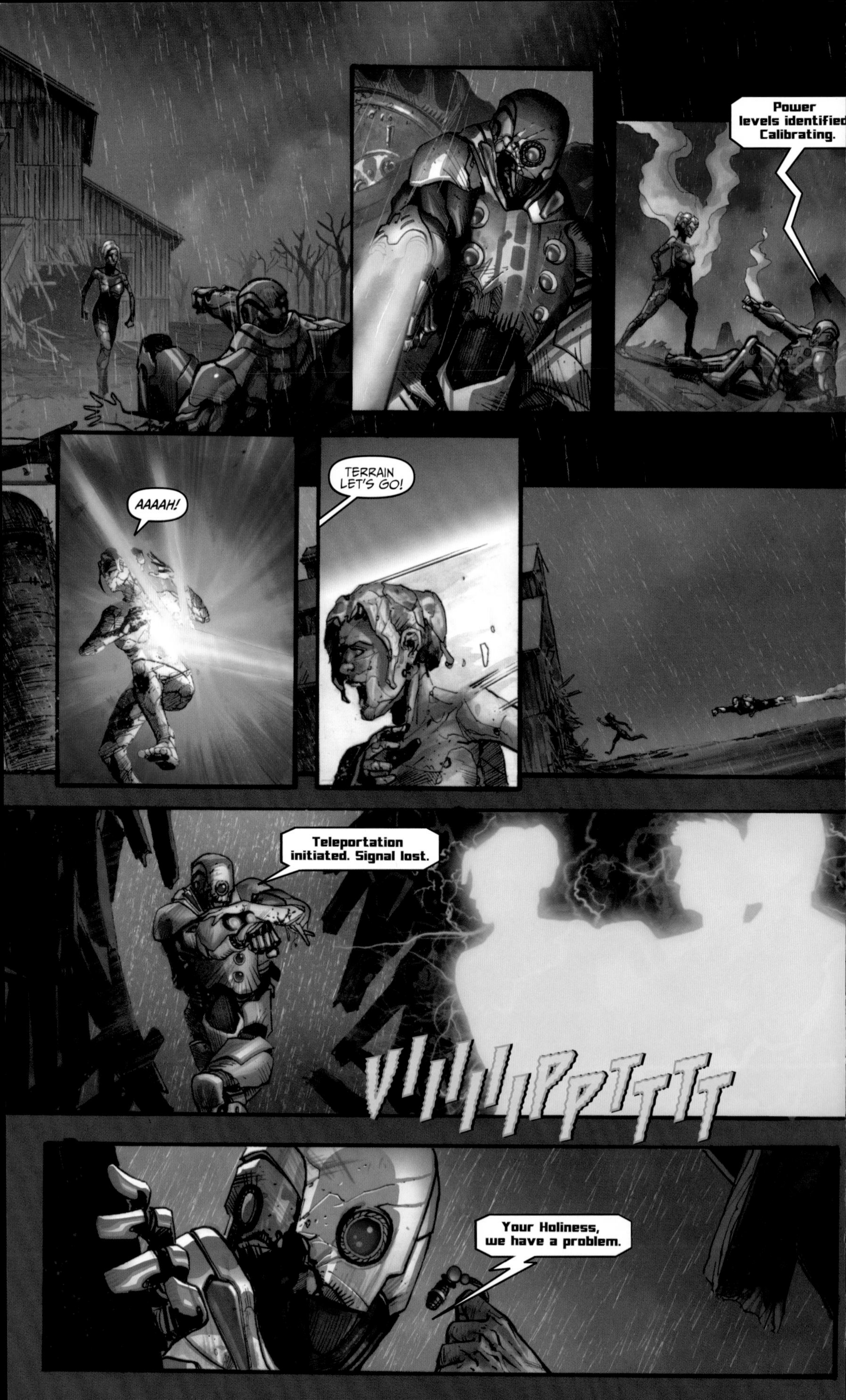
Power
levels identified
Calibrating.
AAAAH!
TERRAIN
LET'S GO!
Teleportation
initiated. Signal lost.
VIIIIIIPPTTTT
Your Holiness,
we have a problem.

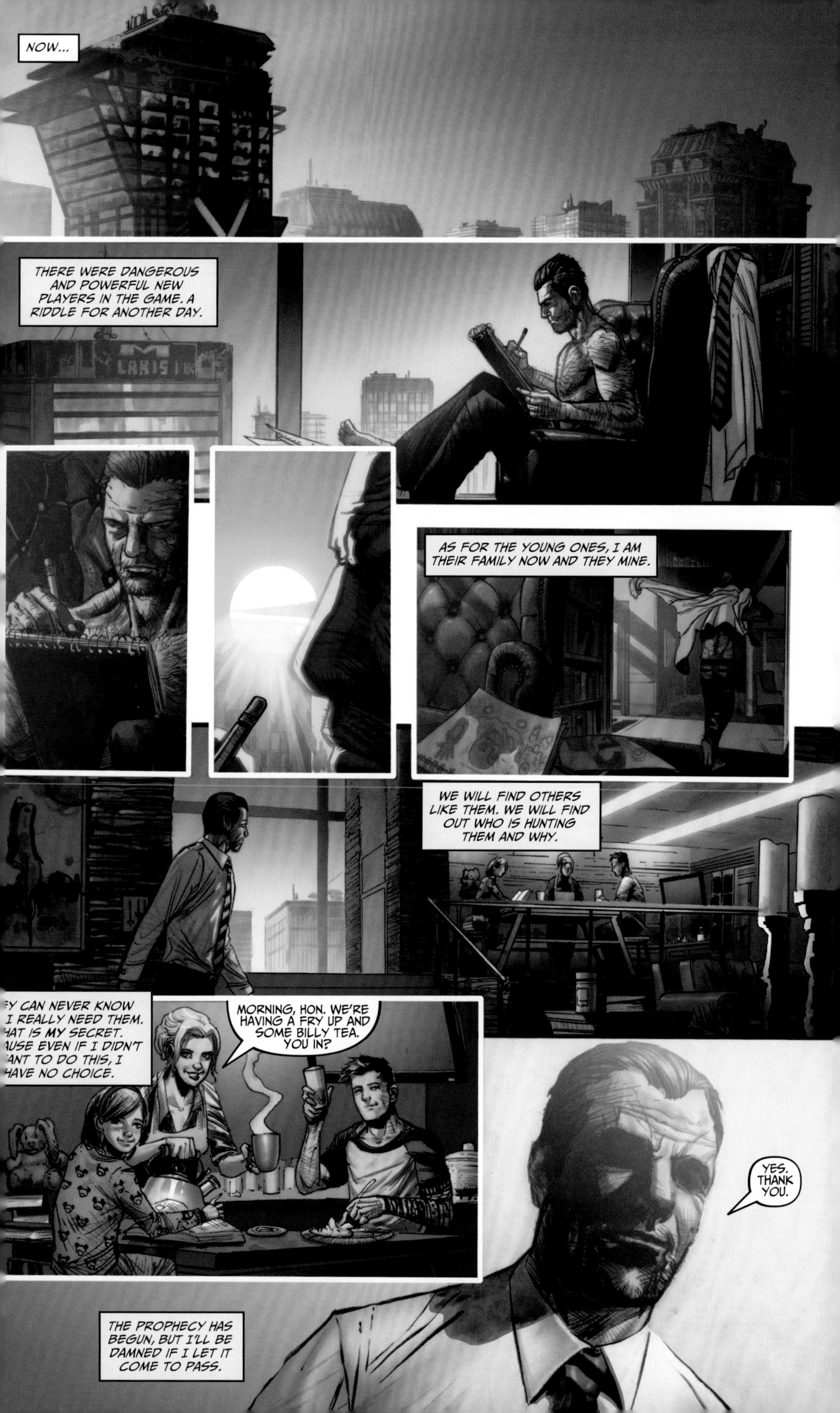
NOW...
THERE WERE DANGEROUS AND POWERFUL NEW PLAYERS IN THE GAME. A RIDDLE FOR ANOTHER DAY.
AS FOR THE YOUNG ONES, I AM THEIR FAMILY NOW AND THEY MINE.
WE WILL FIND OTHERS LIKE THEM. WE WILL FIND OUT WHO IS HUNTING THEM AND WHY.
EY CAN NEVER KNOW I REALLY NEED THEM. HAT IS MY SECRET. AUSE EVEN IF I DIDN'T ANT TO DO THIS, I HAVE NO CHOICE.
MORNING, HON. WE'RE HAVING A FRY UP AND SOME BILLY TEA. YOU IN?
YES. THANK YOU.
THE PROPHECY HAS BEGUN, BUT I'LL BE DAMNED IF I LET IT COME TO PASS.

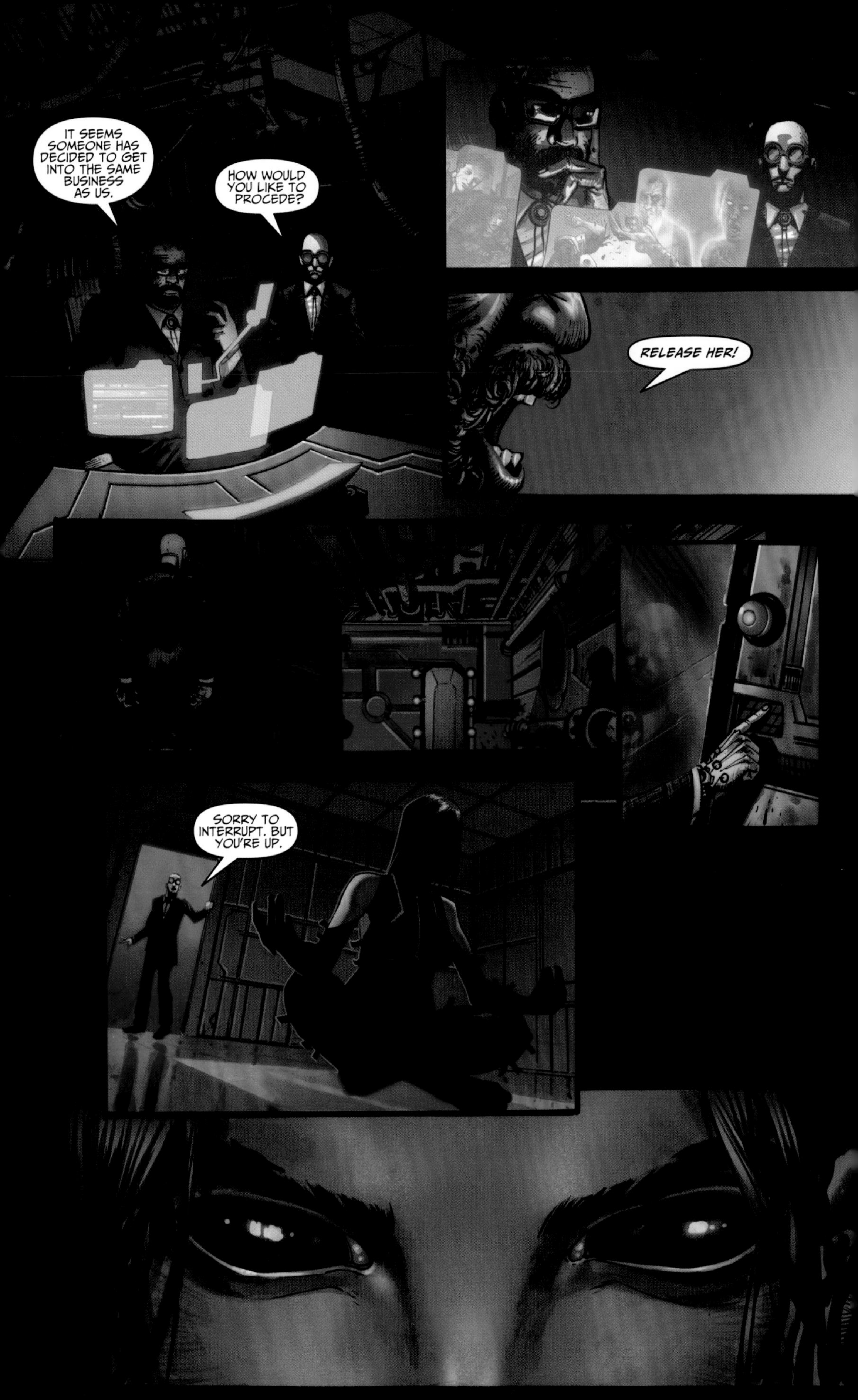
IT SEEMS SOMEONE HAS DECIDED TO GET INTO THE SAME BUSINESS AS US.
HOW WOULD YOU LIKE TO PROCEDE?
RELEASE HER!
SORRY TO INTERRUPT. BUT YOU'RE UP.

NOW...

MY NAME IS TORRENCE JANE-WILLIS, I'M 19 YEARS OLD.

I NEVER THOUGHT I'D SAY SOMETHING LIKE THIS, THE FACT IT'S EVEN HAPPENING IS COMPLETELY WEIRDING ME OUT.

BUT REST ASSURED...

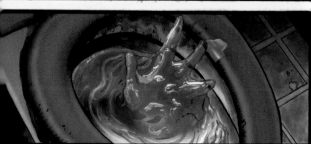

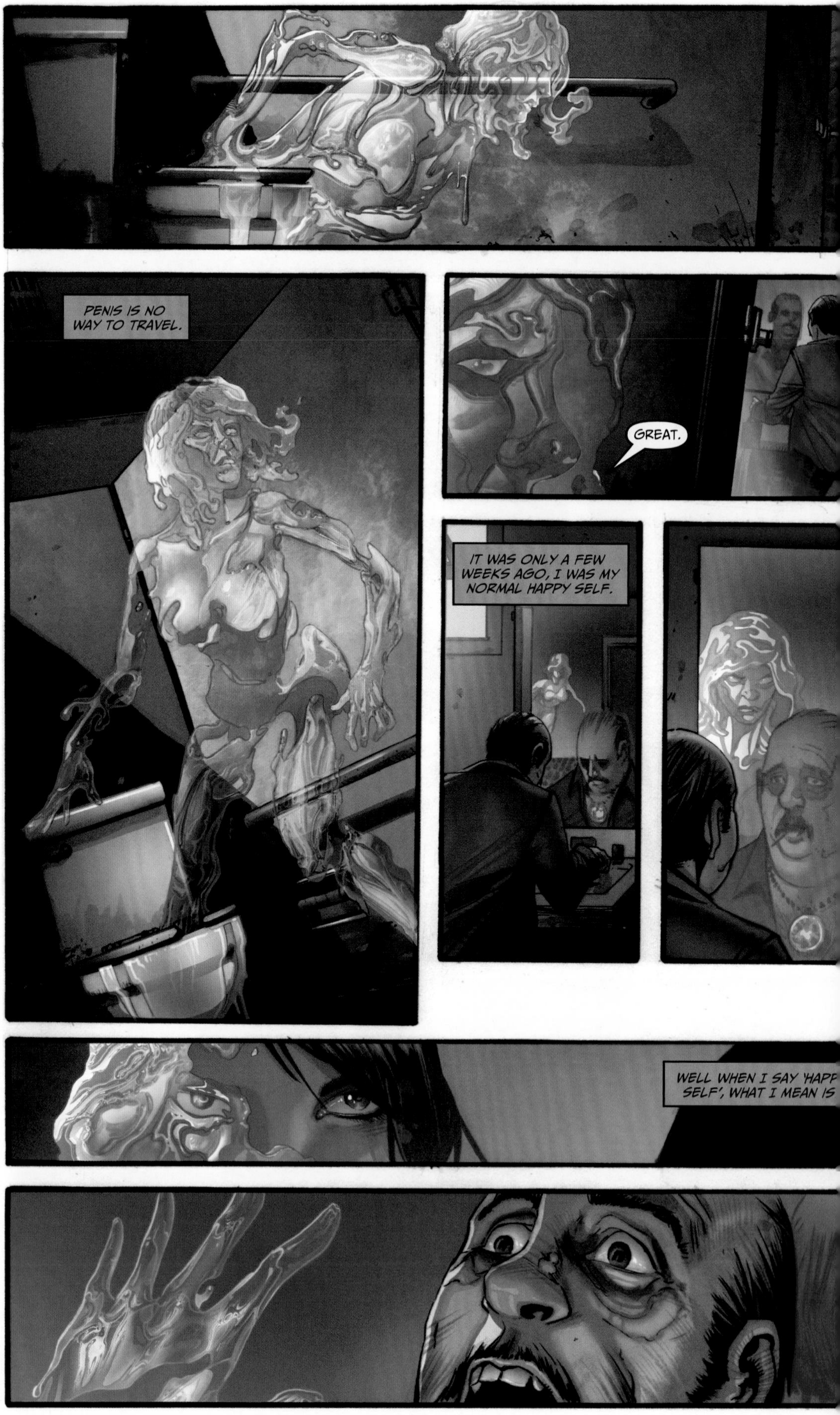
PENIS IS NO
WAY TO TRAVEL.
GREAT.
IT WAS ONLY A FEW
WEEKS AGO, I WAS MY
NORMAL HAPPY SELF.
WELL WHEN I SAY 'HAPP
SELF', WHAT I MEAN IS

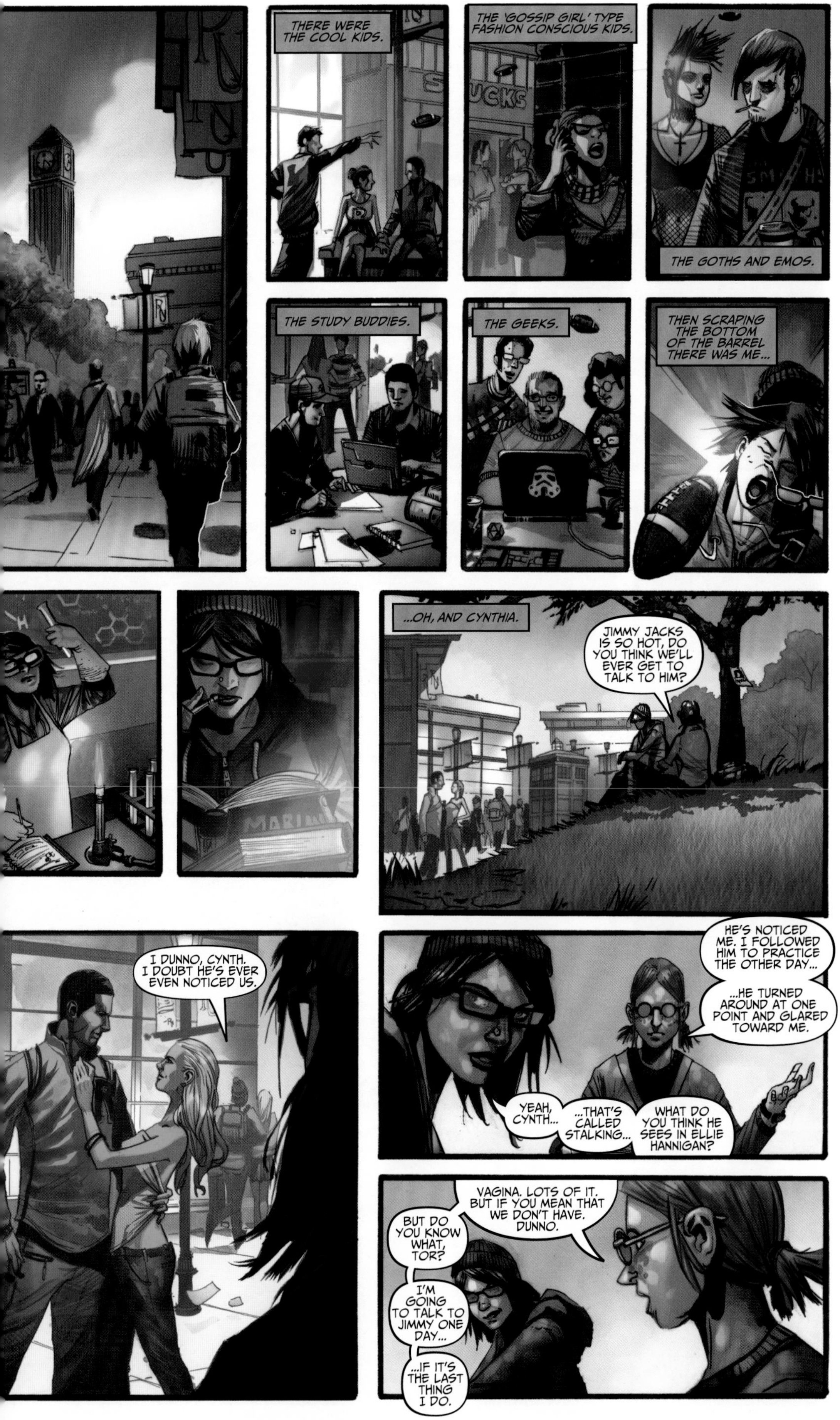
THERE WERE THE COOL KIDS.
THE 'GOSSIP GIRL' TYPE FASHION CONSCIOUS KIDS.
THE GOTHS AND EMOS.
THE STUDY BUDDIES.
THE GEEKS.
THEN SCRAPING THE BOTTOM OF THE BARREL THERE WAS ME...
...OH, AND CYNTHIA.
JIMMY JACKS IS SO HOT, DO YOU THINK WE'LL EVER GET TO TALK TO HIM?
I DUNNO, CYNTH. I DOUBT HE'S EVER EVEN NOTICED US.
HE'S NOTICED ME. I FOLLOWED HIM TO PRACTICE THE OTHER DAY...
...HE TURNED AROUND AT ONE POINT AND GLARED TOWARD ME.
YEAH, CYNTH...
...THAT'S CALLED STALKING...
WHAT DO YOU THINK HE SEES IN ELLIE HANNIGAN?
VAGINA. LOTS OF IT. BUT IF YOU MEAN THAT WE DON'T HAVE. DUNNO.
BUT DO YOU KNOW WHAT, TOR?
I'M GOING TO TALK TO JIMMY ONE DAY...
...IF IT'S THE LAST THING I DO.

CYNTHIA?

CYNTHIA?!

CYNTHIA, OH MY GOD!

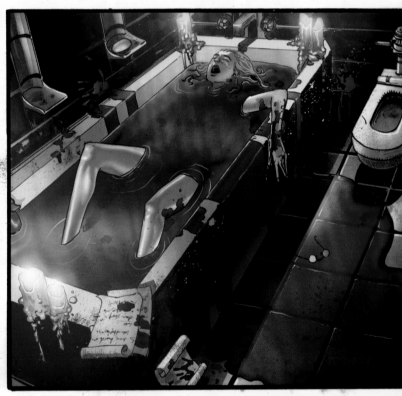

YEAH... CYNTHIA, SHE WAS COOL. TO ME ANYWAY. SHE WAS MY ONLY REAL FRIEND.

WEEKS LATER...

NOW MY WORLD ONLY SEEMED FILLED WITH PEOPLE I COULDN'T BE, OR COULDN'T BE WITH.

WILLIS!

WHEN YOU GOT INTO THE COLLEGE IT WAS UNDER WHAT SCHOLARSHIP?

UMMM... SWIMMING, COACH?

HERE WAS ONLY ONE THING I KNEW I COULD STILL DO BETTER THAN ALMOST ANYONE ELSE I KNEW...

SO, WHY IS IT SINCE FIRST PRACTISE...

...YOU HAVE FAILED TO PUT A SINGLE TOE IN ANY POOL OF WATER ON THIS ENTIRE CAMPUS?

UMMM. OVER THE SUMMER...

...I WENT THROUGH SOME CHANGES AND...

THE ONLY CHANGE I FORESEE IS THE ONE WHERE YOU'RE NO LONGER AT SCHOOL AND END UP FLIPPING BREAKFAST MUFFINS UNTIL YOU'RE 35 THEN LIVING ON YOUR OWN IN A HOUSE FULL OF CATS.

I DON'T LIKE CATS.

GOOD. WE'RE IN COMPETITION TOMORROW. YOU WILL SWIM. AND I'LL BE WATCHING, WILLIS. IF I SEE YOU SHOWER OR SO MUCH AS STEP IN A PUDDLE WITHOUT A BATHING SUIT ON, YOU'RE ON YOUR WAY TO BEING THAT CAT LADY. GOT IT?

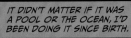

SWIM.

IT DIDN'T MATTER IF IT WAS A POOL OR THE OCEAN, I'D BEEN DOING IT SINCE BIRTH.

I COULD'VE MADE THE OLYMPICS, BUT LAST SUMMER MY BODY CHANGED AND I HAVEN'T SWAM SINCE.

HOPEFULLY IT WON'T BE TOO MUCH OF A DISTRACTION.

THE FUCKING BITCHES AT THAT STUPID SCHOOL THINK THEY'RE SO GREAT. YOU KNOW WHY? COS THEY'VE BEATEN US FIVE TIMES IN A ROW. BUT THIS TIME WE'RE GONNA TAKE THEM... WE HAVE TO...

...WE'RE AT HOME, THIS IS OUR POOL, THIS IS OUR HOUSE...

SWIM TEAM.

...WE'RE BETTER THAN THEM, WE'RE FITTER THAN THEM, SMARTER THAN THEM AND WE ARE DAMN SURE SEXIER THAN THEM...

LET'S DO IT!

RRRRIDGEMOUNT!

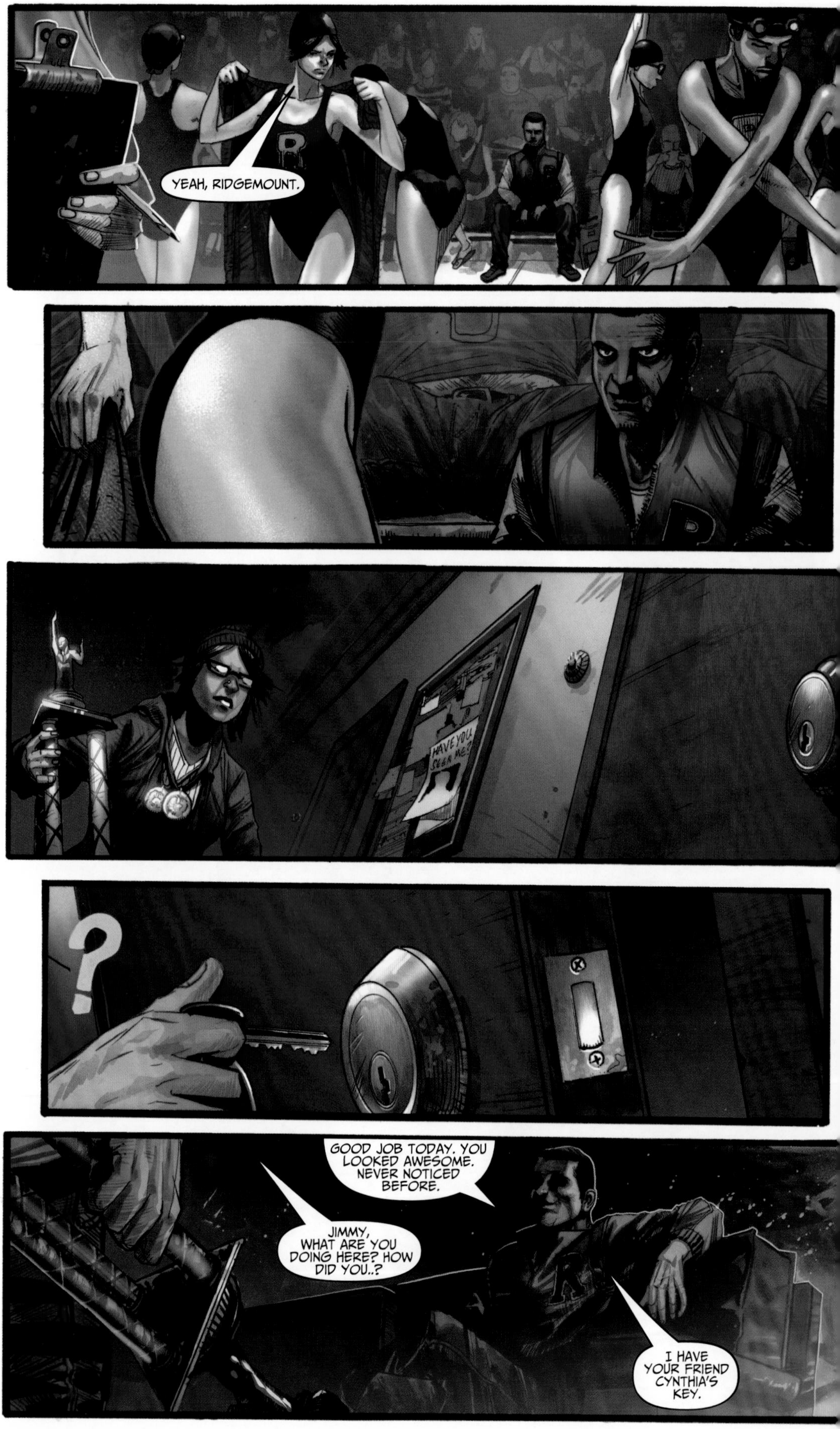
YEAH, RIDGEMOUNT.
HAVE YOU SEEN ME?
?
GOOD JOB TODAY. YOU LOOKED AWESOME. NEVER NOTICED BEFORE.
JIMMY, WHAT ARE YOU DOING HERE? HOW DID YOU..?
I HAVE YOUR FRIEND CYNTHIA'S KEY.

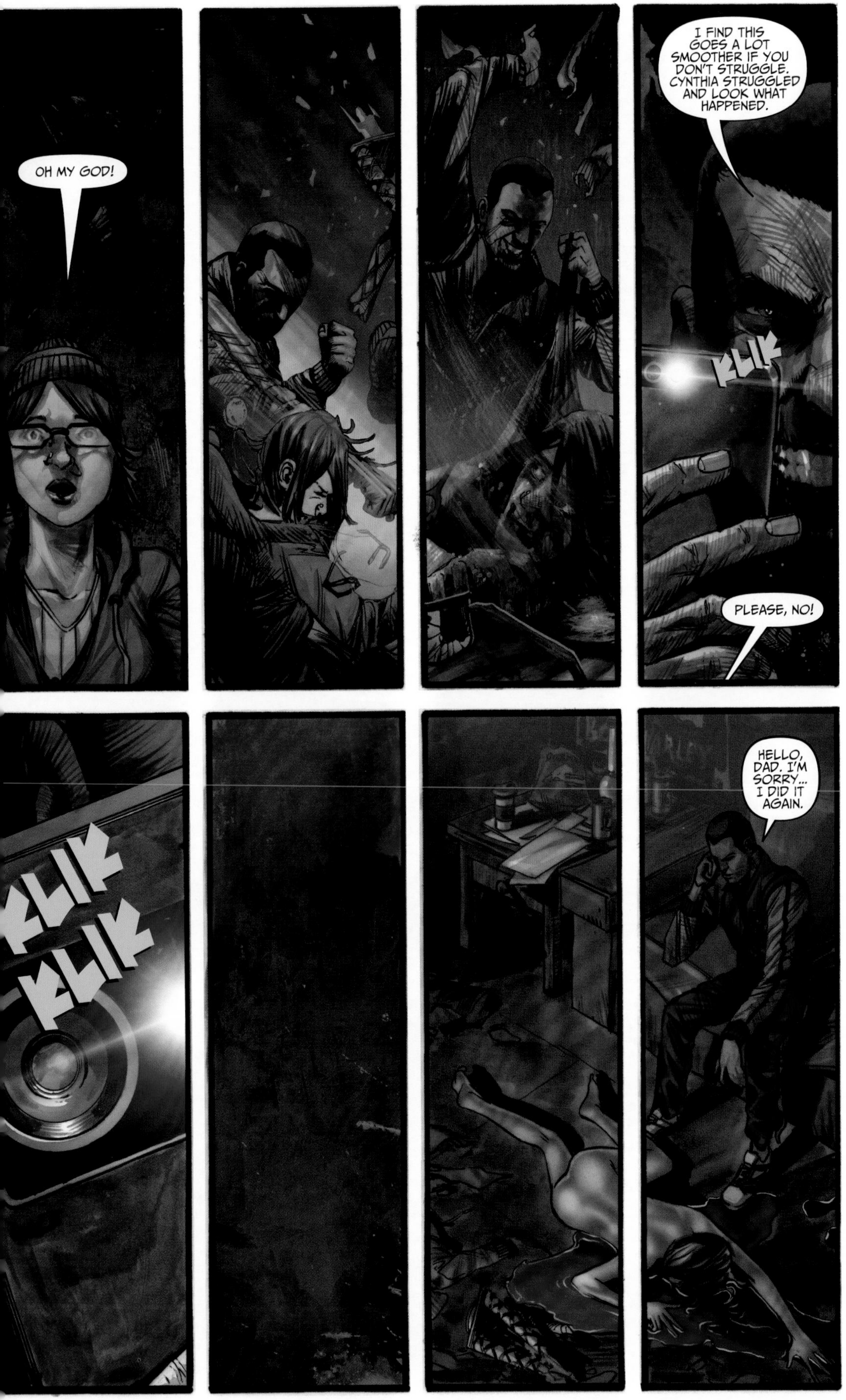
OH MY GOD!
I FIND THIS GOES A LOT SMOOTHER IF YOU DON'T STRUGGLE. CYNTHIA STRUGGLED AND LOOK WHAT HAPPENED.
KLIK
PLEASE, NO!
KLIK
KLIK
HELLO, DAD. I'M SORRY... I DID IT AGAIN.

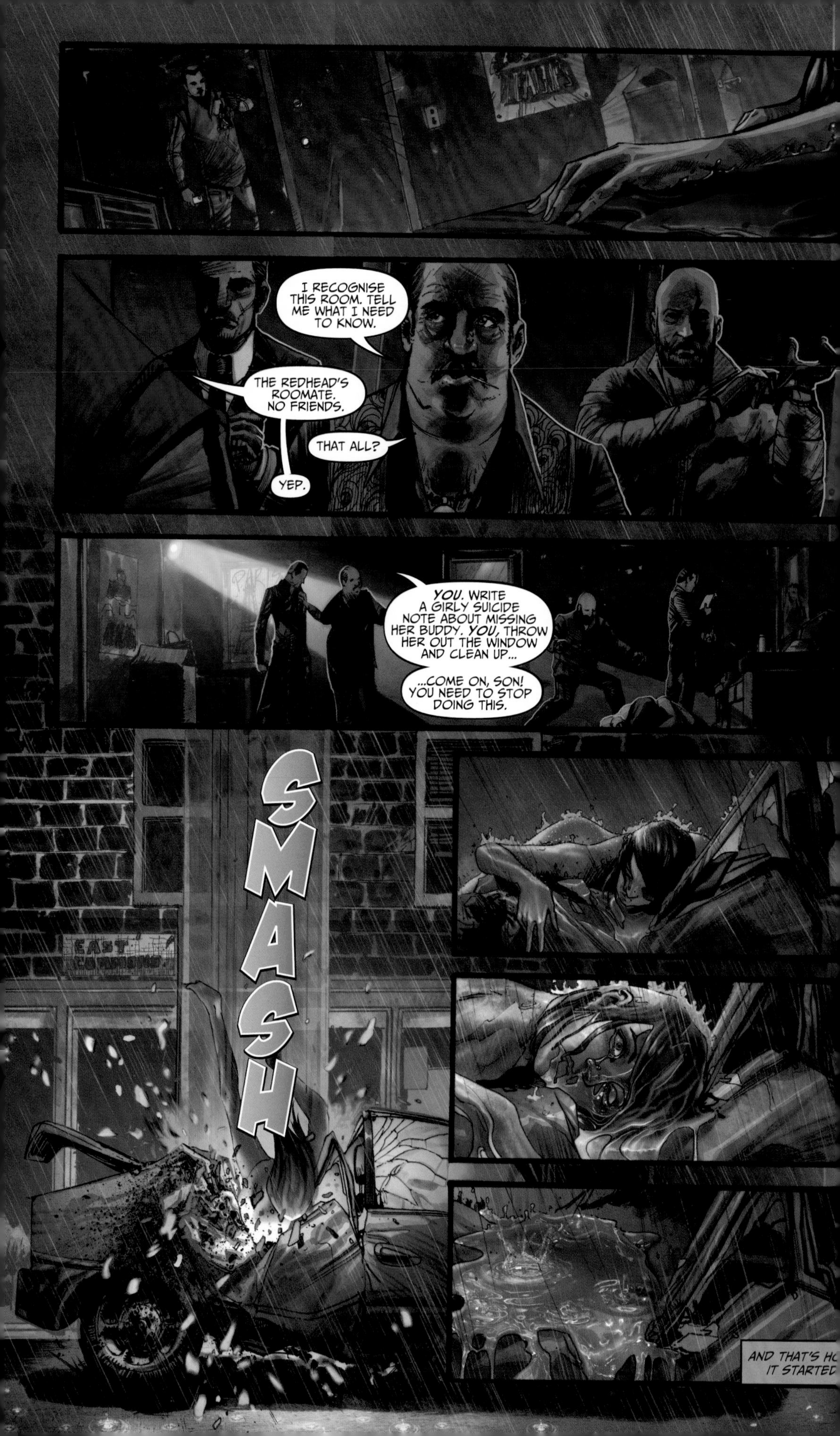
I RECOGNISE THIS ROOM. TELL ME WHAT I NEED TO KNOW.
THE REDHEAD'S ROOMATE. NO FRIENDS.
THAT ALL?
YEP.
YOU. WRITE A GIRLY SUICIDE NOTE ABOUT MISSING HER BUDDY. YOU, THROW HER OUT THE WINDOW AND CLEAN UP...
...COME ON, SON! YOU NEED TO STOP DOING THIS.
SMASH
EAST
AND THAT'S HO
IT STARTED

IBEP...
USSRS...
SIT. BEP
...USSRS...
SIT.

...OH!
HE SAID
REVERSE
IT!

TA-DA!

YOU'RE GETTING
GOOD AT THAT.
WHAT THE
FUCK *WAS*
IT?

SEVERE
IMPETIGO.

THAT
HURT. HOW
MANY DISEASES
HAVE YOU GIVEN
ME THESE LAST
SIX WEEKS?

The multi-billionaire has revealed that not only is
he intending to colonize Mars but is working on
technology that will enable travel beyond the
Solar System...

I THOUGHT
EDWARDS WAS A
MEDIA GUY WHO OWNED
TV NETWORKS.

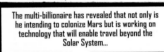

I OWN
LOTS OF THINGS.
AMASSED OVER A LOT
OF YEARS. INCLUDING
TV NETWORKS...

...THAT'S
NOT ONE OF
MINE.

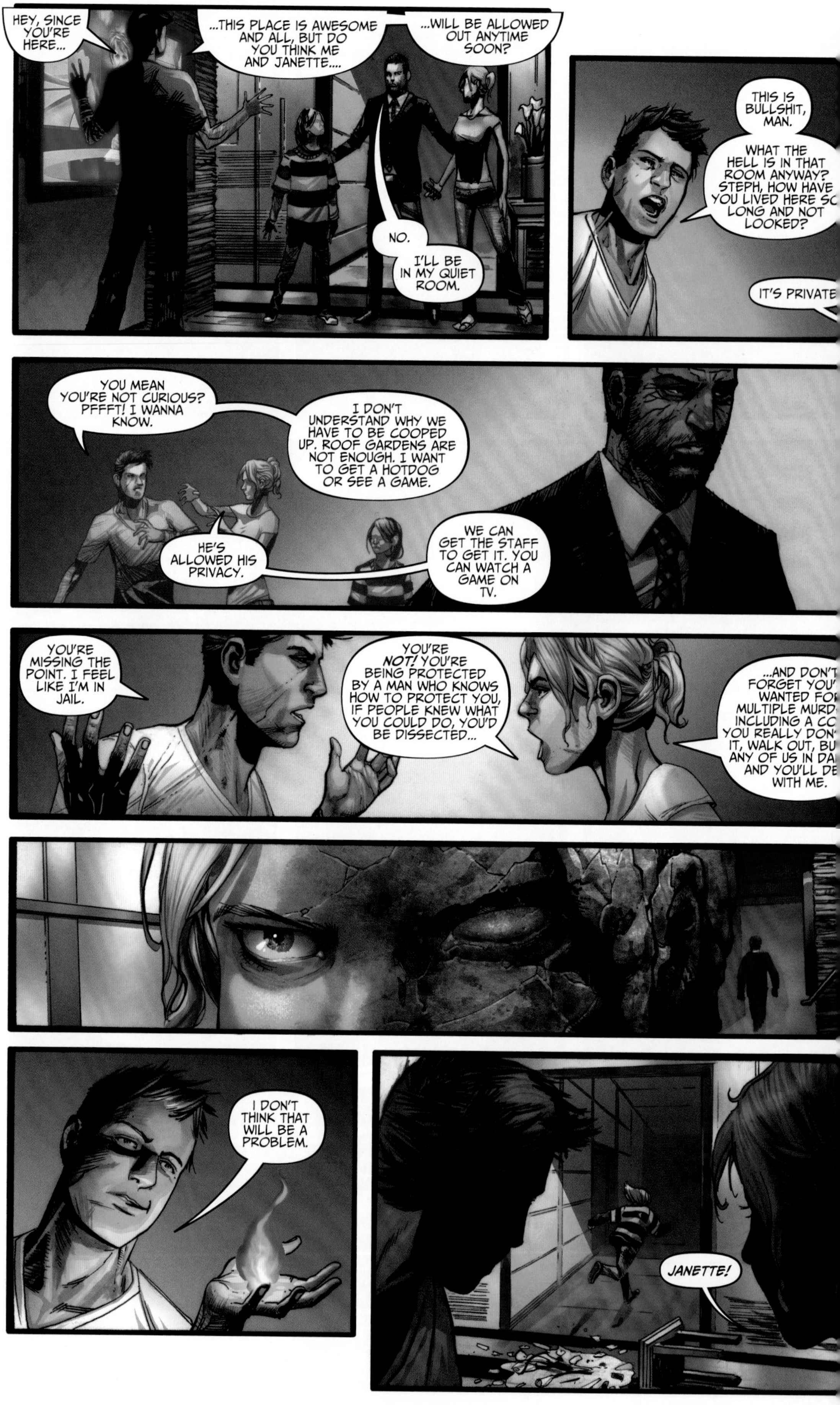

HEY, SINCE YOU'RE HERE...
...THIS PLACE IS AWESOME AND ALL, BUT DO YOU THINK ME AND JANETTE....
...WILL BE ALLOWED OUT ANYTIME SOON?
NO.
I'LL BE IN MY QUIET ROOM.
THIS IS BULLSHIT, MAN.
WHAT THE HELL IS IN THAT ROOM ANYWAY? STEPH, HOW HAVE YOU LIVED HERE SO LONG AND NOT LOOKED?
IT'S PRIVATE
YOU MEAN YOU'RE NOT CURIOUS? PFFFT! I WANNA KNOW.
I DON'T UNDERSTAND WHY WE HAVE TO BE COOPED UP. ROOF GARDENS ARE NOT ENOUGH. I WANT TO GET A HOTDOG OR SEE A GAME.
HE'S ALLOWED HIS PRIVACY.
WE CAN GET THE STAFF TO GET IT. YOU CAN WATCH A GAME ON TV.
YOU'RE MISSING THE POINT. I FEEL LIKE I'M IN JAIL.
YOU'RE NOT! YOU'RE BEING PROTECTED BY A MAN WHO KNOWS HOW TO PROTECT YOU, IF PEOPLE KNEW WHAT YOU COULD DO, YOU'D BE DISSECTED...
...AND DON'T FORGET YOU' WANTED FOR MULTIPLE MURD INCLUDING A CO YOU REALLY DON' IT, WALK OUT, BU ANY OF US IN DA AND YOU'LL DE WITH ME.
I DON'T THINK THAT WILL BE A PROBLEM.
JANETTE!

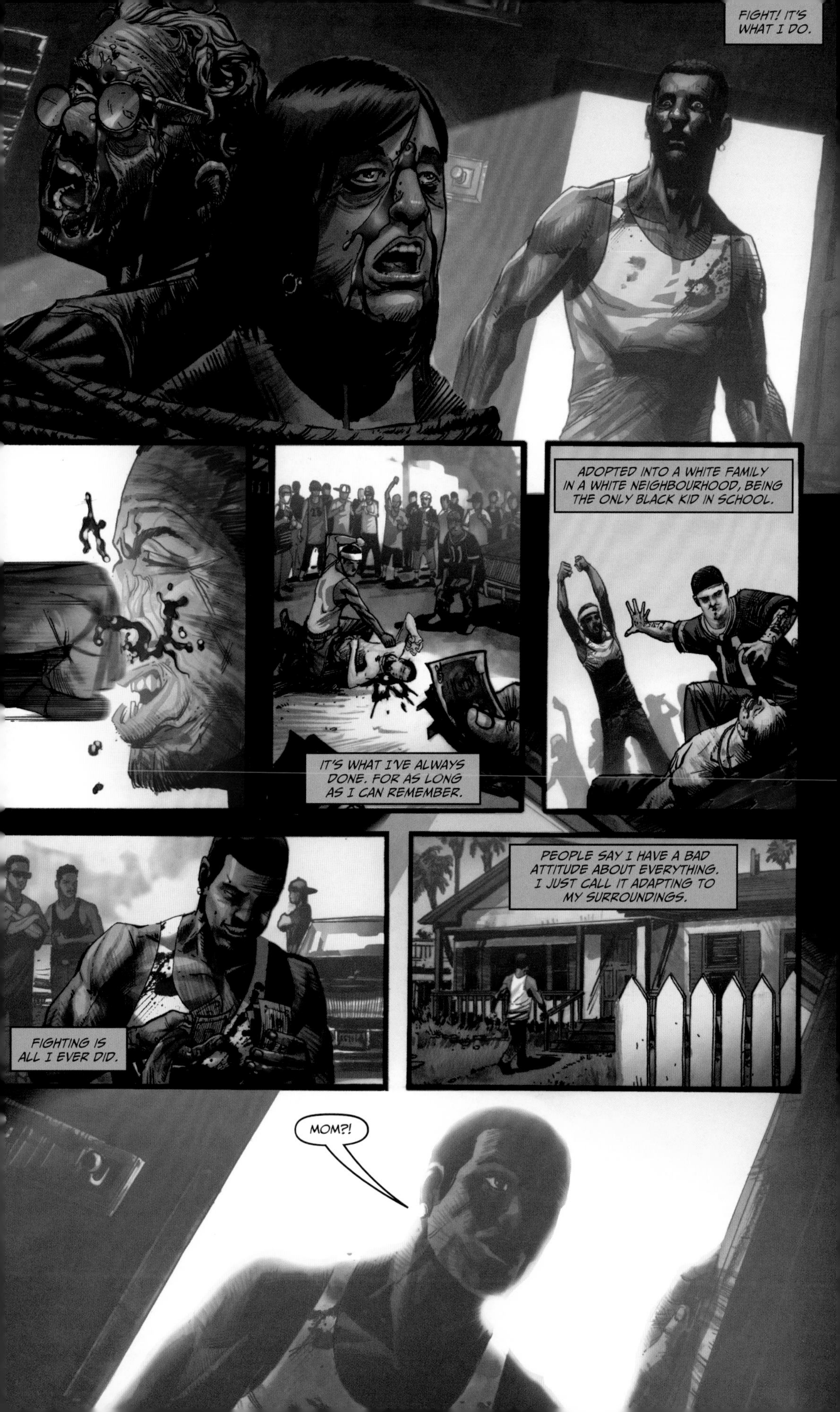
FIGHT! IT'S WHAT I DO.
IT'S WHAT I'VE ALWAYS DONE. FOR AS LONG AS I CAN REMEMBER.
ADOPTED INTO A WHITE FAMILY IN A WHITE NEIGHBOURHOOD, BEING THE ONLY BLACK KID IN SCHOOL.
FIGHTING IS ALL I EVER DID.
PEOPLE SAY I HAVE A BAD ATTITUDE ABOUT EVERYTHING. I JUST CALL IT ADAPTING TO MY SURROUNDINGS.
MOM?!

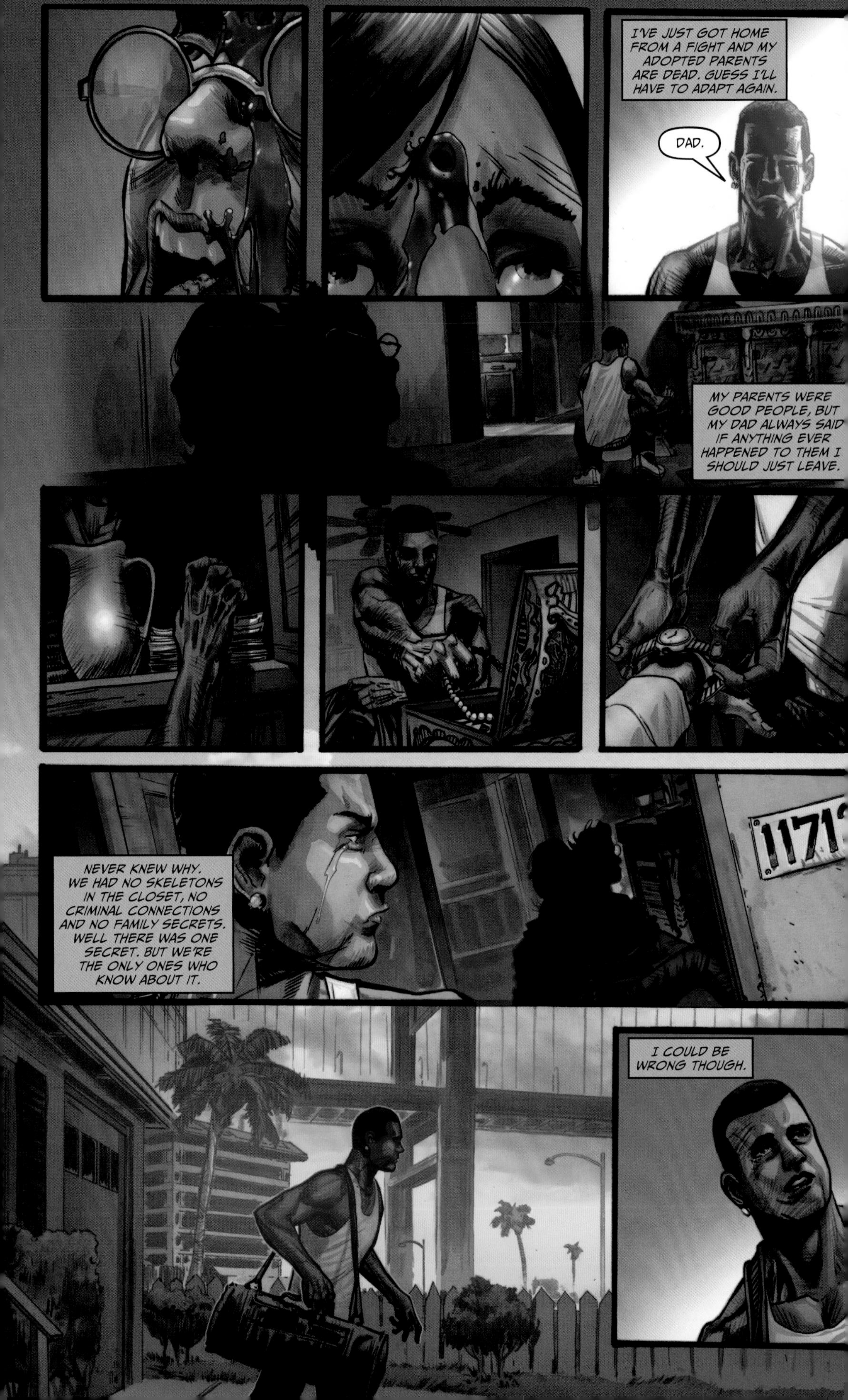
I'VE JUST GOT HOME FROM A FIGHT AND MY ADOPTED PARENTS ARE DEAD. GUESS I'LL HAVE TO ADAPT AGAIN.
DAD.
MY PARENTS WERE GOOD PEOPLE, BUT MY DAD ALWAYS SAID IF ANYTHING EVER HAPPENED TO THEM I SHOULD JUST LEAVE.
NEVER KNEW WHY. WE HAD NO SKELETONS IN THE CLOSET, NO CRIMINAL CONNECTIONS AND NO FAMILY SECRETS. WELL THERE WAS ONE SECRET. BUT WE'RE THE ONLY ONES WHO KNOW ABOUT IT.
I COULD BE WRONG THOUGH.

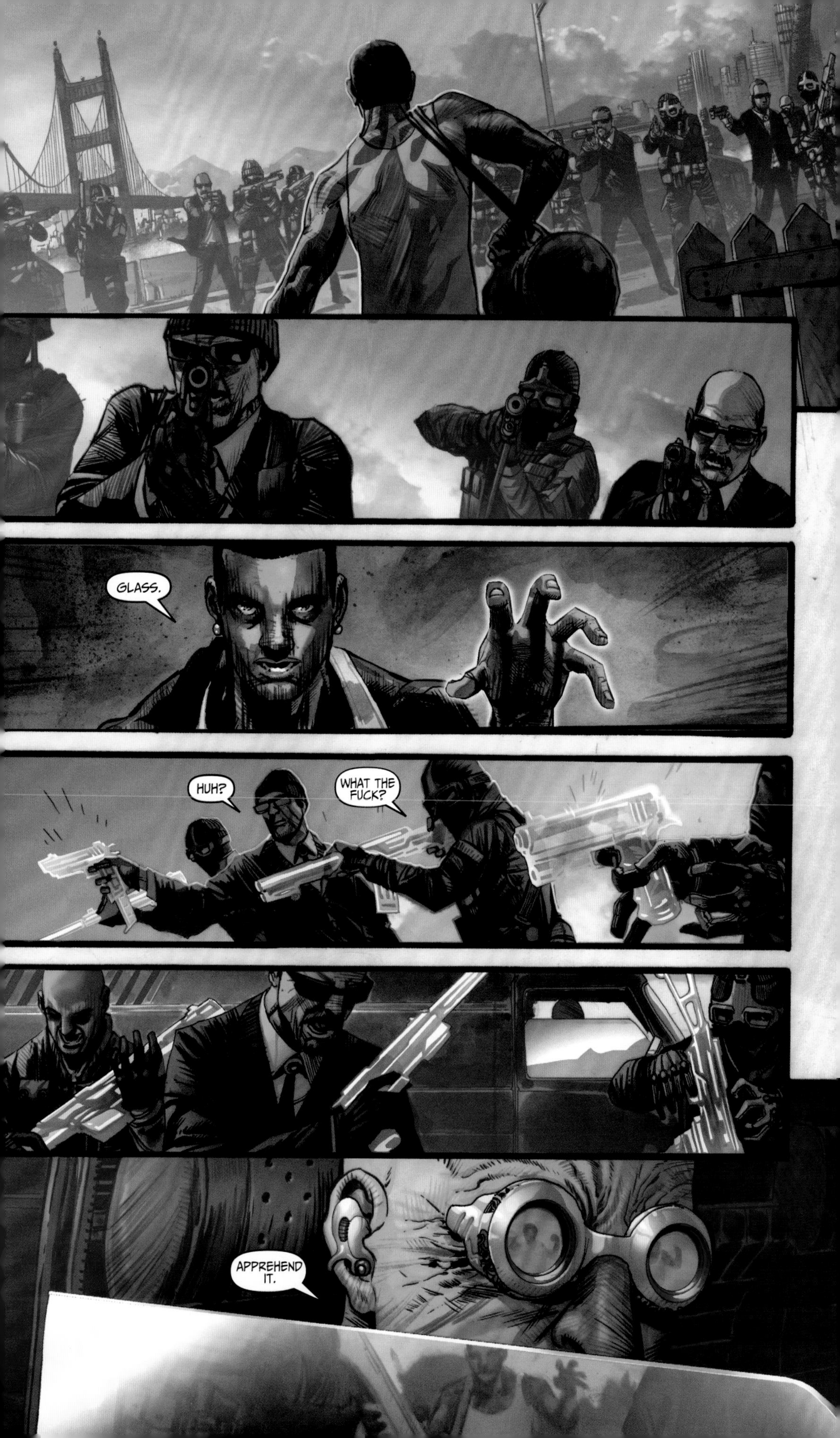
GLASS.
HUH?
WHAT THE FUCK?
APPREHEND IT.

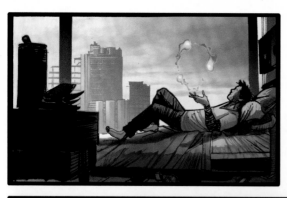

DON'T OPEN THIS DOOR.

I GET I CAN'T JUST GO WHERE I WANT. SO I WANNA KNOW EVERYTHING ABOUT THE PLACE I'M IN...

...INCLUDING WHY ELON MUSK HERE WON'T LET ANYONE IN THAT ROOM.

I'LL TELEPORT YOU OUT AT THE FIRST SIGN OF TROUBLE.

YOU'RE RIGHT!

MAY I'M BE OVERLY YOU SH BE ALLO OUTSI

...I'V BOOK THE T OF YC TABLE DINNER PECAN

HA THE DR TAKE Y

FYI. NEVER, EV GO INTO M ROOM.

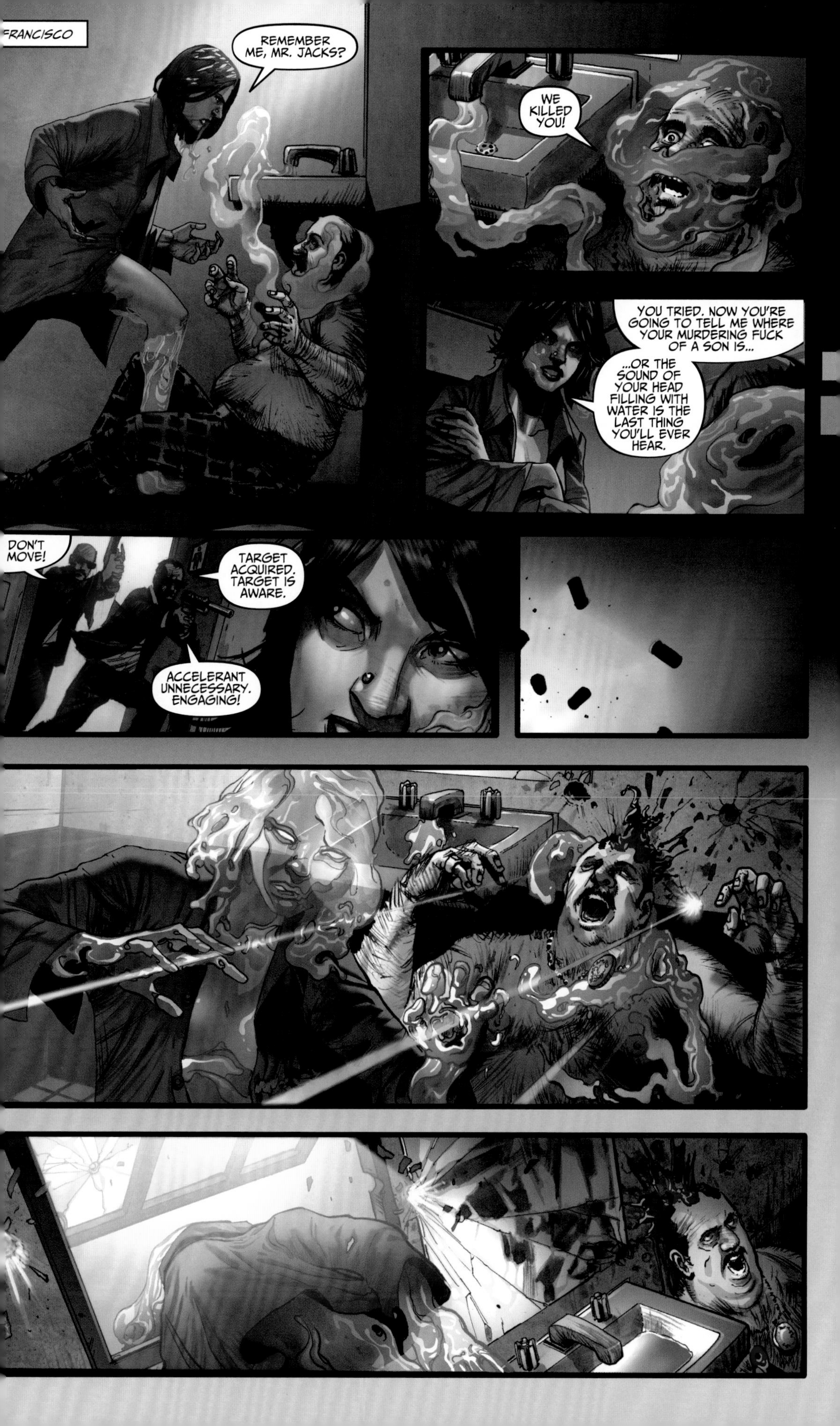
FRANCISCO
REMEMBER ME, MR. JACKS?
WE KILLED YOU!
YOU TRIED. NOW YOU'RE GOING TO TELL ME WHERE YOUR MURDERING FUCK OF A SON IS...
...OR THE SOUND OF YOUR HEAD FILLING WITH WATER IS THE LAST THING YOU'LL EVER HEAR.
DON'T MOVE!
TARGET ACQUIRED. TARGET IS AWARE.
ACCELERANT UNNECESSARY. ENGAGING!

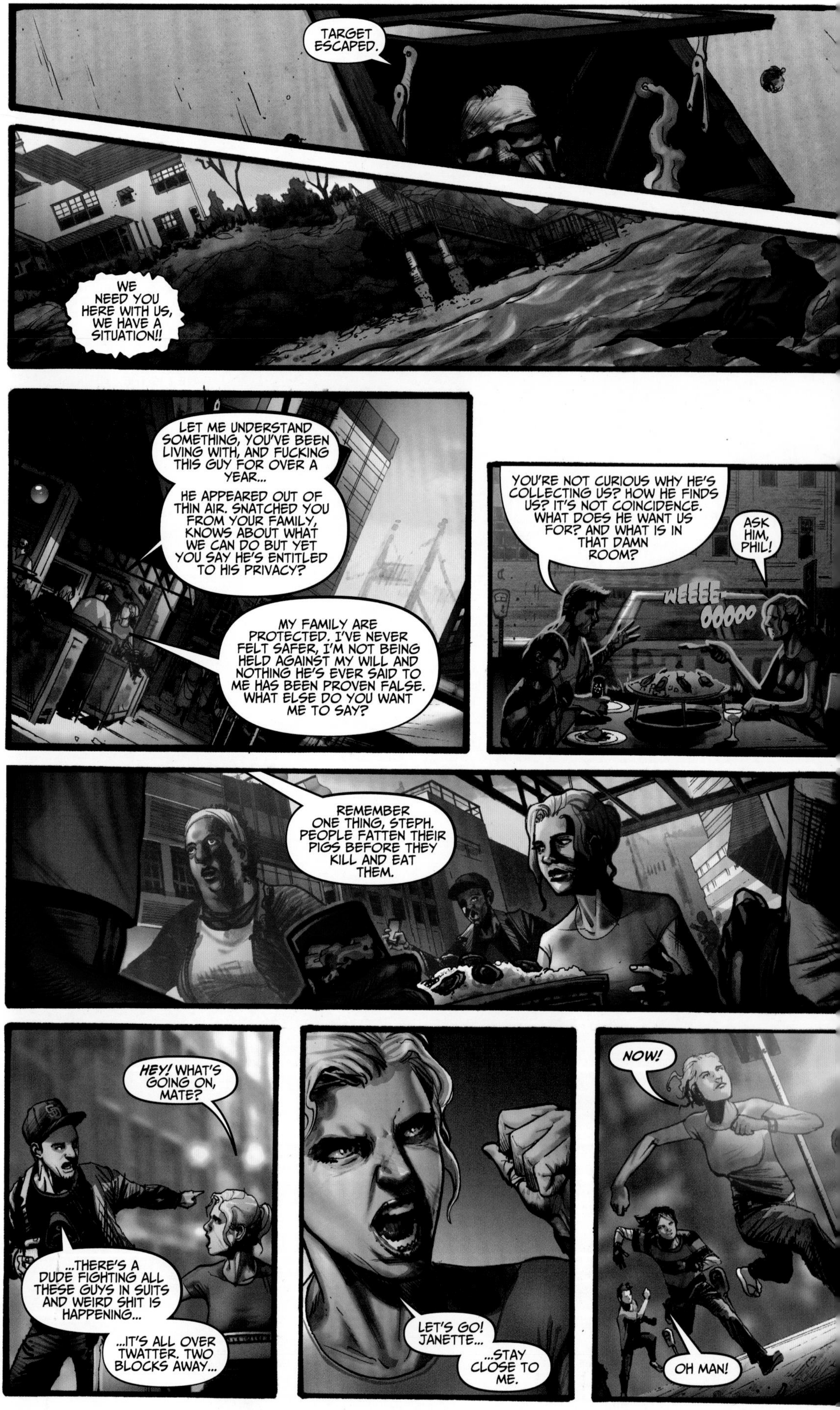
TARGET ESCAPED.
WE NEED YOU HERE WITH US, WE HAVE A SITUATION!!
LET ME UNDERSTAND SOMETHING, YOU'VE BEEN LIVING WITH, AND FUCKING THIS GUY FOR OVER A YEAR...
HE APPEARED OUT OF THIN AIR. SNATCHED YOU FROM YOUR FAMILY, KNOWS ABOUT WHAT WE CAN DO BUT YET YOU SAY HE'S ENTITLED TO HIS PRIVACY?
MY FAMILY ARE PROTECTED. I'VE NEVER FELT SAFER, I'M NOT BEING HELD AGAINST MY WILL AND NOTHING HE'S EVER SAID TO ME HAS BEEN PROVEN FALSE. WHAT ELSE DO YOU WANT ME TO SAY?
YOU'RE NOT CURIOUS WHY HE'S COLLECTING US? HOW HE FINDS US? IT'S NOT COINCIDENCE. WHAT DOES HE WANT US FOR? AND WHAT IS IN THAT DAMN ROOM?
ASK HIM, PHIL!
WEEEE
OOOOO
REMEMBER ONE THING, STEPH. PEOPLE FATTEN THEIR PIGS BEFORE THEY KILL AND EAT THEM.
HEY! WHAT'S GOING ON, MATE?
...THERE'S A DUDE FIGHTING ALL THESE GUYS IN SUITS AND WEIRD SHIT IS HAPPENING...
...IT'S ALL OVER TWATTER. TWO BLOCKS AWAY...
LET'S GO! JANETTE...
...STAY CLOSE TO ME.
NOW!
OH MAN!

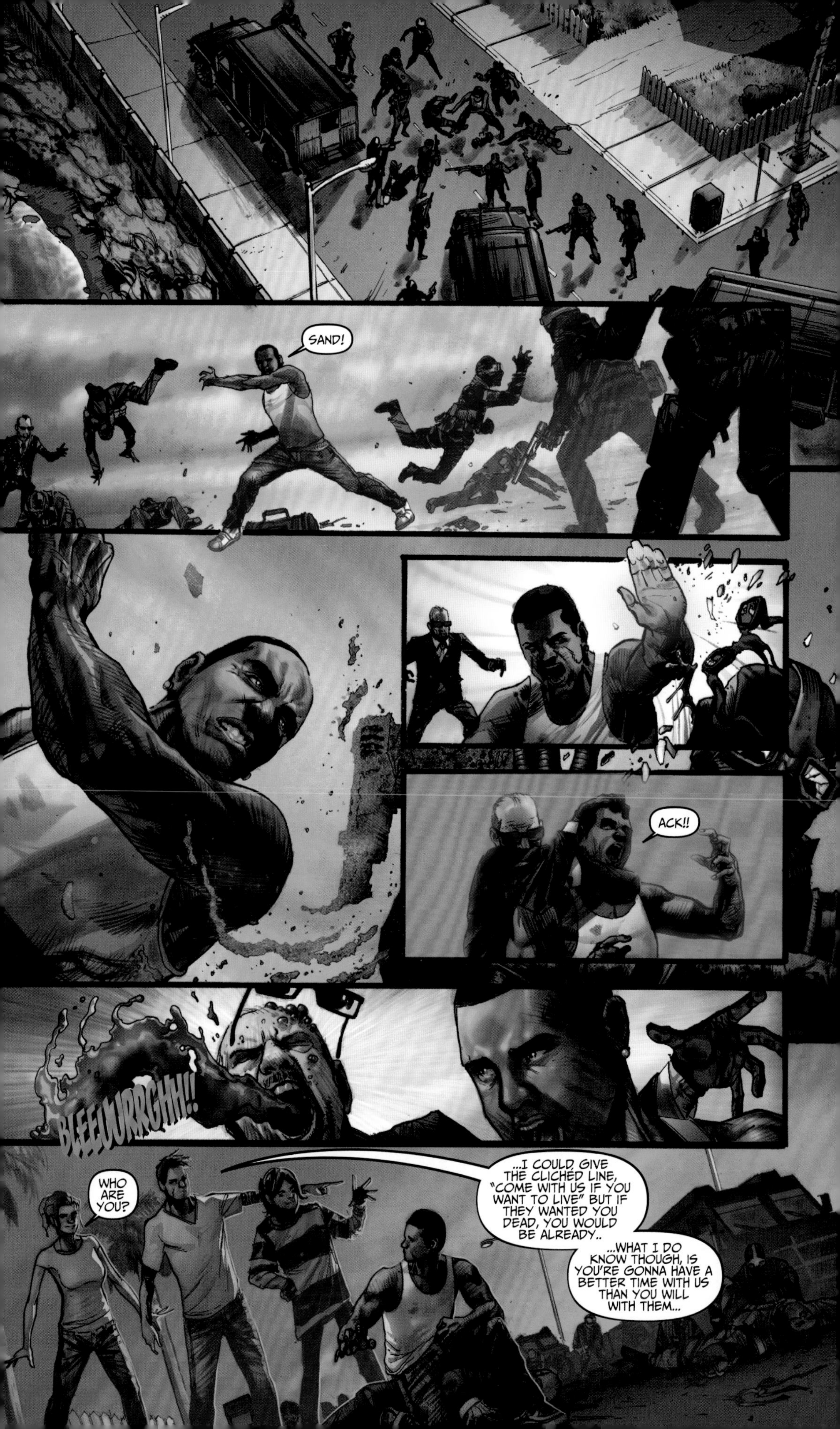
SAND!
ACK!!
BLEEUURRGHH!!
WHO ARE YOU?
...I COULD GIVE THE CLICHÉD LINE, "COME WITH US IF YOU WANT TO LIVE" BUT IF THEY WANTED YOU DEAD, YOU WOULD BE ALREADY..
...WHAT I DO KNOW THOUGH, IS YOU'RE GONNA HAVE A BETTER TIME WITH US THAN YOU WILL WITH THEM...

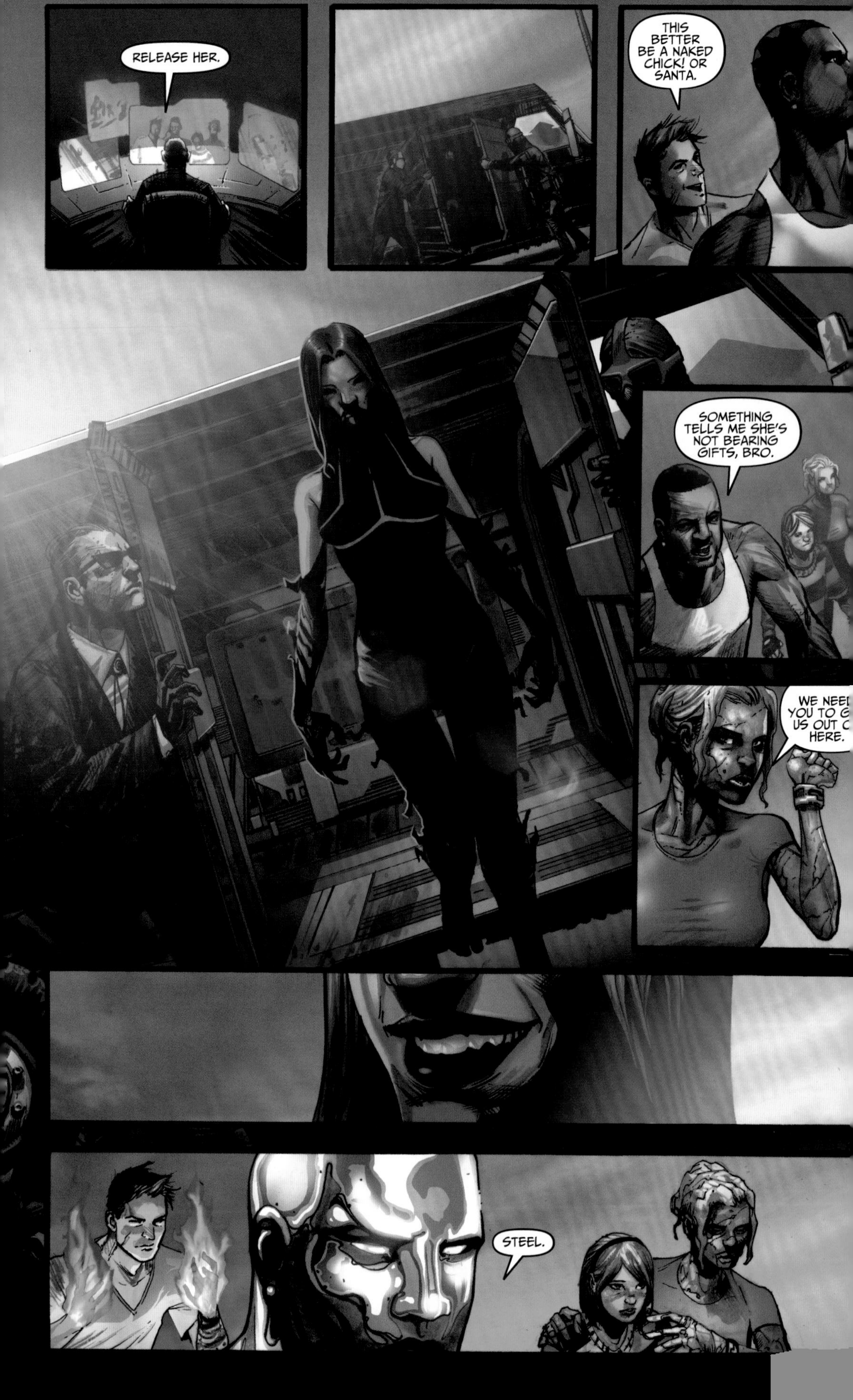
RELEASE HER.
THIS BETTER BE A NAKED CHICK! OR SANTA.
SOMETHING TELLS ME SHE'S NOT BEARING GIFTS, BRO.
WE NEE YOU TO G US OUT HERE.
STEEL.

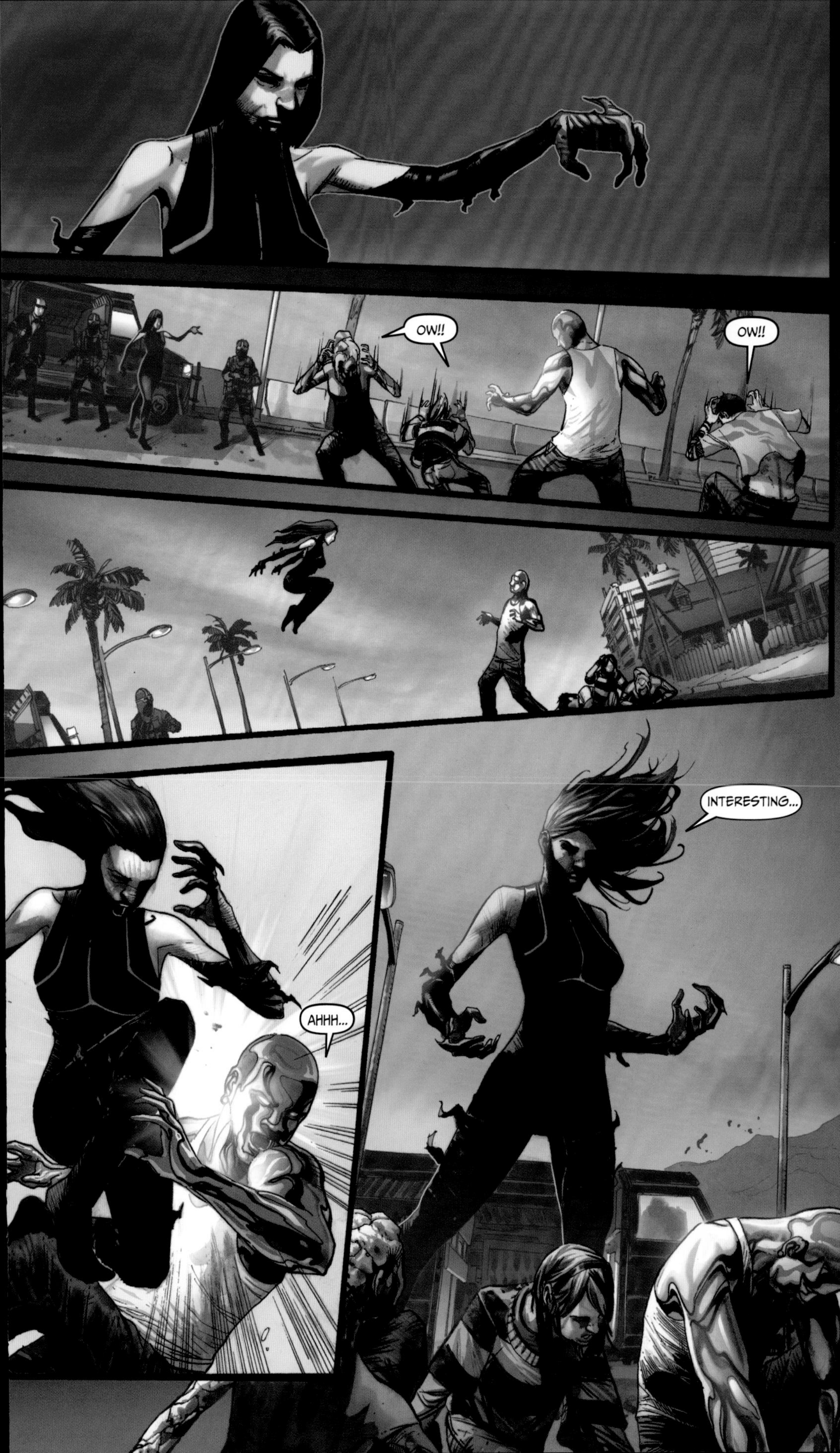
OW!!
OW!!
INTERESTING...
AHHH...

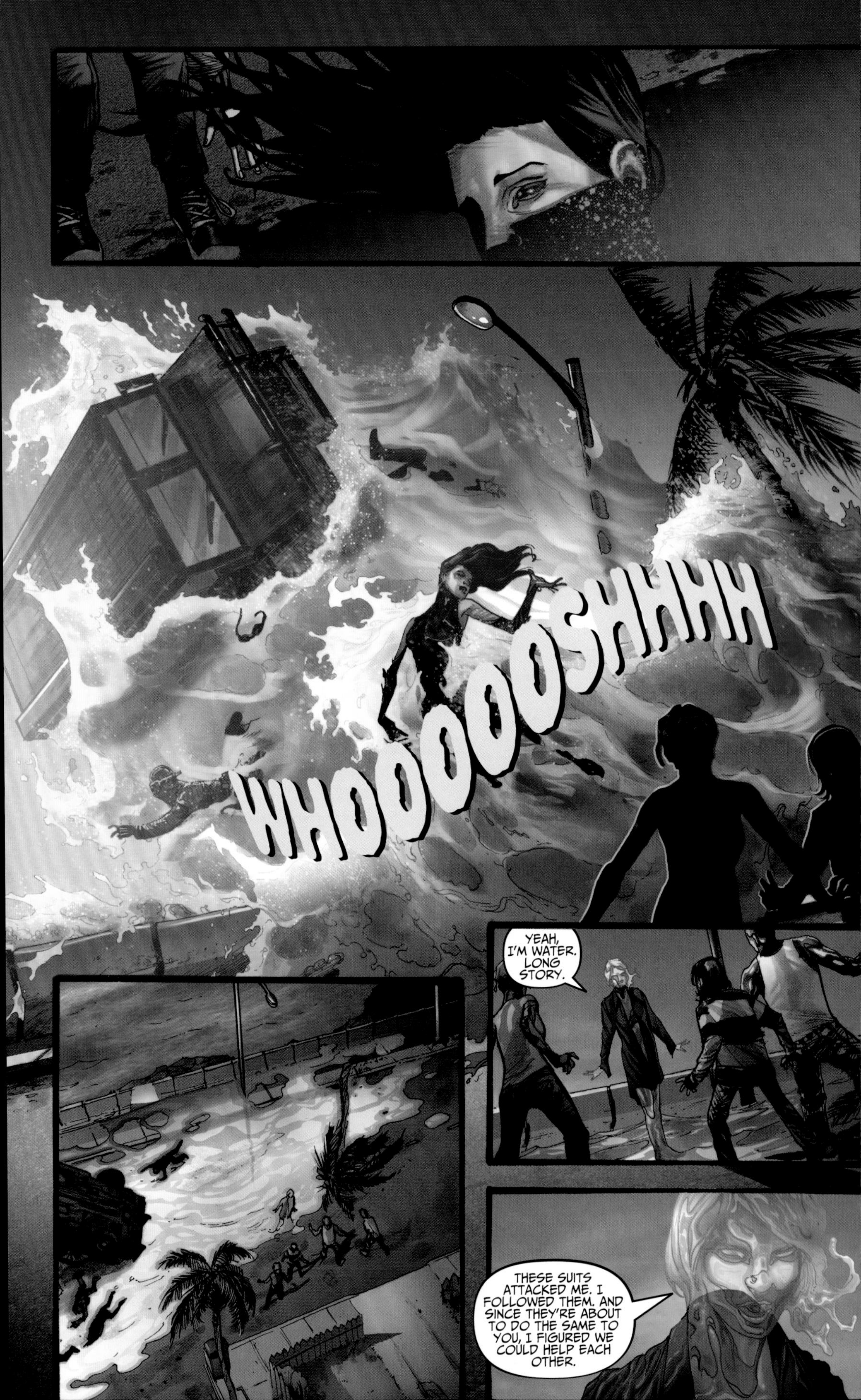
WHOOOOOOSHHHH
YEAH, I'M WATER. LONG STORY.
THESE SUITS ATTACKED ME. I FOLLOWED THEM. AND SINCE THEY'RE ABOUT TO DO THE SAME TO YOU, I FIGURED WE COULD HELP EACH OTHER.

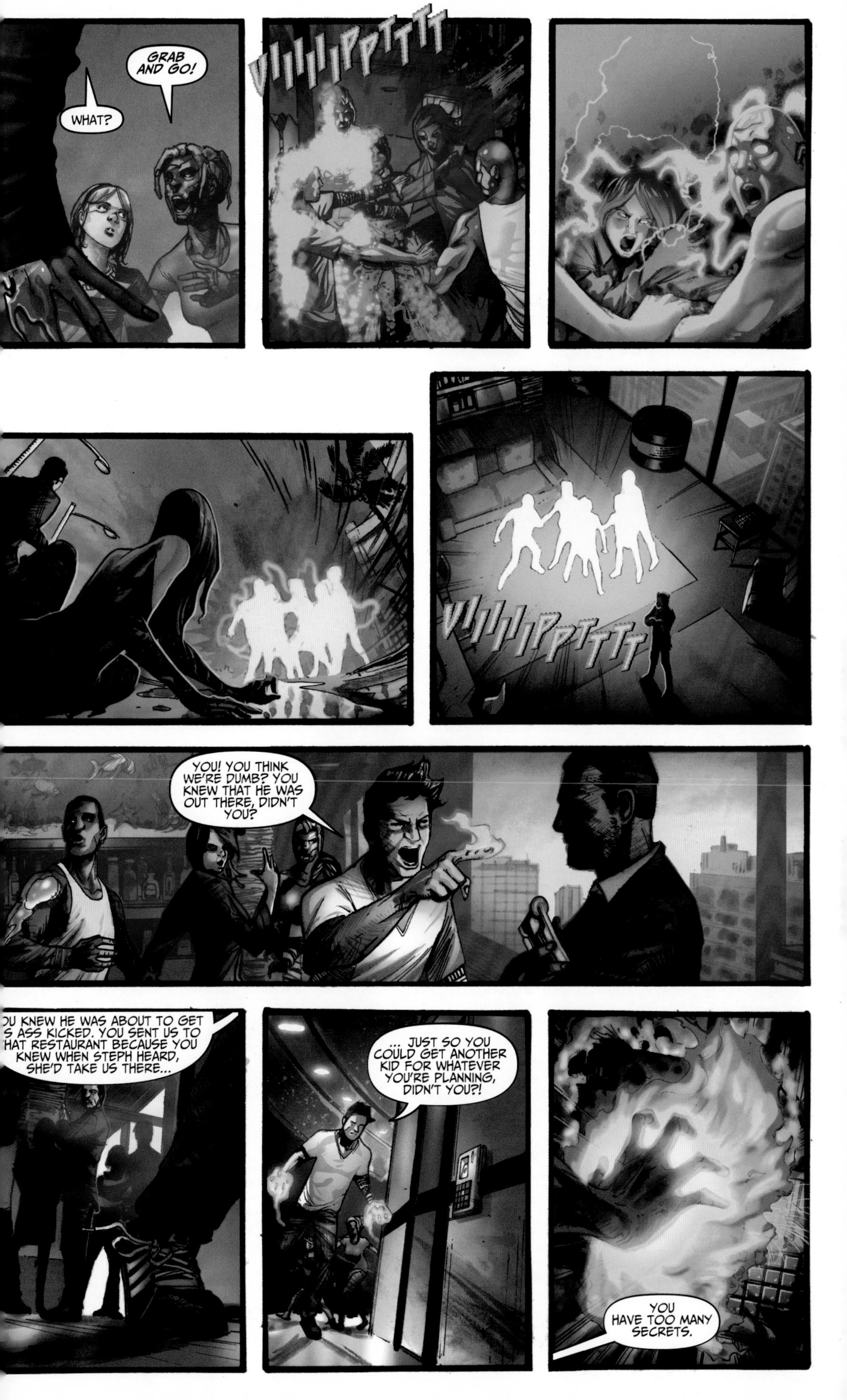
GRAB AND GO!
WHAT?
VIIIIIIPPTTTT
VIIIIIIPPTTTTT
YOU! YOU THINK WE'RE DUMB? YOU KNEW THAT HE WAS OUT THERE, DIDN'T YOU?
OU KNEW HE WAS ABOUT TO GET S ASS KICKED. YOU SENT US TO HAT RESTAURANT BECAUSE YOU KNEW WHEN STEPH HEARD, SHE'D TAKE US THERE...
... JUST SO YOU COULD GET ANOTHER KID FOR WHATEVER YOU'RE PLANNING, DIDN'T YOU?!
YOU HAVE TOO MANY SECRETS.

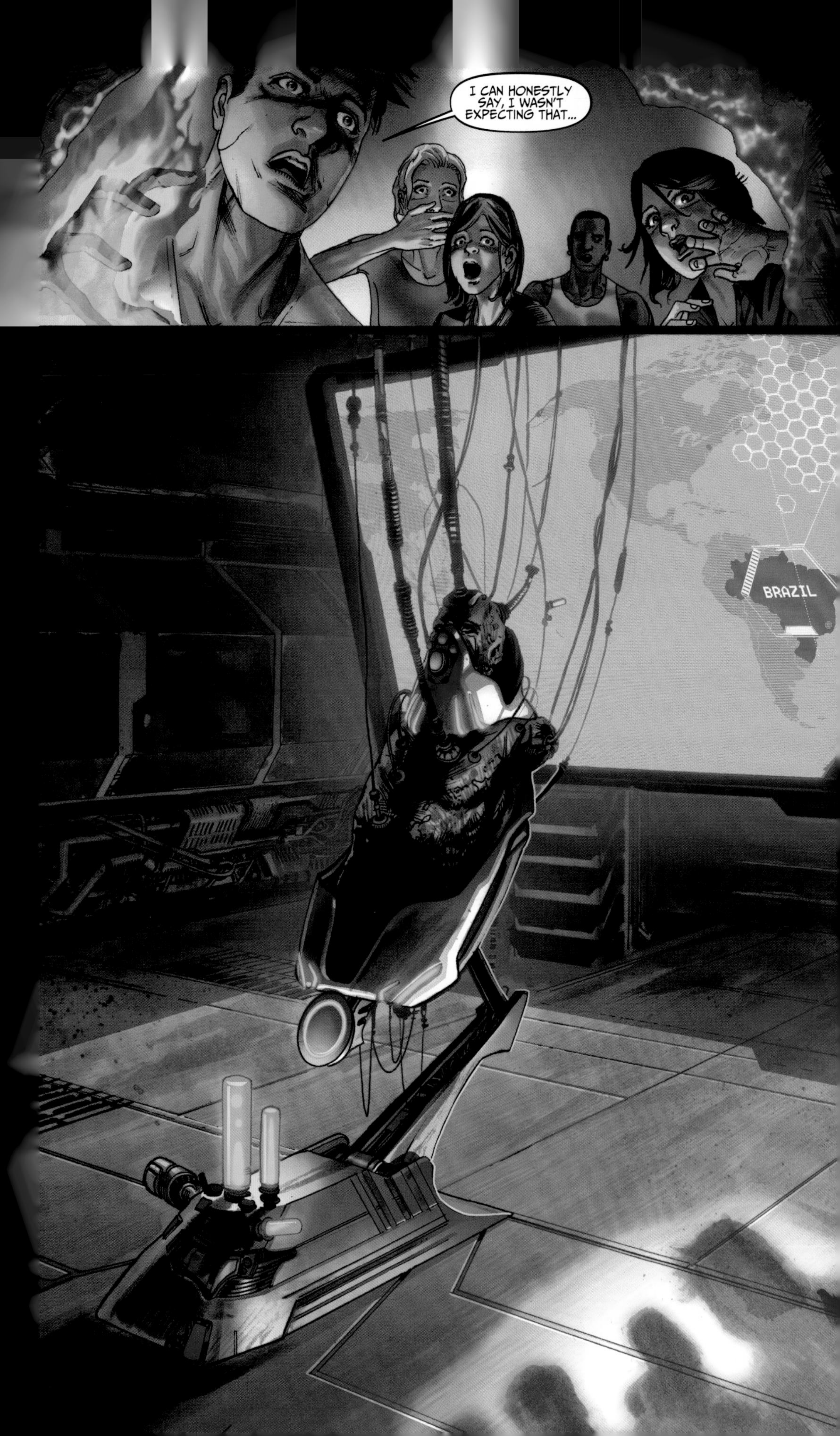
I CAN HONESTLY SAY, I WASN'T EXPECTING THAT...
BRAZIL

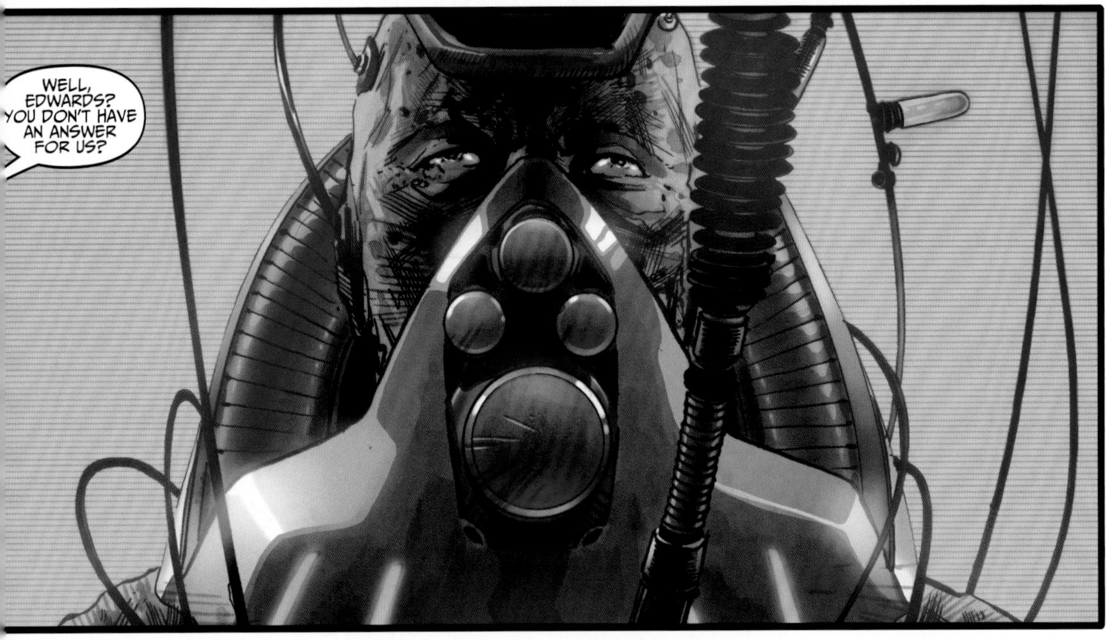
WELL, EDWARDS? YOU DON'T HAVE AN ANSWER FOR US?

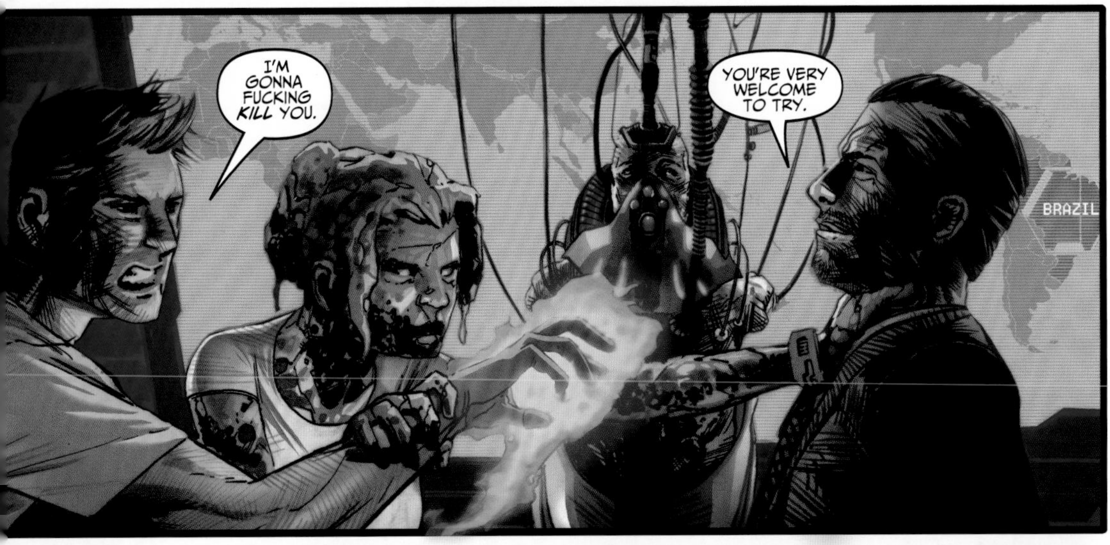
I'M GONNA FUCKING *KILL* YOU.
YOU'RE VERY WELCOME TO TRY.
BRAZIL

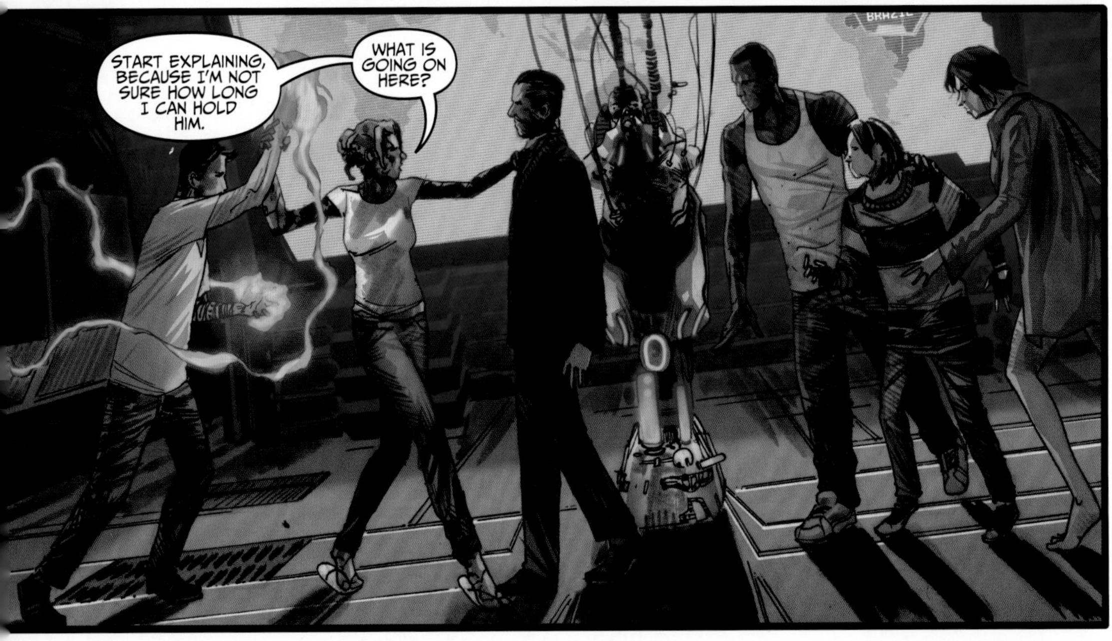
START EXPLAINING, BECAUSE I'M NOT SURE HOW LONG I CAN HOLD HIM.
WHAT IS GOING ON HERE?

THOSE PEOPLE IN THE CLICHÉ SUITS CHASING YOU. THEY'RE CALLED ILLUSION.

THEY KILLED MY PARENTS.

ALIENS? FUCK THIS BULLSHIT...

...LET ME BAKE THIS ASSHOLE.

THEY'RE A HUNDRED TIMES MORE SECRET THAN THE CIA, NSA, MAJESTIC... WHATEVER YOU THINK YOU KNOW, YOU DON'T...

...THEY DO. THEY'RE THE PLANET'S LEADER IN COVERT OPERATIONS, GENETICS, SPLICING HUMANS WITH OFF-WORLD DNA IN THE HOPE OF CREATING AN ARMY OF EVOLVED HUMANS.

SO YOU CAN ACCEPT THAT SHE TURNS TO ROCK, YOU CATCH FIRE, SHE TURNS TO WATER?

YOU TAKE IT AS UNASSAILABLE FACT THAT A YOUNG GIRL CAN INFECT YOU WITH ANY VIRUS SHE KNOWS THE MECHANICS OF, BUT NOT THAT THERE ARE THINGS ON AND NOT ON THIS WORLD THAT HAVE MORE POWER THAN YOU CAN IMAGINE? YOU'RE A VERY NAIVE LITTLE BOY.

22 YEARS AGO, ILLUSION CONDUCTED A CONTAINED EXPERIMENT...

...THEY CREATED A SERUM. THEY INFECTED A 747 FULL OF PEOPLE WITH OFF-WORLD EMBRYONIC STEM CELLS. YOU ARE THE CHILDREN OF SOME OF THOSE PEOPLE.

HOW DO YOU KNOW ABOUT US, DUDE?

I'M THE THIRD RICHEST PERSON ON THE PLANET. I KNOW ABOUT EVERYTHING...

...I'VE DEAL GENETIC FOR YEAR

...I HEARD ABOU THE EXPERIMEN HEARD KIDS LIK YOU MAY EXIST, E I WANT TO STO WHAT THEY'RE DOING...

...BECAUSE WHOEVER HAS THAT LIST OF PASSENGERS AND IS NOW HUNTING THEIR CHILDREN, DOESN'T HAVE THE BEST OF INTENTIONS.

THAT'S A CUTE LITTLE STORY, BUT THAT WASN'T WHAT I WAS ASKING. IF THEY HAVE BAD INTENTIONS, THEN WHAT DO YOU CALL THAT?

AND, MORE IMPORTANTLY, WHO IS HE?

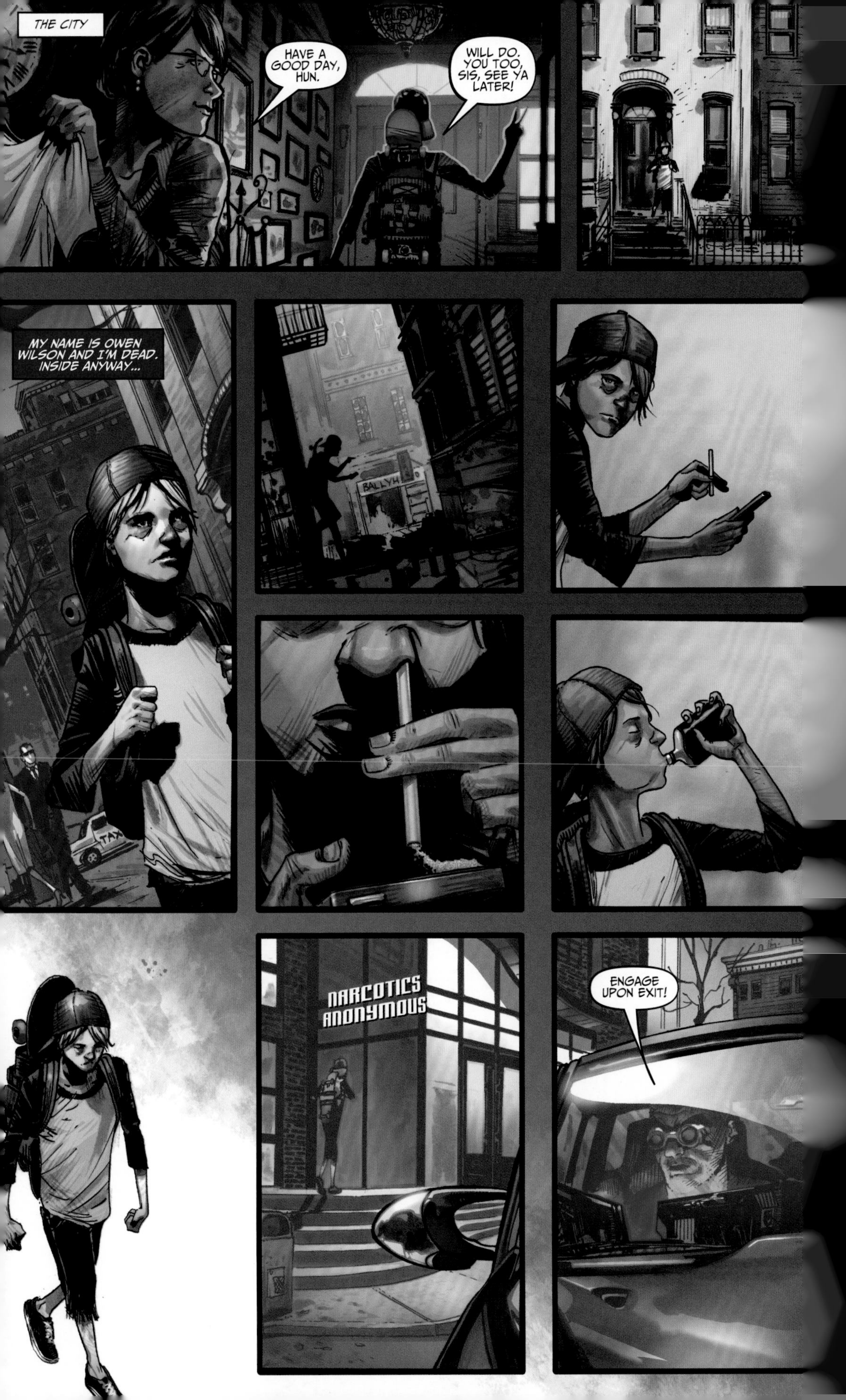
THE CITY
HAVE A GOOD DAY, HUN.
WILL DO. YOU TOO, SIS, SEE YA LATER!
MY NAME IS OWEN WILSON AND I'M DEAD. INSIDE ANYWAY...
TAXI
NARCOTICS ANONYMOUS
ENGAGE UPON EXIT!

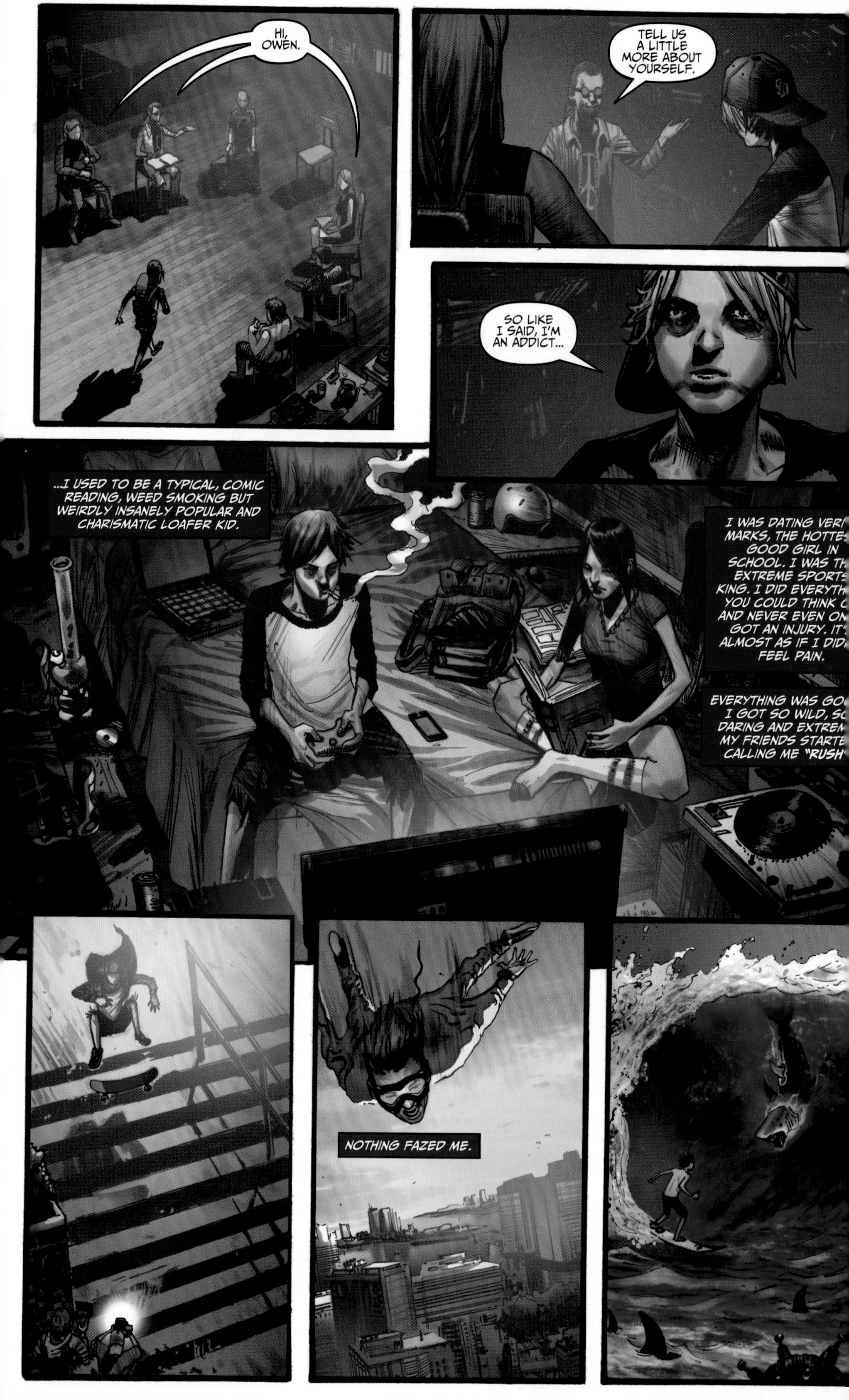
HI, OWEN.
TELL US A LITTLE MORE ABOUT YOURSELF.
SO LIKE I SAID, I'M AN ADDICT...
...I USED TO BE A TYPICAL, COMIC READING, WEED SMOKING BUT WEIRDLY INSANELY POPULAR AND CHARISMATIC LOAFER KID.
I WAS DATING VERI MARKS, THE HOTTES GOOD GIRL IN SCHOOL. I WAS TH EXTREME SPORTS KING. I DID EVERYTH YOU COULD THINK O AND NEVER EVEN ON GOT AN INJURY. IT'S ALMOST AS IF I DID FEEL PAIN.
EVERYTHING WAS GO I GOT SO WILD, SO DARING AND EXTREM MY FRIENDS STARTE CALLING ME "RUSH
NOTHING FAZED ME.

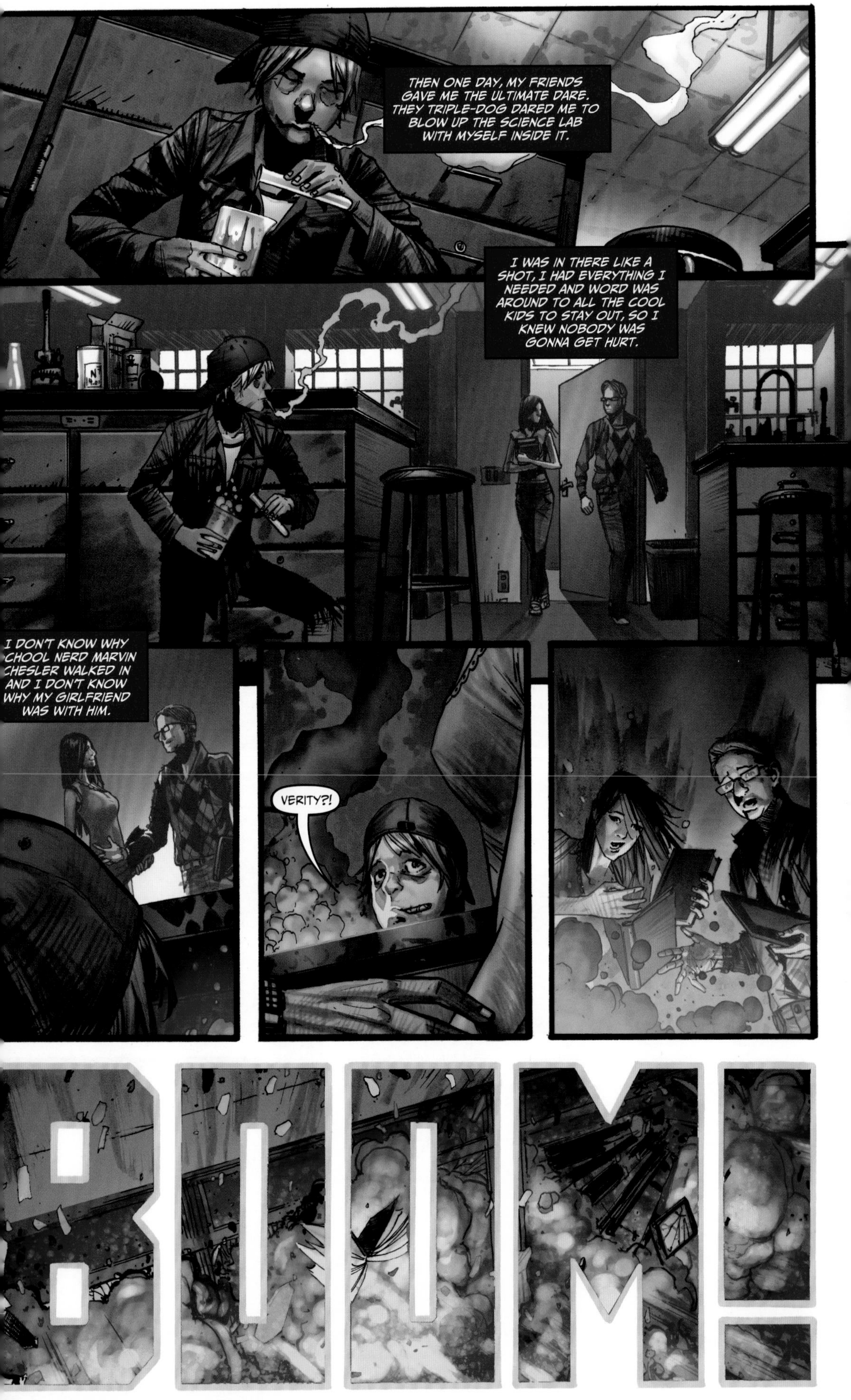
THEN ONE DAY, MY FRIENDS GAVE ME THE ULTIMATE DARE. THEY TRIPLE-DOG DARED ME TO BLOW UP THE SCIENCE LAB WITH MYSELF INSIDE IT.
I WAS IN THERE LIKE A SHOT, I HAD EVERYTHING I NEEDED AND WORD WAS AROUND TO ALL THE COOL KIDS TO STAY OUT, SO I KNEW NOBODY WAS GONNA GET HURT.
I DON'T KNOW WHY CHOOL NERD MARVIN CHESLER WALKED IN AND I DON'T KNOW WHY MY GIRLFRIEND WAS WITH HIM.
VERITY?!
BOOM!

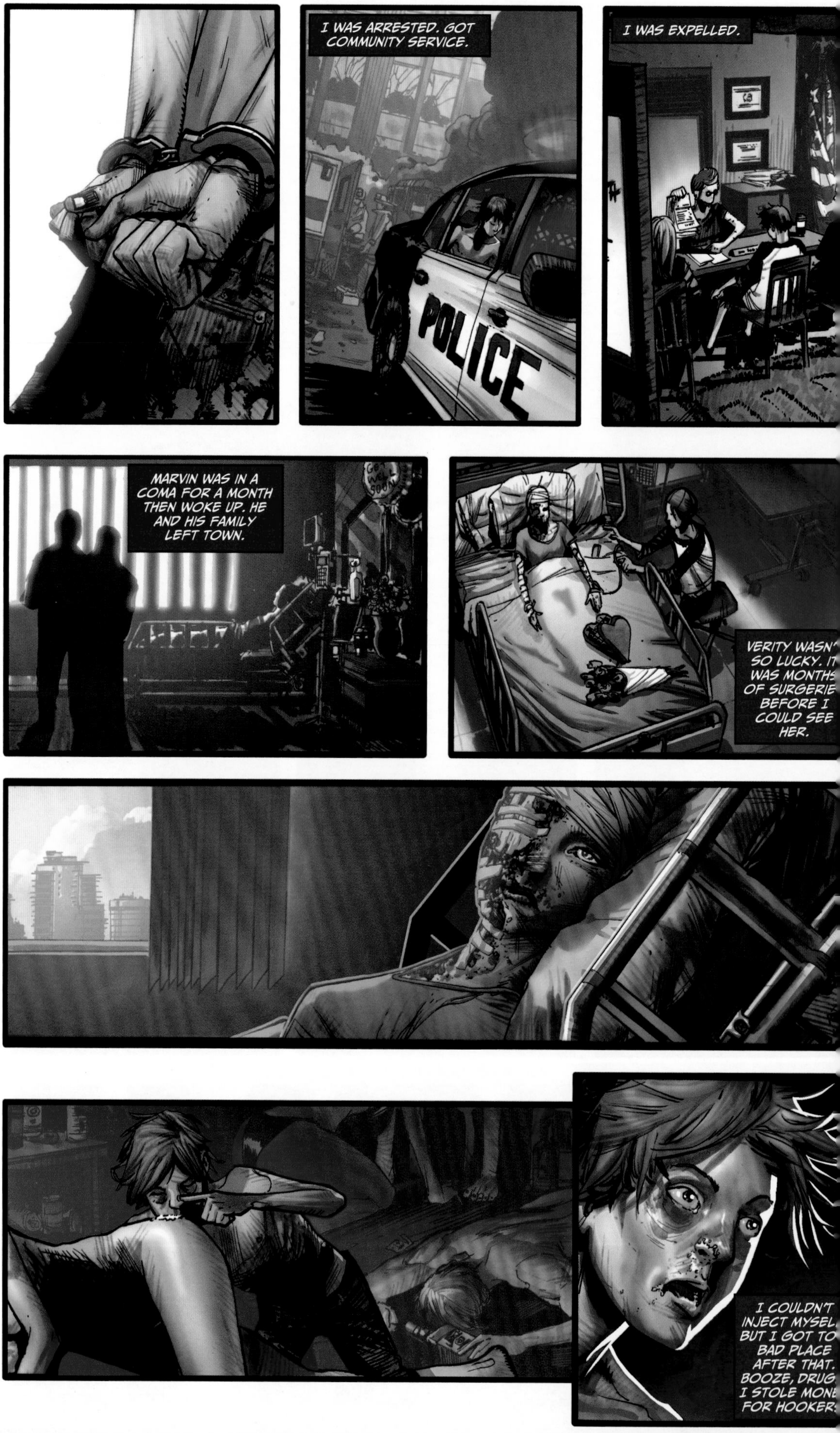
I WAS ARRESTED. GOT COMMUNITY SERVICE.
POLICE
I WAS EXPELLED.
MARVIN WAS IN A COMA FOR A MONTH THEN WOKE UP. HE AND HIS FAMILY LEFT TOWN.
VERITY WASN' SO LUCKY. IT WAS MONTHS OF SURGERIE BEFORE I COULD SEE HER.
I COULDN'T INJECT MYSEL BUT I GOT TO BAD PLACE AFTER THAT. BOOZE, DRUG I STOLE MONE FOR HOOKER

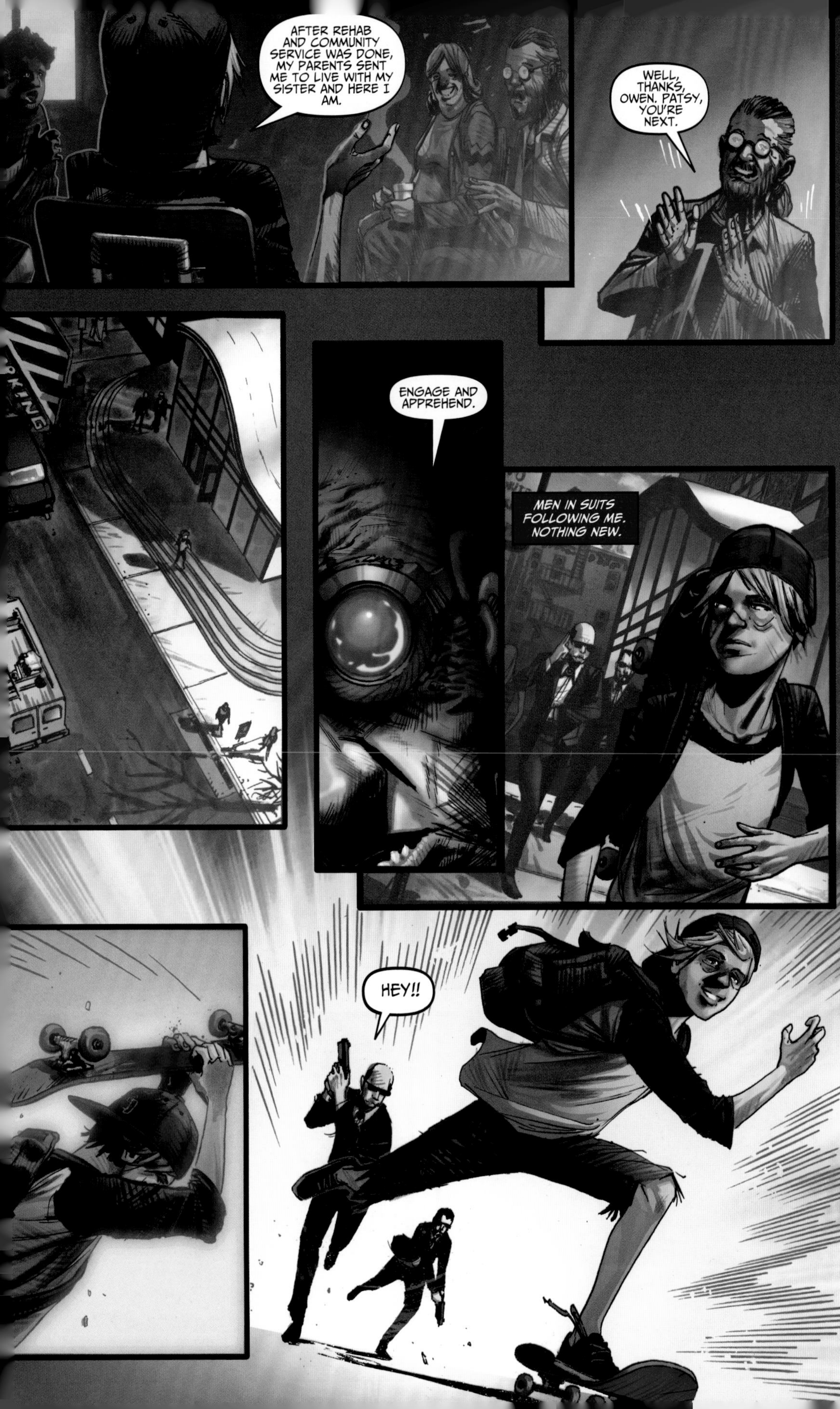
AFTER REHAB AND COMMUNITY SERVICE WAS DONE, MY PARENTS SENT ME TO LIVE WITH MY SISTER AND HERE I AM.
WELL, THANKS, OWEN. PATSY, YOU'RE NEXT.
ENGAGE AND APPREHEND.
MEN IN SUITS FOLLOWING ME. NOTHING NEW.
HEY!!

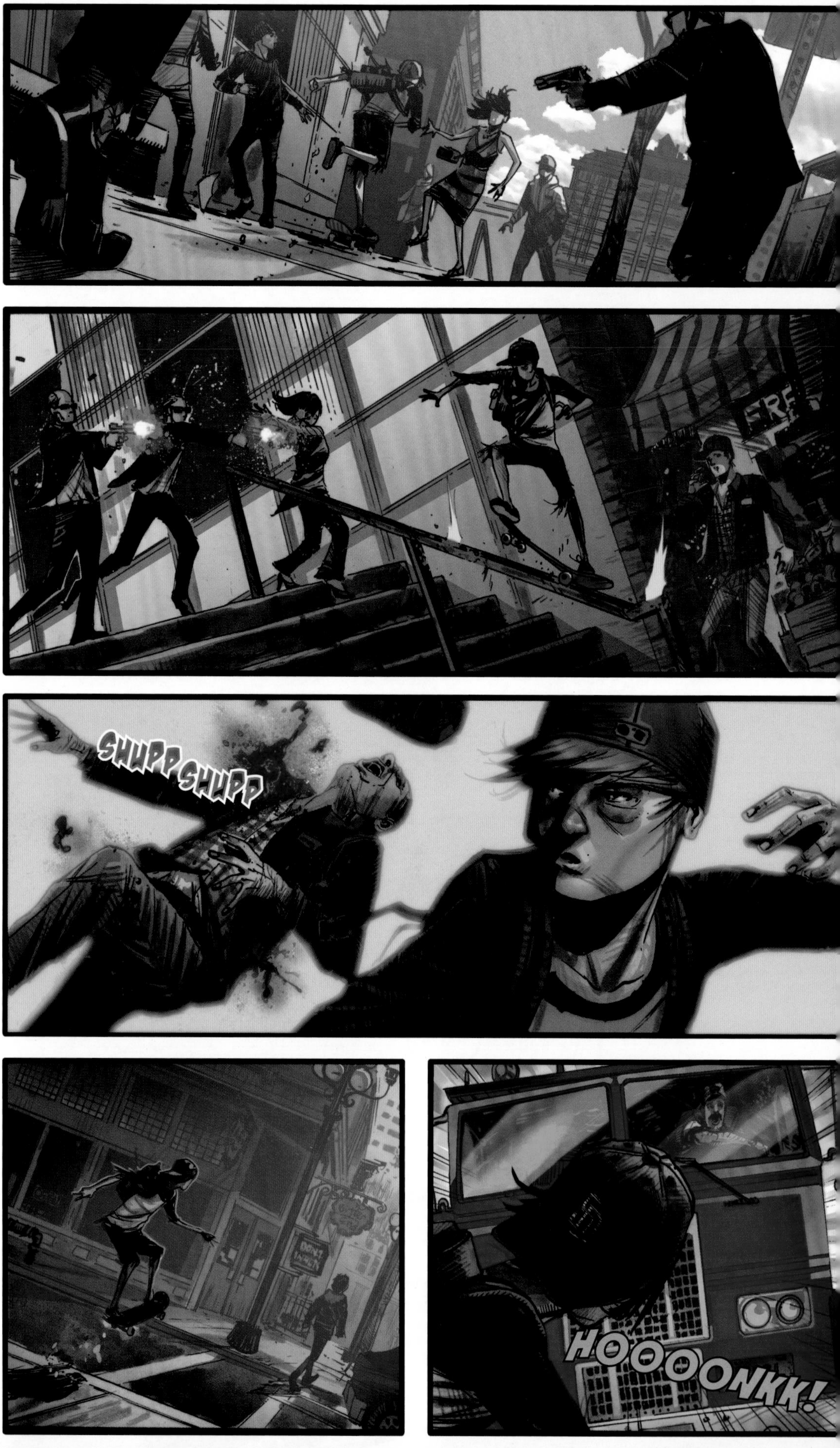
SHUPP SHUPP
HOOOONKK!

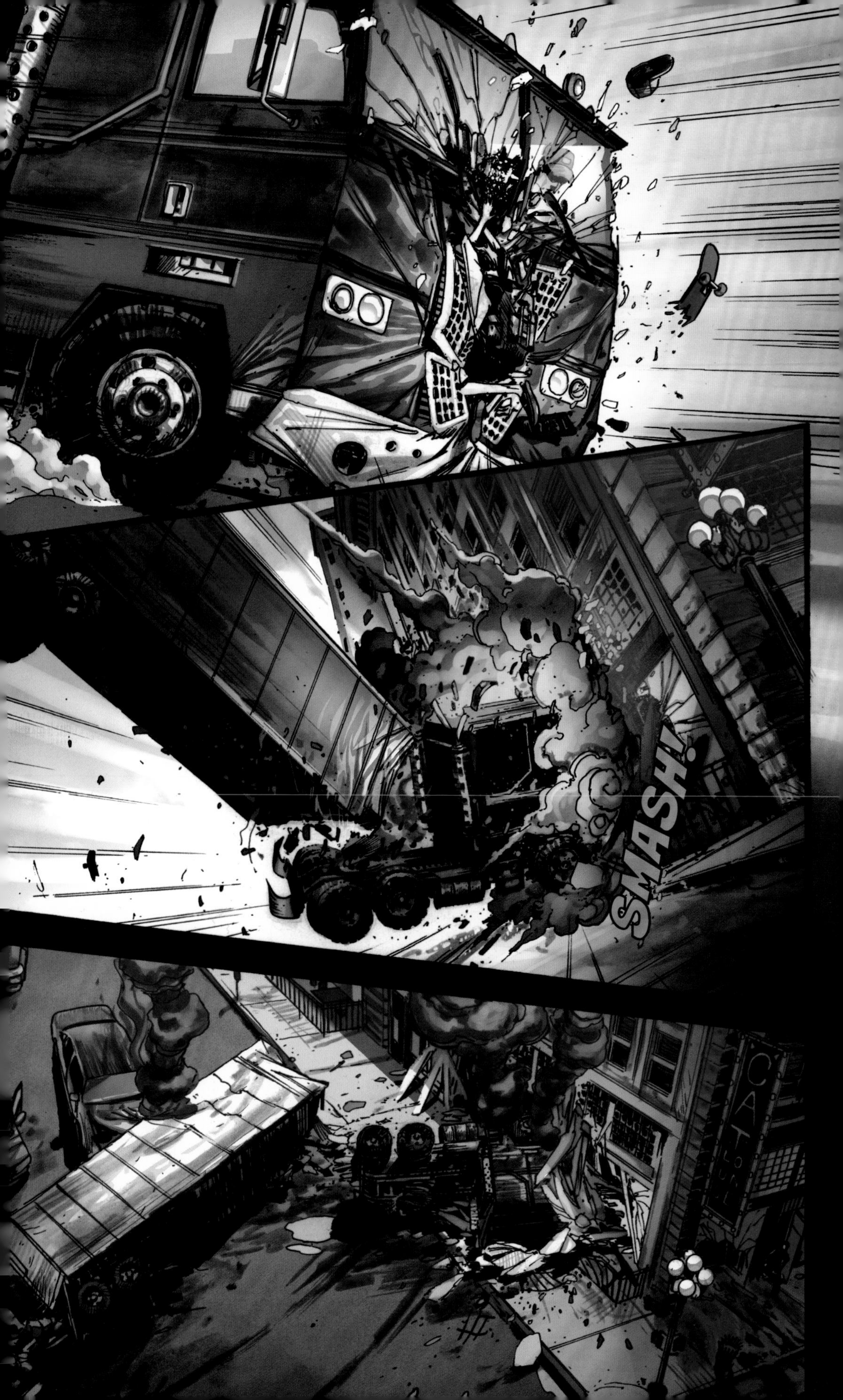
SMASH!

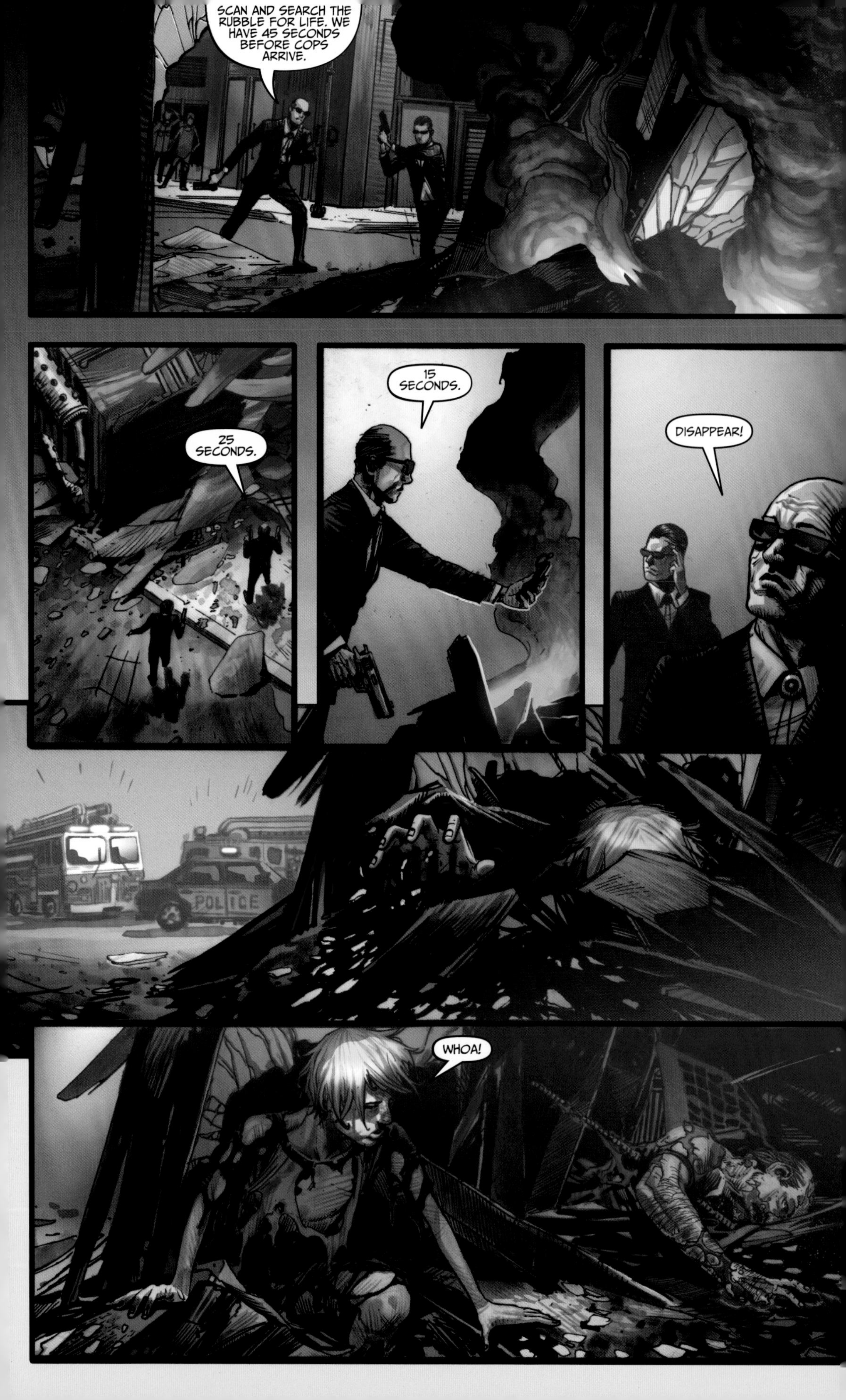
SCAN AND SEARCH THE RUBBLE FOR LIFE. WE HAVE 45 SECONDS BEFORE COPS ARRIVE.
25 SECONDS.
15 SECONDS.
DISAPPEAR!
POLICE
WHOA!

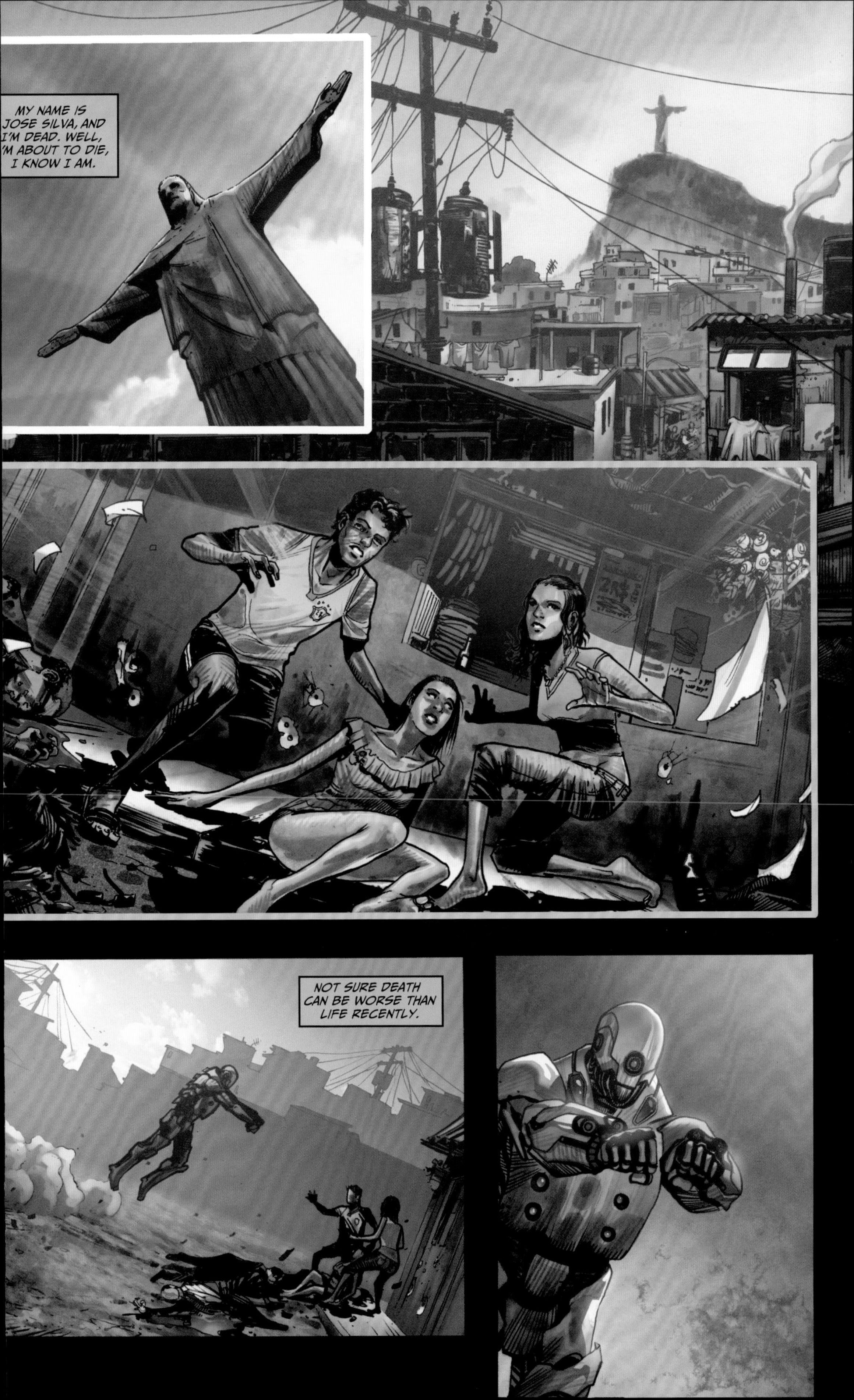
MY NAME IS JOSE SILVA, AND I'M DEAD. WELL, I'M ABOUT TO DIE, I KNOW I AM.
NOT SURE DEATH CAN BE WORSE THAN LIFE RECENTLY.

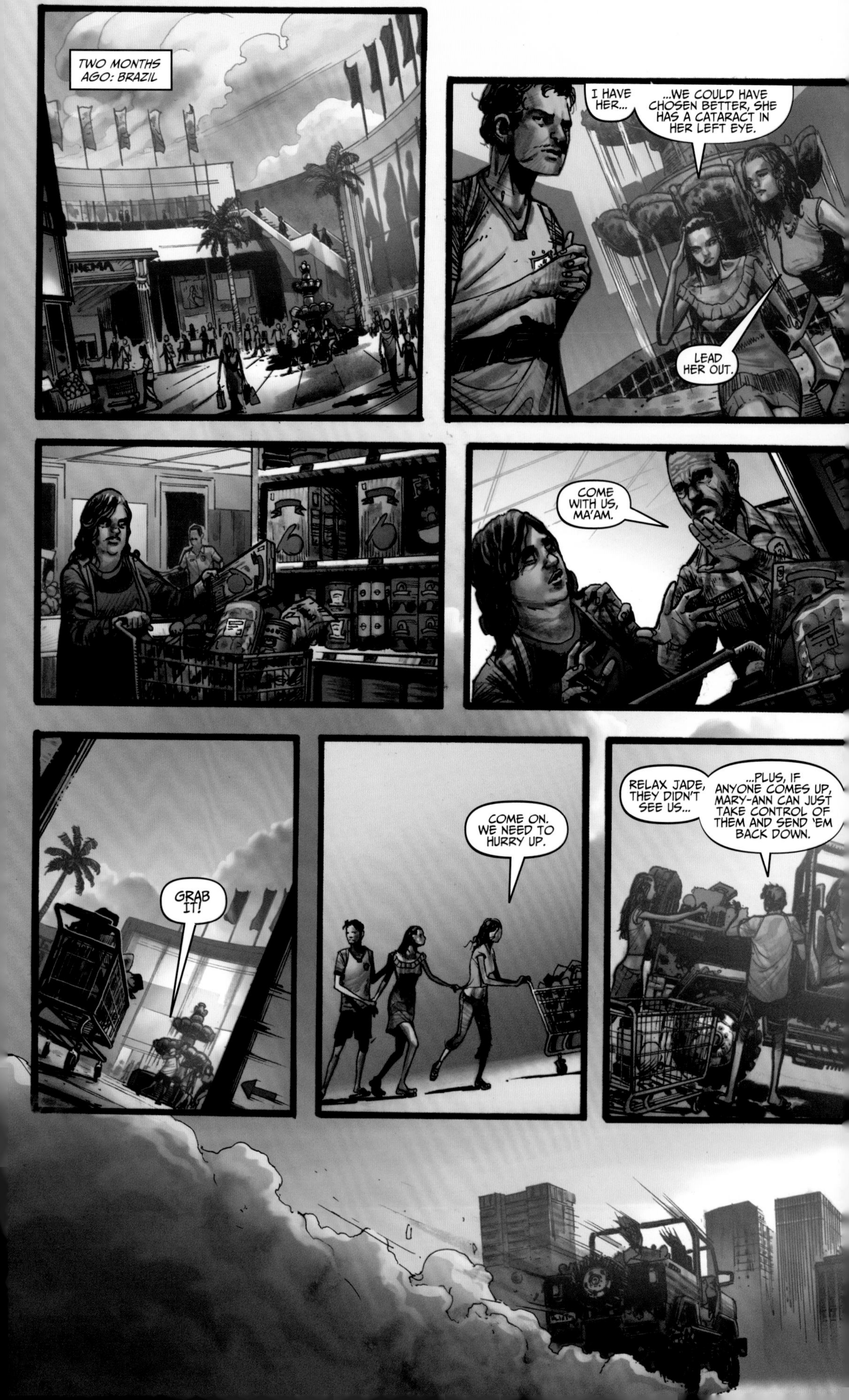
TWO MONTHS AGO: BRAZIL
I HAVE HER...
...WE COULD HAVE CHOSEN BETTER, SHE HAS A CATARACT IN HER LEFT EYE.
LEAD HER OUT.
COME WITH US, MA'AM.
GRAB IT!
COME ON. WE NEED TO HURRY UP.
RELAX JADE, THEY DIDN'T SEE US...
...PLUS, IF ANYONE COMES UP, MARY-ANN CAN JUST TAKE CONTROL OF THEM AND SEND 'EM BACK DOWN.

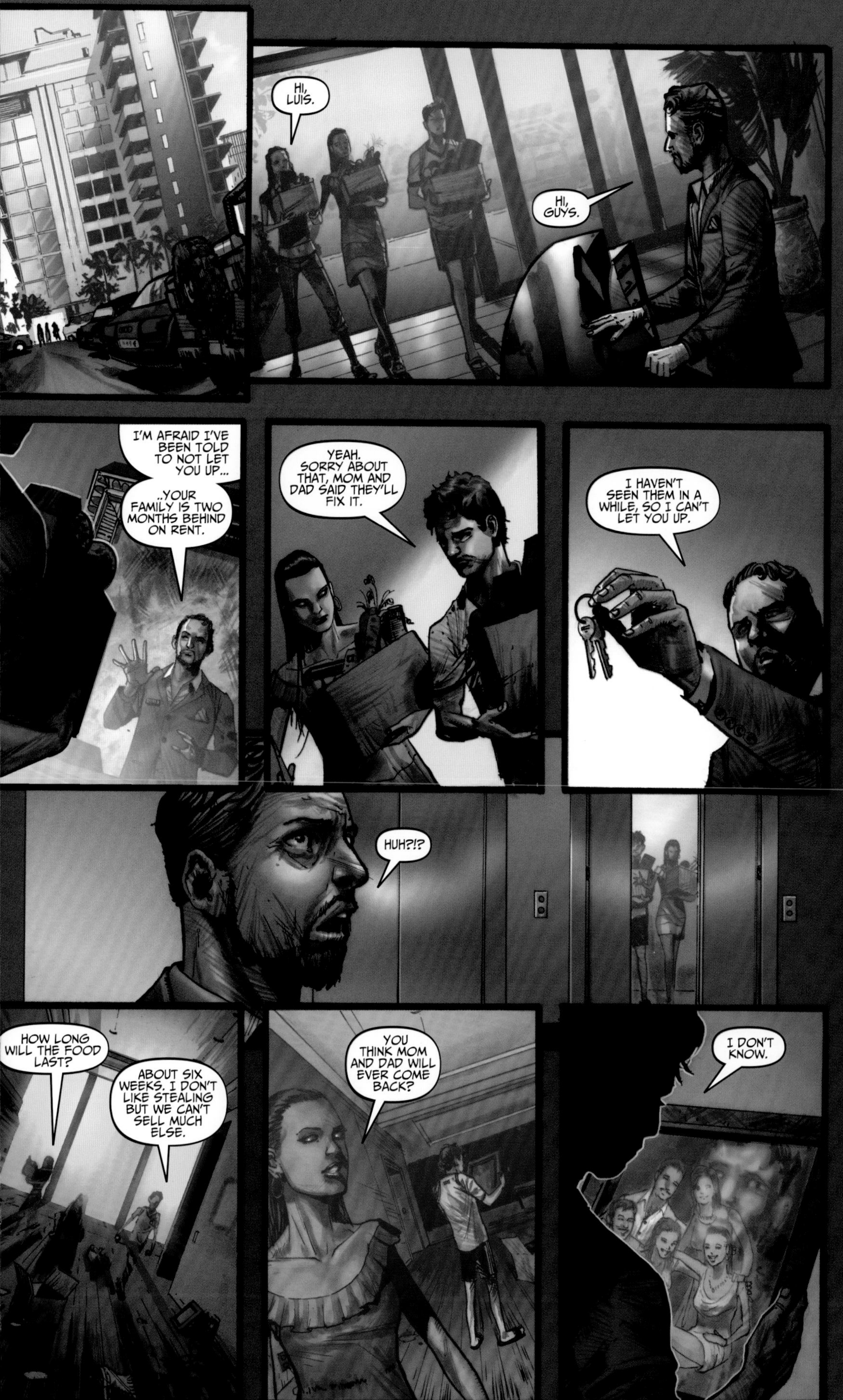
HI, LUIS.
HI, GUYS.
I'M AFRAID I'VE BEEN TOLD TO NOT LET YOU UP...
..YOUR FAMILY IS TWO MONTHS BEHIND ON RENT.
YEAH. SORRY ABOUT THAT, MOM AND DAD SAID THEY'LL FIX IT.
I HAVEN'T SEEN THEM IN A WHILE, SO I CAN'T LET YOU UP.
HUH?!?
HOW LONG WILL THE FOOD LAST?
ABOUT SIX WEEKS. I DON'T LIKE STEALING BUT WE CAN'T SELL MUCH ELSE.
YOU THINK MOM AND DAD WILL EVER COME BACK?
I DON'T KNOW.

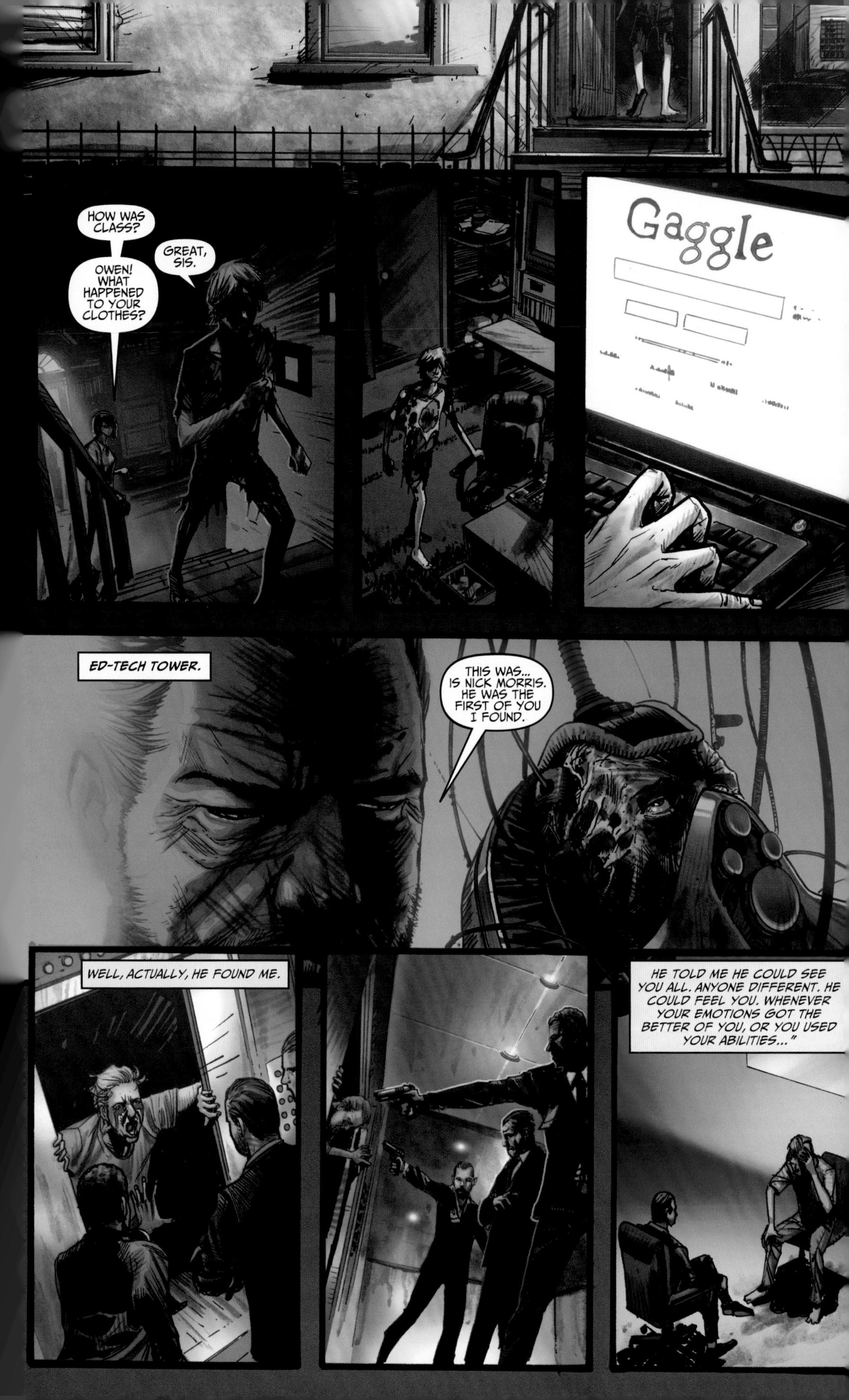

HOW WAS CLASS?
GREAT, SIS.
OWEN! WHAT HAPPENED TO YOUR CLOTHES?
Gaggle
ED-TECH TOWER.
THIS WAS... IS NICK MORRIS. HE WAS THE FIRST OF YOU I FOUND.
WELL, ACTUALLY, HE FOUND ME.
HE TOLD ME HE COULD SEE YOU ALL. ANYONE DIFFERENT. HE COULD FEEL YOU. WHENEVER YOUR EMOTIONS GOT THE BETTER OF YOU, OR YOU USED YOUR ABILITIES..."

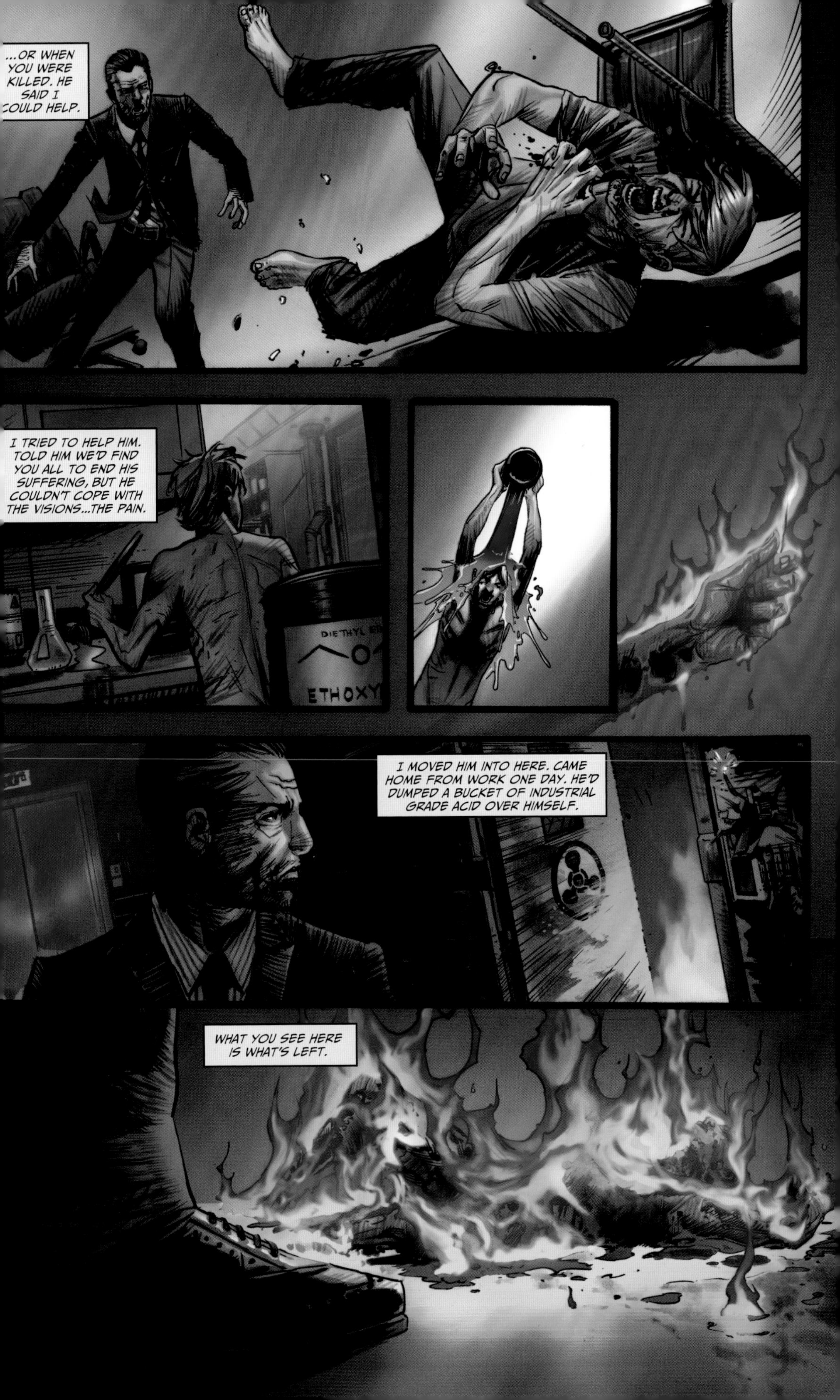
...OR WHEN YOU WERE KILLED. HE SAID I COULD HELP.
I TRIED TO HELP HIM. TOLD HIM WE'D FIND YOU ALL TO END HIS SUFFERING, BUT HE COULDN'T COPE WITH THE VISIONS...THE PAIN.
DIETHYL
ETHOXY
I MOVED HIM INTO HERE. CAME HOME FROM WORK ONE DAY. HE'D DUMPED A BUCKET OF INDUSTRIAL GRADE ACID OVER HIMSELF.
WHAT YOU SEE HERE IS WHAT'S LEFT.

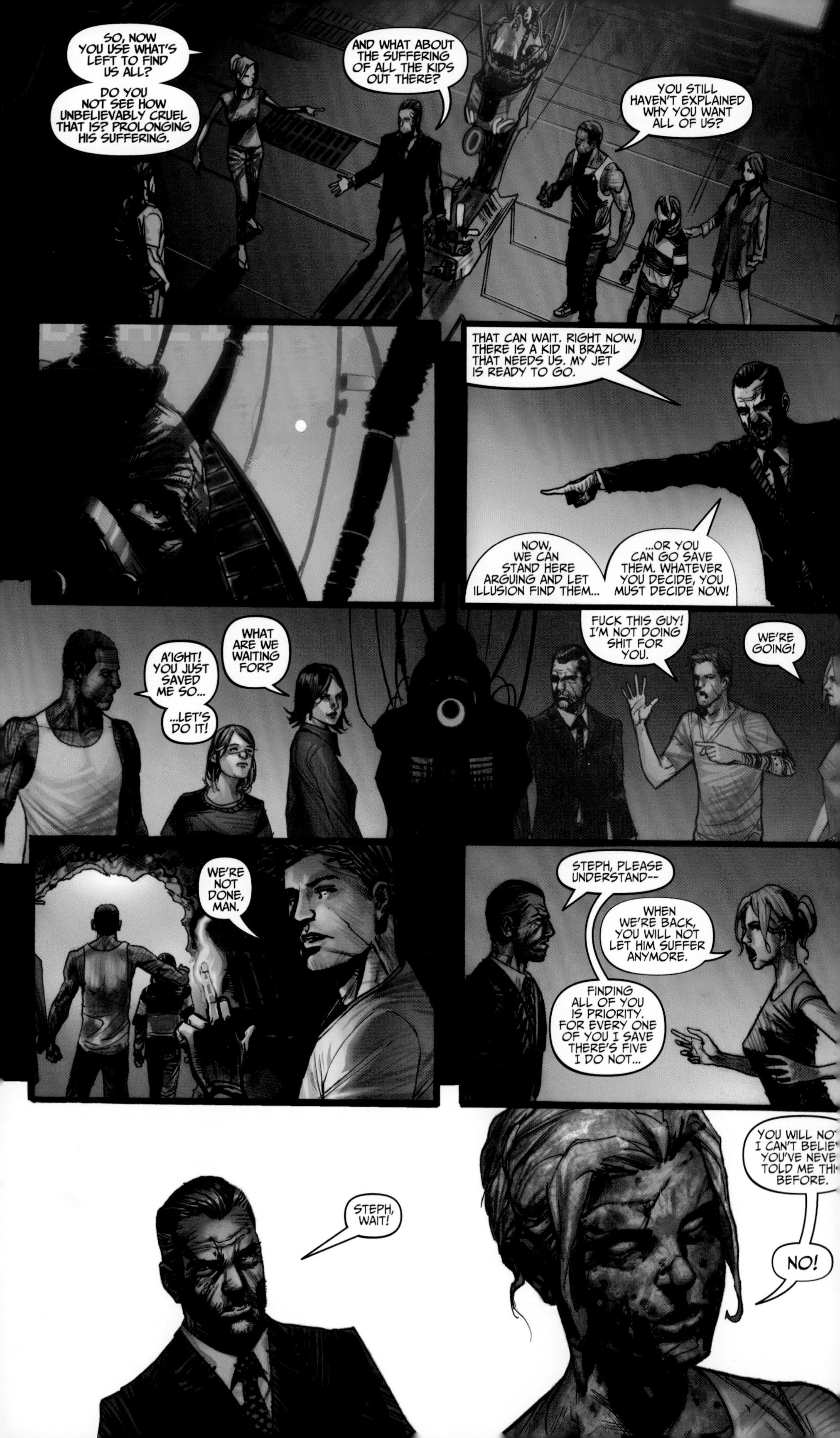
SO, NOW YOU USE WHAT'S LEFT TO FIND US ALL?
DO YOU NOT SEE HOW UNBELIEVABLY CRUEL THAT IS? PROLONGING HIS SUFFERING.
AND WHAT ABOUT THE SUFFERING OF ALL THE KIDS OUT THERE?
YOU STILL HAVEN'T EXPLAINED WHY YOU WANT ALL OF US?
THAT CAN WAIT. RIGHT NOW, THERE IS A KID IN BRAZIL THAT NEEDS US. MY JET IS READY TO GO.
NOW, WE CAN STAND HERE ARGUING AND LET ILLUSION FIND THEM...
...OR YOU CAN GO SAVE THEM. WHATEVER YOU DECIDE, YOU MUST DECIDE NOW!
A'IGHT! YOU JUST SAVED ME SO...
...LET'S DO IT!
WHAT ARE WE WAITING FOR?
FUCK THIS GUY! I'M NOT DOING SHIT FOR YOU.
WE'RE GOING!
WE'RE NOT DONE, MAN.
STEPH, PLEASE UNDERSTAND--
WHEN WE'RE BACK, YOU WILL NOT LET HIM SUFFER ANYMORE.
FINDING ALL OF YOU IS PRIORITY. FOR EVERY ONE OF YOU I SAVE THERE'S FIVE I DO NOT...
STEPH, WAIT!
NO!

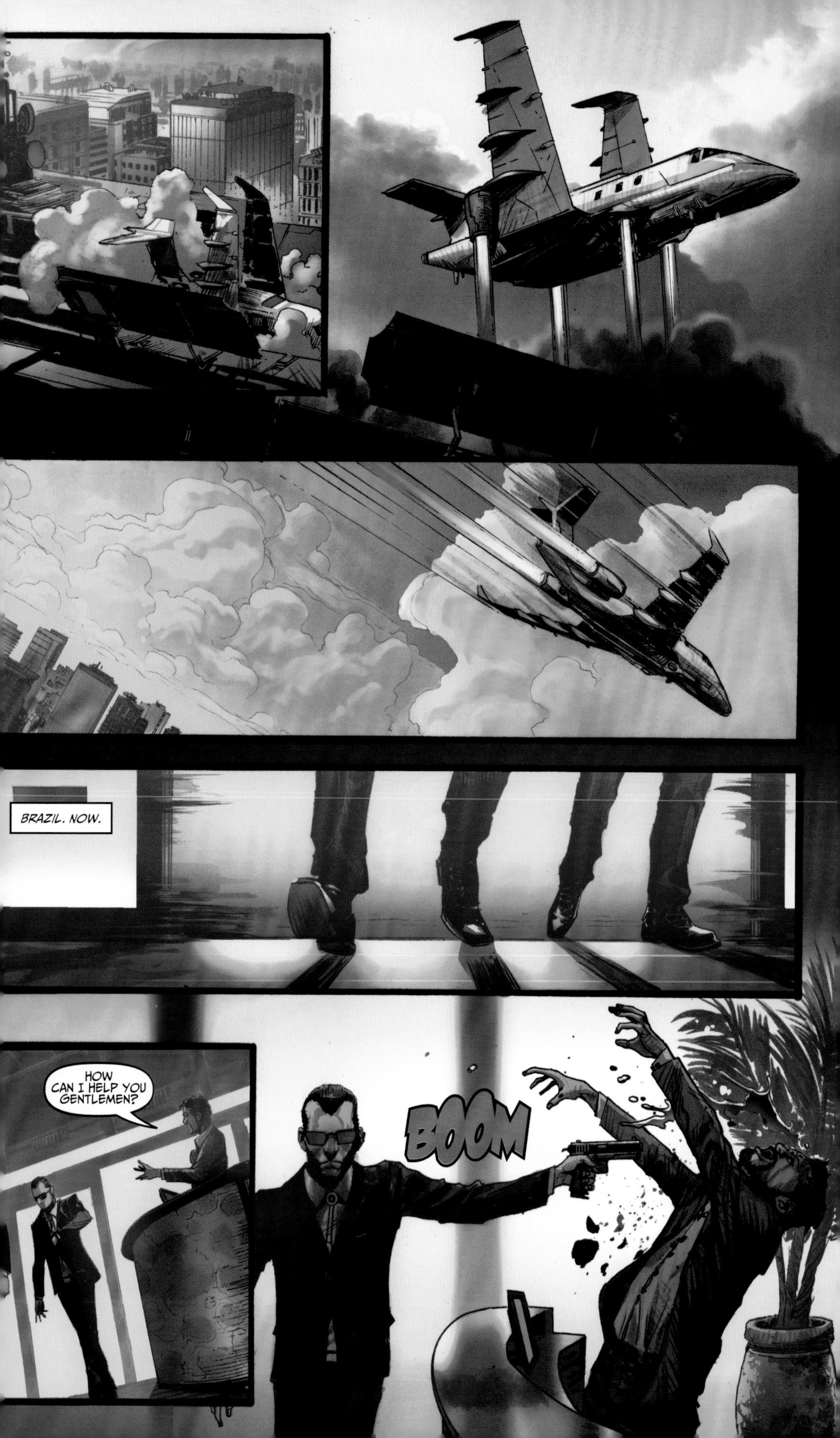
BRAZIL. NOW.
HOW CAN I HELP YOU GENTLEMEN?
BOOM

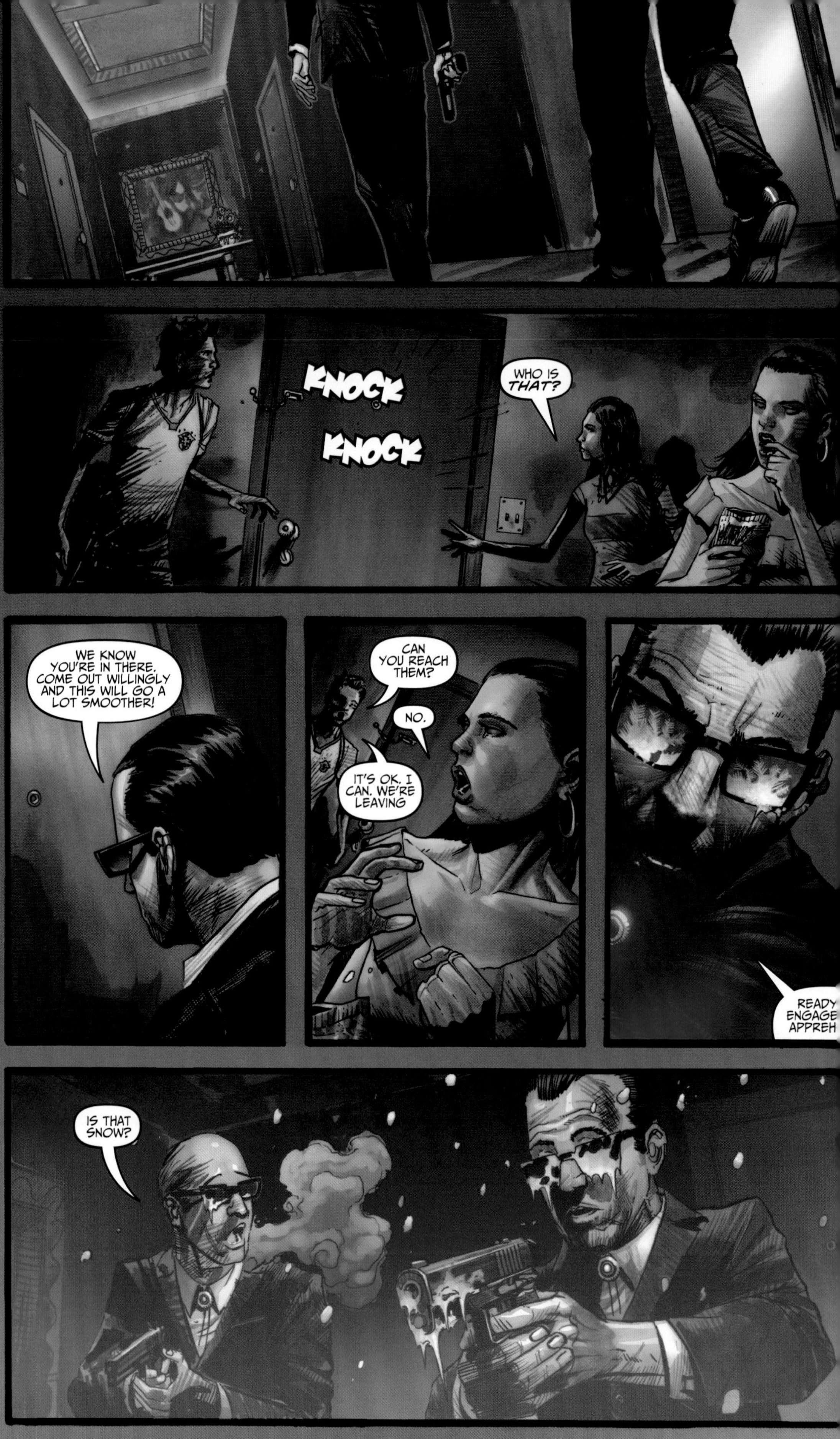
KNOCK
KNOCK
WHO IS THAT?
WE KNOW YOU'RE IN THERE. COME OUT WILLINGLY AND THIS WILL GO A LOT SMOOTHER!
CAN YOU REACH THEM?
NO.
IT'S OK. I CAN. WE'RE LEAVING
READY ENGAGE APPREH
IS THAT SNOW?

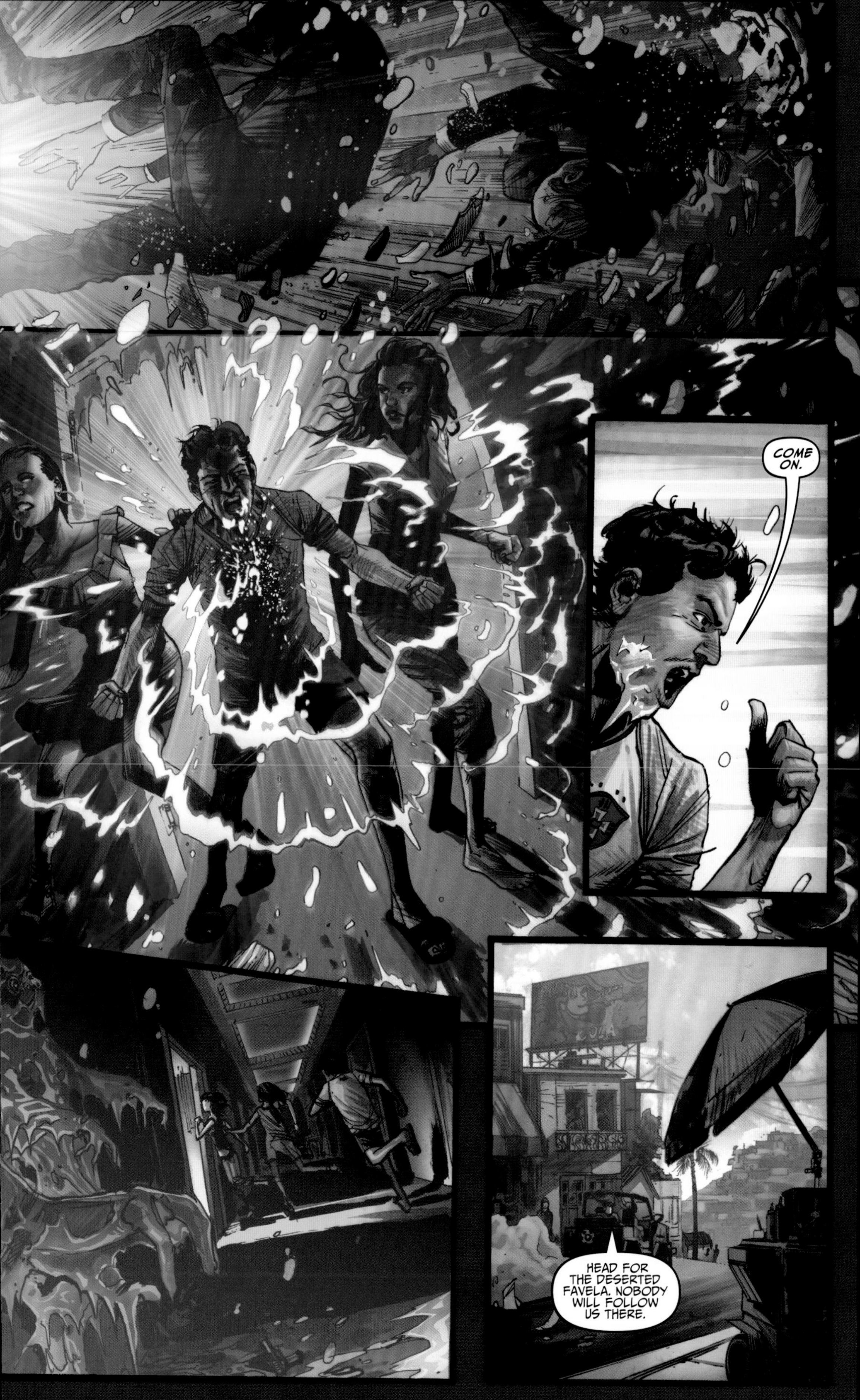
COME ON.
HEAD FOR THE DESERTED FAVELA. NOBODY WILL FOLLOW US THERE.

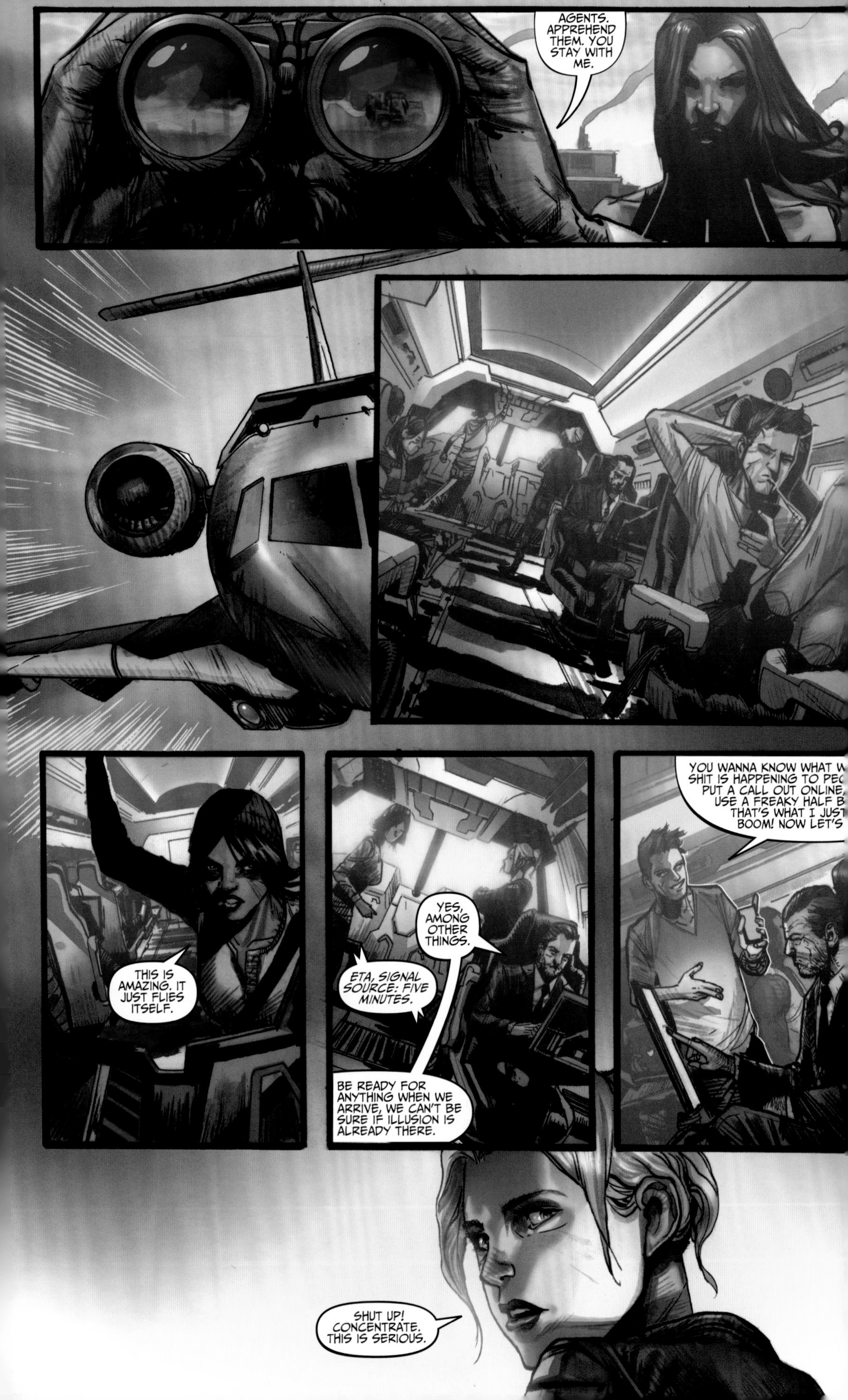
AGENTS. APPREHEND THEM. YOU STAY WITH ME.
THIS IS AMAZING. IT JUST FLIES ITSELF.
ETA, SIGNAL SOURCE: FIVE MINUTES.
YES, AMONG OTHER THINGS.
BE READY FOR ANYTHING WHEN WE ARRIVE, WE CAN'T BE SURE IF ILLUSION IS ALREADY THERE.
YOU WANNA KNOW WHAT W SHIT IS HAPPENING TO PEO PUT A CALL OUT ONLINE, USE A FREAKY HALF B THAT'S WHAT I JUST BOOM! NOW LET'S
SHUT UP! CONCENTRATE. THIS IS SERIOUS.

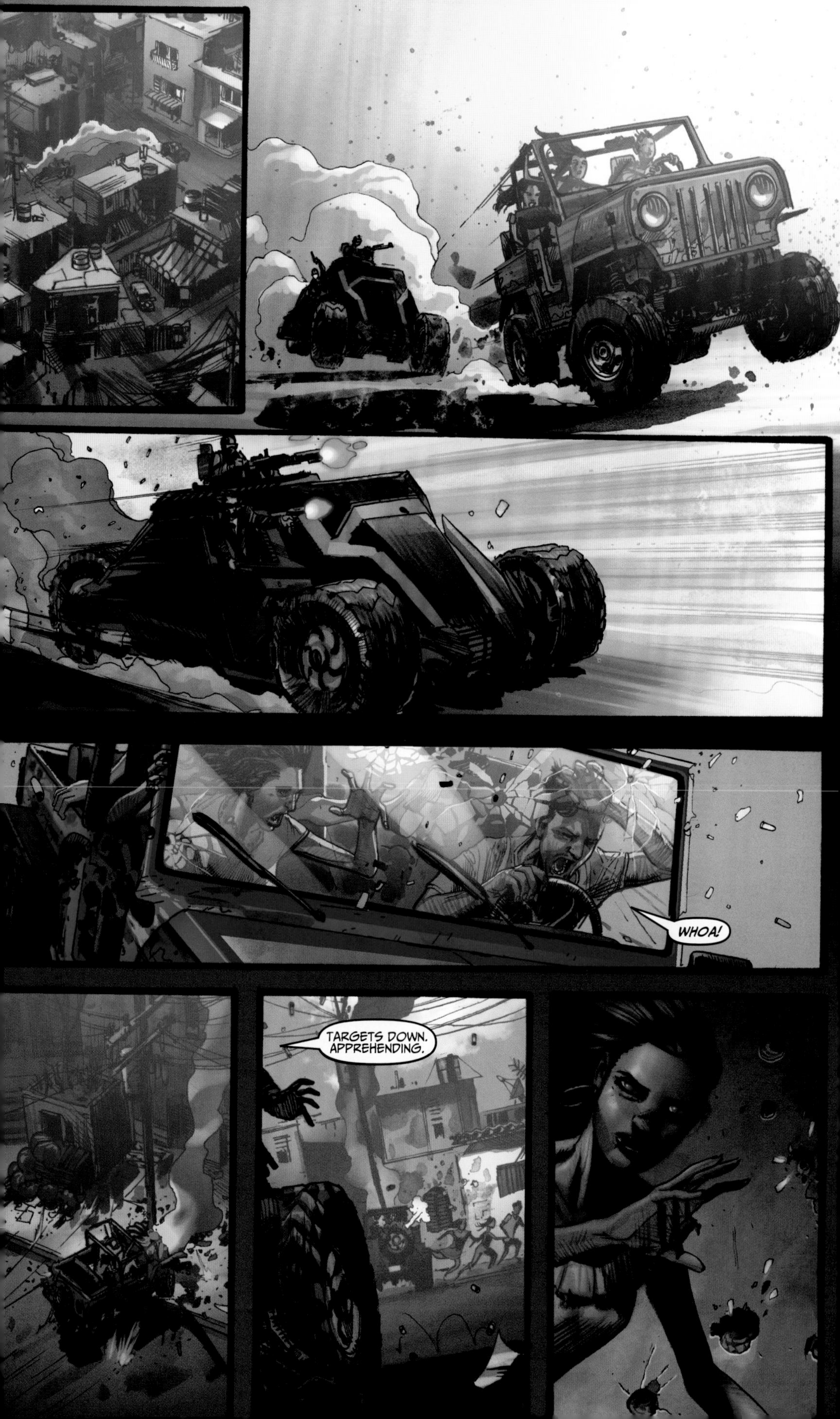
WHOA!
TARGETS DOWN. APPREHENDING.

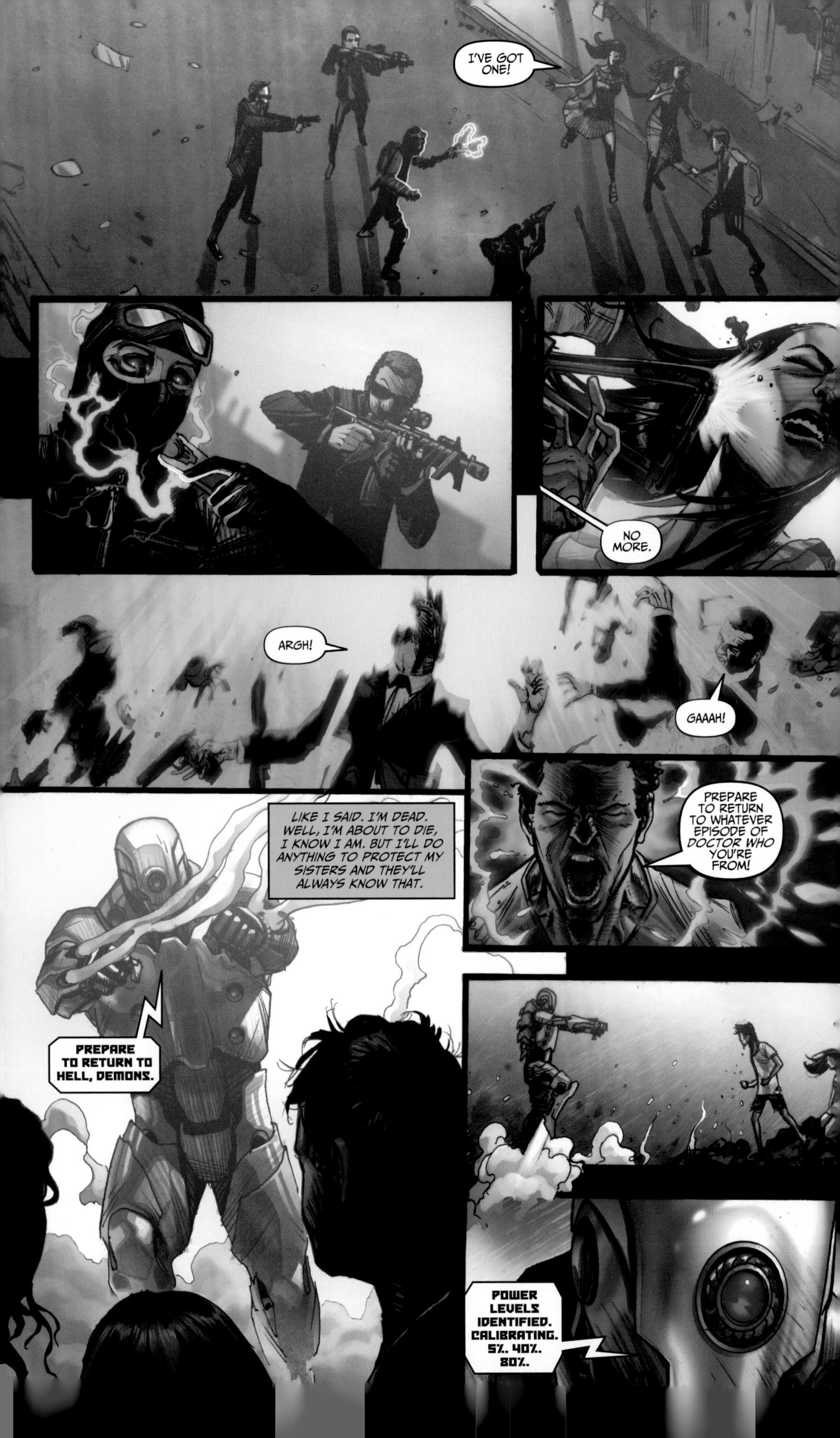
I'VE GOT ONE!
NO MORE.
ARGH!
GAAAH!
LIKE I SAID. I'M DEAD. WELL, I'M ABOUT TO DIE, I KNOW I AM. BUT I'LL DO ANYTHING TO PROTECT MY SISTERS AND THEY'LL ALWAYS KNOW THAT.
PREPARE TO RETURN TO WHATEVER EPISODE OF DOCTOR WHO YOU'RE FROM!
PREPARE TO RETURN TO HELL, DEMONS.
POWER LEVELS IDENTIFIED. CALIBRATING. 5%. 40%. 80%.

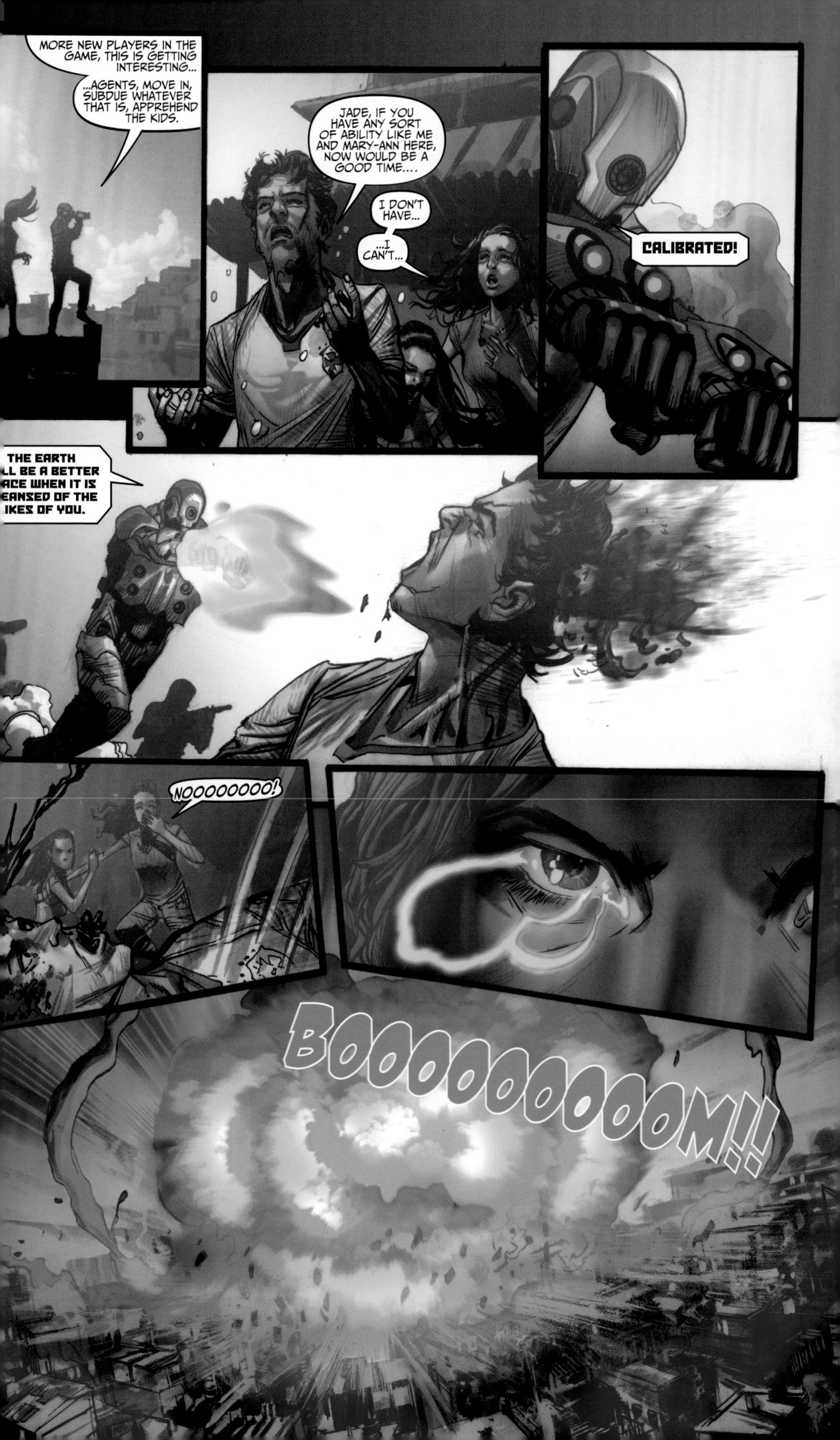
MORE NEW PLAYERS IN THE GAME, THIS IS GETTING INTERESTING...
...AGENTS, MOVE IN, SUBDUE WHATEVER THAT IS, APPREHEND THE KIDS.
JADE, IF YOU HAVE ANY SORT OF ABILITY LIKE ME AND MARY-ANN HERE, NOW WOULD BE A GOOD TIME....
I DON'T HAVE...
...I CAN'T...
CALIBRATED!
THE EARTH LL BE A BETTER ACE WHEN IT IS EANSED OF THE IKES OF YOU.
NOOOOOOOO!
BOOOOOOOOOM!!

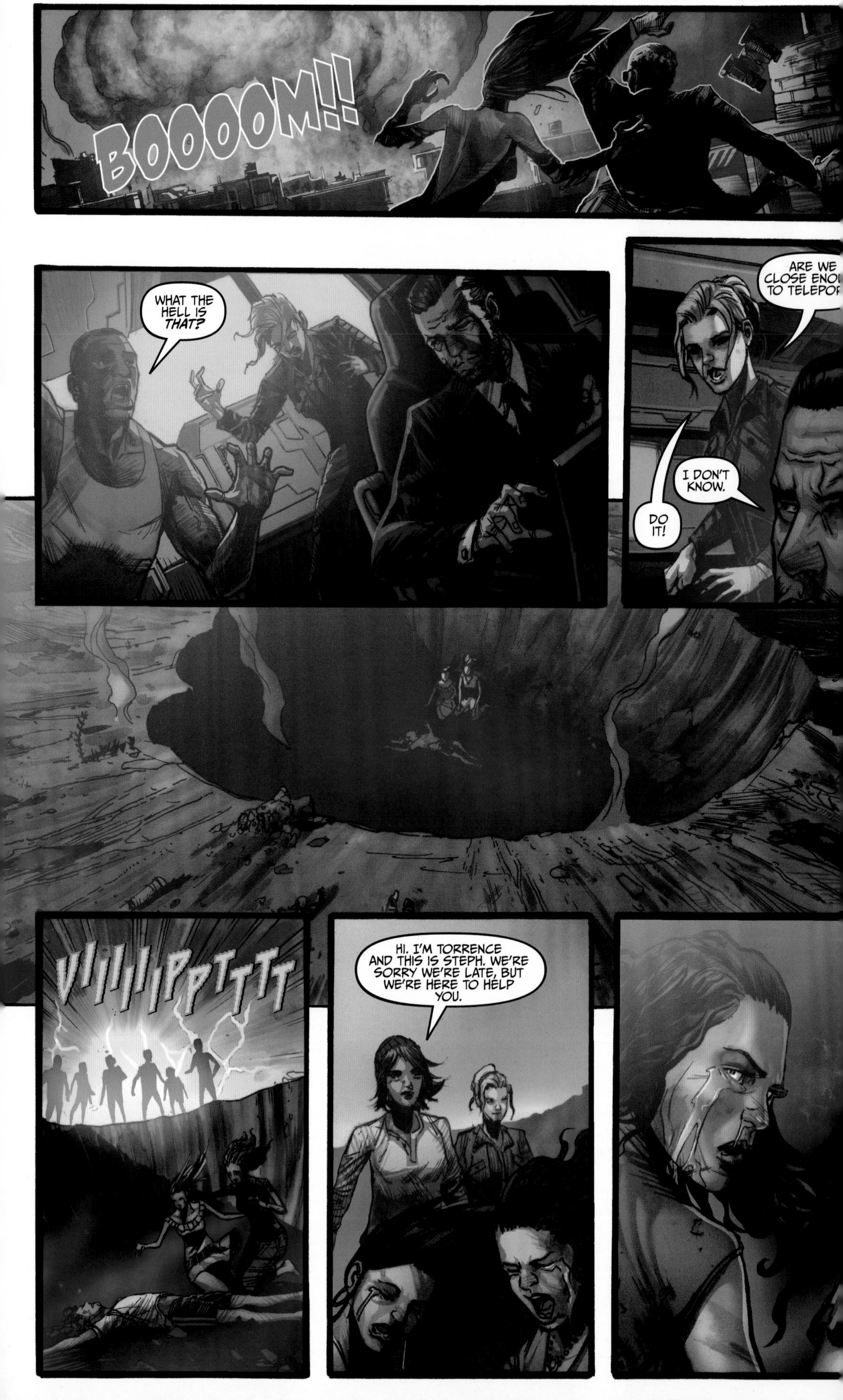
BOOOOM!!
WHAT THE HELL IS THAT?
ARE WE CLOSE ENO
TO TELEPOR
I DON'T KNOW.
DO IT!
VIIIIIIPPTTTTT
HI. I'M TORRENCE AND THIS IS STEPH. WE'RE SORRY WE'RE LATE, BUT WE'RE HERE TO HELP YOU.

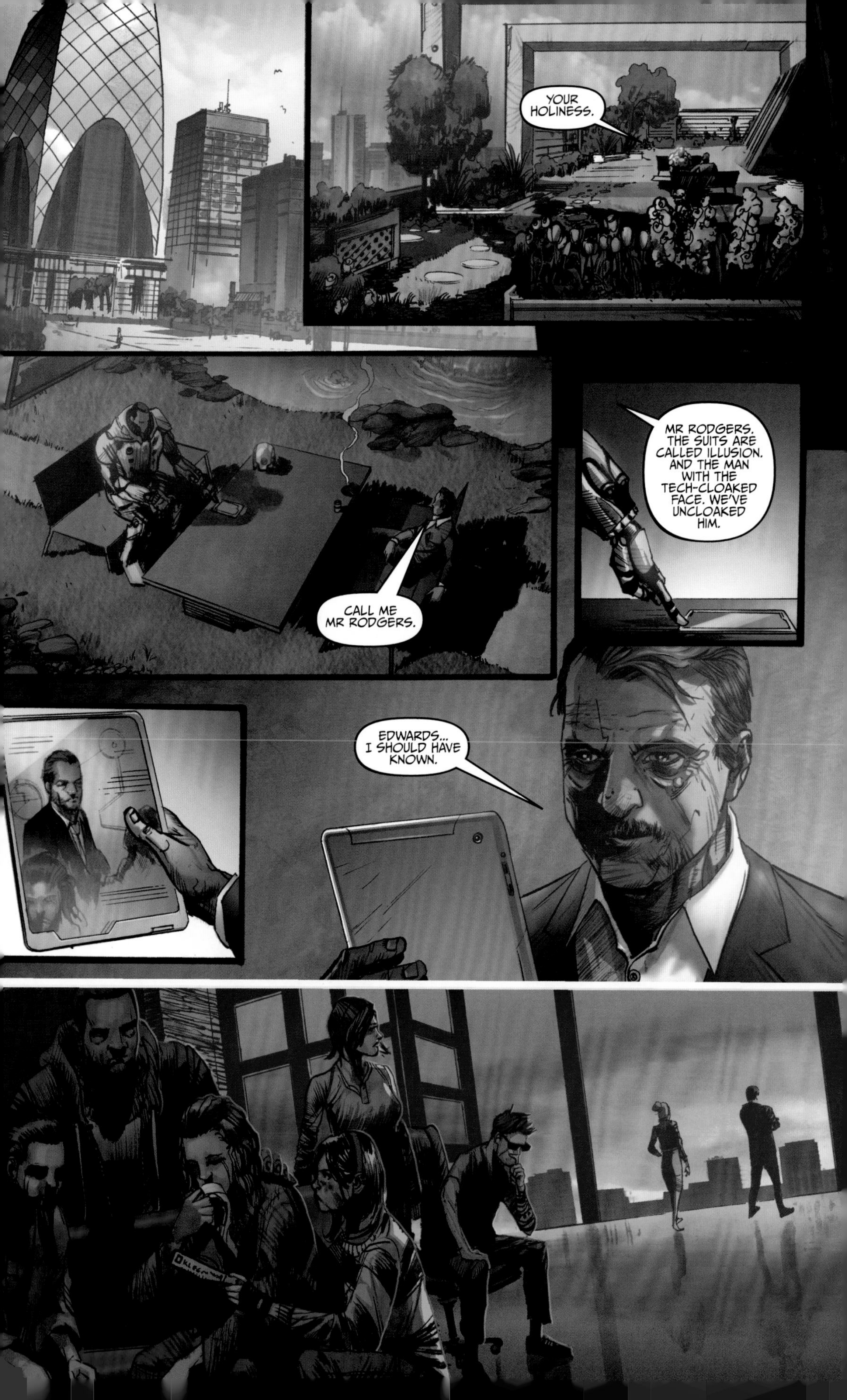
YOUR HOLINESS.
CALL ME MR RODGERS.
MR RODGERS. THE SUITS ARE CALLED ILLUSION. AND THE MAN WITH THE TECH-CLOAKED FACE. WE'VE UNCLOAKED HIM.
EDWARDS... I SHOULD HAVE KNOWN.

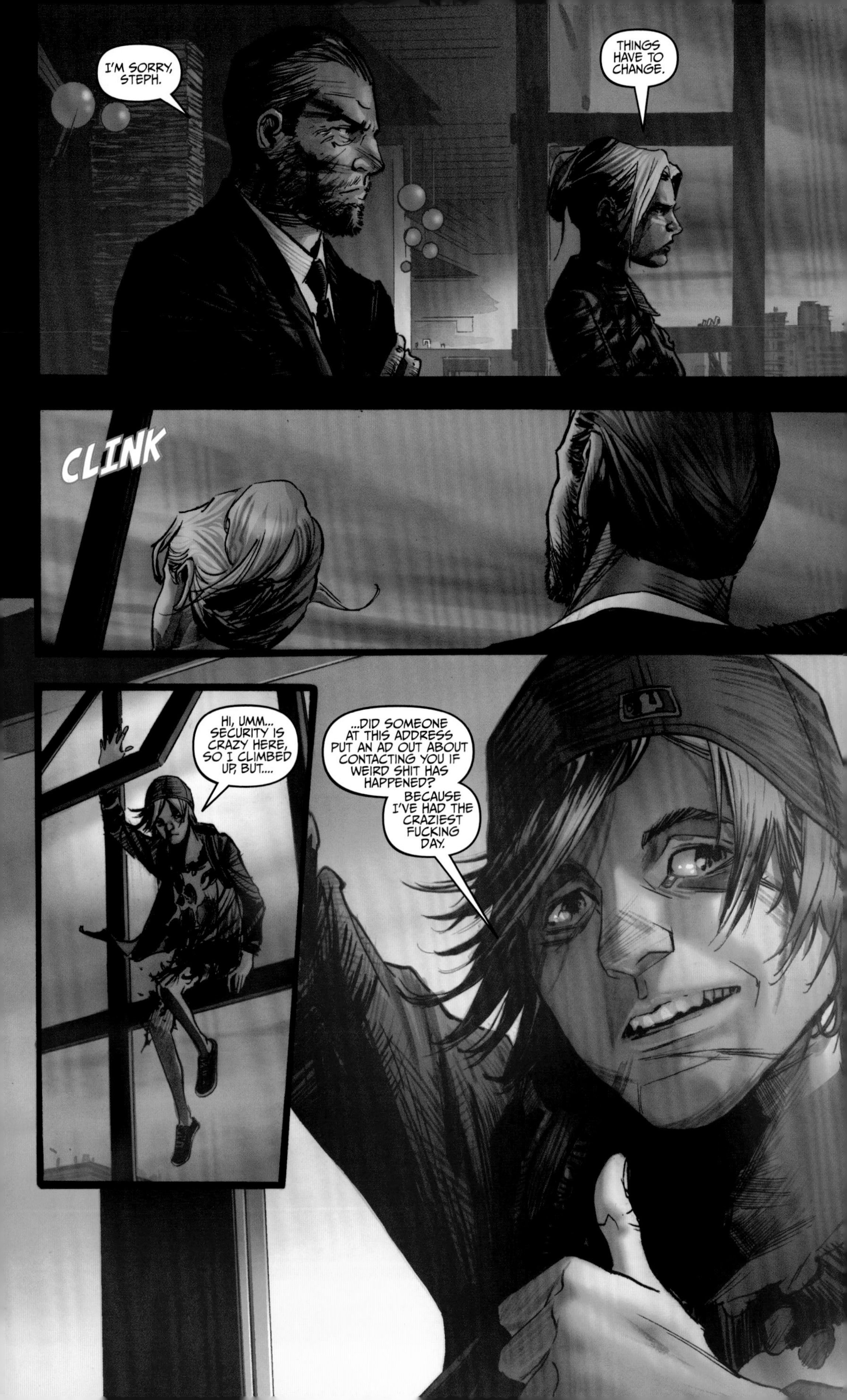
I'M SORRY, STEPH.
THINGS HAVE TO CHANGE.
CLINK
HI, UMM... SECURITY IS CRAZY HERE, SO I CLIMBED UP, BUT....
...DID SOMEONE AT THIS ADDRESS PUT AN AD OUT ABOUT CONTACTING YOU IF WEIRD SHIT HAS HAPPENED?
BECAUSE I'VE HAD THE CRAZIEST FUCKING DAY.

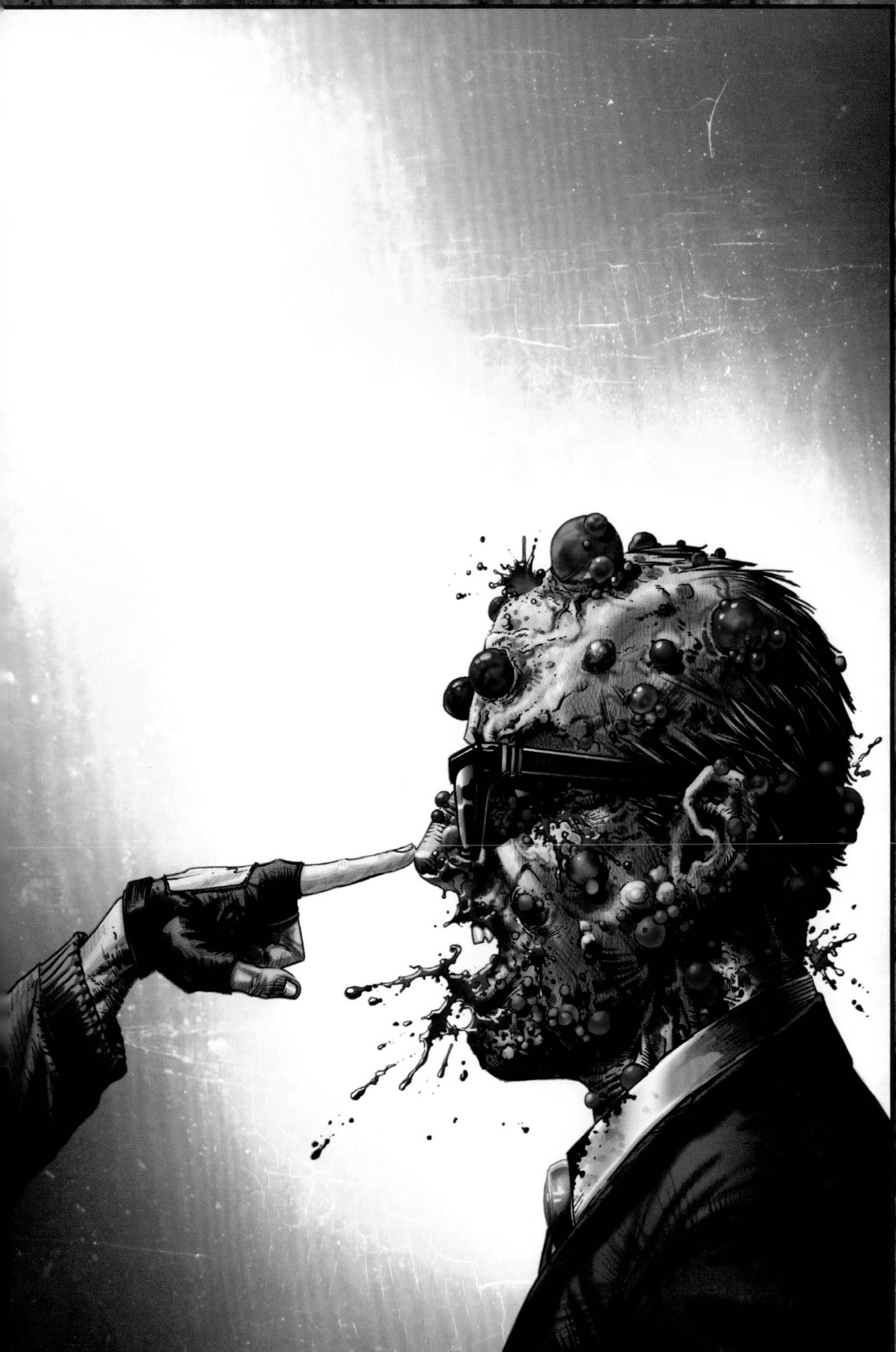

ISSUE 4 COVER A - BY JOSHUA CASSARA & LUIS GUERRERO

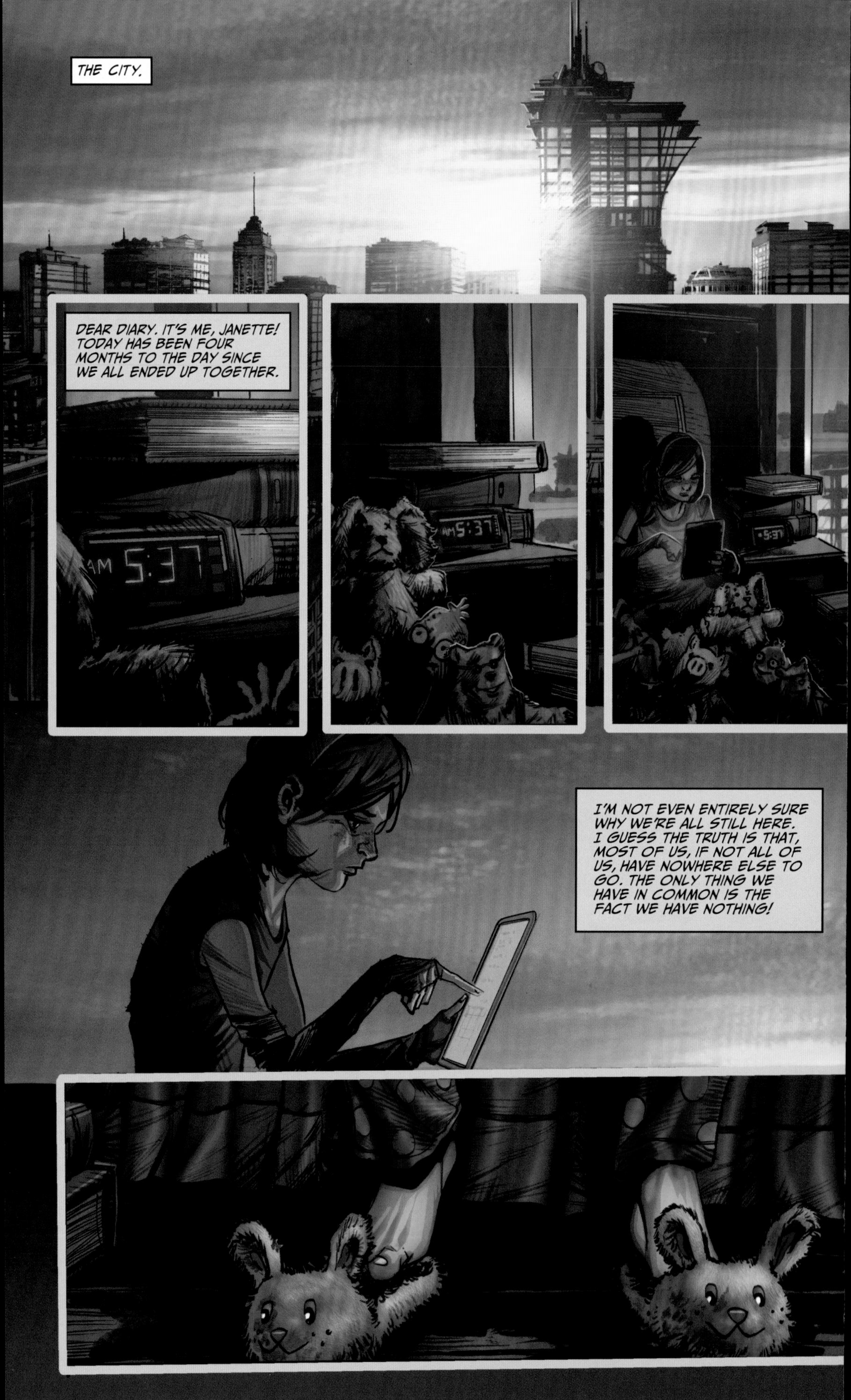

THE CITY.
DEAR DIARY. IT'S ME, JANETTE! TODAY HAS BEEN FOUR MONTHS TO THE DAY SINCE WE ALL ENDED UP TOGETHER.
AM 5:37
AM 5:37
I'M NOT EVEN ENTIRELY SURE WHY WE'RE ALL STILL HERE. I GUESS THE TRUTH IS THAT, MOST OF US, IF NOT ALL OF US, HAVE NOWHERE ELSE TO GO. THE ONLY THING WE HAVE IN COMMON IS THE FACT WE HAVE NOTHING!

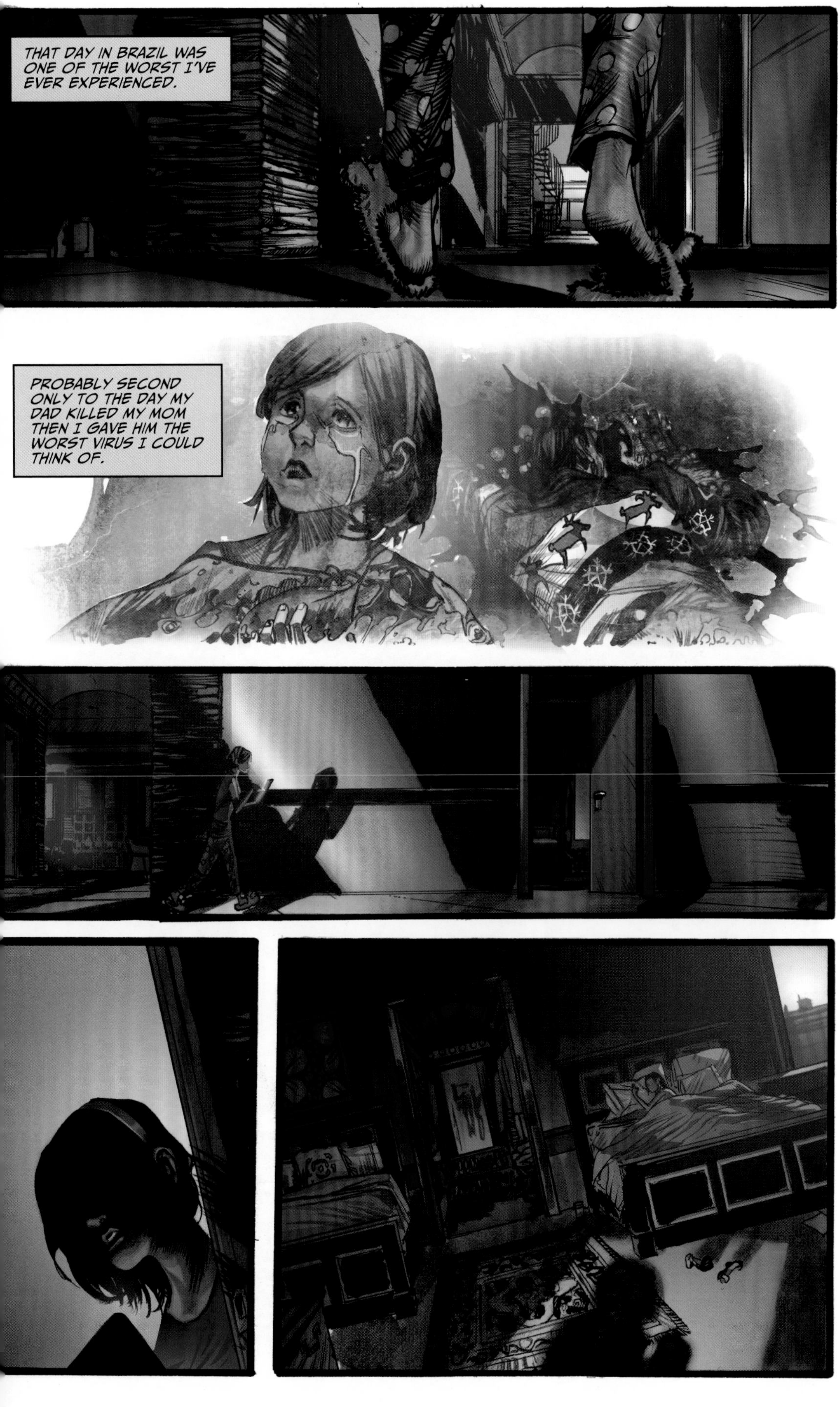
THAT DAY IN BRAZIL WAS ONE OF THE WORST I'VE EVER EXPERIENCED.
PROBABLY SECOND ONLY TO THE DAY MY DAD KILLED MY MOM THEN I GAVE HIM THE WORST VIRUS I COULD THINK OF.

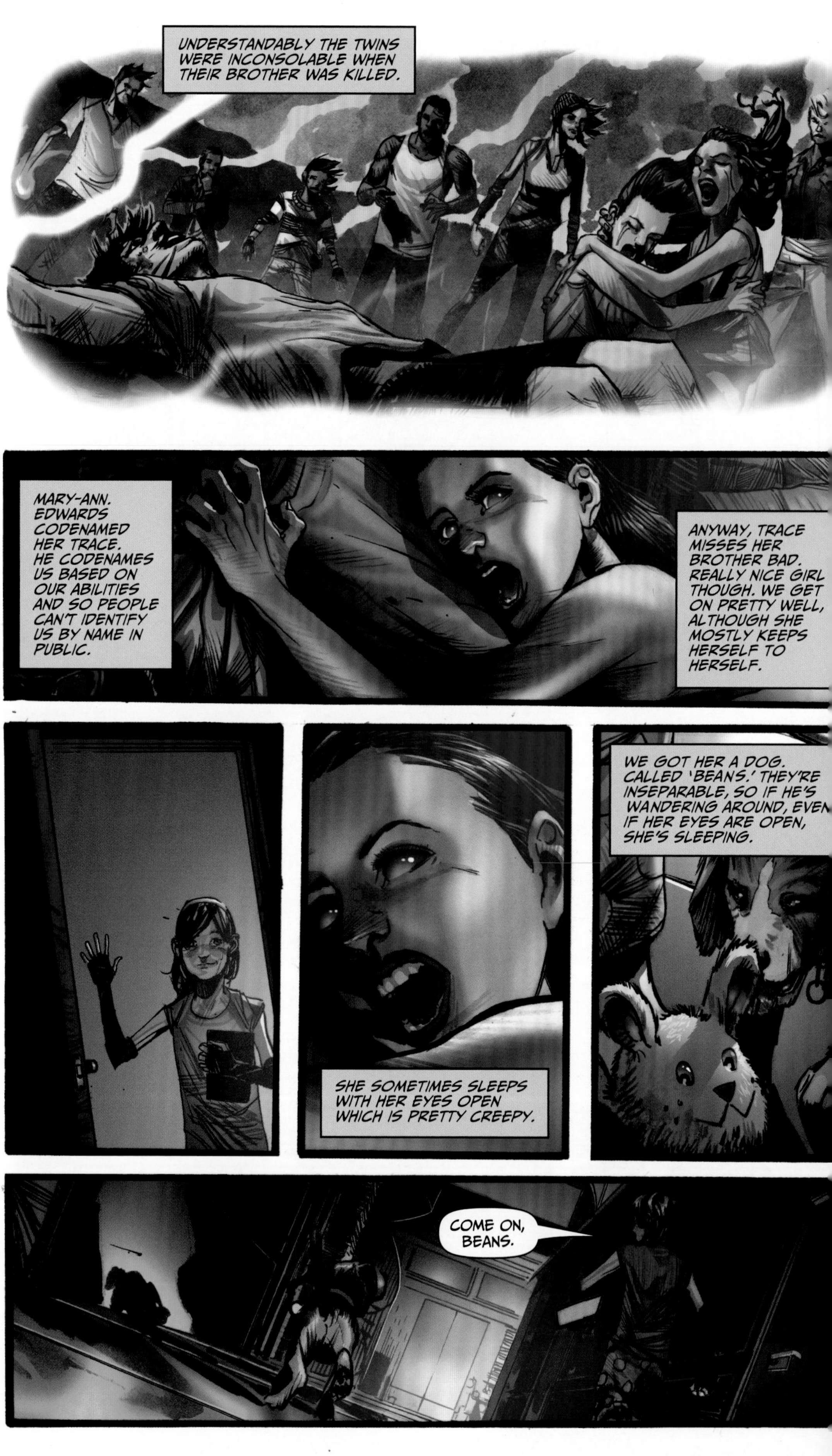
UNDERSTANDABLY THE TWINS WERE INCONSOLABLE WHEN THEIR BROTHER WAS KILLED.
MARY-ANN. EDWARDS CODENAMED HER TRACE. HE CODENAMES US BASED ON OUR ABILITIES AND SO PEOPLE CAN'T IDENTIFY US BY NAME IN PUBLIC.
ANYWAY, TRACE MISSES HER BROTHER BAD. REALLY NICE GIRL THOUGH. WE GET ON PRETTY WELL, ALTHOUGH SHE MOSTLY KEEPS HERSELF TO HERSELF.
SHE SOMETIMES SLEEPS WITH HER EYES OPEN WHICH IS PRETTY CREEPY.
WE GOT HER A DOG. CALLED 'BEANS.' THEY'RE INSEPARABLE, SO IF HE'S WANDERING AROUND, EVEN IF HER EYES ARE OPEN, SHE'S SLEEPING.
COME ON, BEANS.

HER TWIN, JADE, AKA, JADE. LONG STORY ON HER KEEPING HER NAME. ANYWAY, SHE'S HANDLED HER GRIEF DIFFERENTLY. SHE DEFINITELY DOESN'T KEEP TO HERSELF. IN FACT, QUITE THE OPPOSITE.

OOOOH GOD...

I'M SURE SHE MISSES HIM BUT SHE HASN'T REALLY SPOKEN ABOUT HER BROTHER AT ALL. INSTEAD SHE'S JUST BEEN FUCKING RAY. AKA, WISH.

I'VE WALKED IN ON THEM AT LEAST THREE OTHER TIMES.

EEEEEEWW!!

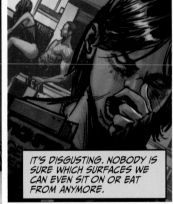

IT'S DISGUSTING. NOBODY IS SURE WHICH SURFACES WE CAN EVEN SIT ON OR EAT FROM ANYMORE.

EEEEEEEEEEEEWWWW!!

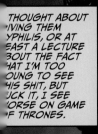

THOUGHT ABOUT ~~~IVING THEM ~~~YPHILIS, OR AT ~~~EAST A LECTURE ~~~BOUT THE FACT ~~~HAT I'M TOO ~~~OUNG TO SEE ~~~HIS SHIT, BUT ~~~UCK IT, I SEE ~~~ORSE ON GAME ~~~F THRONES.

COULD HAVE SWORN JADE'S EYES WERE GREEN. WHATEVER!

shut

I PROBABLY SHOULD JUST TEACH THEM ABOUT MANNERS OR CLOSING DOORS. AT LEAST EDWARDS AND STEPH ARE DISCRETE.

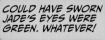

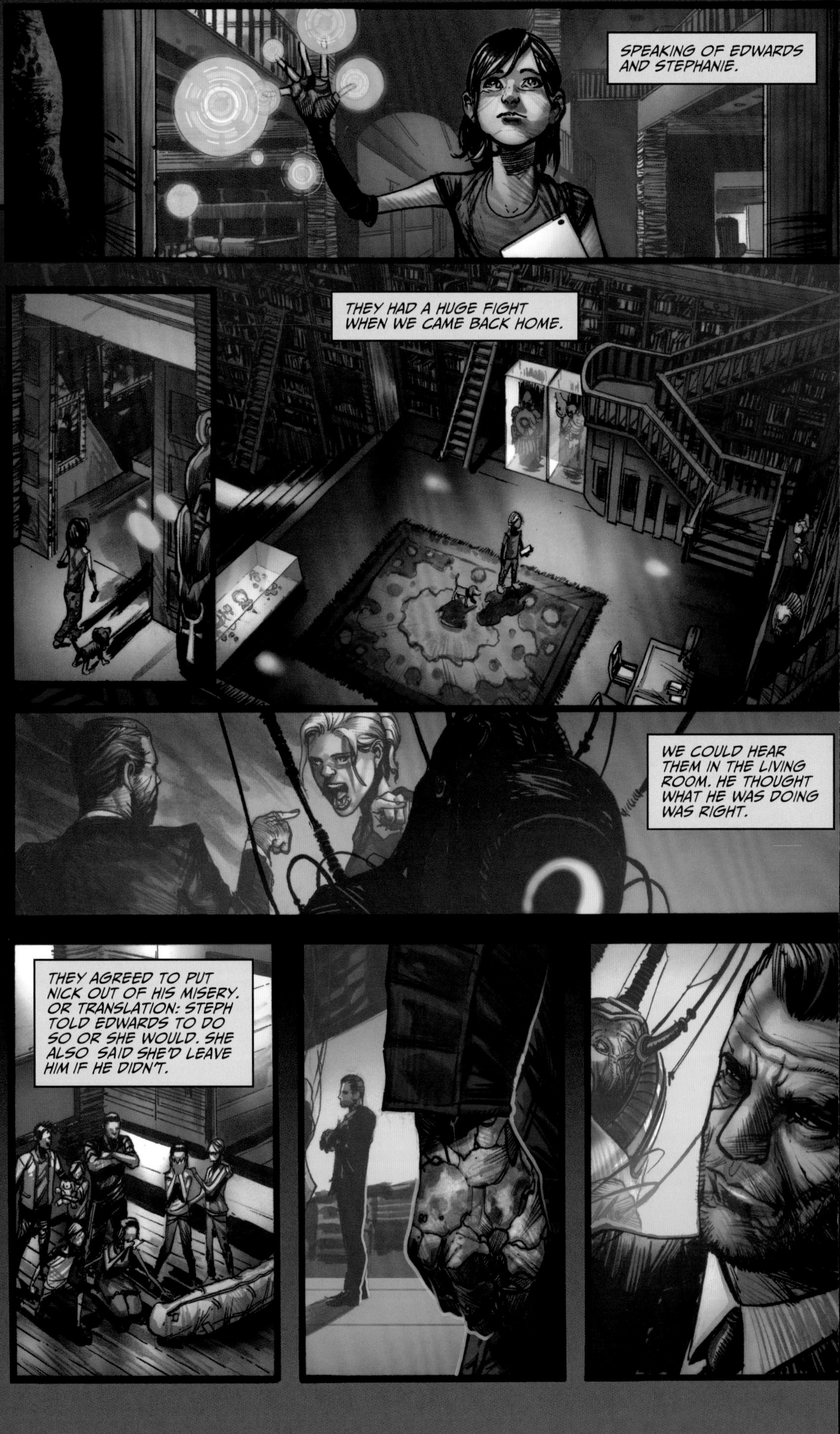
SPEAKING OF EDWARDS AND STEPHANIE.
THEY HAD A HUGE FIGHT WHEN WE CAME BACK HOME.
WE COULD HEAR THEM IN THE LIVING ROOM. HE THOUGHT WHAT HE WAS DOING WAS RIGHT.
THEY AGREED TO PUT NICK OUT OF HIS MISERY. OR TRANSLATION: STEPH TOLD EDWARDS TO DO SO OR SHE WOULD. SHE ALSO SAID SHE'D LEAVE HIM IF HE DIDN'T.

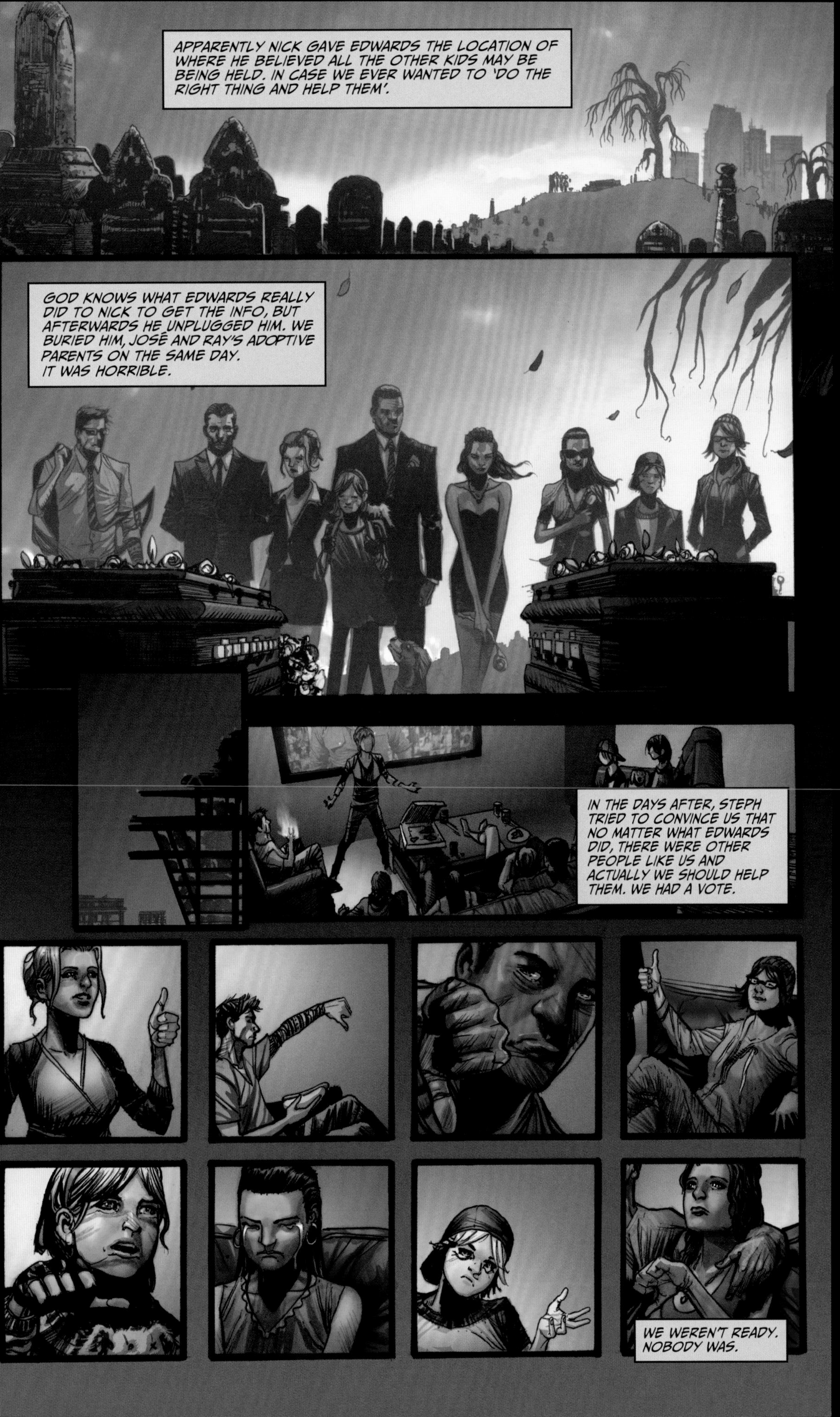

APPARENTLY NICK GAVE EDWARDS THE LOCATION OF WHERE HE BELIEVED ALL THE OTHER KIDS MAY BE BEING HELD. IN CASE WE EVER WANTED TO 'DO THE RIGHT THING AND HELP THEM'.
GOD KNOWS WHAT EDWARDS REALLY DID TO NICK TO GET THE INFO, BUT AFTERWARDS HE UNPLUGGED HIM. WE BURIED HIM, JOSÉ AND RAY'S ADOPTIVE PARENTS ON THE SAME DAY. IT WAS HORRIBLE.
IN THE DAYS AFTER, STEPH TRIED TO CONVINCE US THAT NO MATTER WHAT EDWARDS DID, THERE WERE OTHER PEOPLE LIKE US AND ACTUALLY WE SHOULD HELP THEM. WE HAD A VOTE.
WE WEREN'T READY. NOBODY WAS.

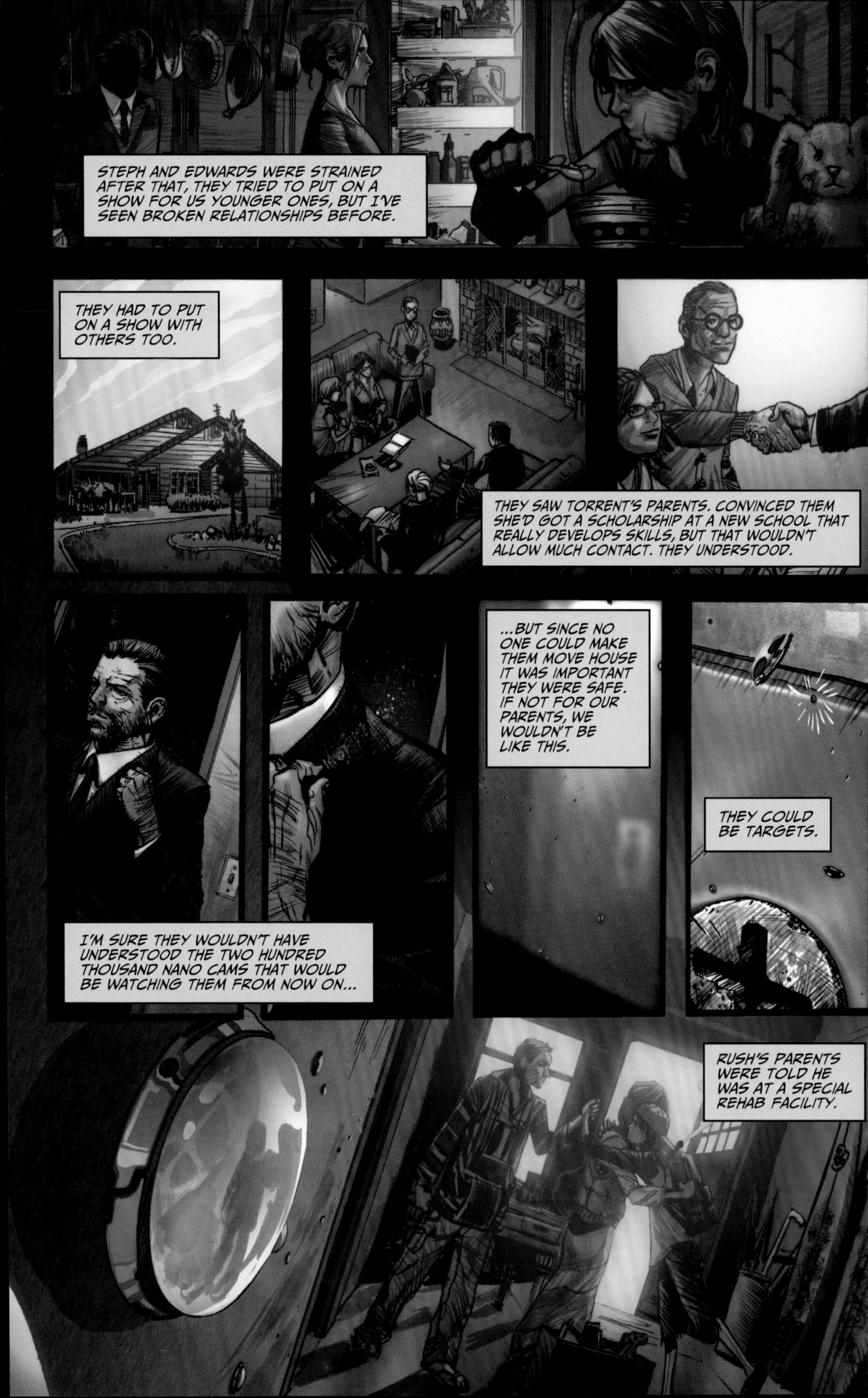
STEPH AND EDWARDS WERE STRAINED AFTER THAT, THEY TRIED TO PUT ON A SHOW FOR US YOUNGER ONES, BUT I'VE SEEN BROKEN RELATIONSHIPS BEFORE.
THEY HAD TO PUT ON A SHOW WITH OTHERS TOO.
THEY SAW TORRENT'S PARENTS. CONVINCED THEM SHE'D GOT A SCHOLARSHIP AT A NEW SCHOOL THAT REALLY DEVELOPS SKILLS, BUT THAT WOULDN'T ALLOW MUCH CONTACT. THEY UNDERSTOOD.
I'M SURE THEY WOULDN'T HAVE UNDERSTOOD THE TWO HUNDRED THOUSAND NANO CAMS THAT WOULD BE WATCHING THEM FROM NOW ON...
...BUT SINCE NO ONE COULD MAKE THEM MOVE HOUSE IT WAS IMPORTANT THEY WERE SAFE. IF NOT FOR OUR PARENTS, WE WOULDN'T BE LIKE THIS.
THEY COULD BE TARGETS.
RUSH'S PARENTS WERE TOLD HE WAS AT A SPECIAL REHAB FACILITY.

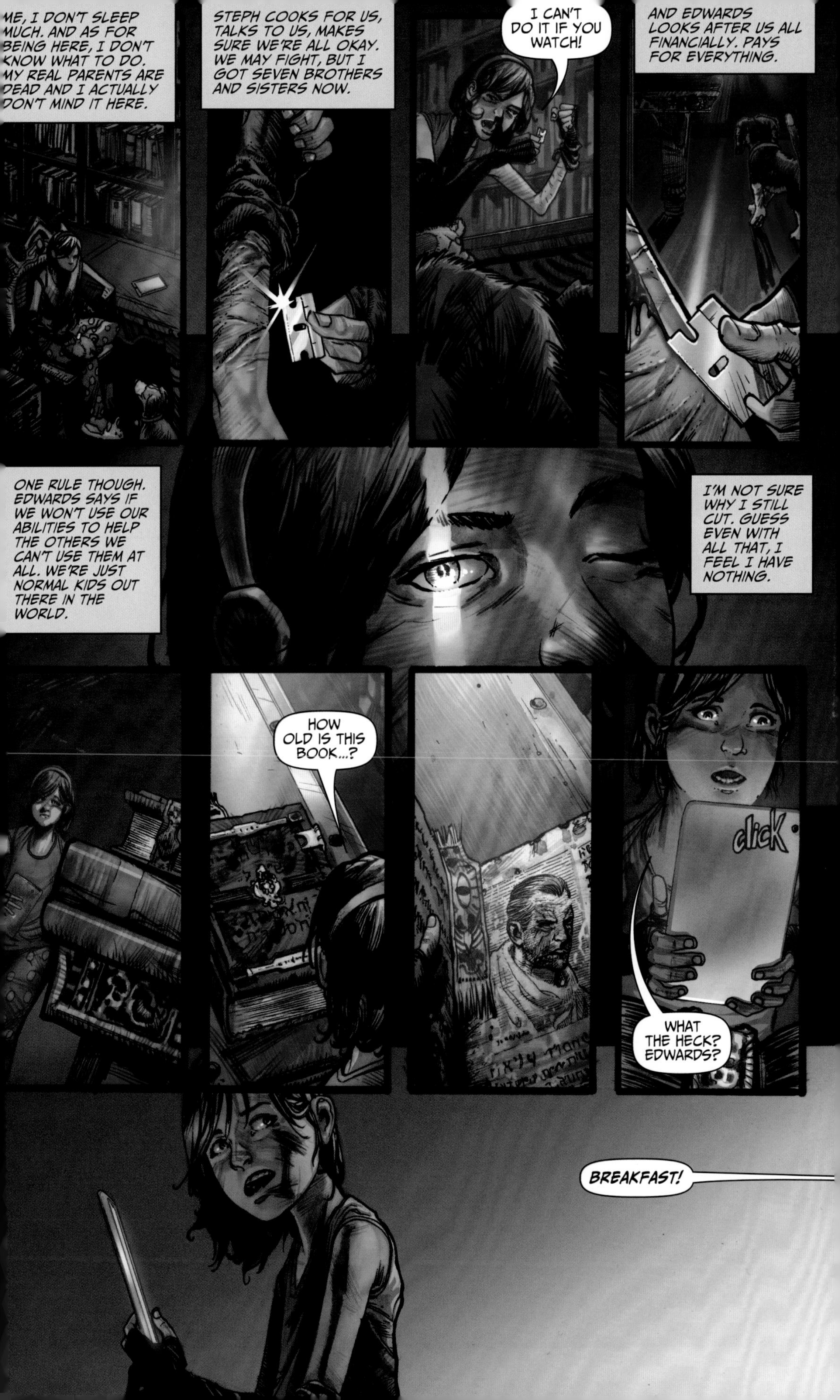
ME, I DON'T SLEEP MUCH. AND AS FOR BEING HERE, I DON'T KNOW WHAT TO DO. MY REAL PARENTS ARE DEAD AND I ACTUALLY DON'T MIND IT HERE.
STEPH COOKS FOR US, TALKS TO US, MAKES SURE WE'RE ALL OKAY. WE MAY FIGHT, BUT I GOT SEVEN BROTHERS AND SISTERS NOW.
I CAN'T DO IT IF YOU WATCH!
AND EDWARDS LOOKS AFTER US ALL FINANCIALLY. PAYS FOR EVERYTHING.
ONE RULE THOUGH. EDWARDS SAYS IF WE WON'T USE OUR ABILITIES TO HELP THE OTHERS WE CAN'T USE THEM AT ALL. WE'RE JUST NORMAL KIDS OUT THERE IN THE WORLD.
I'M NOT SURE WHY I STILL CUT. GUESS EVEN WITH ALL THAT, I FEEL I HAVE NOTHING.
HOW OLD IS THIS BOOK...?
click
WHAT THE HECK? EDWARDS?
BREAKFAST!

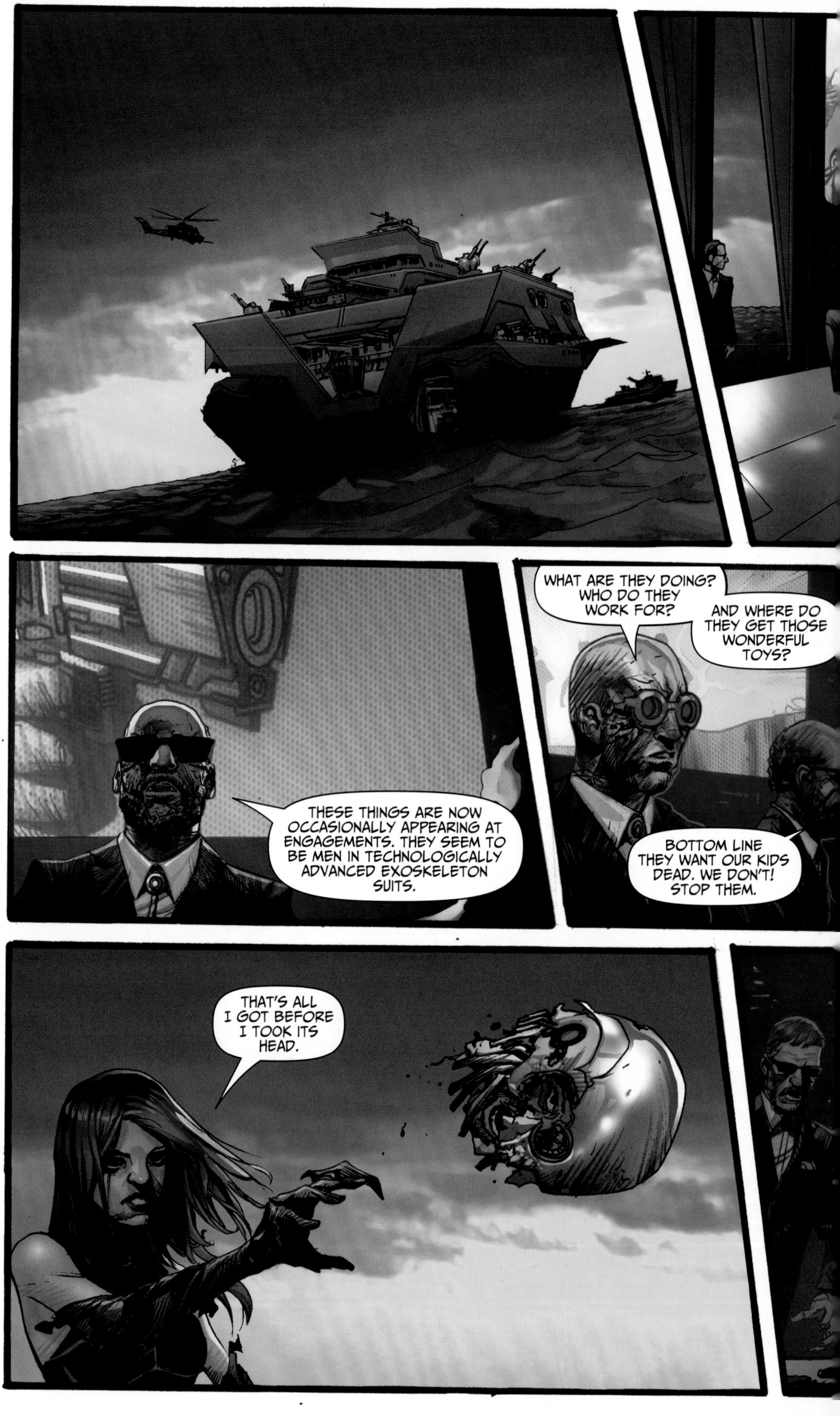
THESE THINGS ARE NOW OCCASIONALLY APPEARING AT ENGAGEMENTS. THEY SEEM TO BE MEN IN TECHNOLOGICALLY ADVANCED EXOSKELETON SUITS.
WHAT ARE THEY DOING? WHO DO THEY WORK FOR?
AND WHERE DO THEY GET THOSE WONDERFUL TOYS?
BOTTOM LINE THEY WANT OUR KIDS DEAD. WE DON'T! STOP THEM.
THAT'S ALL I GOT BEFORE I TOOK ITS HEAD.

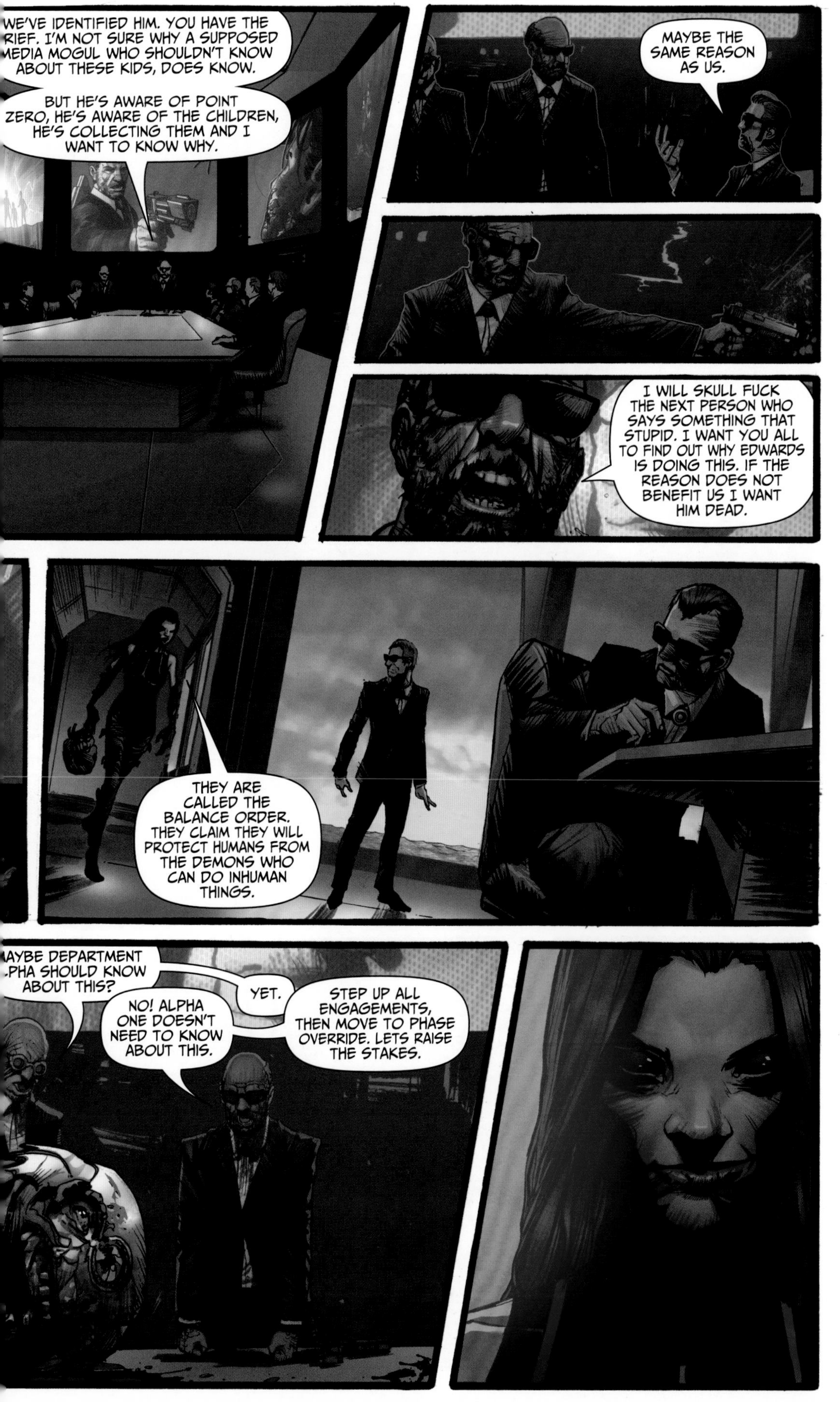
WE'VE IDENTIFIED HIM. YOU HAVE THE RIEF. I'M NOT SURE WHY A SUPPOSED MEDIA MOGUL WHO SHOULDN'T KNOW ABOUT THESE KIDS, DOES KNOW.
BUT HE'S AWARE OF POINT ZERO, HE'S AWARE OF THE CHILDREN, HE'S COLLECTING THEM AND I WANT TO KNOW WHY.
MAYBE THE SAME REASON AS US.
I WILL SKULL FUCK THE NEXT PERSON WHO SAYS SOMETHING THAT STUPID. I WANT YOU ALL TO FIND OUT WHY EDWARDS IS DOING THIS. IF THE REASON DOES NOT BENEFIT US I WANT HIM DEAD.
THEY ARE CALLED THE BALANCE ORDER. THEY CLAIM THEY WILL PROTECT HUMANS FROM THE DEMONS WHO CAN DO INHUMAN THINGS.
AYBE DEPARTMENT PHA SHOULD KNOW ABOUT THIS?
NO! ALPHA ONE DOESN'T NEED TO KNOW ABOUT THIS.
YET.
STEP UP ALL ENGAGEMENTS, THEN MOVE TO PHASE OVERRIDE. LETS RAISE THE STAKES.

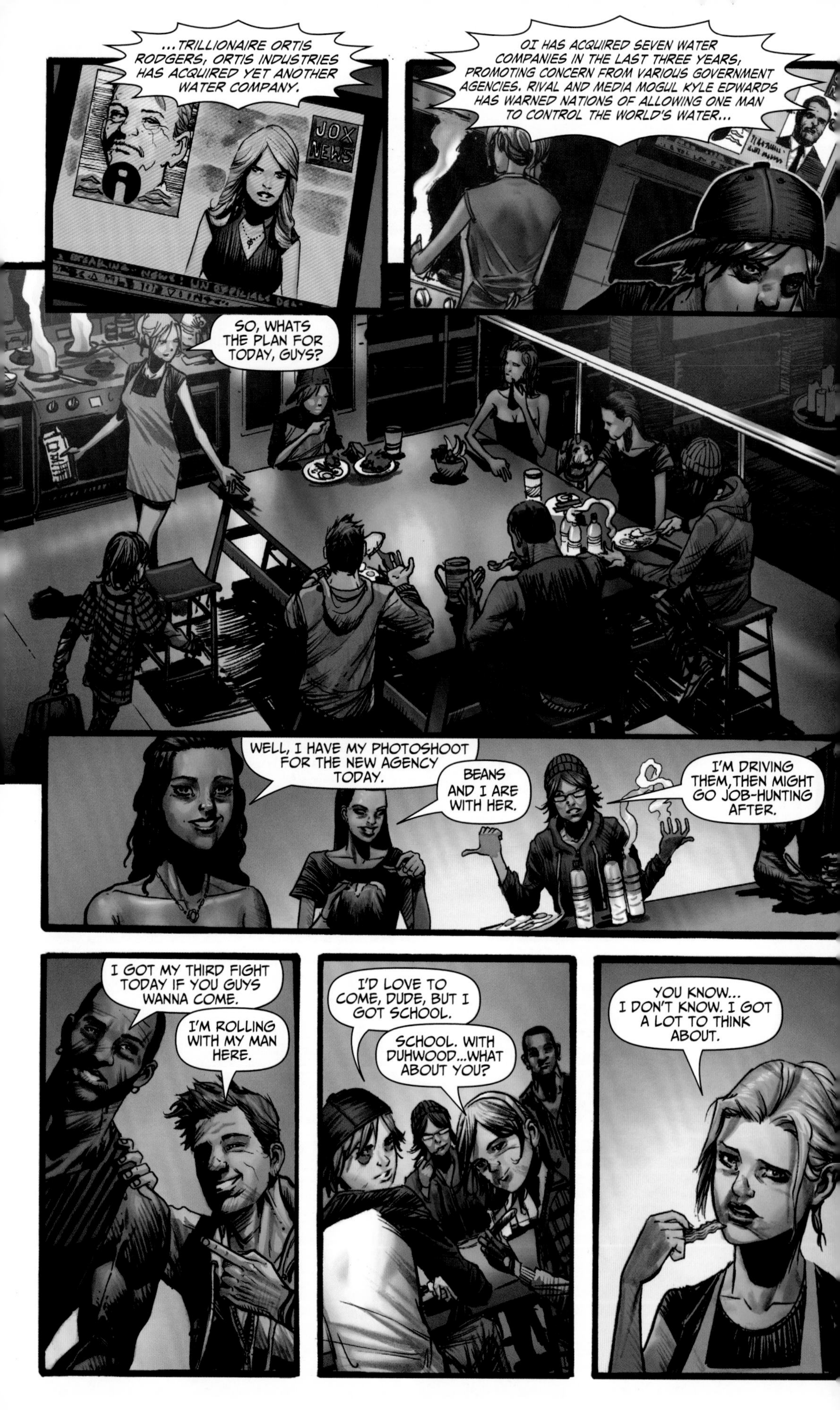
...TRILLIONAIRE ORTIS RODGERS, ORTIS INDUSTRIES HAS ACQUIRED YET ANOTHER WATER COMPANY.
JOX NEWS
OI HAS ACQUIRED SEVEN WATER COMPANIES IN THE LAST THREE YEARS, PROMOTING CONCERN FROM VARIOUS GOVERNMENT AGENCIES. RIVAL AND MEDIA MOGUL KYLE EDWARDS HAS WARNED NATIONS OF ALLOWING ONE MAN TO CONTROL THE WORLD'S WATER...
SO, WHATS THE PLAN FOR TODAY, GUYS?
WELL, I HAVE MY PHOTOSHOOT FOR THE NEW AGENCY TODAY.
BEANS AND I ARE WITH HER.
I'M DRIVING THEM, THEN MIGHT GO JOB-HUNTING AFTER.
I GOT MY THIRD FIGHT TODAY IF YOU GUYS WANNA COME.
I'M ROLLING WITH MY MAN HERE.
I'D LOVE TO COME, DUDE, BUT I GOT SCHOOL.
SCHOOL. WITH DUHWOOD...WHAT ABOUT YOU?
YOU KNOW... I DON'T KNOW. I GOT A LOT TO THINK ABOUT.

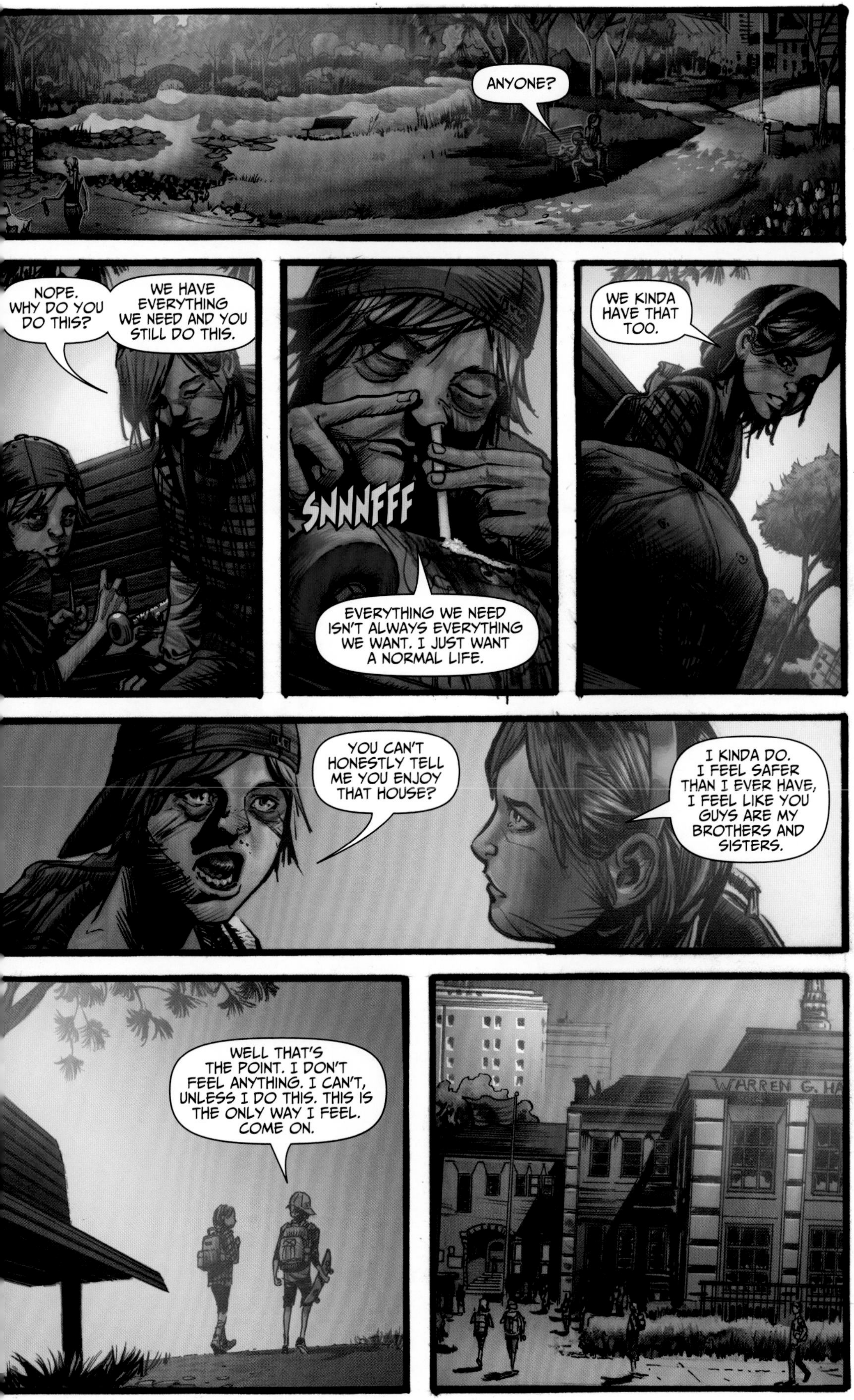

ANYONE?
NOPE. WHY DO YOU DO THIS?
WE HAVE EVERYTHING WE NEED AND YOU STILL DO THIS.
SNNNFFF
EVERYTHING WE NEED ISN'T ALWAYS EVERYTHING WE WANT. I JUST WANT A NORMAL LIFE.
WE KINDA HAVE THAT TOO.
YOU CAN'T HONESTLY TELL ME YOU ENJOY THAT HOUSE?
I KINDA DO. I FEEL SAFER THAN I EVER HAVE, I FEEL LIKE YOU GUYS ARE MY BROTHERS AND SISTERS.
WELL THAT'S THE POINT. I DON'T FEEL ANYTHING. I CAN'T, UNLESS I DO THIS. THIS IS THE ONLY WAY I FEEL. COME ON.
WARREN G. HA

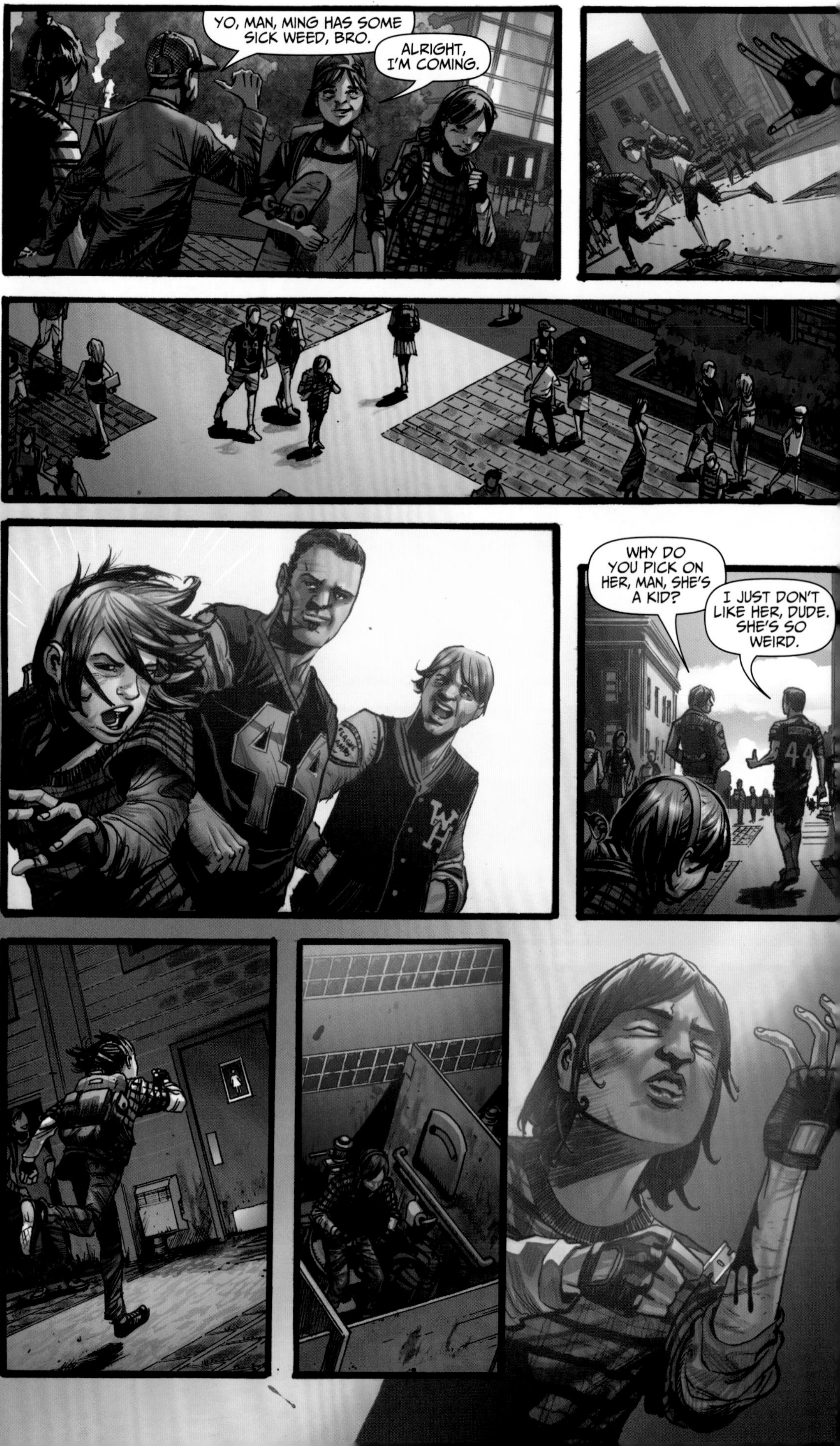
YO, MAN, MING HAS SOME SICK WEED, BRO.
ALRIGHT, I'M COMING.
WHY DO YOU PICK ON HER, MAN, SHE'S A KID?
I JUST DON'T LIKE HER, DUDE. SHE'S SO WEIRD.

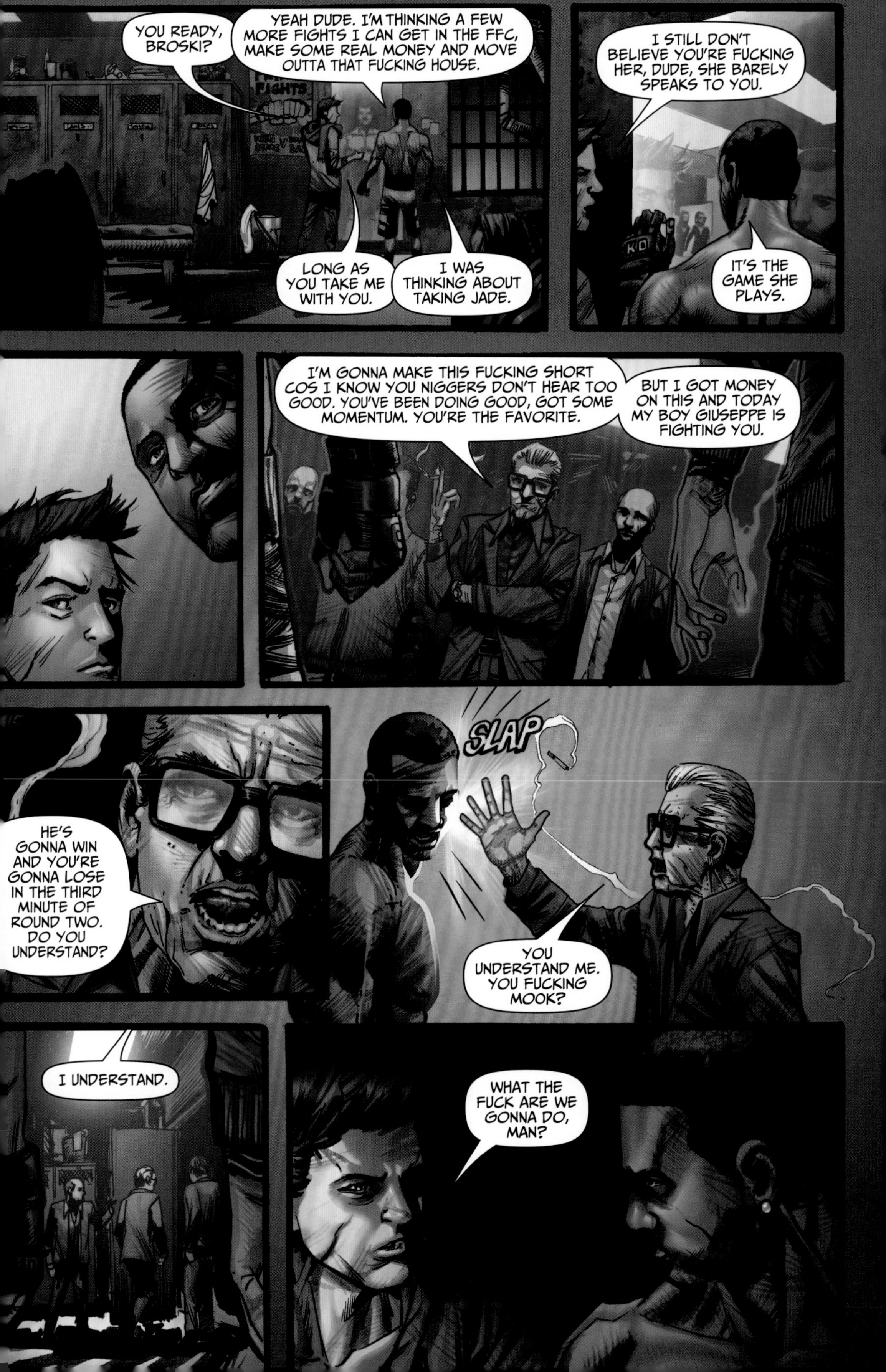
YOU READY, BROSKI?
YEAH DUDE. I'M THINKING A FEW MORE FIGHTS I CAN GET IN THE FFC, MAKE SOME REAL MONEY AND MOVE OUTTA THAT FUCKING HOUSE.
LONG AS YOU TAKE ME WITH YOU.
I WAS THINKING ABOUT TAKING JADE.
I STILL DON'T BELIEVE YOU'RE FUCKING HER, DUDE, SHE BARELY SPEAKS TO YOU.
IT'S THE GAME SHE PLAYS.
I'M GONNA MAKE THIS FUCKING SHORT COS I KNOW YOU NIGGERS DON'T HEAR TOO GOOD. YOU'VE BEEN DOING GOOD, GOT SOME MOMENTUM. YOU'RE THE FAVORITE.
BUT I GOT MONEY ON THIS AND TODAY MY BOY GIUSEPPE IS FIGHTING YOU.
HE'S GONNA WIN AND YOU'RE GONNA LOSE IN THE THIRD MINUTE OF ROUND TWO. DO YOU UNDERSTAND?
SLAP
YOU UNDERSTAND ME. YOU FUCKING MOOK?
I UNDERSTAND.
WHAT THE FUCK ARE WE GONNA DO, MAN?

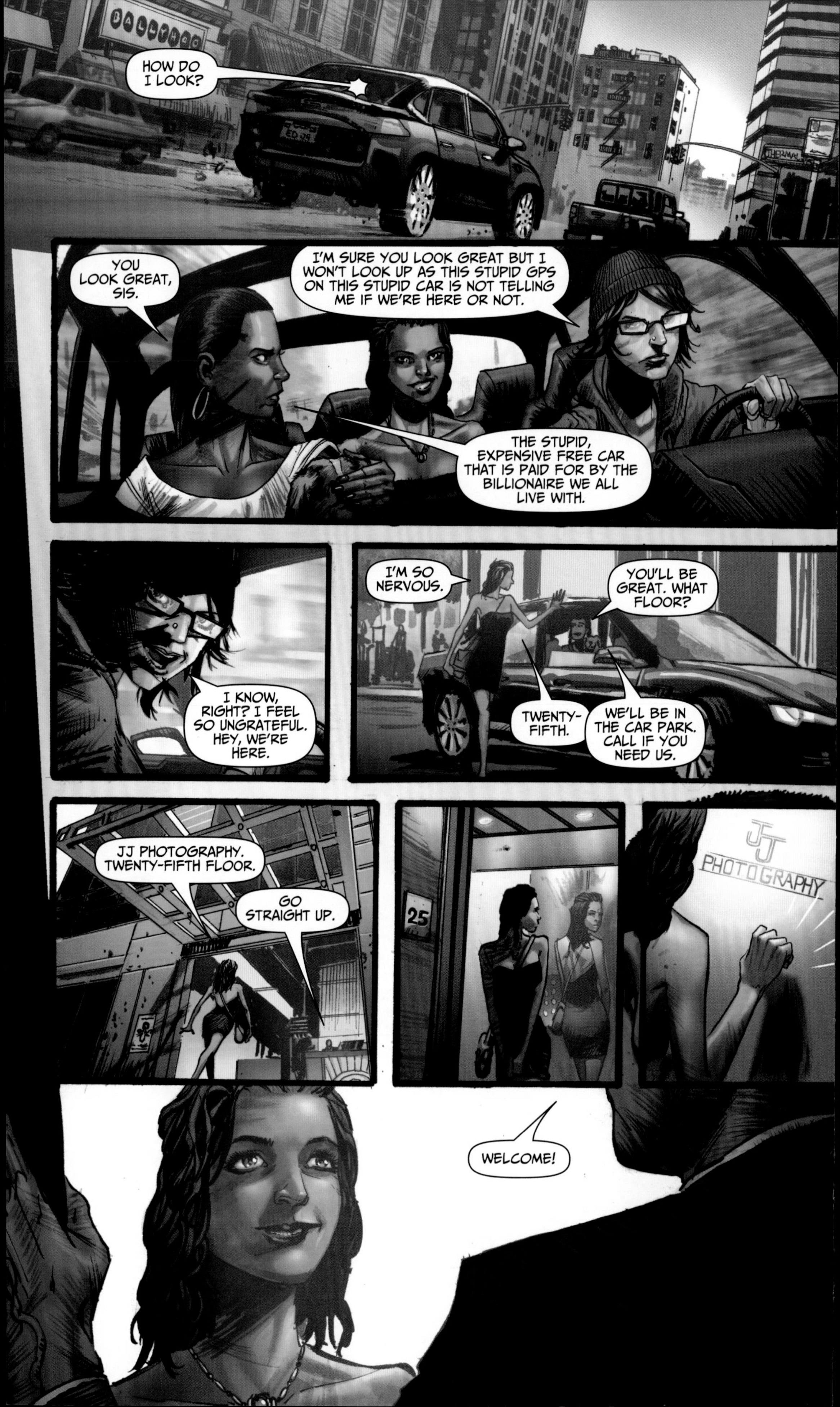

HOW DO I LOOK?
YOU LOOK GREAT, SIS.
I'M SURE YOU LOOK GREAT BUT I WON'T LOOK UP AS THIS STUPID GPS ON THIS STUPID CAR IS NOT TELLING ME IF WE'RE HERE OR NOT.
THE STUPID, EXPENSIVE FREE CAR THAT IS PAID FOR BY THE BILLIONAIRE WE ALL LIVE WITH.
I KNOW, RIGHT? I FEEL SO UNGRATEFUL. HEY, WE'RE HERE.
I'M SO NERVOUS.
YOU'LL BE GREAT. WHAT FLOOR?
TWENTY-FIFTH.
WE'LL BE IN THE CAR PARK. CALL IF YOU NEED US.
JJ PHOTOGRAPHY. TWENTY-FIFTH FLOOR.
GO STRAIGHT UP.
25
JJ PHOTOGRAPHY
WELCOME!

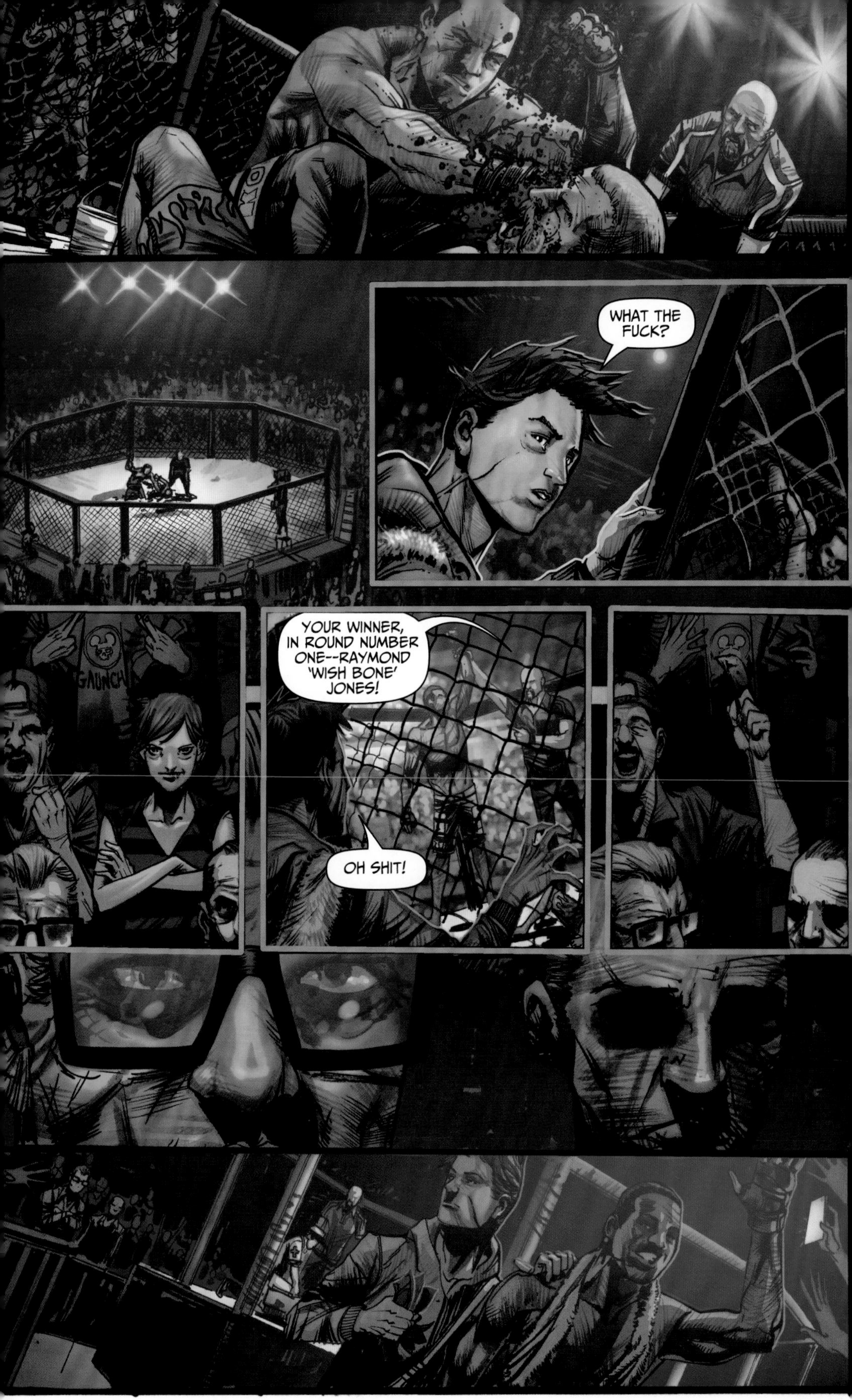
WHAT THE FUCK?
YOUR WINNER, IN ROUND NUMBER ONE--RAYMOND 'WISH BONE' JONES!
OH SHIT!
GAUNCH

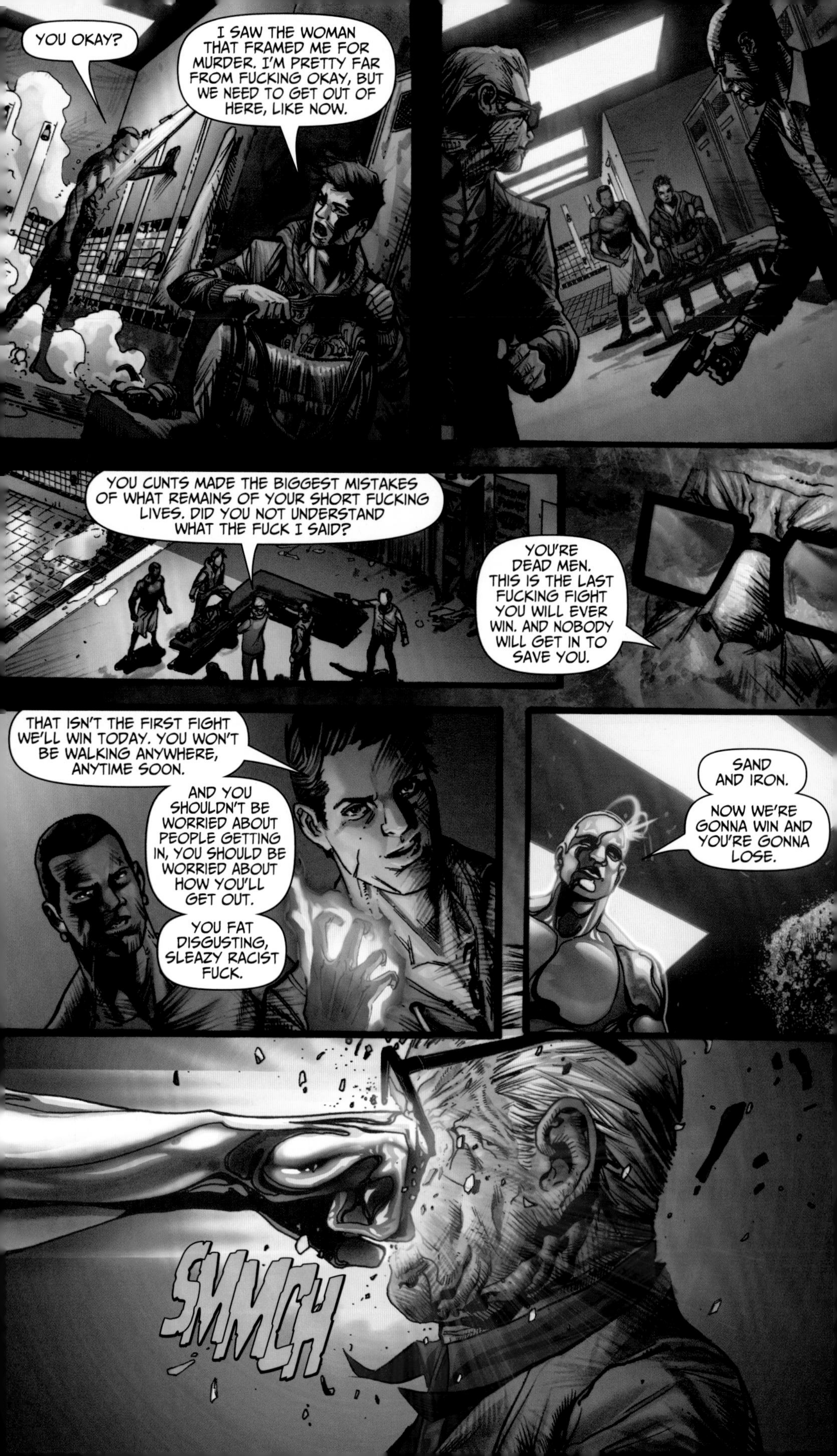
YOU OKAY?
I SAW THE WOMAN THAT FRAMED ME FOR MURDER. I'M PRETTY FAR FROM FUCKING OKAY, BUT WE NEED TO GET OUT OF HERE, LIKE NOW.
YOU CUNTS MADE THE BIGGEST MISTAKES OF WHAT REMAINS OF YOUR SHORT FUCKING LIVES. DID YOU NOT UNDERSTAND WHAT THE FUCK I SAID?
YOU'RE DEAD MEN. THIS IS THE LAST FUCKING FIGHT YOU WILL EVER WIN. AND NOBODY WILL GET IN TO SAVE YOU.
THAT ISN'T THE FIRST FIGHT WE'LL WIN TODAY. YOU WON'T BE WALKING ANYWHERE, ANYTIME SOON.
AND YOU SHOULDN'T BE WORRIED ABOUT PEOPLE GETTING IN, YOU SHOULD BE WORRIED ABOUT HOW YOU'LL GET OUT.
YOU FAT DISGUSTING, SLEAZY RACIST FUCK.
SAND AND IRON.
NOW WE'RE GONNA WIN AND YOU'RE GONNA LOSE.
SMMCH

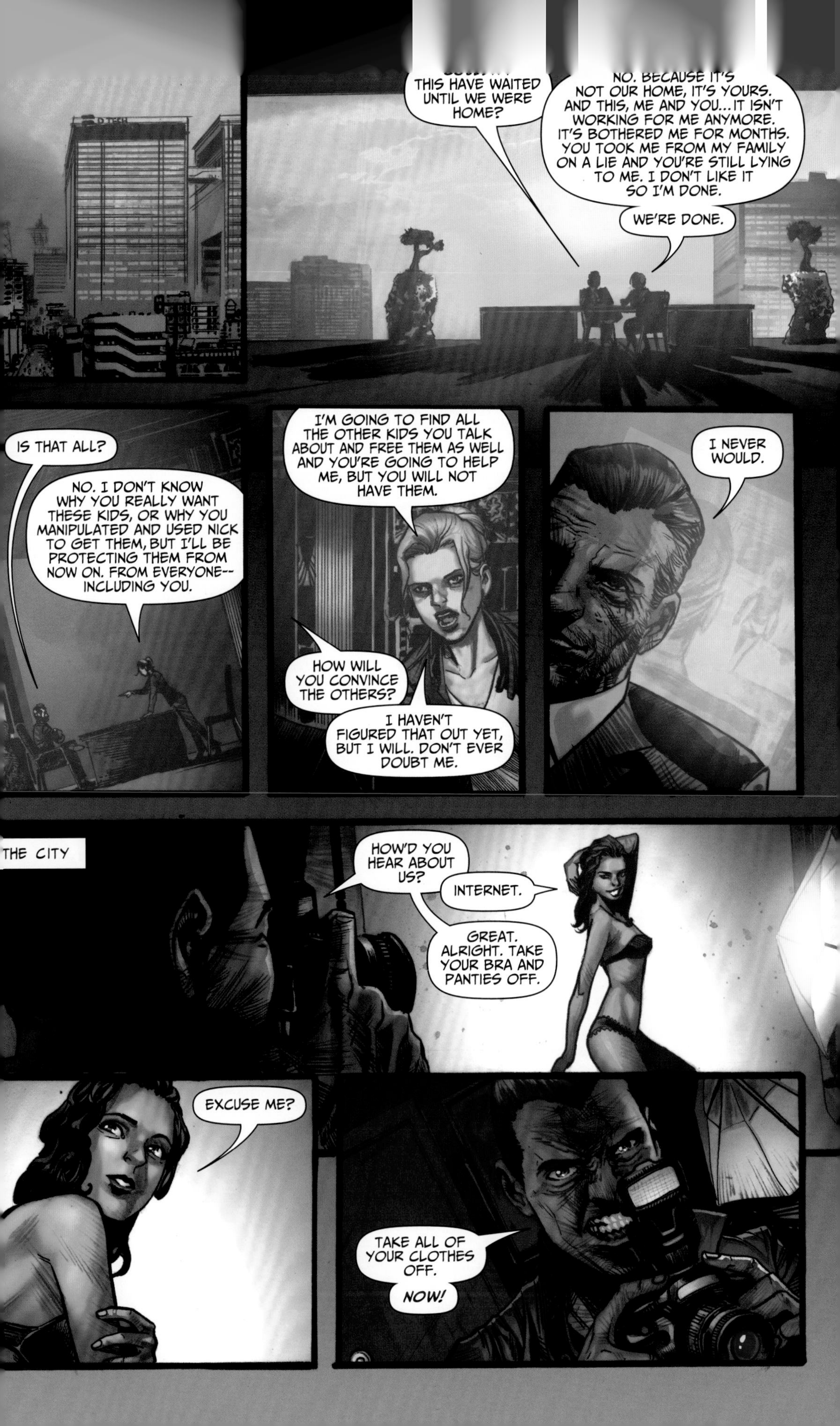

THIS HAVE WAITED UNTIL WE WERE HOME?
NO. BECAUSE IT'S NOT OUR HOME, IT'S YOURS. AND THIS, ME AND YOU... IT ISN'T WORKING FOR ME ANYMORE. IT'S BOTHERED ME FOR MONTHS. YOU TOOK ME FROM MY FAMILY ON A LIE AND YOU'RE STILL LYING TO ME. I DON'T LIKE IT SO I'M DONE.
WE'RE DONE.
IS THAT ALL?
NO. I DON'T KNOW WHY YOU REALLY WANT THESE KIDS, OR WHY YOU MANIPULATED AND USED NICK TO GET THEM, BUT I'LL BE PROTECTING THEM FROM NOW ON. FROM EVERYONE-- INCLUDING YOU.
I'M GOING TO FIND ALL THE OTHER KIDS YOU TALK ABOUT AND FREE THEM AS WELL AND YOU'RE GOING TO HELP ME, BUT YOU WILL NOT HAVE THEM.
HOW WILL YOU CONVINCE THE OTHERS?
I HAVEN'T FIGURED THAT OUT YET, BUT I WILL. DON'T EVER DOUBT ME.
I NEVER WOULD.
THE CITY
HOW'D YOU HEAR ABOUT US?
INTERNET.
GREAT. ALRIGHT. TAKE YOUR BRA AND PANTIES OFF.
EXCUSE ME?
TAKE ALL OF YOUR CLOTHES OFF.
NOW!

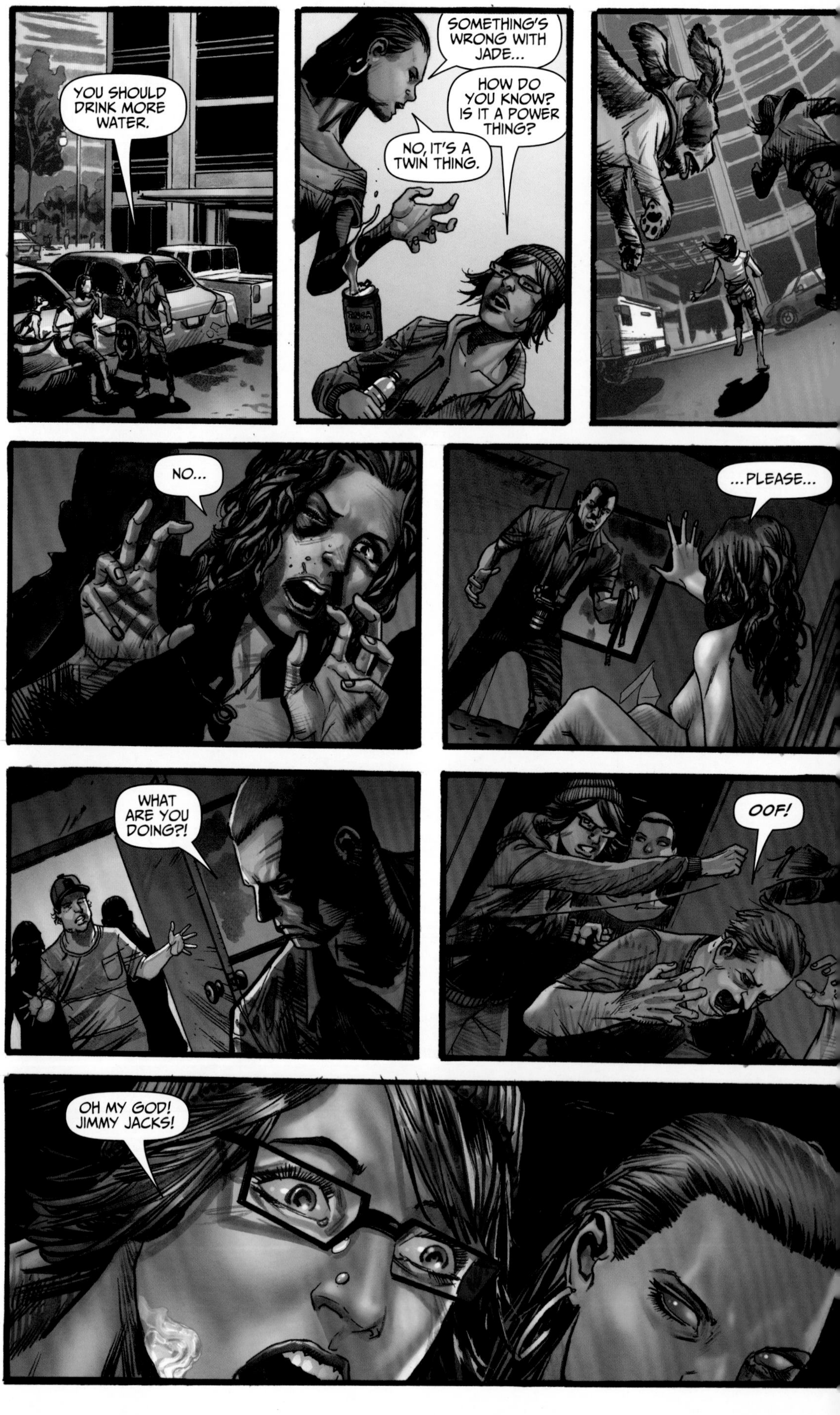
YOU SHOULD DRINK MORE WATER.
SOMETHING'S WRONG WITH JADE...
HOW DO YOU KNOW? IS IT A POWER THING?
NO, IT'S A TWIN THING.
NO...
...PLEASE...
WHAT ARE YOU DOING?!
OOF!
OH MY GOD! JIMMY JACKS!

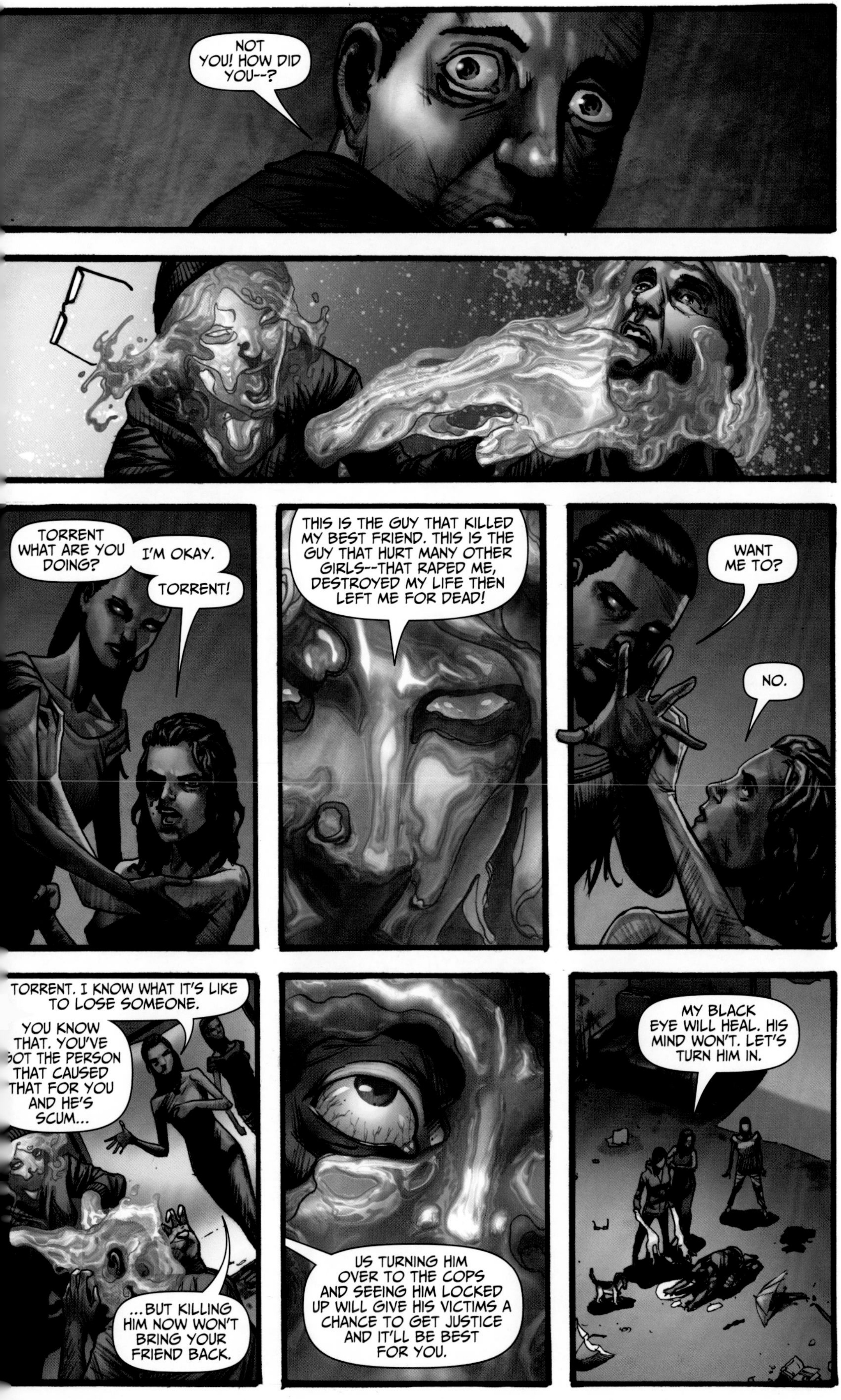
NOT YOU! HOW DID YOU--?
TORRENT WHAT ARE YOU DOING?
I'M OKAY.
TORRENT!
THIS IS THE GUY THAT KILLED MY BEST FRIEND. THIS IS THE GUY THAT HURT MANY OTHER GIRLS--THAT RAPED ME, DESTROYED MY LIFE THEN LEFT ME FOR DEAD!
WANT ME TO?
NO.
TORRENT. I KNOW WHAT IT'S LIKE TO LOSE SOMEONE.
YOU KNOW THAT. YOU'VE GOT THE PERSON THAT CAUSED THAT FOR YOU AND HE'S SCUM...
...BUT KILLING HIM NOW WON'T BRING YOUR FRIEND BACK.
US TURNING HIM OVER TO THE COPS AND SEEING HIM LOCKED UP WILL GIVE HIS VICTIMS A CHANCE TO GET JUSTICE AND IT'LL BE BEST FOR YOU.
MY BLACK EYE WILL HEAL. HIS MIND WON'T. LET'S TURN HIM IN.

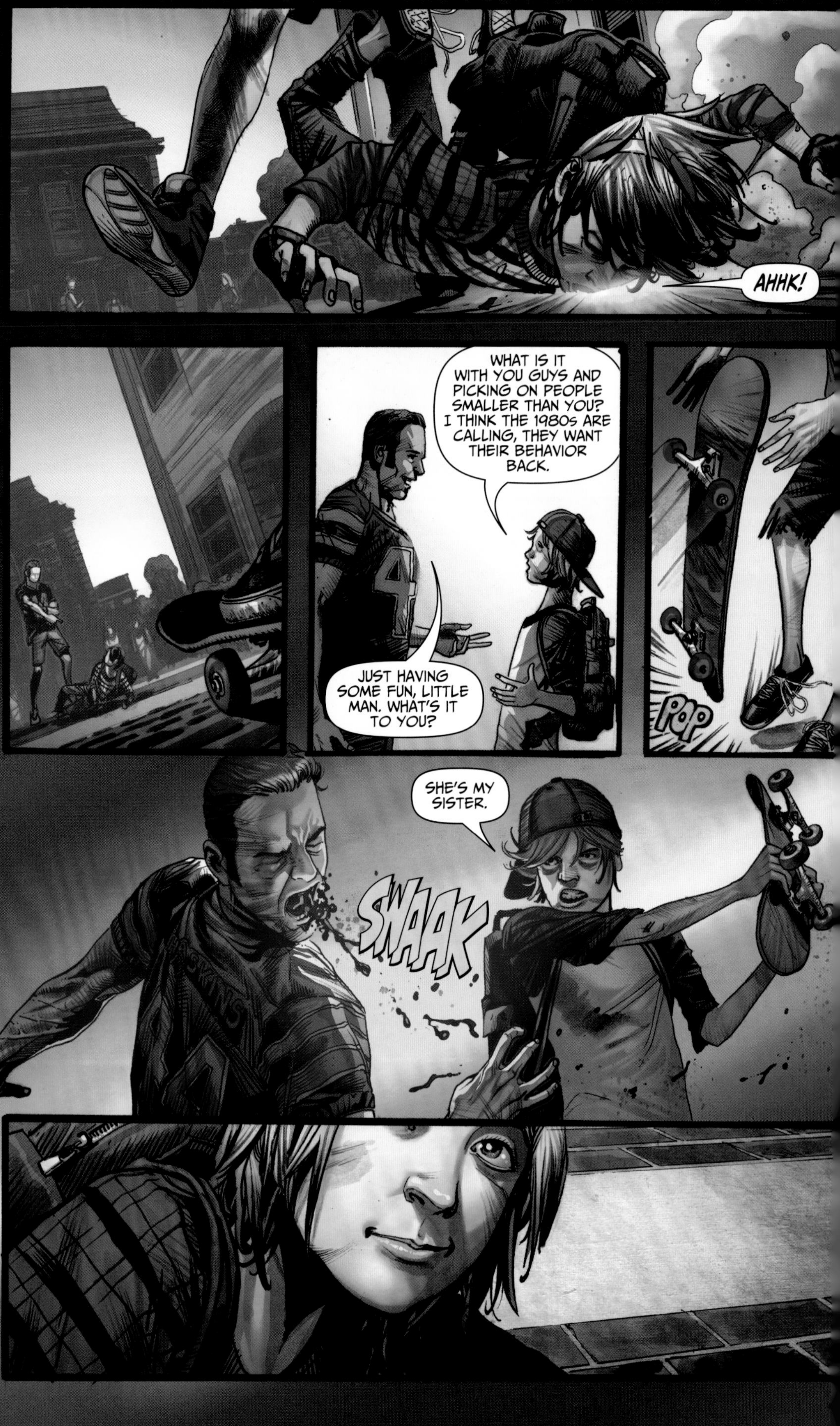
AHHK!
WHAT IS IT WITH YOU GUYS AND PICKING ON PEOPLE SMALLER THAN YOU? I THINK THE 1980s ARE CALLING, THEY WANT THEIR BEHAVIOR BACK.
JUST HAVING SOME FUN, LITTLE MAN. WHAT'S IT TO YOU?
POP
SHE'S MY SISTER.
SNAAK

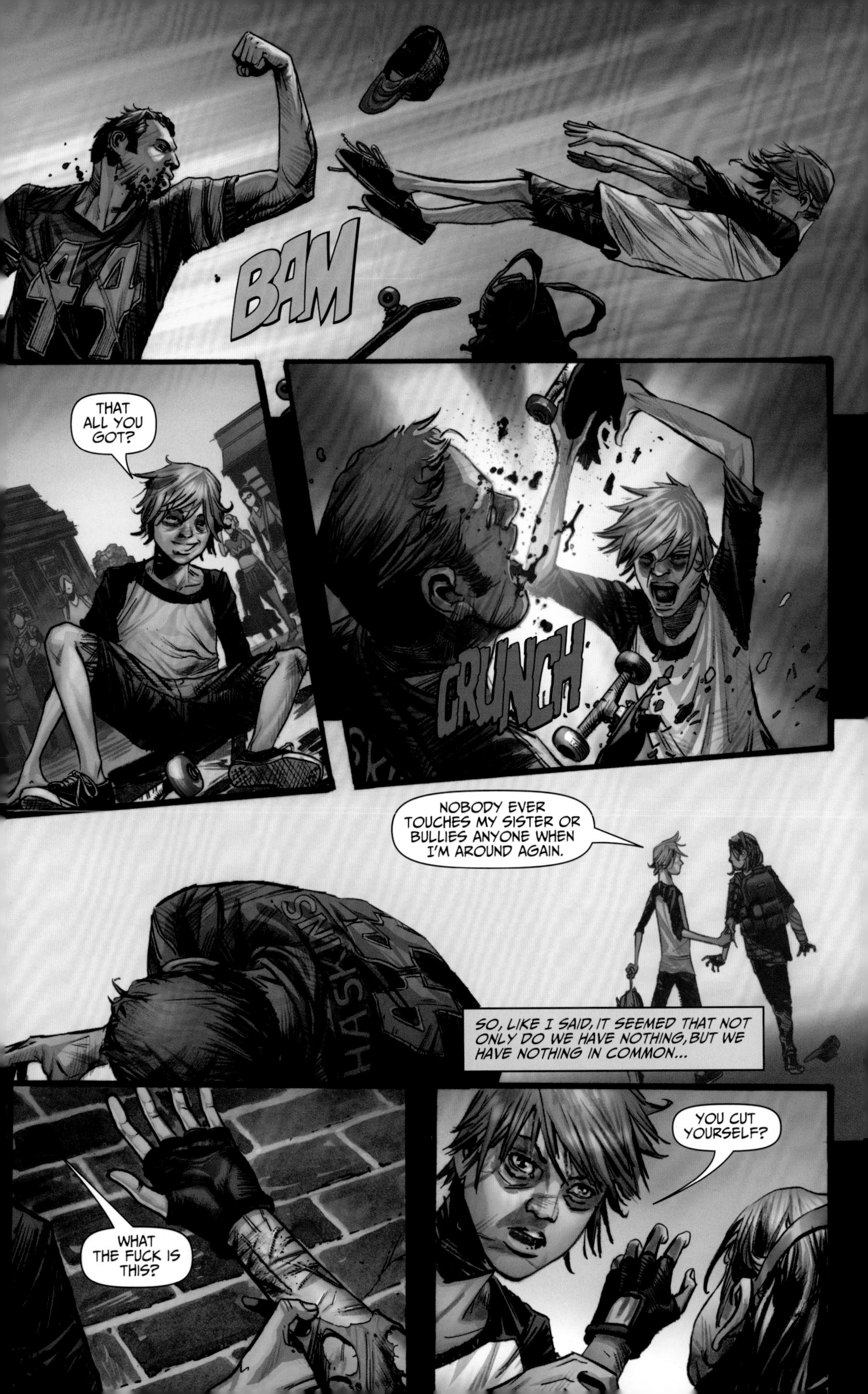
BAM
THAT ALL YOU GOT?
CRUNCH
NOBODY EVER TOUCHES MY SISTER OR BULLIES ANYONE WHEN I'M AROUND AGAIN.
SO, LIKE I SAID, IT SEEMED THAT NOT ONLY DO WE HAVE NOTHING, BUT WE HAVE NOTHING IN COMMON...
WHAT THE FUCK IS THIS?
YOU CUT YOURSELF?

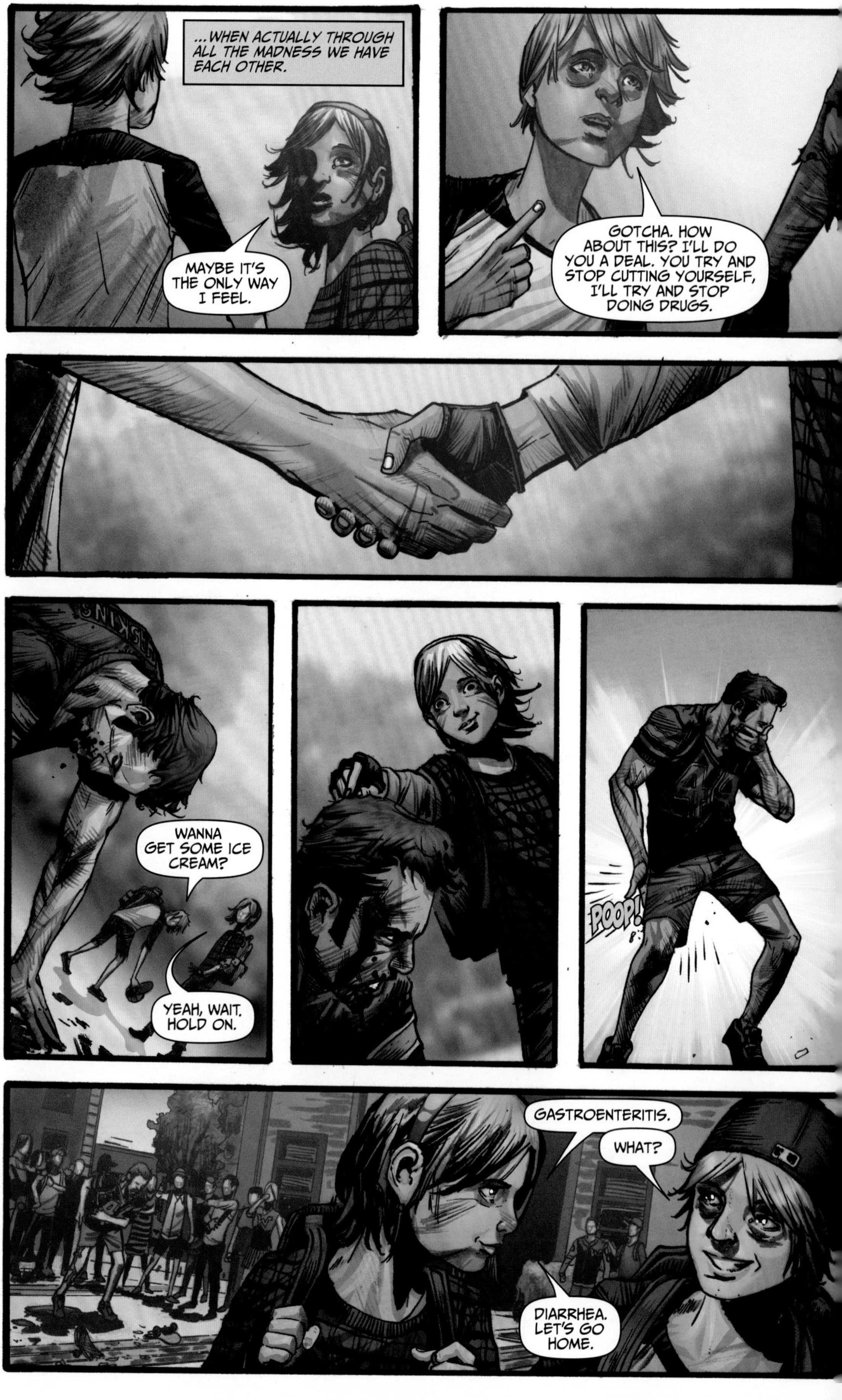
...WHEN ACTUALLY THROUGH ALL THE MADNESS WE HAVE EACH OTHER.
MAYBE IT'S THE ONLY WAY I FEEL.
GOTCHA. HOW ABOUT THIS? I'LL DO YOU A DEAL. YOU TRY AND STOP CUTTING YOURSELF, I'LL TRY AND STOP DOING DRUGS.
WANNA GET SOME ICE CREAM?
YEAH, WAIT. HOLD ON.
POOP!
GASTROENTERITIS.
WHAT?
DIARRHEA. LET'S GO HOME.

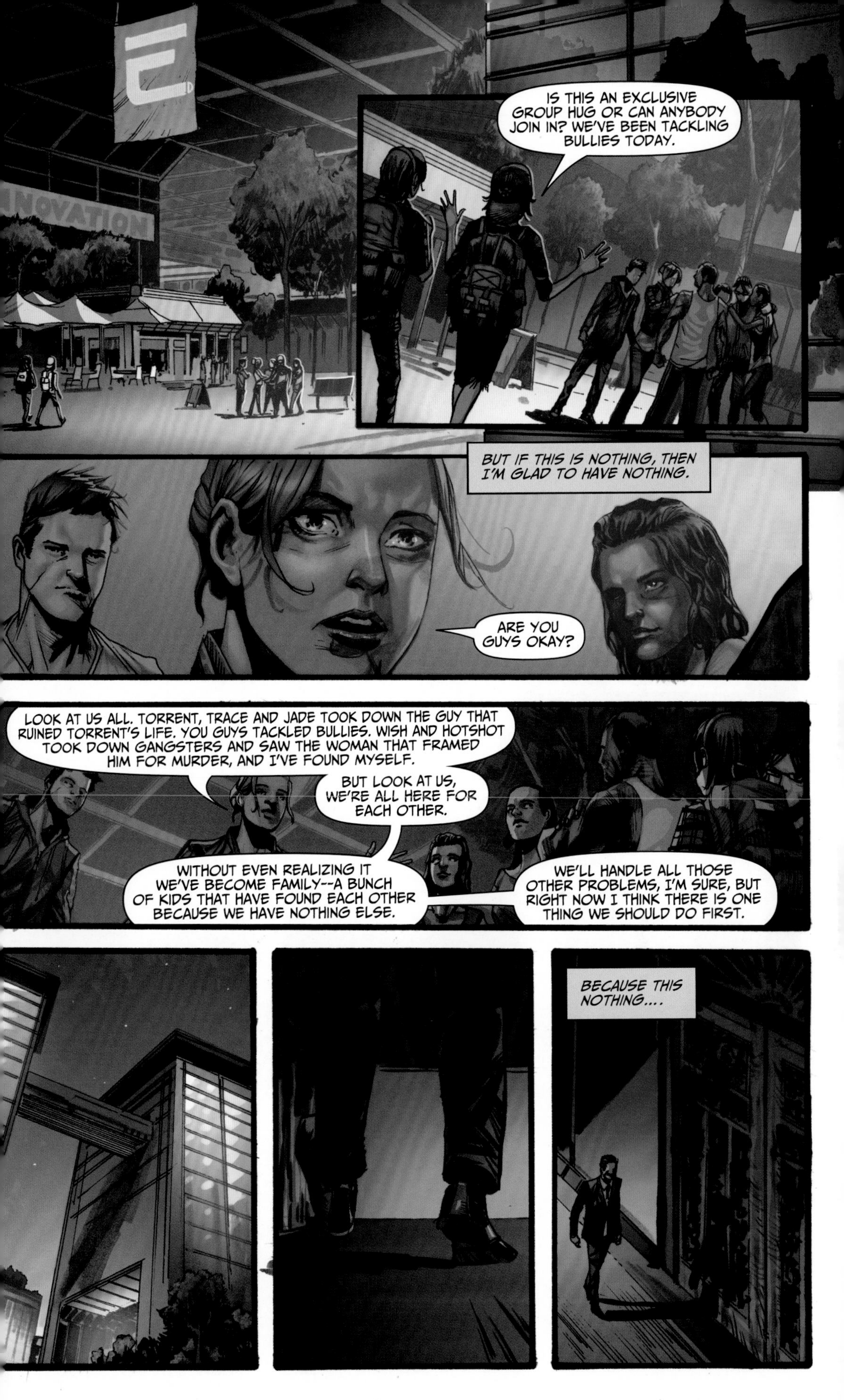
IS THIS AN EXCLUSIVE GROUP HUG OR CAN ANYBODY JOIN IN? WE'VE BEEN TACKLING BULLIES TODAY.
BUT IF THIS IS NOTHING, THEN I'M GLAD TO HAVE NOTHING.
ARE YOU GUYS OKAY?
LOOK AT US ALL. TORRENT, TRACE AND JADE TOOK DOWN THE GUY THAT RUINED TORRENT'S LIFE. YOU GUYS TACKLED BULLIES. WISH AND HOTSHOT TOOK DOWN GANGSTERS AND SAW THE WOMAN THAT FRAMED HIM FOR MURDER, AND I'VE FOUND MYSELF.
BUT LOOK AT US, WE'RE ALL HERE FOR EACH OTHER.
WITHOUT EVEN REALIZING IT WE'VE BECOME FAMILY--A BUNCH OF KIDS THAT HAVE FOUND EACH OTHER BECAUSE WE HAVE NOTHING ELSE.
WE'LL HANDLE ALL THOSE OTHER PROBLEMS, I'M SURE, BUT RIGHT NOW I THINK THERE IS ONE THING WE SHOULD DO FIRST.
BECAUSE THIS NOTHING....

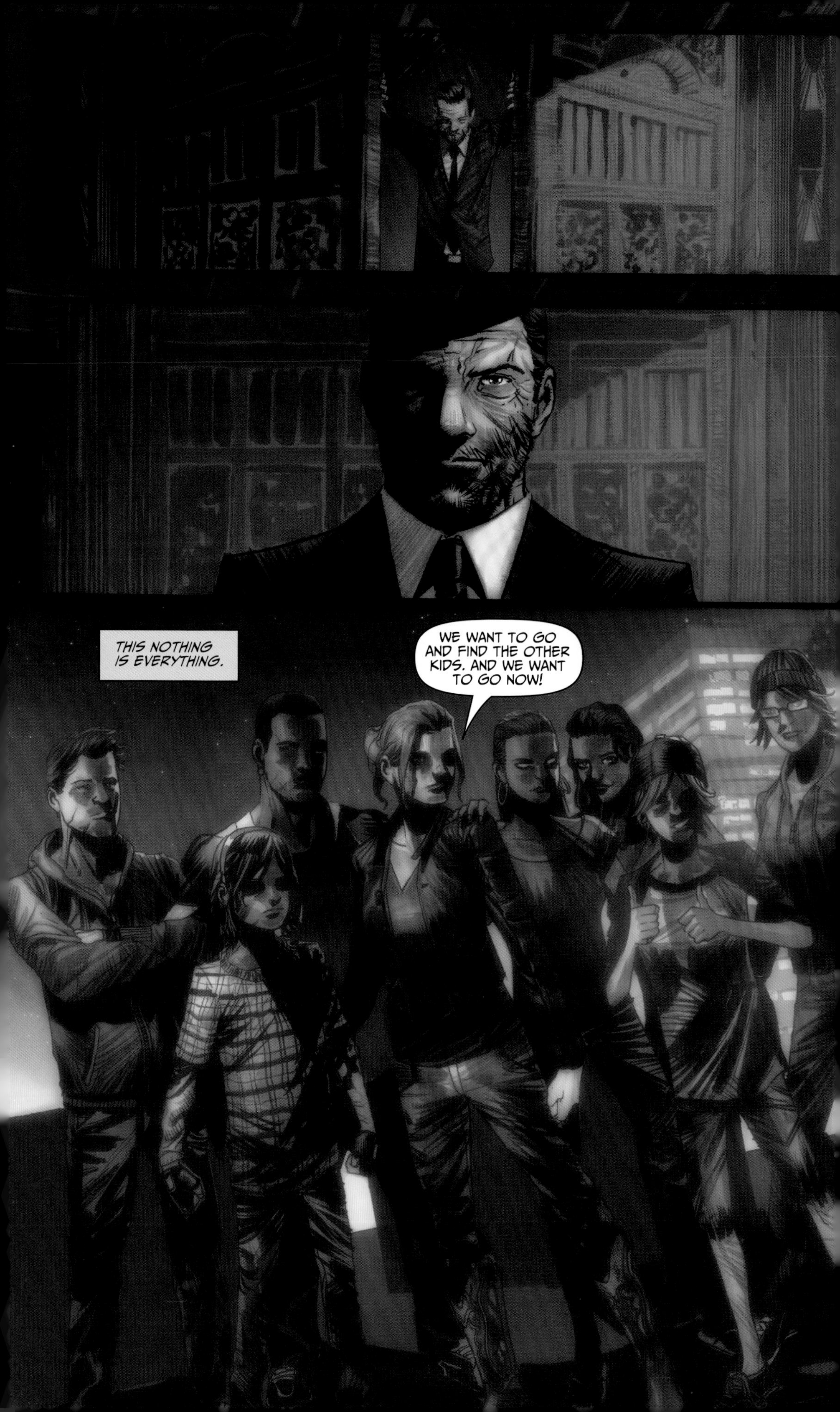
THIS NOTHING IS EVERYTHING.
WE WANT TO GO AND FIND THE OTHER KIDS. AND WE WANT TO GO NOW!

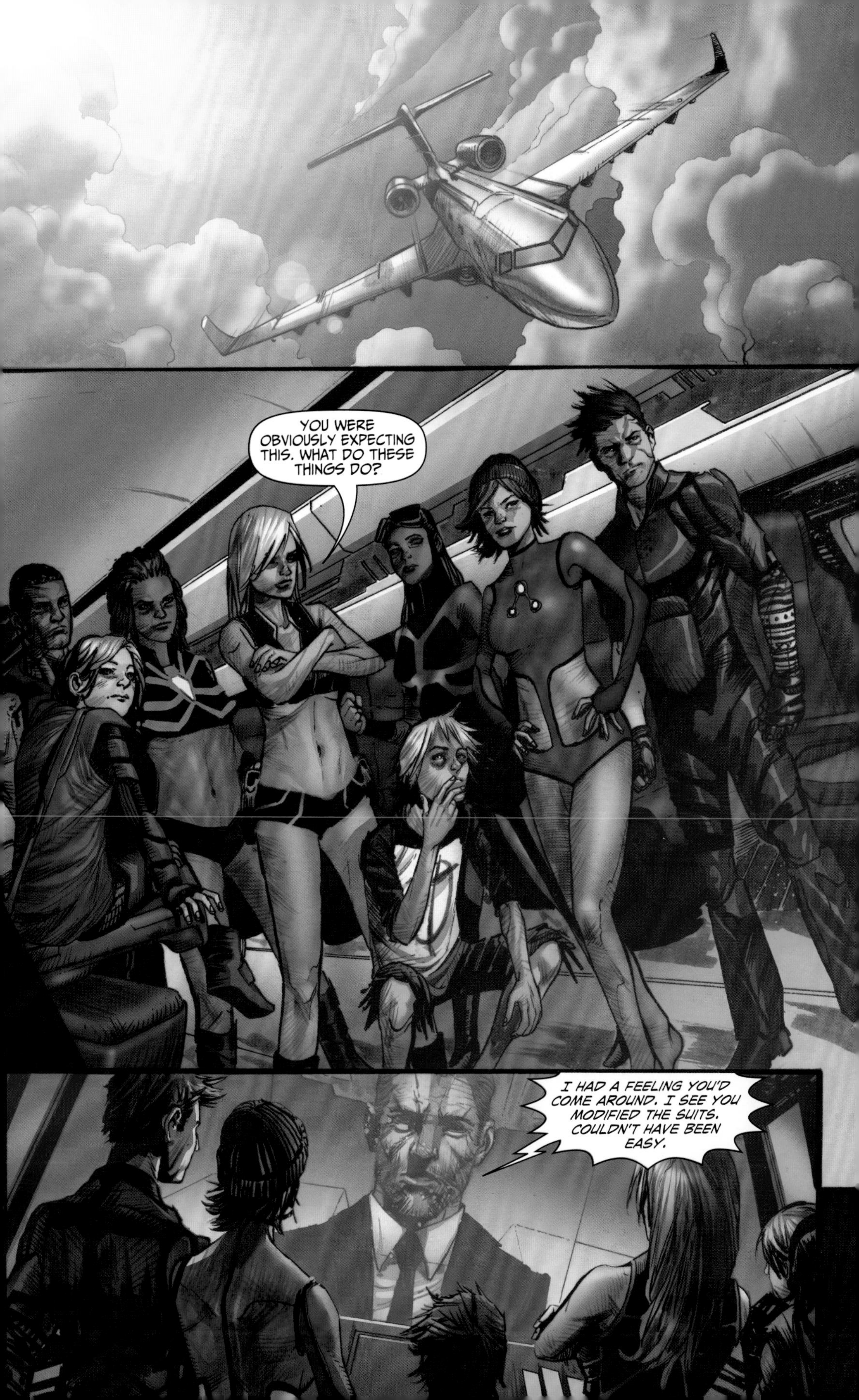
YOU WERE OBVIOUSLY EXPECTING THIS. WHAT DO THESE THINGS DO?
I HAD A FEELING YOU'D COME AROUND. I SEE YOU MODIFIED THE SUITS. COULDN'T HAVE BEEN EASY.

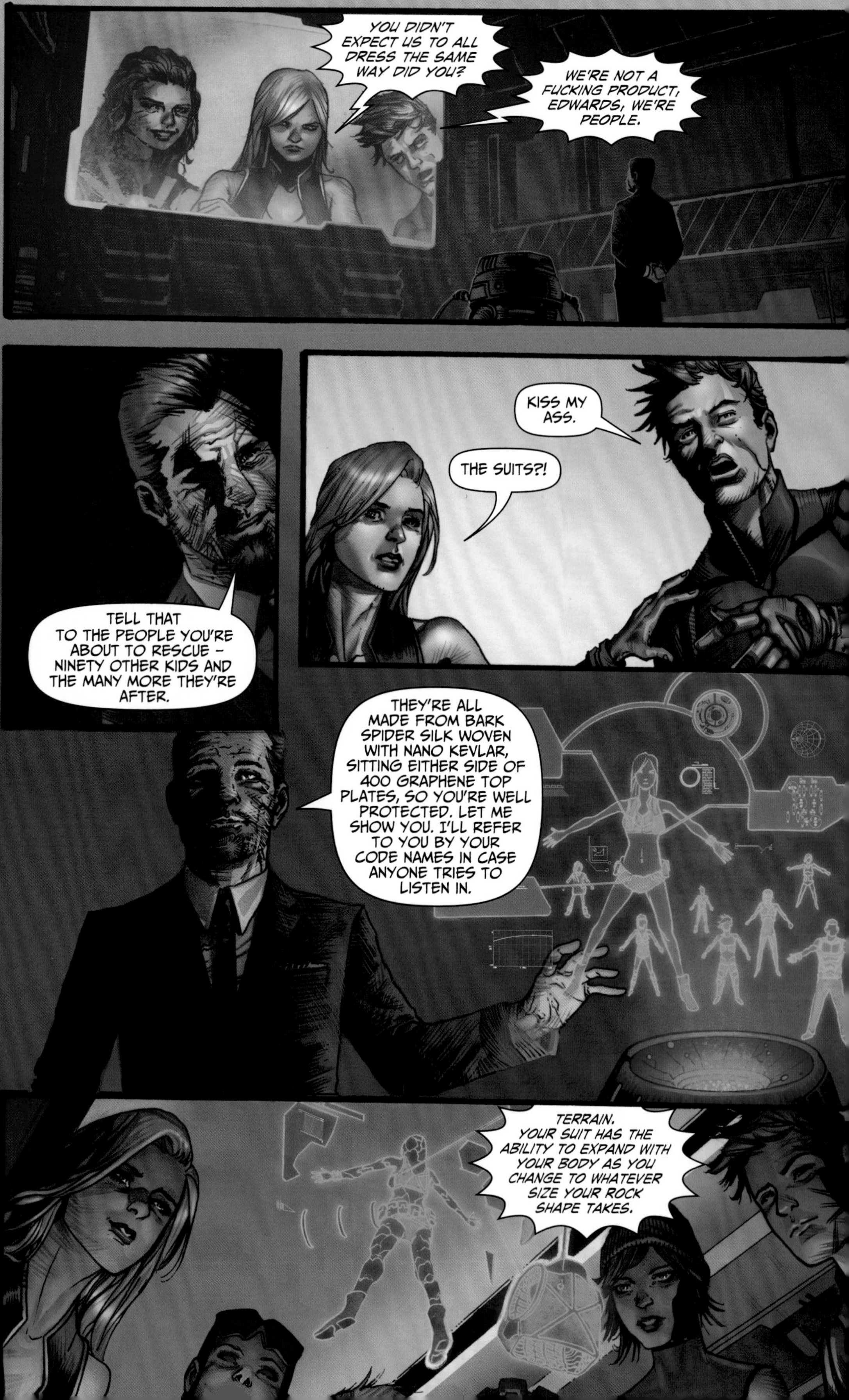
YOU DIDN'T EXPECT US TO ALL DRESS THE SAME WAY DID YOU?
WE'RE NOT A FUCKING PRODUCT, EDWARDS, WE'RE PEOPLE.
TELL THAT TO THE PEOPLE YOU'RE ABOUT TO RESCUE – NINETY OTHER KIDS AND THE MANY MORE THEY'RE AFTER.
KISS MY ASS.
THE SUITS?!
THEY'RE ALL MADE FROM BARK SPIDER SILK WOVEN WITH NANO KEVLAR, SITTING EITHER SIDE OF 400 GRAPHENE TOP PLATES, SO YOU'RE WELL PROTECTED. LET ME SHOW YOU. I'LL REFER TO YOU BY YOUR CODE NAMES IN CASE ANYONE TRIES TO LISTEN IN.
TERRAIN. YOUR SUIT HAS THE ABILITY TO EXPAND WITH YOUR BODY AS YOU CHANGE TO WHATEVER SIZE YOUR ROCK SHAPE TAKES.

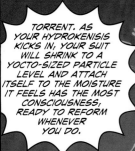

TORRENT. AS YOUR HYDROKENISIS KICKS IN, YOUR SUIT WILL SHRINK TO A YOCTO-SIZED PARTICLE LEVEL AND ATTACH ITSELF TO THE MOISTURE IT FEELS HAS THE MOST CONSCIOUSNESS, READY TO REFORM WHENEVER YOU DO.

WISH. FIGHT GLOVES ARE A NICE TOUCH. YOUR SUIT CAN DO WHAT BOTH THE GIRLS' CAN, DEPENDING ON WHETHER YOU'RE CHANGING TO SOMETHING LIKE METAL OR SOMETHING LIKE SAND.

THE TWINS. JADE, I'VE PLACED BRACKETS AND A TITANIUM-ZIRCONIUM ALLOY FRAME AROUND YOUR SUIT, BECAUSE WHATEVER TYPE OF RADIATION YOU EMIT NEEDS CONDUCTING FOR BLASTS. THE CONDUCTIVE GLOVES AND CHEST PLATE WILL HELP THAT.

TRACE. YOUR HEADPIECE AND EYE WEAR WILL ALLOW YOU FULL CONTROL OF YOUR HOST, WHILE RETAINING INSTINCTUAL CONTROL OF YOURSELF AND REMOVING HEADACHES.

HOTSHOT.

FUCK YOU, EDWARDS.

THE GAUNTLETS ON YOUR HANDS AND FEET WILL ALLOW YOU TO CONTROL WHERE FLAMES ARE DIRECTED; ENABLING YOU TO DIRECT BLASTS AND FLY.

VIRUS. YOUR SUIT PROTECTS YOUR WHOLE BODY, HAS A POUCH FOR MEDICAL ENCYCLOPEDIA-LOADED IPAD.

FINGERLESS GLOVES WILL ALLOW YOU TO INFECT WHOEVER DESERVES IT.

AND RUSH?

THE SUIT DIDN'T FIT RIGHT SO I KINDA DID MY OWN THING. INVULNERABILITY KINDA MAKES THE SUIT MOSTLY USELESS ANYWAY.

YOUR LIVES AND THE LIVES OF THE KIDS ONBOARD THAT VESSEL ARE DEPENDING ON YOU. YOU ARE THE SPECIAL ONES WHO GOT AWAY. THIS IS YOUR CHANCE TO FREE THE OTHERS.

IF IT'S SO IMPORTANT, WHY AREN'T YOU HERE?

I HAVE OTHER EQUALLY IMPORTANT MATTERS TO ATTEND TO. I'VE SENT SCHEMATICS FOR THEIR WHOLE FACILITY AND I PAID A LOT FOR THIS INFORMATION. GET IN CLEAN.

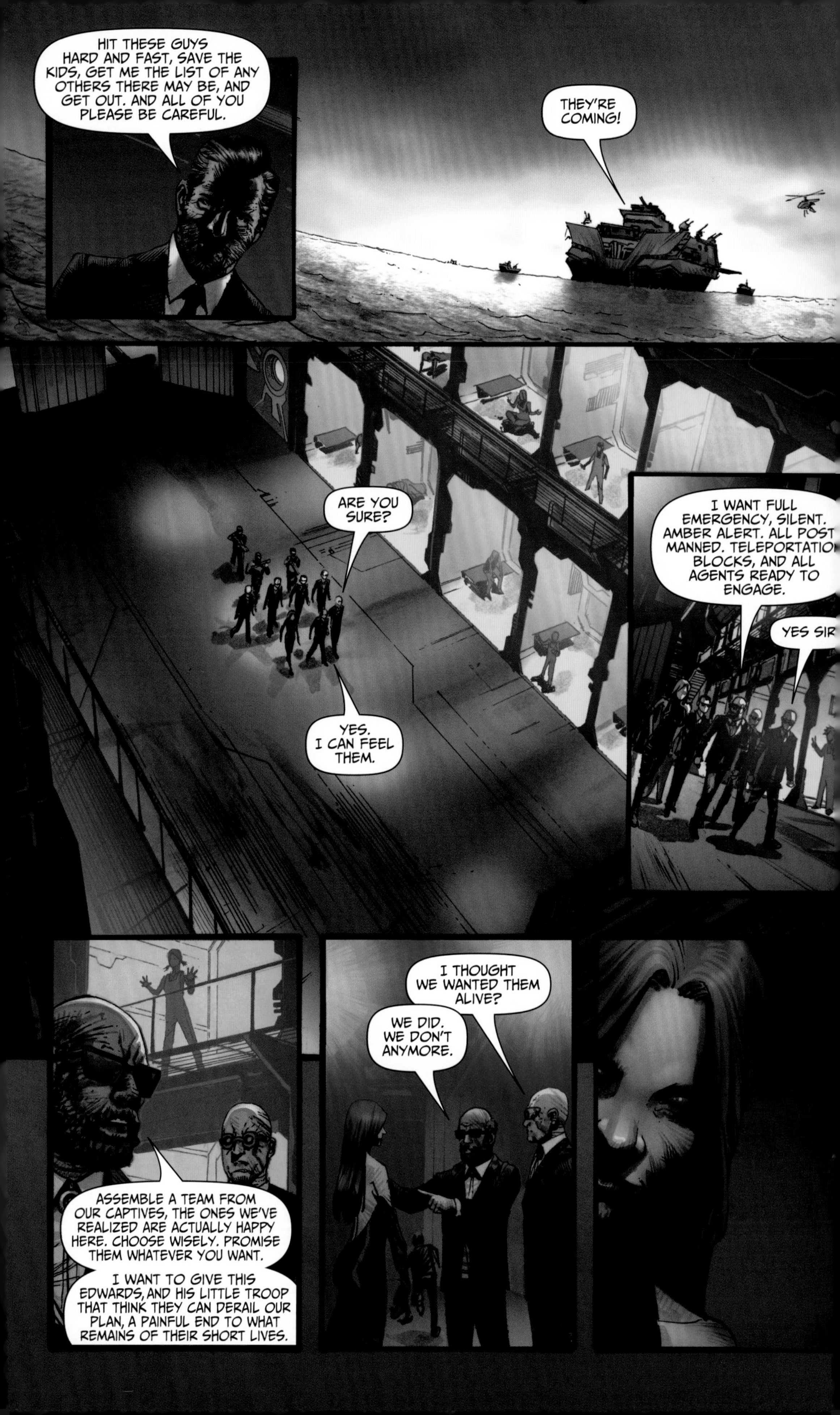
HIT THESE GUYS HARD AND FAST, SAVE THE KIDS, GET ME THE LIST OF ANY OTHERS THERE MAY BE, AND GET OUT. AND ALL OF YOU PLEASE BE CAREFUL.
THEY'RE COMING!
ARE YOU SURE?
YES. I CAN FEEL THEM.
I WANT FULL EMERGENCY, SILENT. AMBER ALERT. ALL POST MANNED. TELEPORTATIO BLOCKS, AND ALL AGENTS READY TO ENGAGE.
YES SIR
ASSEMBLE A TEAM FROM OUR CAPTIVES, THE ONES WE'VE REALIZED ARE ACTUALLY HAPPY HERE. CHOOSE WISELY. PROMISE THEM WHATEVER YOU WANT.
I WANT TO GIVE THIS EDWARDS, AND HIS LITTLE TROOP THAT THINK THEY CAN DERAIL OUR PLAN, A PAINFUL END TO WHAT REMAINS OF THEIR SHORT LIVES.
I THOUGHT WE WANTED THEM ALIVE?
WE DID. WE DON'T ANYMORE.

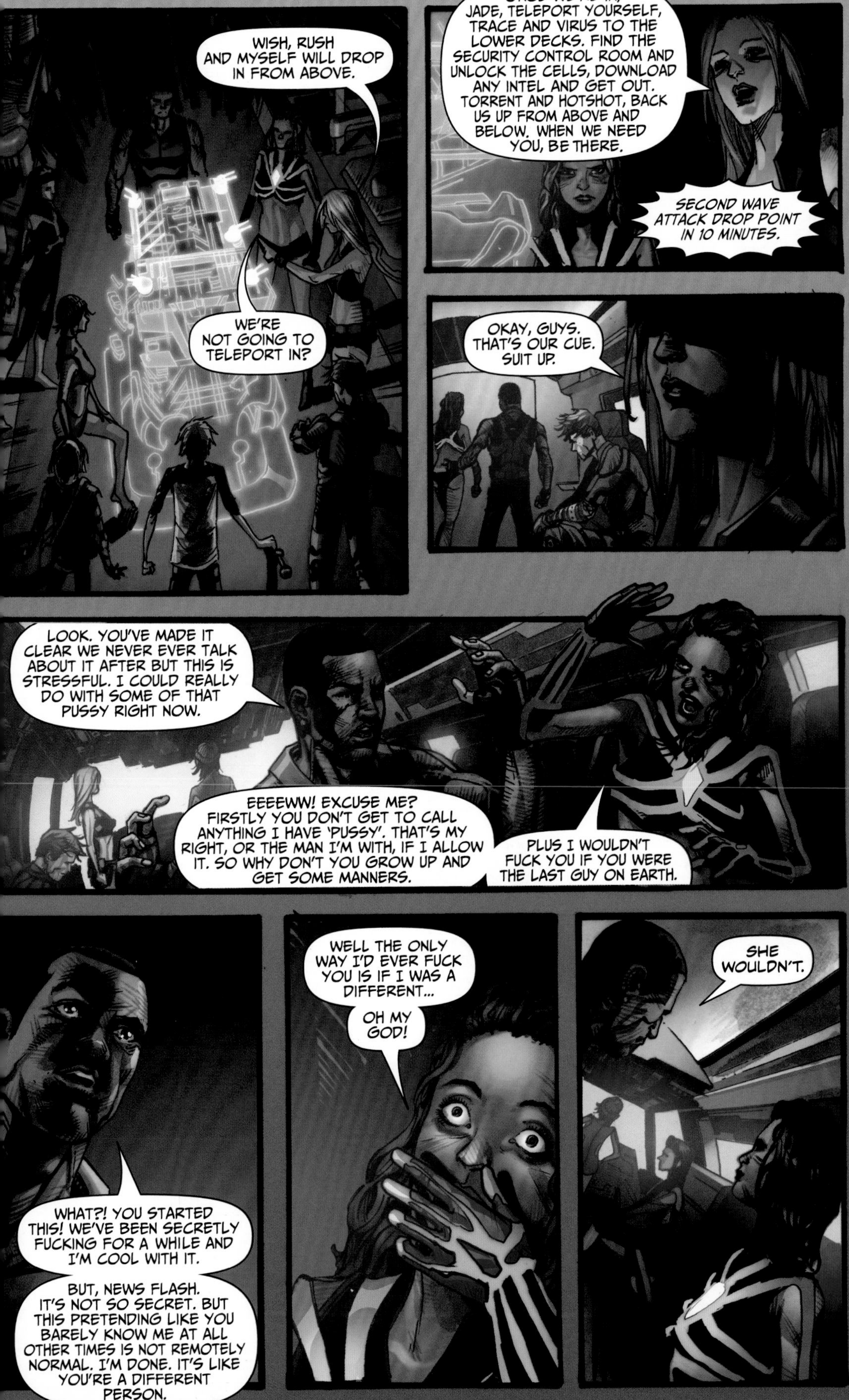
WISH, RUSH AND MYSELF WILL DROP IN FROM ABOVE.
WE'RE NOT GOING TO TELEPORT IN?
ONCE WE'RE IN, JADE, TELEPORT YOURSELF, TRACE AND VIRUS TO THE LOWER DECKS. FIND THE SECURITY CONTROL ROOM AND UNLOCK THE CELLS, DOWNLOAD ANY INTEL AND GET OUT. TORRENT AND HOTSHOT, BACK US UP FROM ABOVE AND BELOW. WHEN WE NEED YOU, BE THERE.
SECOND WAVE ATTACK DROP POINT IN 10 MINUTES.
OKAY, GUYS. THAT'S OUR CUE. SUIT UP.
LOOK. YOU'VE MADE IT CLEAR WE NEVER EVER TALK ABOUT IT AFTER BUT THIS IS STRESSFUL. I COULD REALLY DO WITH SOME OF THAT PUSSY RIGHT NOW.
EEEEWW! EXCUSE ME? FIRSTLY YOU DON'T GET TO CALL ANYTHING I HAVE 'PUSSY'. THAT'S MY RIGHT, OR THE MAN I'M WITH, IF I ALLOW IT. SO WHY DON'T YOU GROW UP AND GET SOME MANNERS.
PLUS I WOULDN'T FUCK YOU IF YOU WERE THE LAST GUY ON EARTH.
WHAT?! YOU STARTED THIS! WE'VE BEEN SECRETLY FUCKING FOR A WHILE AND I'M COOL WITH IT.
BUT, NEWS FLASH. IT'S NOT SO SECRET. BUT THIS PRETENDING LIKE YOU BARELY KNOW ME AT ALL OTHER TIMES IS NOT REMOTELY NORMAL. I'M DONE. IT'S LIKE YOU'RE A DIFFERENT PERSON.
WELL THE ONLY WAY I'D EVER FUCK YOU IS IF I WAS A DIFFERENT...
OH MY GOD!
SHE WOULDN'T.

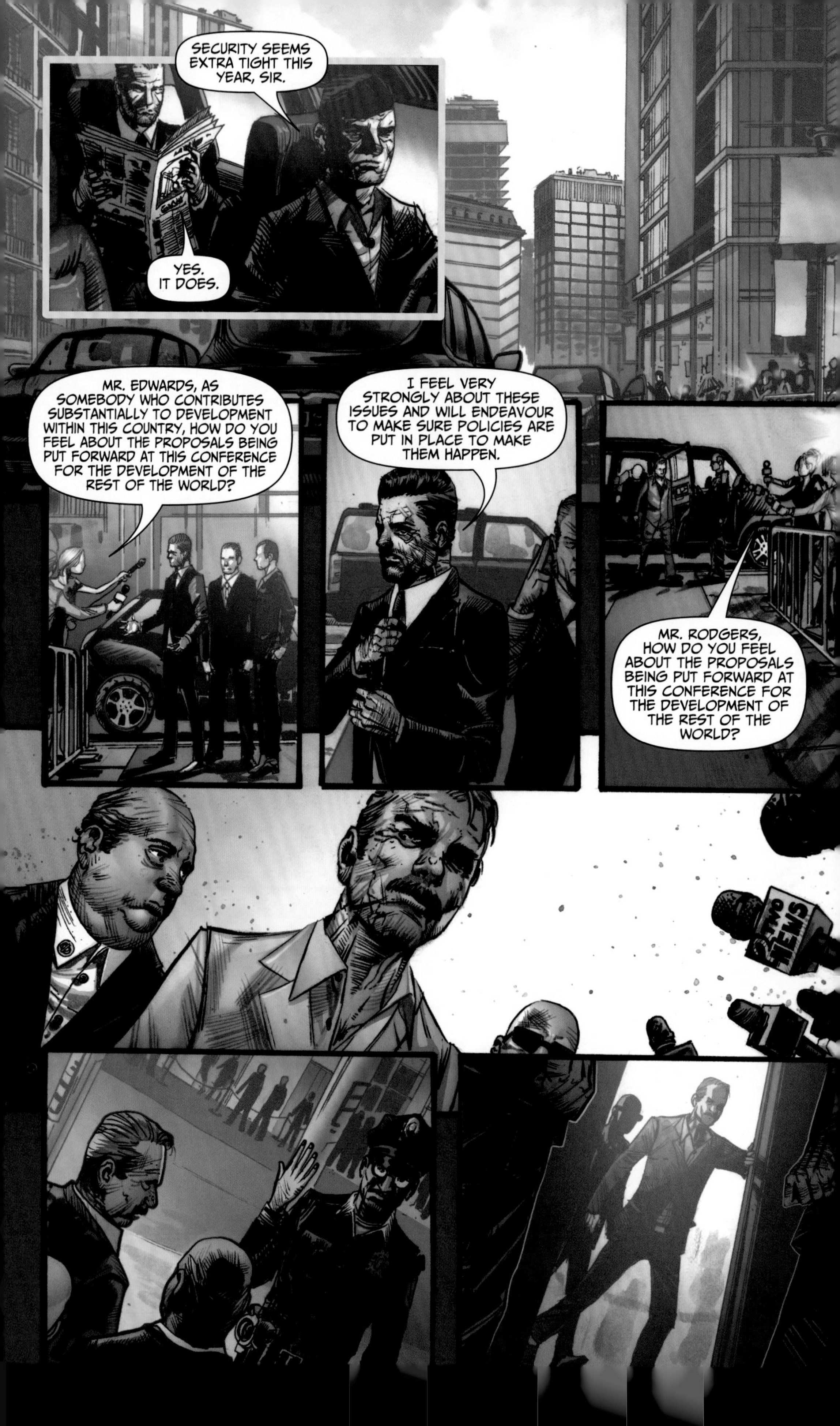
SECURITY SEEMS EXTRA TIGHT THIS YEAR, SIR.
YES. IT DOES.
MR. EDWARDS, AS SOMEBODY WHO CONTRIBUTES SUBSTANTIALLY TO DEVELOPMENT WITHIN THIS COUNTRY, HOW DO YOU FEEL ABOUT THE PROPOSALS BEING PUT FORWARD AT THIS CONFERENCE FOR THE DEVELOPMENT OF THE REST OF THE WORLD?
I FEEL VERY STRONGLY ABOUT THESE ISSUES AND WILL ENDEAVOUR TO MAKE SURE POLICIES ARE PUT IN PLACE TO MAKE THEM HAPPEN.
MR. RODGERS, HOW DO YOU FEEL ABOUT THE PROPOSALS BEING PUT FORWARD AT THIS CONFERENCE FOR THE DEVELOPMENT OF THE REST OF THE WORLD?
NEWS

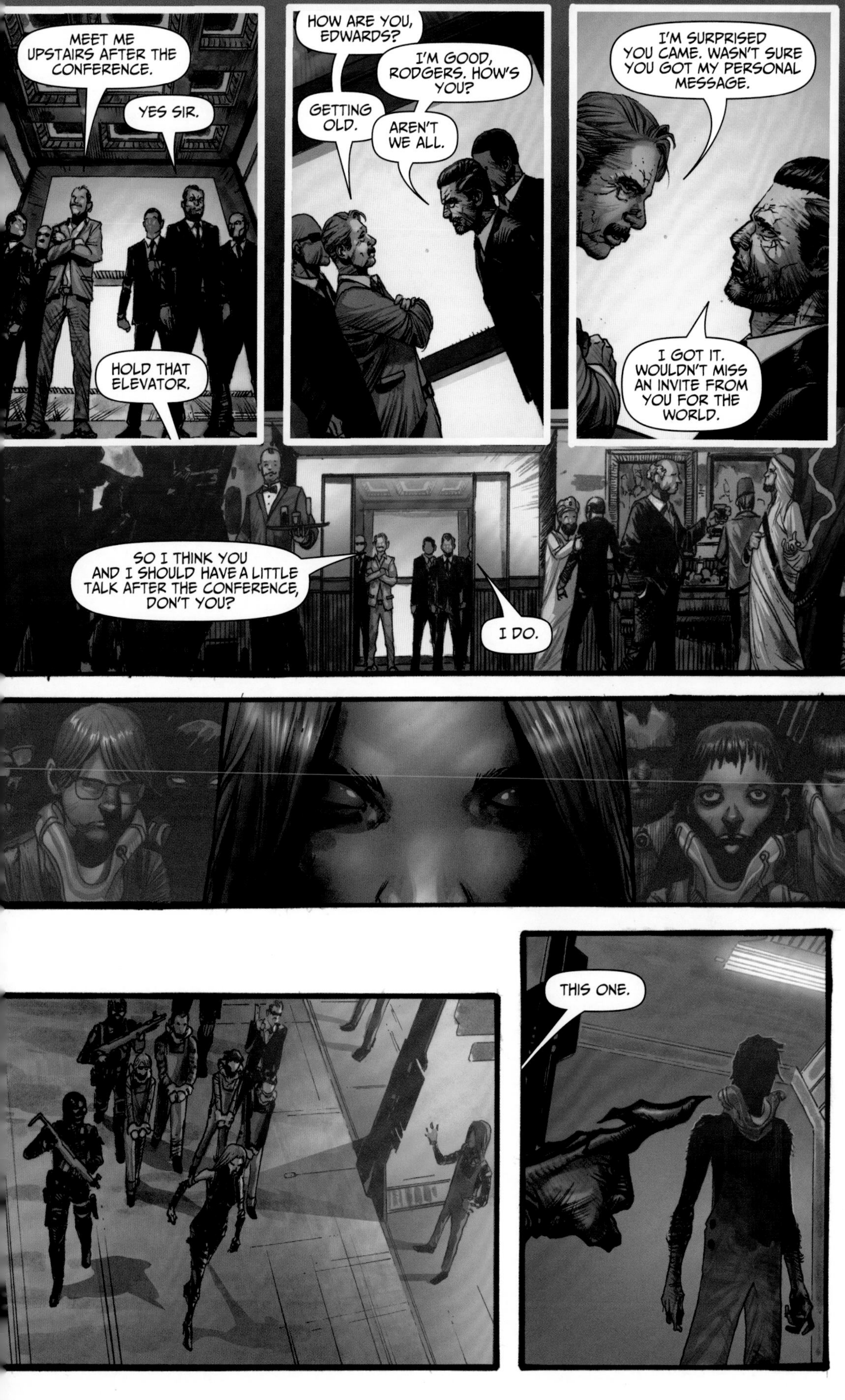
MEET ME UPSTAIRS AFTER THE CONFERENCE.
YES SIR.
HOLD THAT ELEVATOR.
HOW ARE YOU, EDWARDS?
I'M GOOD, RODGERS. HOW'S YOU?
GETTING OLD.
AREN'T WE ALL.
I'M SURPRISED YOU CAME. WASN'T SURE YOU GOT MY PERSONAL MESSAGE.
I GOT IT. WOULDN'T MISS AN INVITE FROM YOU FOR THE WORLD.
SO I THINK YOU AND I SHOULD HAVE A LITTLE TALK AFTER THE CONFERENCE, DON'T YOU?
I DO.
THIS ONE.

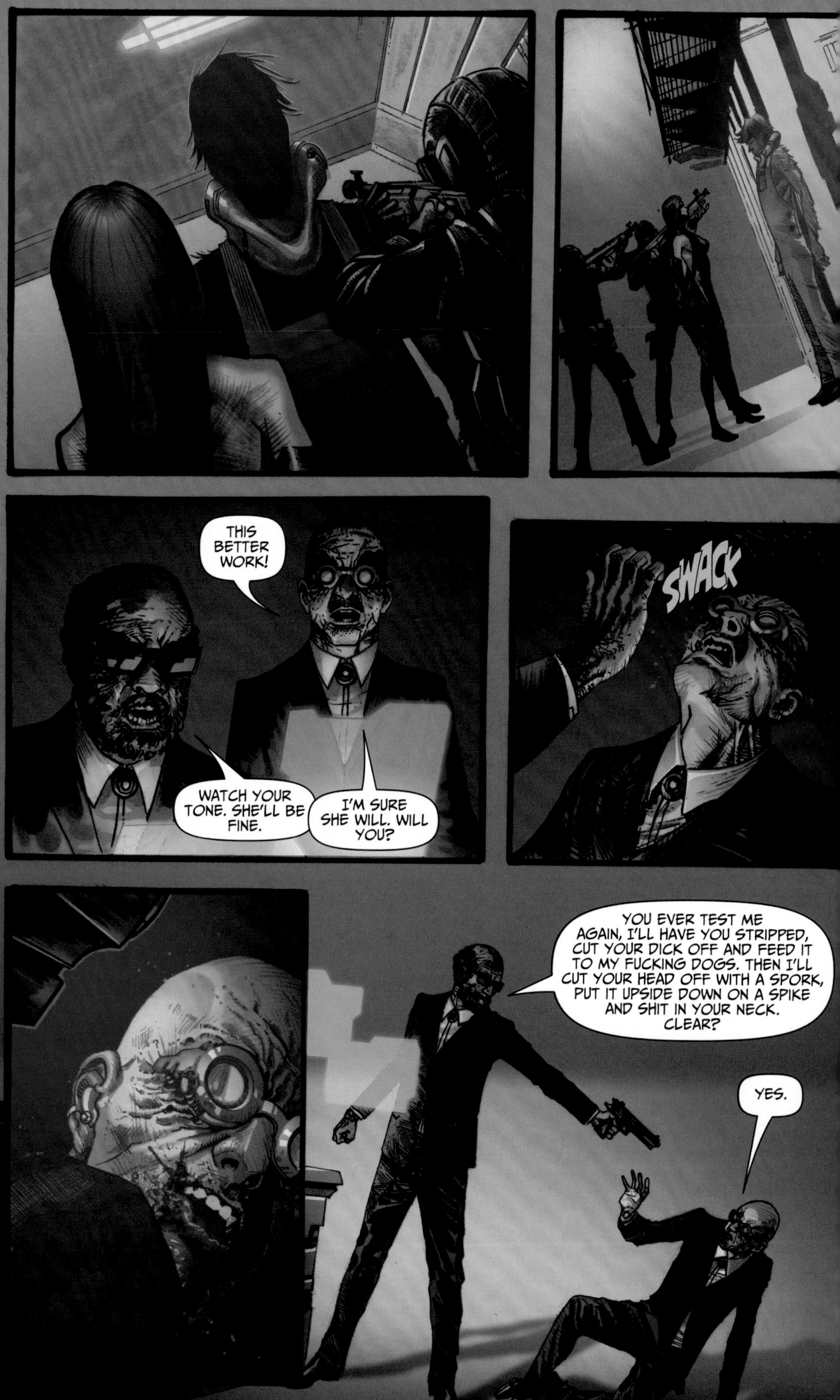
THIS BETTER WORK!
WATCH YOUR TONE. SHE'LL BE FINE.
I'M SURE SHE WILL. WILL YOU?
SWACK
YOU EVER TEST ME AGAIN, I'LL HAVE YOU STRIPPED, CUT YOUR DICK OFF AND FEED IT TO MY FUCKING DOGS. THEN I'LL CUT YOUR HEAD OFF WITH A SPORK, PUT IT UPSIDE DOWN ON A SPIKE AND SHIT IN YOUR NECK. CLEAR?
YES.

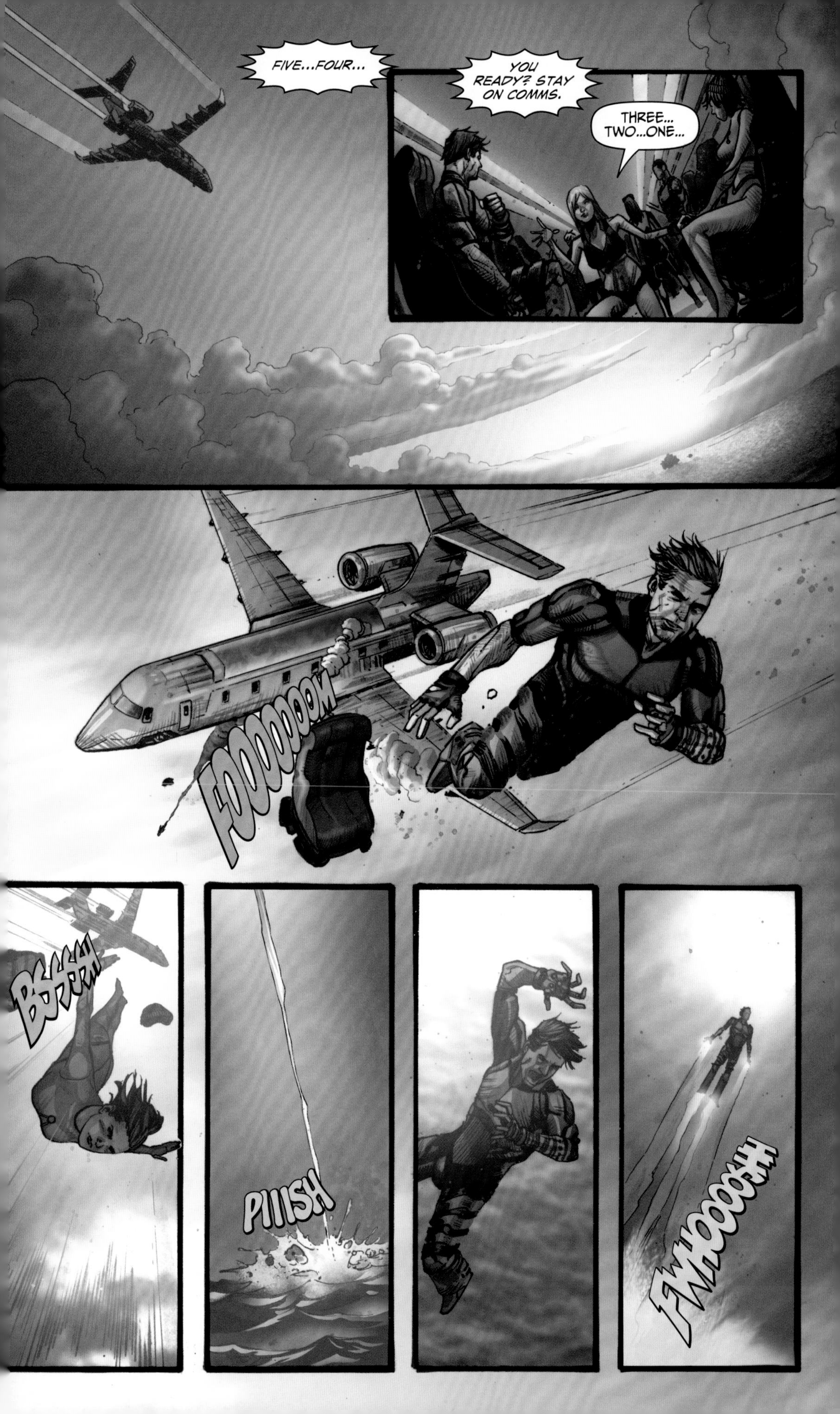
FIVE...FOUR...
YOU READY? STAY ON COMMS.
THREE... TWO...ONE...
FOOOOOOM
BSSSHH
PIIISH
FWHOOOOSHH

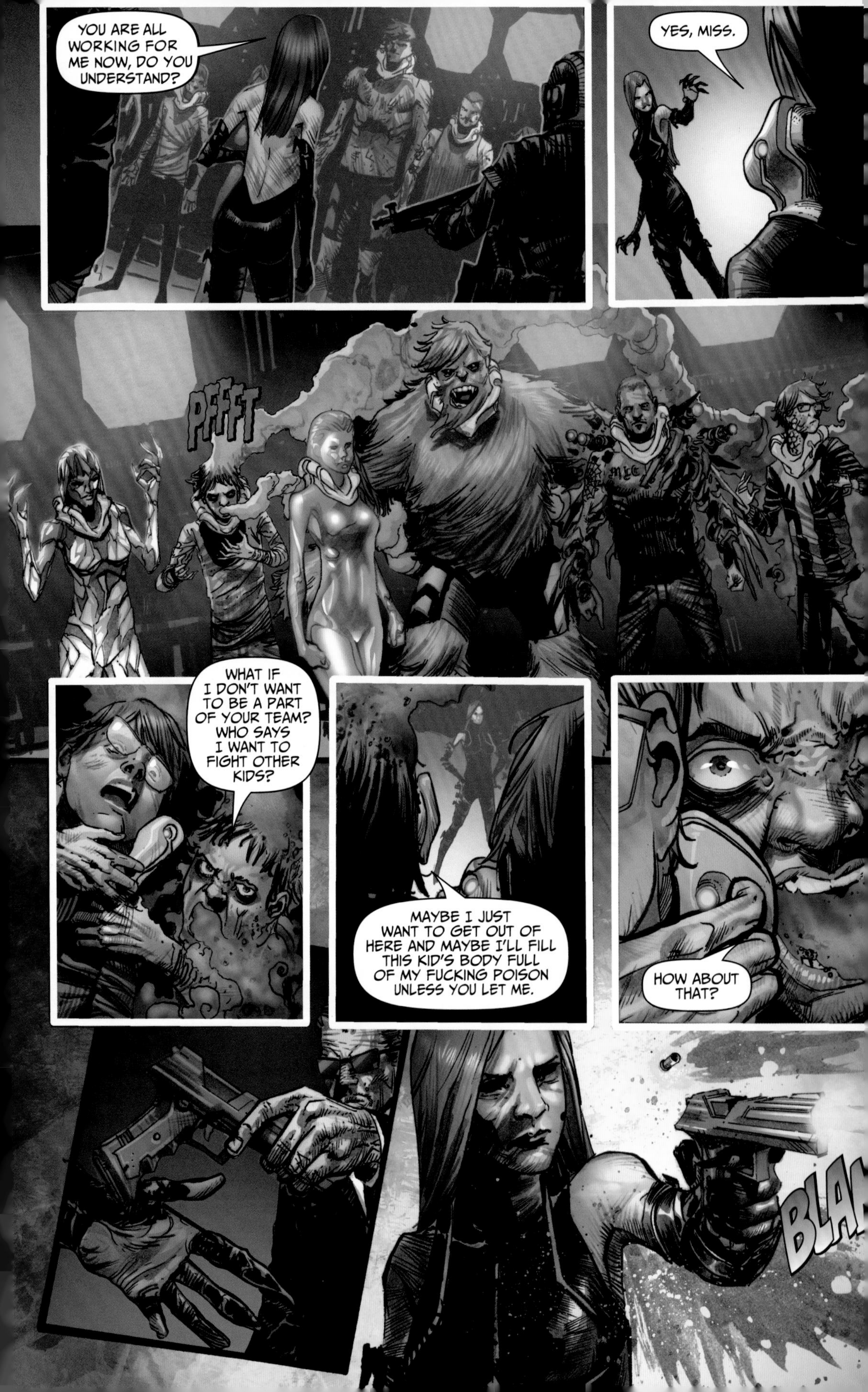

YOU ARE ALL WORKING FOR ME NOW, DO YOU UNDERSTAND?
YES, MISS.
PFFFT
WHAT IF I DON'T WANT TO BE A PART OF YOUR TEAM? WHO SAYS I WANT TO FIGHT OTHER KIDS?
MAYBE I JUST WANT TO GET OUT OF HERE AND MAYBE I'LL FILL THIS KID'S BODY FULL OF MY FUCKING POISON UNLESS YOU LET ME.
HOW ABOUT THAT?

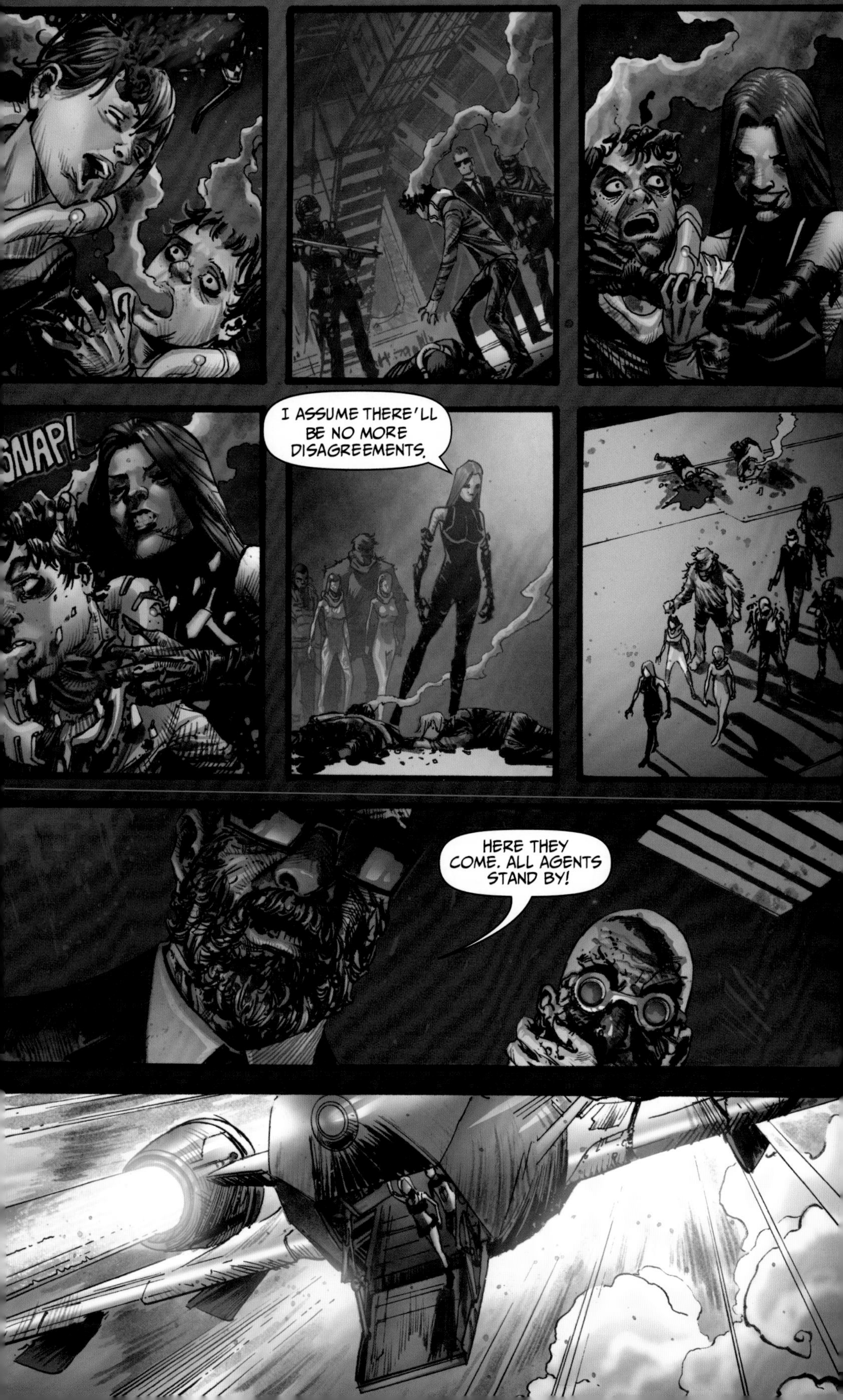
SNAP!
I ASSUME THERE'LL BE NO MORE DISAGREEMENTS.
HERE THEY COME. ALL AGENTS STAND BY!

THE OTHERS ARE READY TO GO.

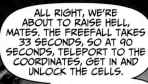

ALL RIGHT, WE'RE ABOUT TO RAISE HELL, MATES. THE FREEFALL TAKES 33 SECONDS, SO AT 90 SECONDS, TELEPORT TO THE COORDINATES, GET IN AND UNLOCK THE CELLS.

STAY ON COMMS. WE'LL MEET BACK ON THE JET.

DO YOU GUYS NEED PODS?

NO.

TITANIUM.

DO YOU EVEN NEED THAT?

NAH, IT'S JUST HABIT. THIS IS GONNA BE A RUSH.

IF WE LIVE, NO DRUGS!

IIIIIIIF WEEEEE LIIIIIIVVEEE, NOOOOO CUUUTTIIIINGG!!!

WOOOOOOOOOOOOO HOOOOOO!

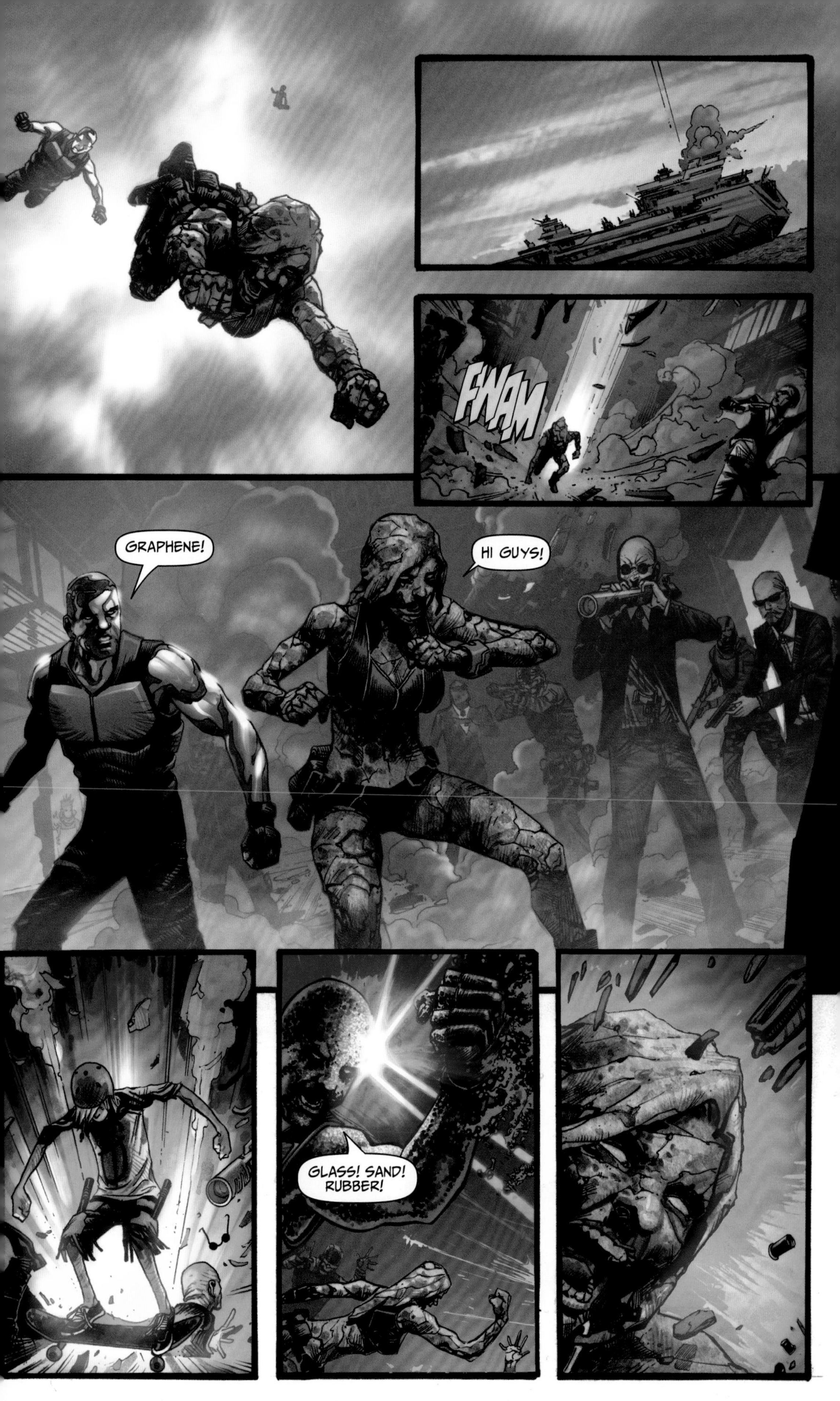
FWAM
GRAPHENE!
HI GUYS!
GLASS! SAND! RUBBER!

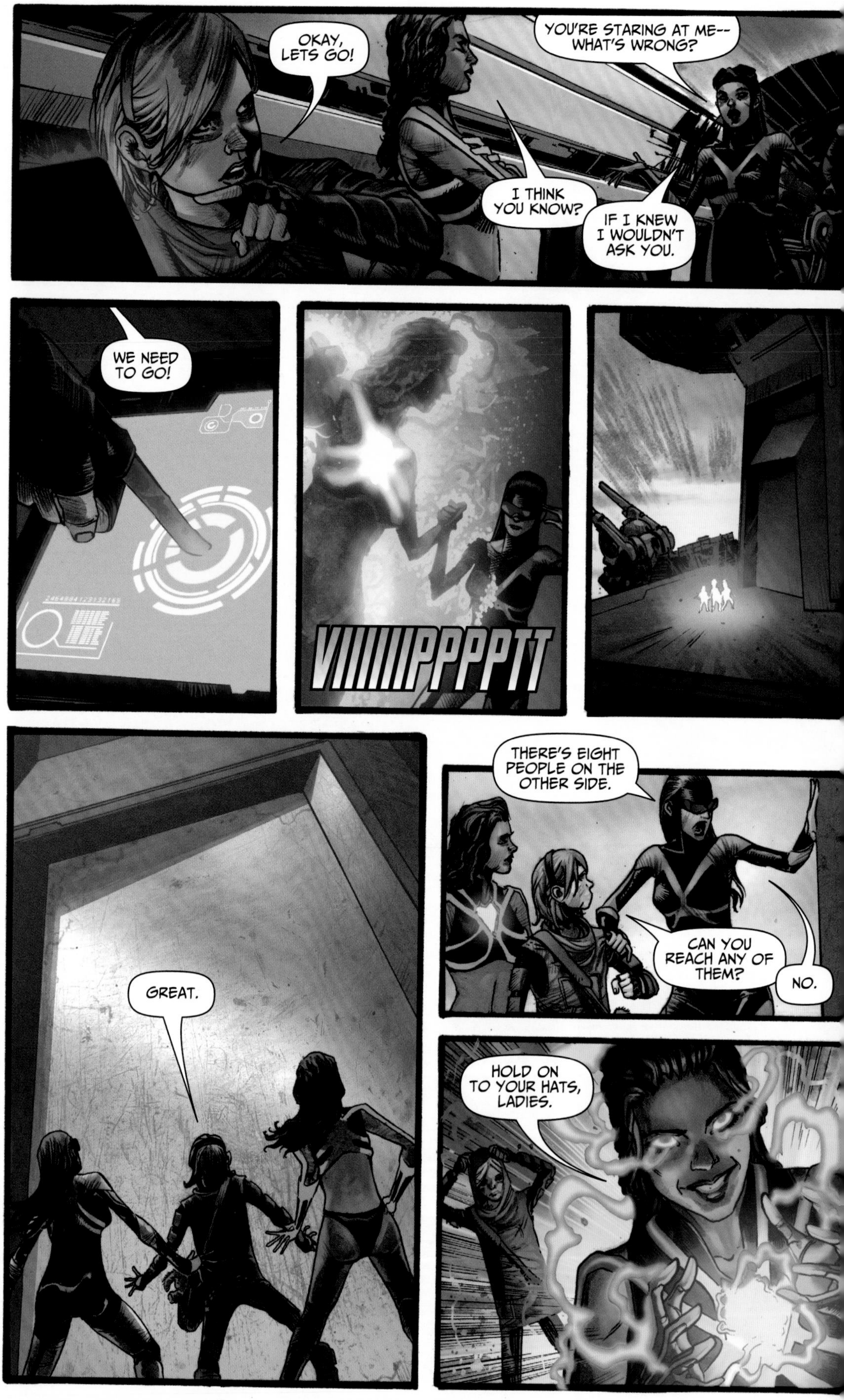

OKAY, LETS GO!
YOU'RE STARING AT ME-- WHAT'S WRONG?
I THINK YOU KNOW?
IF I KNEW I WOULDN'T ASK YOU.
WE NEED TO GO!
VIIIIIIPPPPTT
THERE'S EIGHT PEOPLE ON THE OTHER SIDE.
GREAT.
CAN YOU REACH ANY OF THEM?
NO.
HOLD ON TO YOUR HATS, LADIES.

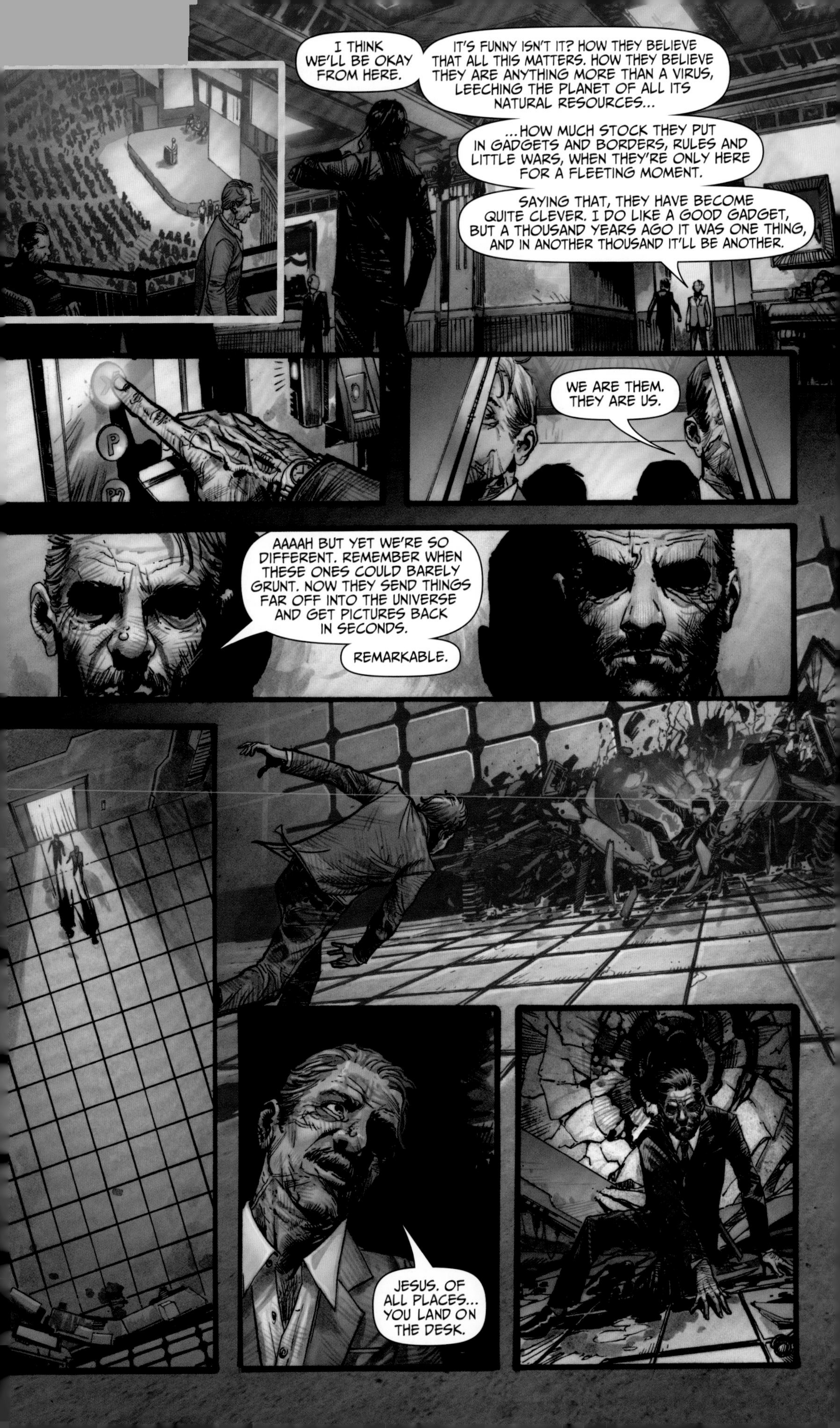
I THINK WE'LL BE OKAY FROM HERE.
IT'S FUNNY ISN'T IT? HOW THEY BELIEVE THAT ALL THIS MATTERS. HOW THEY BELIEVE THEY ARE ANYTHING MORE THAN A VIRUS, LEECHING THE PLANET OF ALL ITS NATURAL RESOURCES...
...HOW MUCH STOCK THEY PUT IN GADGETS AND BORDERS, RULES AND LITTLE WARS, WHEN THEY'RE ONLY HERE FOR A FLEETING MOMENT.
SAYING THAT, THEY HAVE BECOME QUITE CLEVER. I DO LIKE A GOOD GADGET, BUT A THOUSAND YEARS AGO IT WAS ONE THING, AND IN ANOTHER THOUSAND IT'LL BE ANOTHER.
WE ARE THEM. THEY ARE US.
AAAAH BUT YET WE'RE SO DIFFERENT. REMEMBER WHEN THESE ONES COULD BARELY GRUNT. NOW THEY SEND THINGS FAR OFF INTO THE UNIVERSE AND GET PICTURES BACK IN SECONDS.
REMARKABLE.
JESUS. OF ALL PLACES... YOU LAND ON THE DESK.

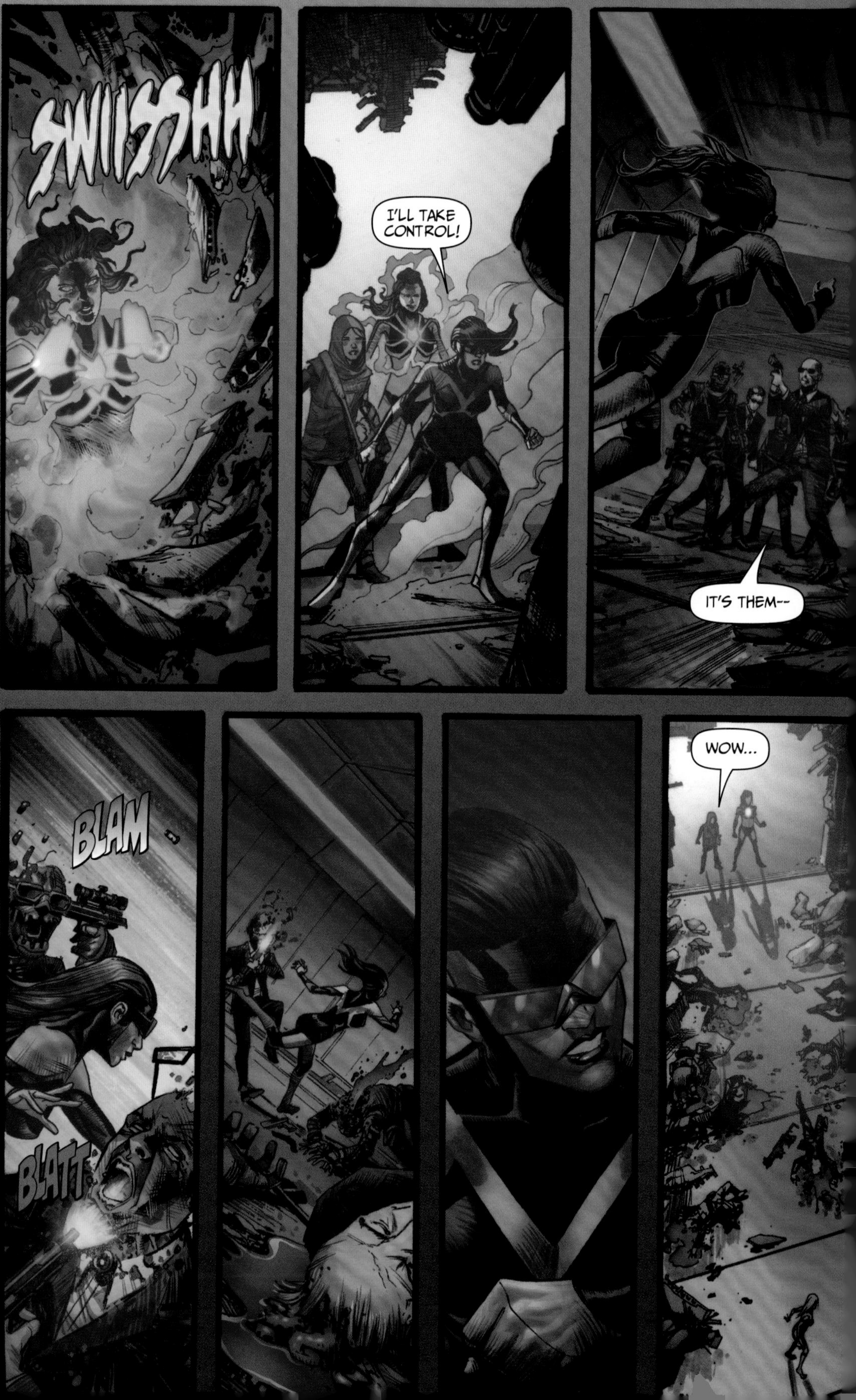
SWIISSHH
I'LL TAKE CONTROL!
IT'S THEM--
BLAM
BLATT
WOW...

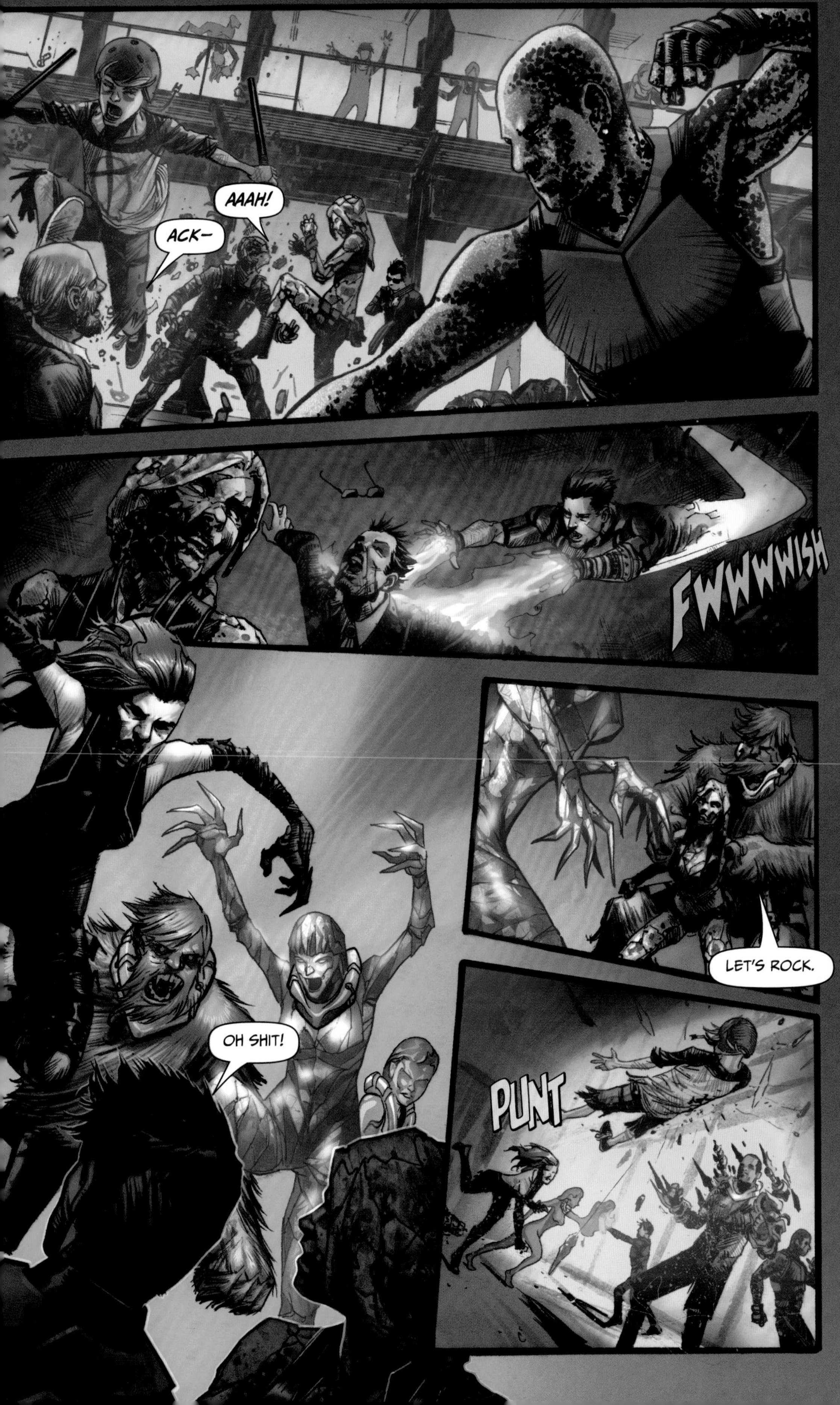
AAAH!
ACK–
FWWWWISH
LET'S ROCK.
OH SHIT!
PUNT

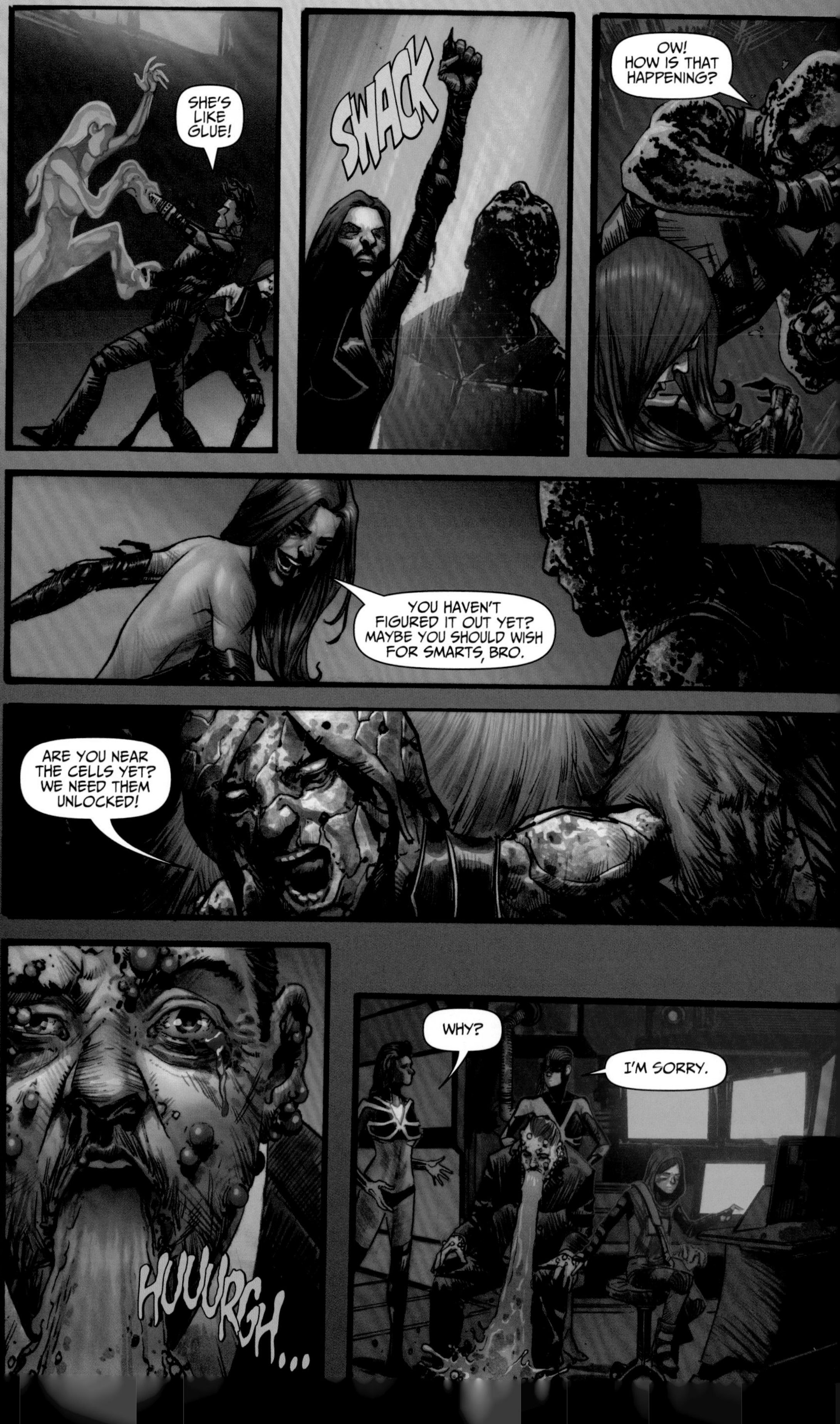
SHE'S LIKE GLUE!
SWACK
OW! HOW IS THAT HAPPENING?
YOU HAVEN'T FIGURED IT OUT YET? MAYBE YOU SHOULD WISH FOR SMARTS, BRO.
ARE YOU NEAR THE CELLS YET? WE NEED THEM UNLOCKED!
HUUURGH...
WHY?
I'M SORRY.

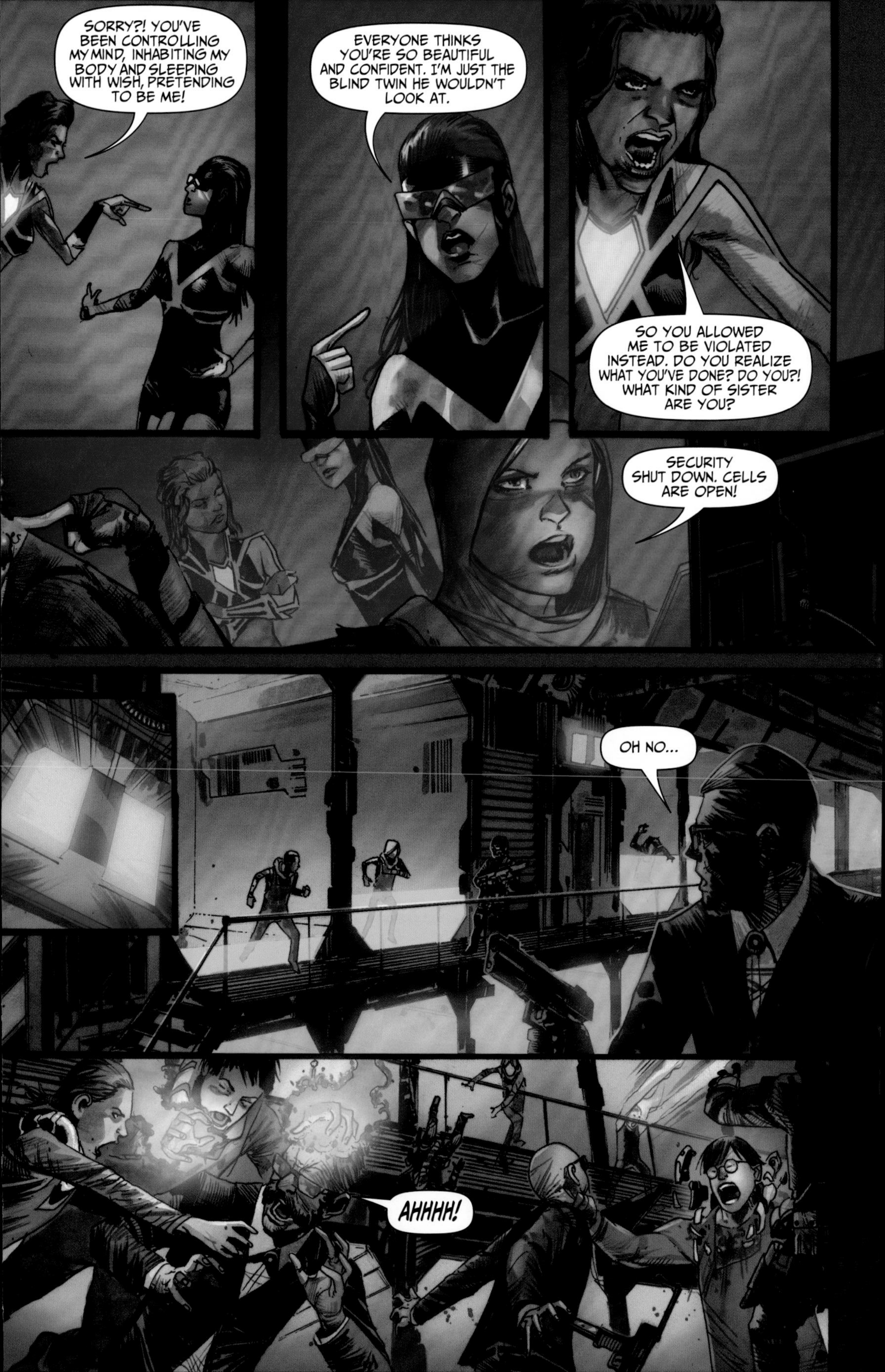
SORRY?! YOU'VE BEEN CONTROLLING MY MIND, INHABITING MY BODY AND SLEEPING WITH WISH, PRETENDING TO BE ME!
EVERYONE THINKS YOU'RE SO BEAUTIFUL AND CONFIDENT. I'M JUST THE BLIND TWIN HE WOULDN'T LOOK AT.
SO YOU ALLOWED ME TO BE VIOLATED INSTEAD. DO YOU REALIZE WHAT YOU'VE DONE? DO YOU?! WHAT KIND OF SISTER ARE YOU?
SECURITY SHUT DOWN. CELLS ARE OPEN!
OH NO...
AHHHH!

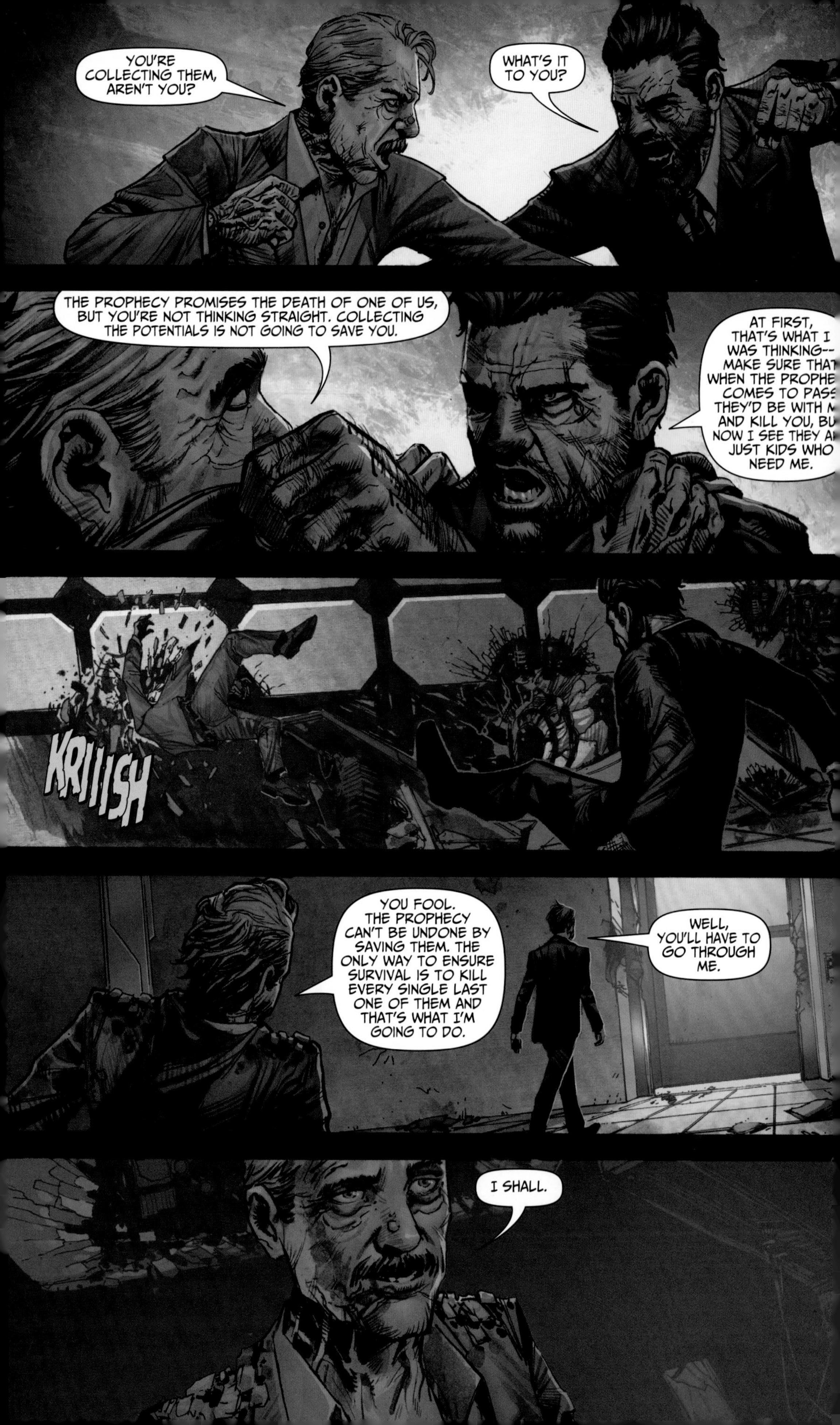

YOU'RE COLLECTING THEM, AREN'T YOU?
WHAT'S IT TO YOU?
THE PROPHECY PROMISES THE DEATH OF ONE OF US, BUT YOU'RE NOT THINKING STRAIGHT. COLLECTING THE POTENTIALS IS NOT GOING TO SAVE YOU.
AT FIRST, THAT'S WHAT I WAS THINKING-- MAKE SURE THAT WHEN THE PROPHE COMES TO PASS THEY'D BE WITH AND KILL YOU, BU NOW I SEE THEY A JUST KIDS WHO NEED ME.
KRIIISH
YOU FOOL. THE PROPHECY CAN'T BE UNDONE BY SAVING THEM. THE ONLY WAY TO ENSURE SURVIVAL IS TO KILL EVERY SINGLE LAST ONE OF THEM AND THAT'S WHAT I'M GOING TO DO.
WELL, YOU'LL HAVE TO GO THROUGH ME.
I SHALL.

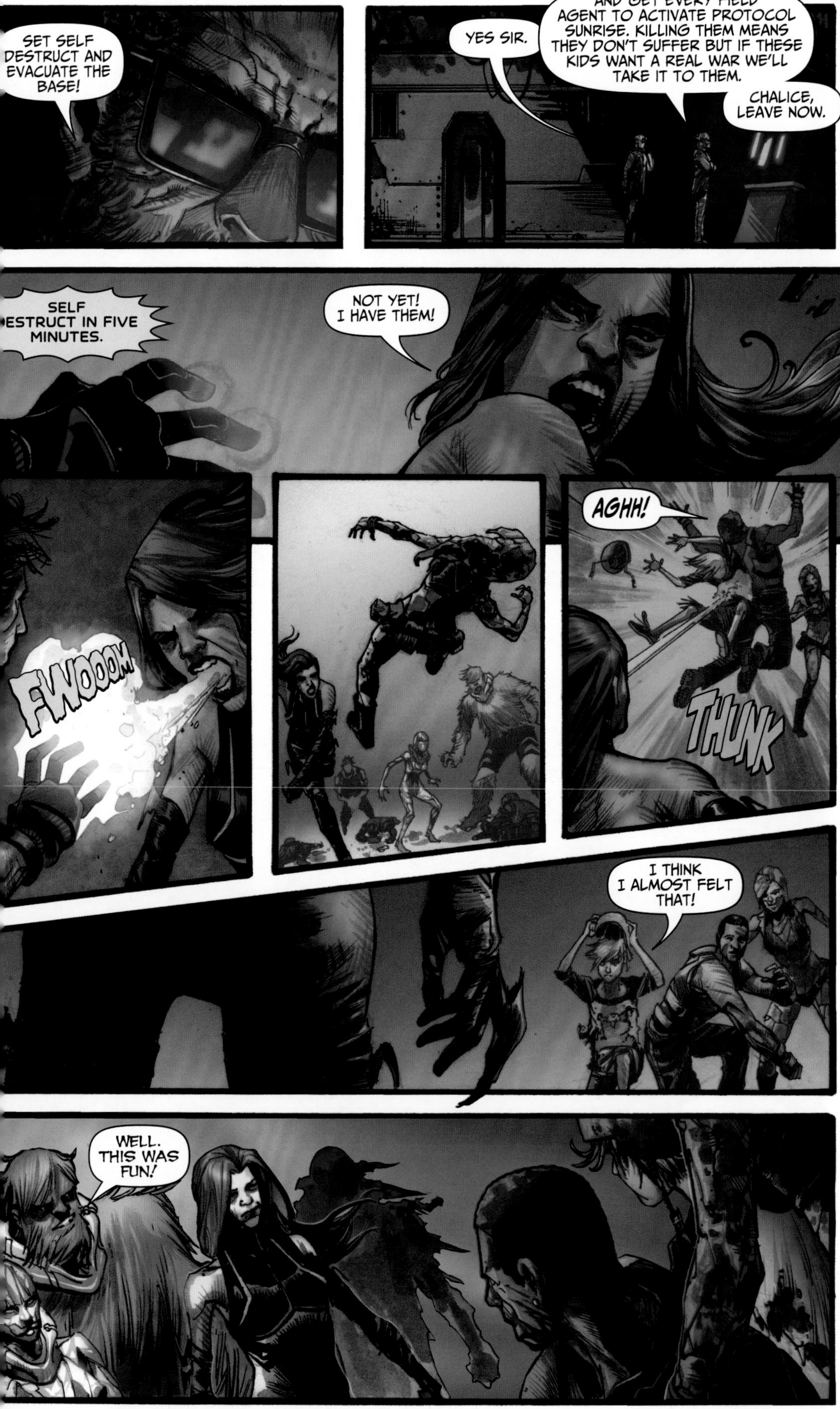
SET SELF DESTRUCT AND EVACUATE THE BASE!
YES SIR.
AND GET EVERY FIELD AGENT TO ACTIVATE PROTOCOL SUNRISE. KILLING THEM MEANS THEY DON'T SUFFER BUT IF THESE KIDS WANT A REAL WAR WE'LL TAKE IT TO THEM.
CHALICE, LEAVE NOW.
SELF ESTRUCT IN FIVE MINUTES.
NOT YET! I HAVE THEM!
FWOOOM
AGHH!
THUNK
I THINK I ALMOST FELT THAT!
WELL. THIS WAS FUN!

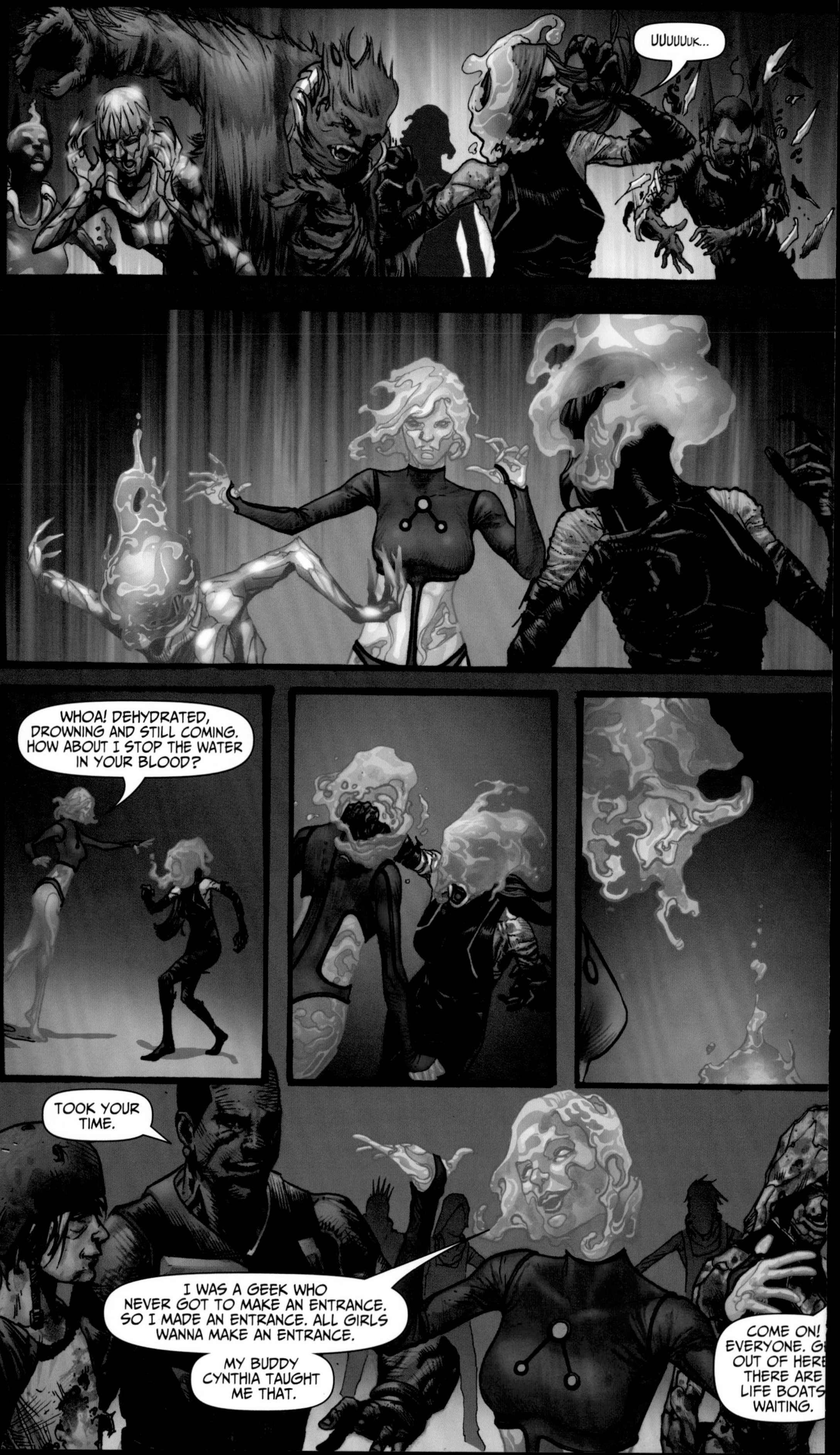
UUUUUUK...
WHOA! DEHYDRATED, DROWNING AND STILL COMING. HOW ABOUT I STOP THE WATER IN YOUR BLOOD?
TOOK YOUR TIME.
I WAS A GEEK WHO NEVER GOT TO MAKE AN ENTRANCE. SO I MADE AN ENTRANCE. ALL GIRLS WANNA MAKE AN ENTRANCE.
MY BUDDY CYNTHIA TAUGHT ME THAT.
COME ON! EVERYONE. G OUT OF HERE THERE ARE LIFE BOATS WAITING.

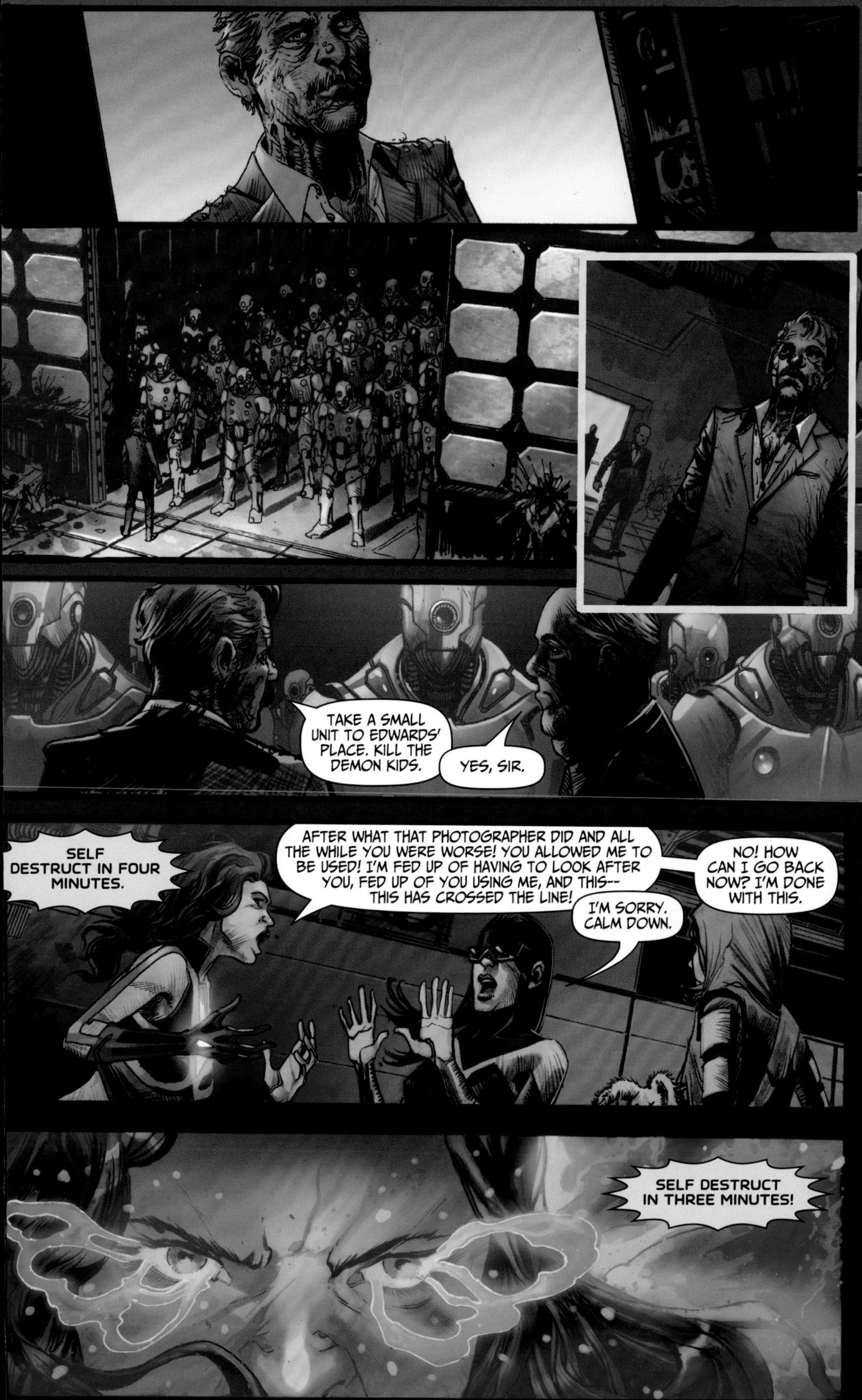
TAKE A SMALL UNIT TO EDWARDS' PLACE. KILL THE DEMON KIDS.
YES, SIR.
SELF DESTRUCT IN FOUR MINUTES.
AFTER WHAT THAT PHOTOGRAPHER DID AND ALL THE WHILE YOU WERE WORSE! YOU ALLOWED ME TO BE USED! I'M FED UP OF HAVING TO LOOK AFTER YOU, FED UP OF YOU USING ME, AND THIS-- THIS HAS CROSSED THE LINE!
I'M SORRY. CALM DOWN.
NO! HOW CAN I GO BACK NOW? I'M DONE WITH THIS.
SELF DESTRUCT IN THREE MINUTES!

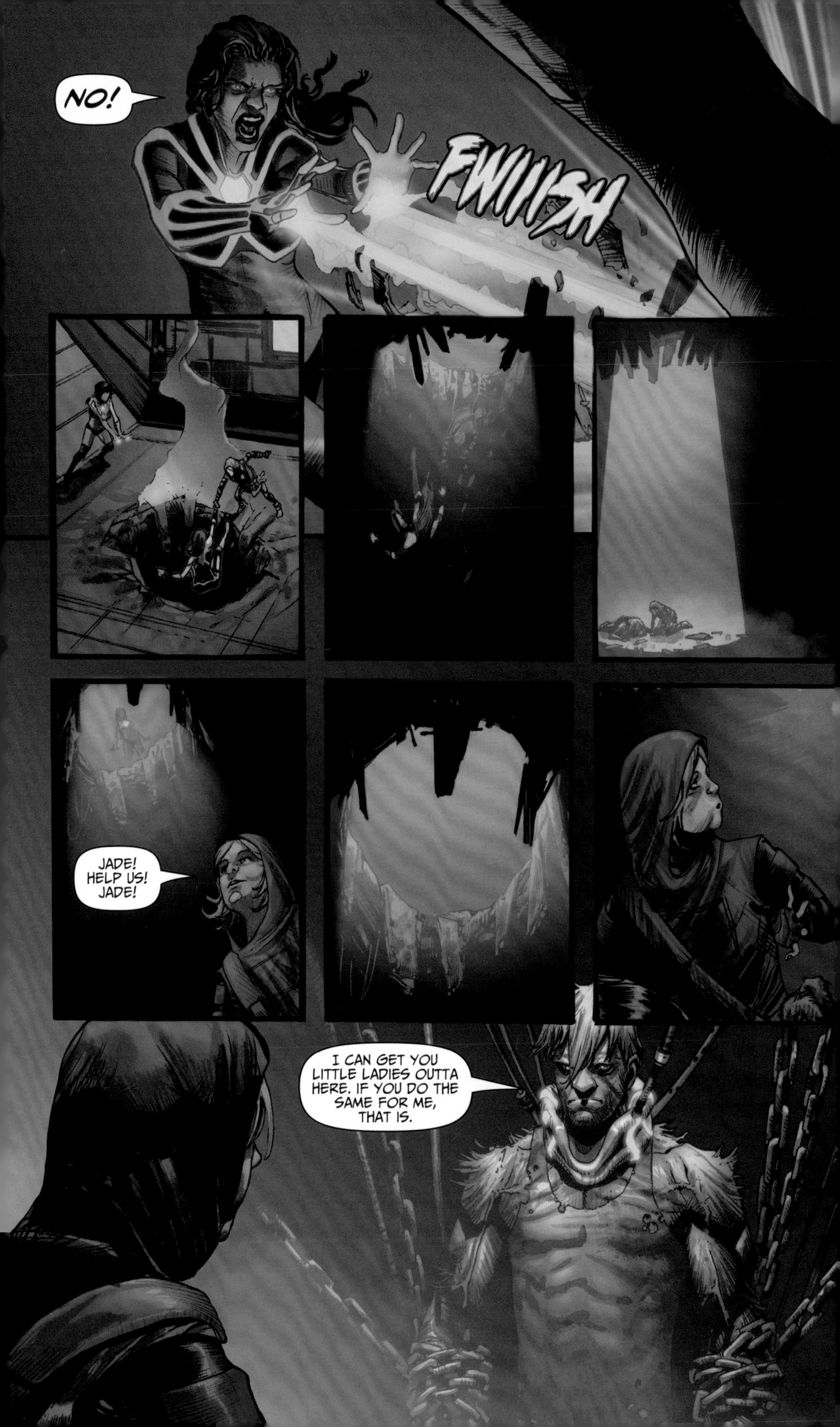
NO!
FWIIISH
JADE! HELP US! JADE!
I CAN GET YOU LITTLE LADIES OUTTA HERE. IF YOU DO THE SAME FOR ME, THAT IS.

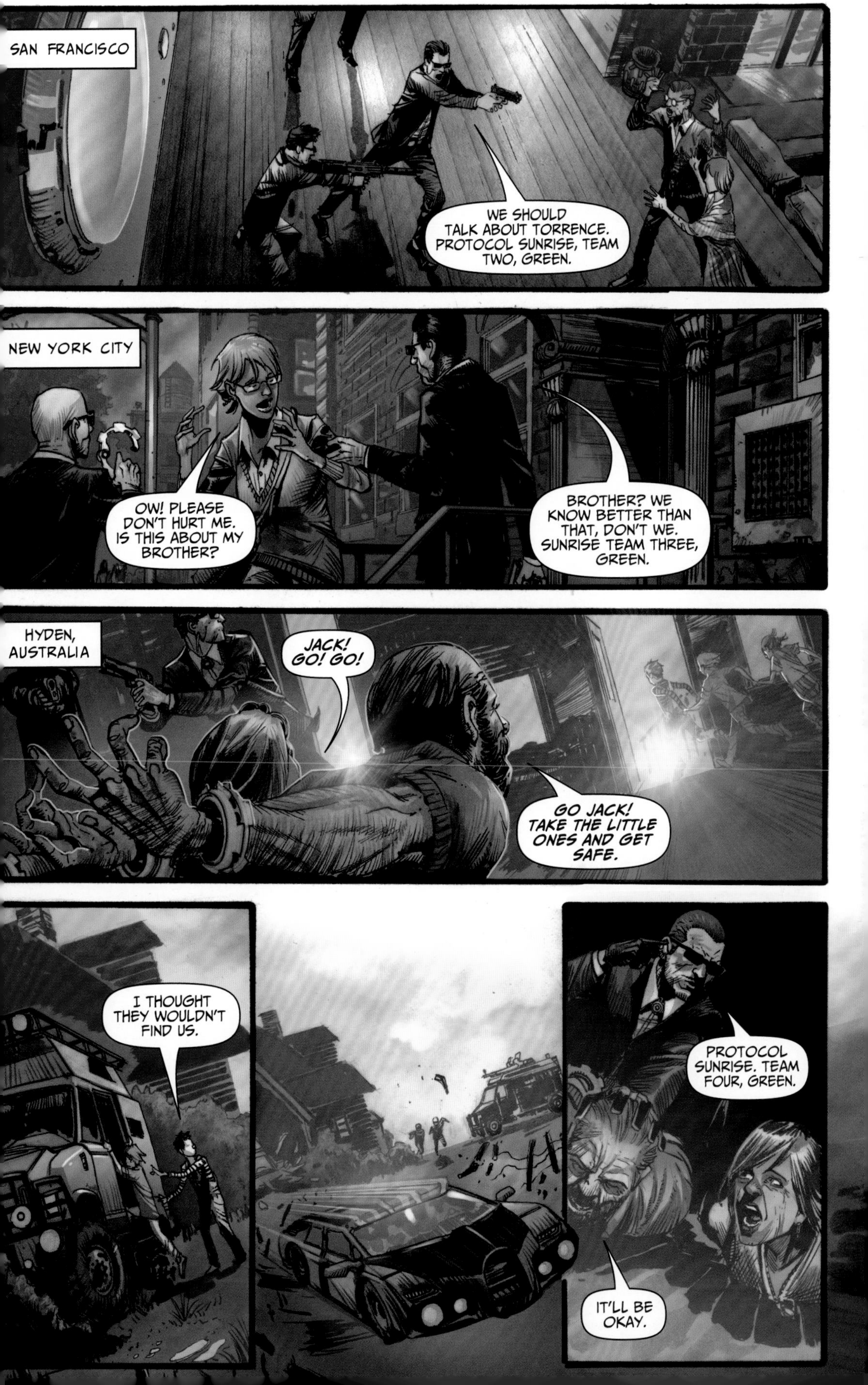
SAN FRANCISCO
WE SHOULD TALK ABOUT TORRENCE. PROTOCOL SUNRISE, TEAM TWO, GREEN.
NEW YORK CITY
OW! PLEASE DON'T HURT ME. IS THIS ABOUT MY BROTHER?
BROTHER? WE KNOW BETTER THAN THAT, DON'T WE. SUNRISE TEAM THREE, GREEN.
HYDEN, AUSTRALIA
JACK! GO! GO!
GO JACK! TAKE THE LITTLE ONES AND GET SAFE.
I THOUGHT THEY WOULDN'T FIND US.
PROTOCOL SUNRISE. TEAM FOUR, GREEN.
IT'LL BE OKAY.

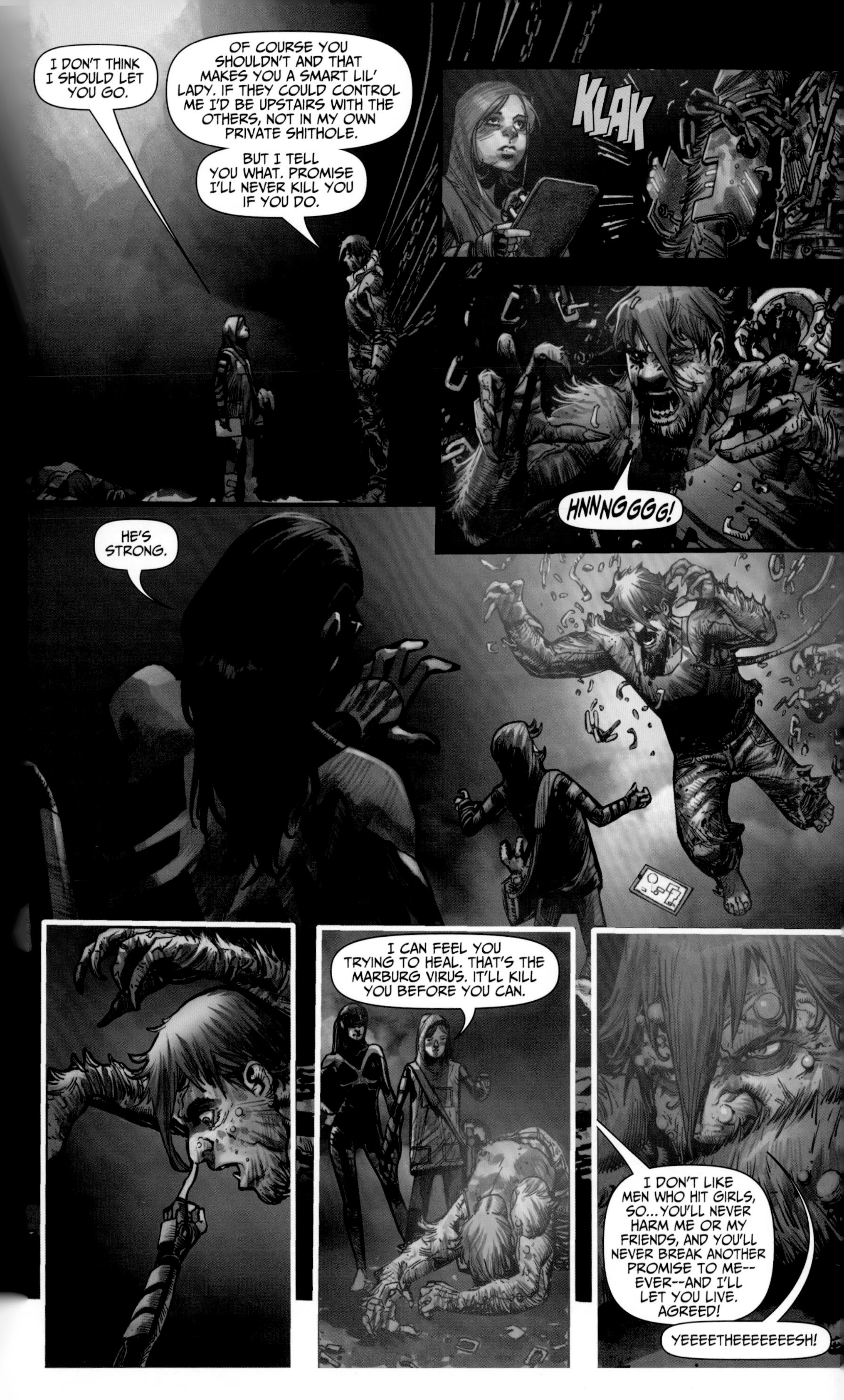
I DON'T THINK I SHOULD LET YOU GO.
OF COURSE YOU SHOULDN'T AND THAT MAKES YOU A SMART LIL' LADY. IF THEY COULD CONTROL ME I'D BE UPSTAIRS WITH THE OTHERS, NOT IN MY OWN PRIVATE SHITHOLE.
BUT I TELL YOU WHAT. PROMISE I'LL NEVER KILL YOU IF YOU DO.
KLAK
HNNNGGGG!
HE'S STRONG.
I CAN FEEL YOU TRYING TO HEAL. THAT'S THE MARBURG VIRUS. IT'LL KILL YOU BEFORE YOU CAN.
I DON'T LIKE MEN WHO HIT GIRLS, SO...YOU'LL NEVER HARM ME OR MY FRIENDS, AND YOU'LL NEVER BREAK ANOTHER PROMISE TO ME--EVER--AND I'LL LET YOU LIVE. AGREED!
YEEEETHEEEEEEESH!

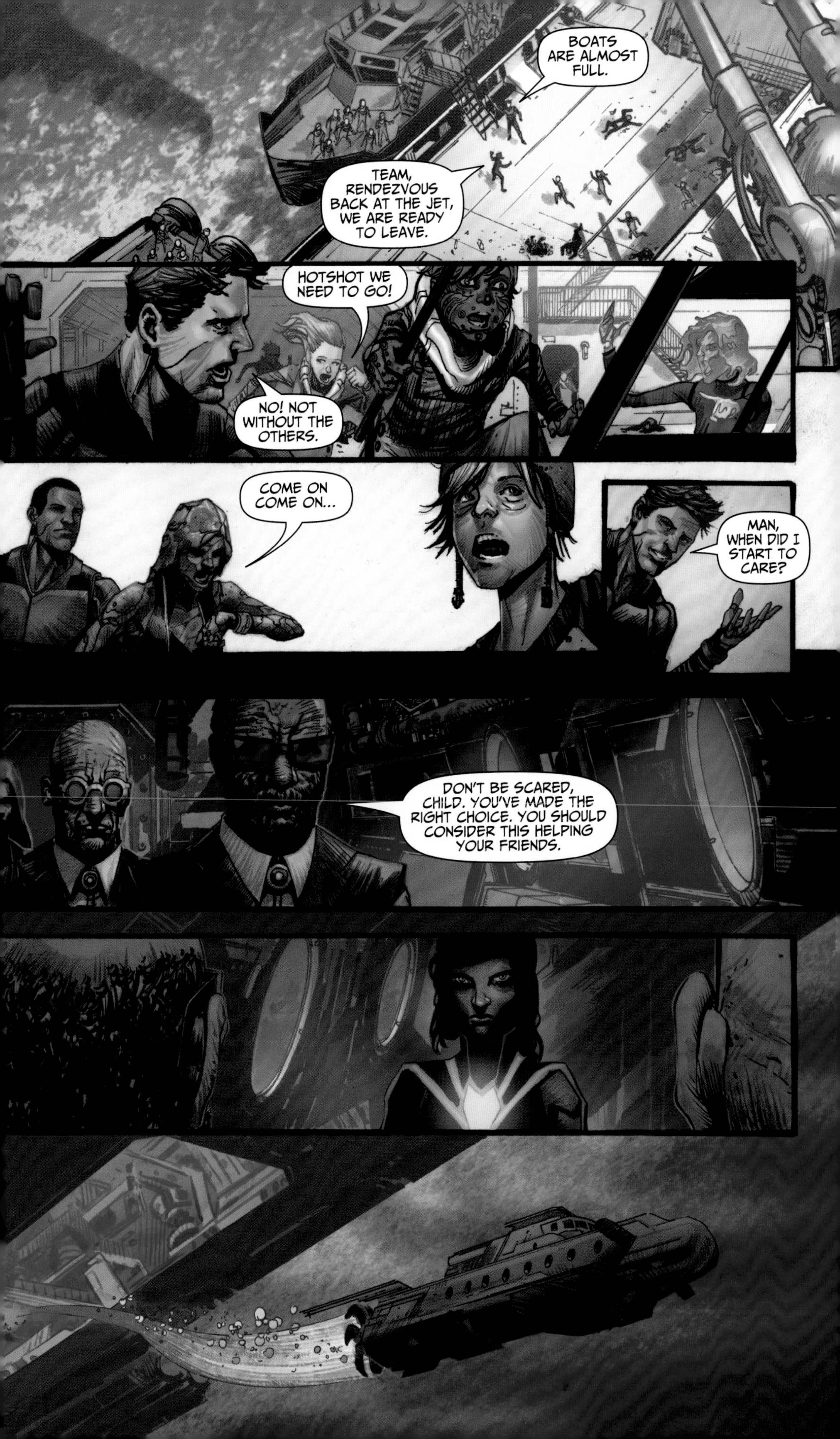
BOATS ARE ALMOST FULL.
TEAM, RENDEZVOUS BACK AT THE JET, WE ARE READY TO LEAVE.
HOTSHOT WE NEED TO GO!
NO! NOT WITHOUT THE OTHERS.
COME ON COME ON...
MAN, WHEN DID I START TO CARE?
DON'T BE SCARED, CHILD. YOU'VE MADE THE RIGHT CHOICE. YOU SHOULD CONSIDER THIS HELPING YOUR FRIENDS.

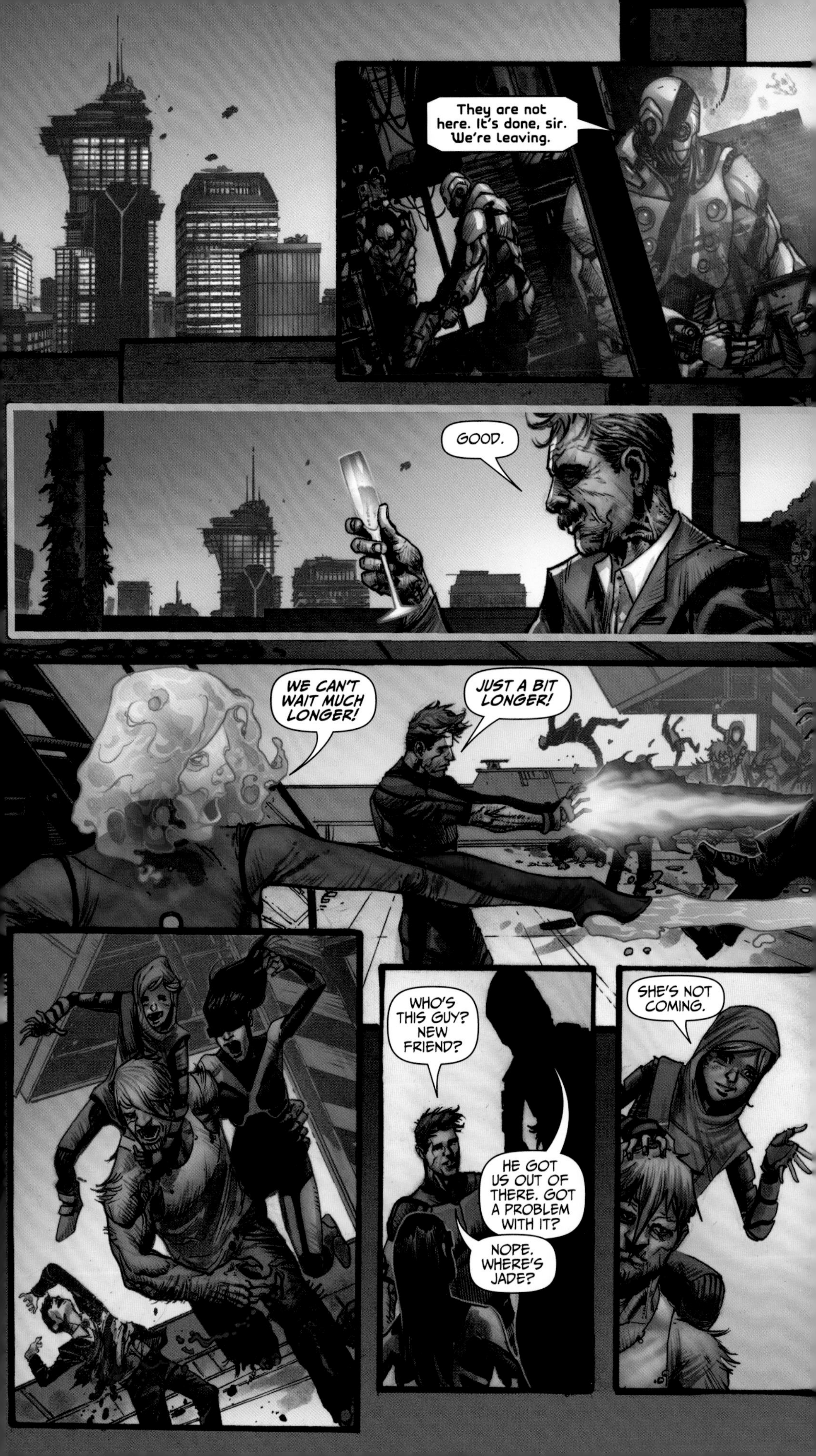
They are not here. It's done, sir. We're leaving.
GOOD.
WE CAN'T WAIT MUCH LONGER!
JUST A BIT LONGER!
WHO'S THIS GUY? NEW FRIEND?
HE GOT US OUT OF THERE. GOT A PROBLEM WITH IT?
NOPE. WHERE'S JADE?
SHE'S NOT COMING.

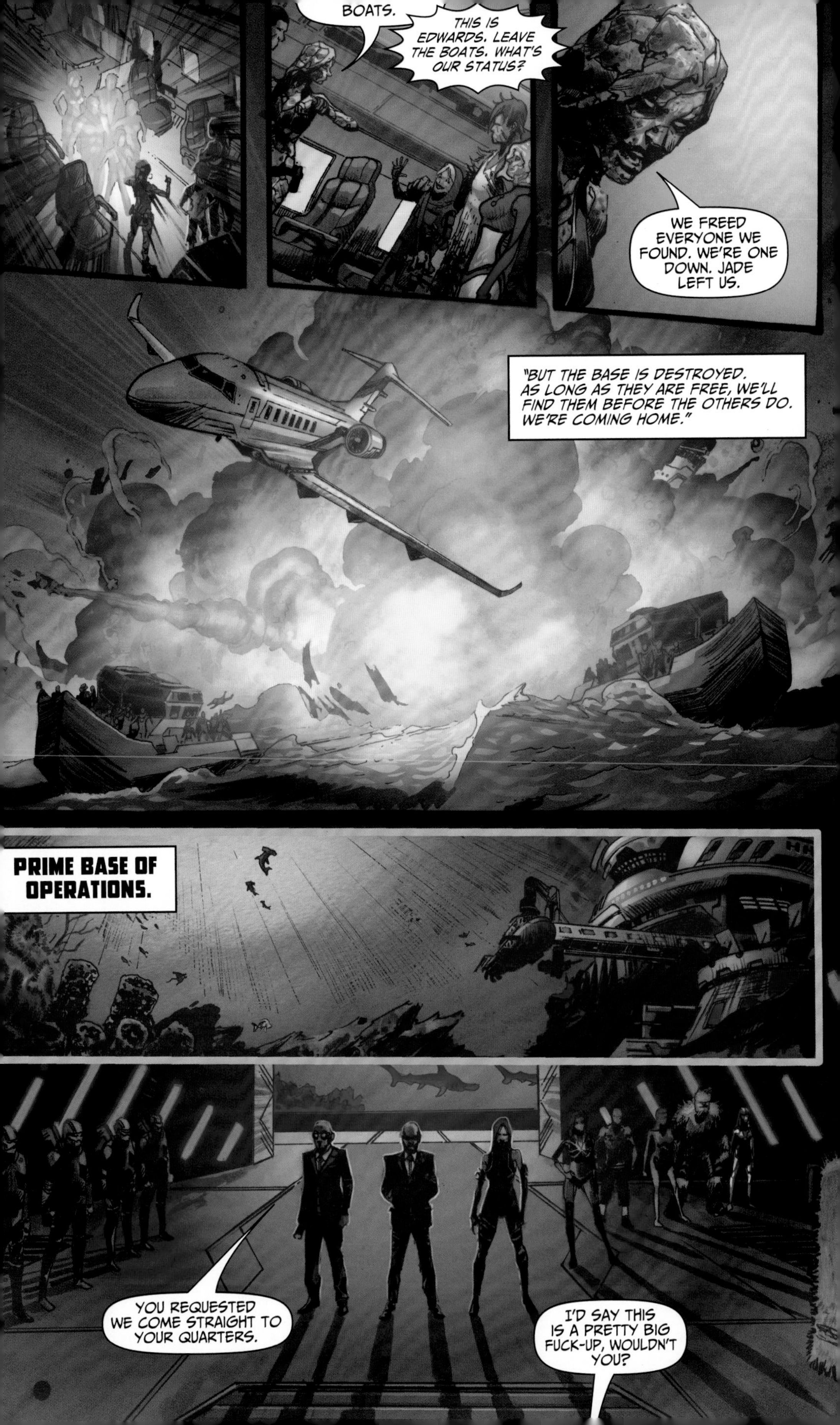
BOATS.
THIS IS EDWARDS. LEAVE THE BOATS. WHAT'S OUR STATUS?
WE FREED EVERYONE WE FOUND. WE'RE ONE DOWN. JADE LEFT US.
"BUT THE BASE IS DESTROYED. AS LONG AS THEY ARE FREE, WE'LL FIND THEM BEFORE THE OTHERS DO. WE'RE COMING HOME."
PRIME BASE OF OPERATIONS.
YOU REQUESTED WE COME STRAIGHT TO YOUR QUARTERS.
I'D SAY THIS IS A PRETTY BIG FUCK-UP, WOULDN'T YOU?

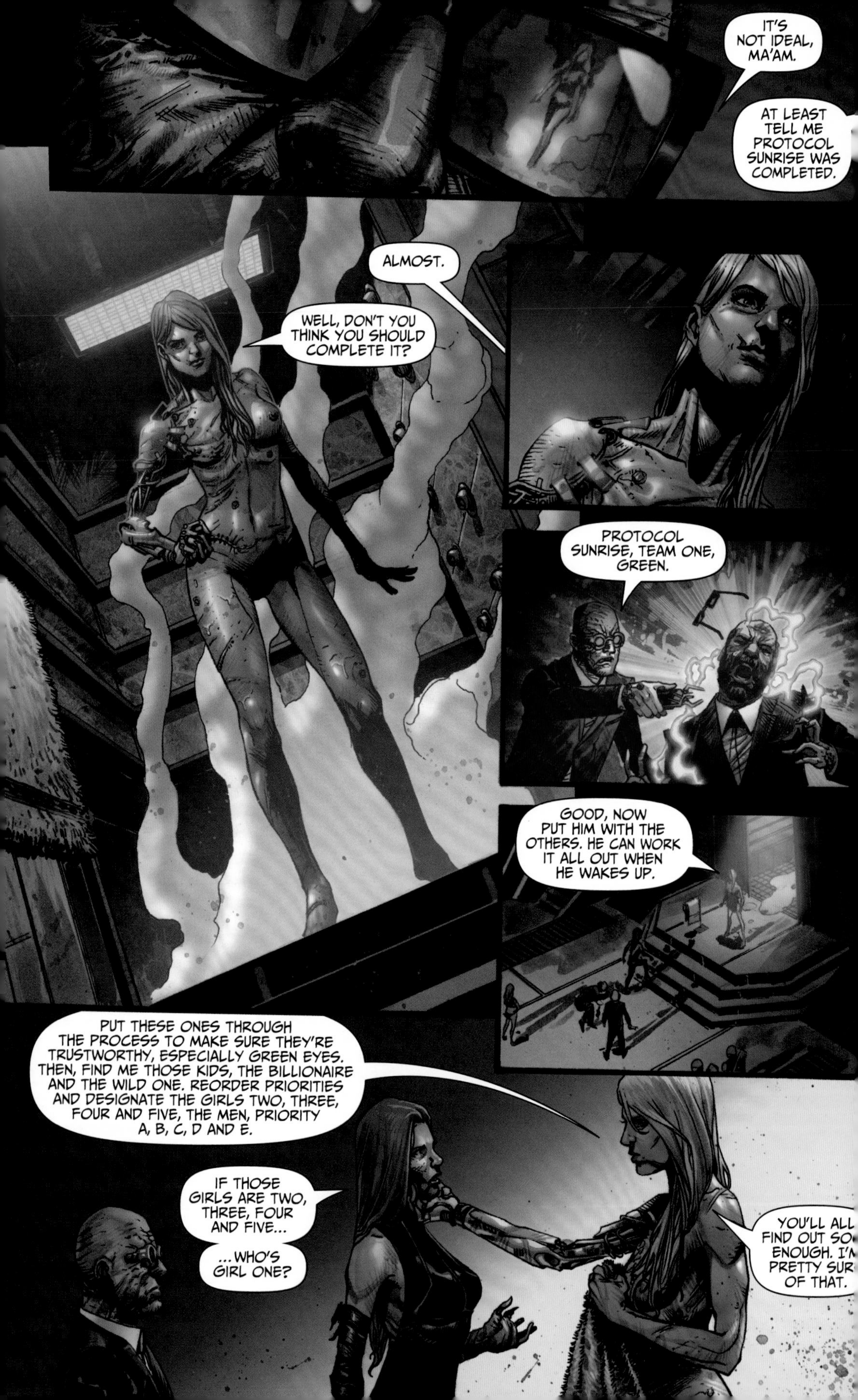
IT'S NOT IDEAL, MA'AM.
AT LEAST TELL ME PROTOCOL SUNRISE WAS COMPLETED.
ALMOST.
WELL, DON'T YOU THINK YOU SHOULD COMPLETE IT?
PROTOCOL SUNRISE, TEAM ONE, GREEN.
GOOD, NOW PUT HIM WITH THE OTHERS. HE CAN WORK IT ALL OUT WHEN HE WAKES UP.
PUT THESE ONES THROUGH THE PROCESS TO MAKE SURE THEY'RE TRUSTWORTHY, ESPECIALLY GREEN EYES. THEN, FIND ME THOSE KIDS, THE BILLIONAIRE AND THE WILD ONE. REORDER PRIORITIES AND DESIGNATE THE GIRLS TWO, THREE, FOUR AND FIVE, THE MEN, PRIORITY A, B, C, D AND E.
IF THOSE GIRLS ARE TWO, THREE, FOUR AND FIVE...
...WHO'S GIRL ONE?

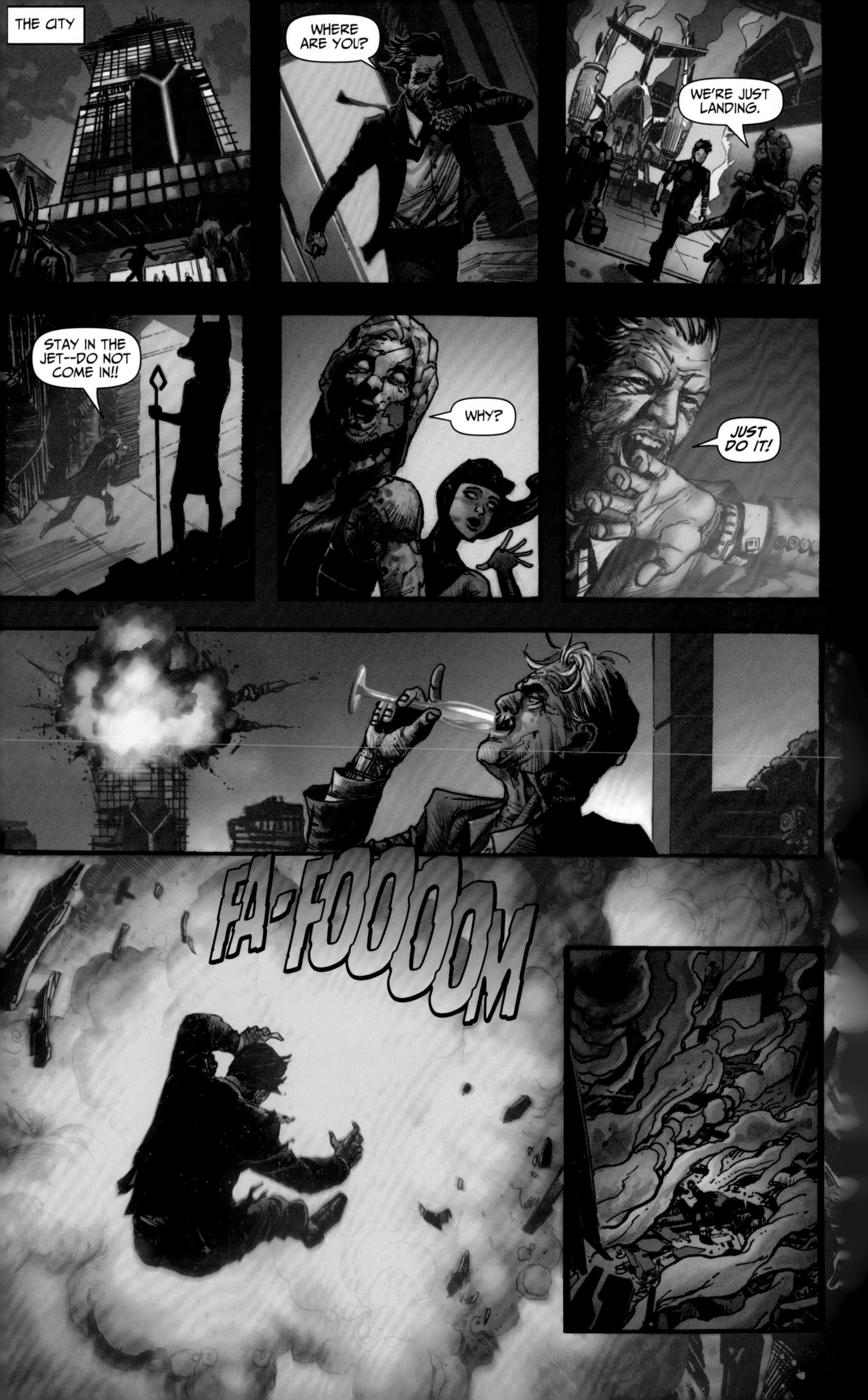
THE CITY
WHERE ARE YOU?
WE'RE JUST LANDING.
STAY IN THE JET--DO NOT COME IN!!
WHY?
JUST DO IT!
FA-FOOOOM

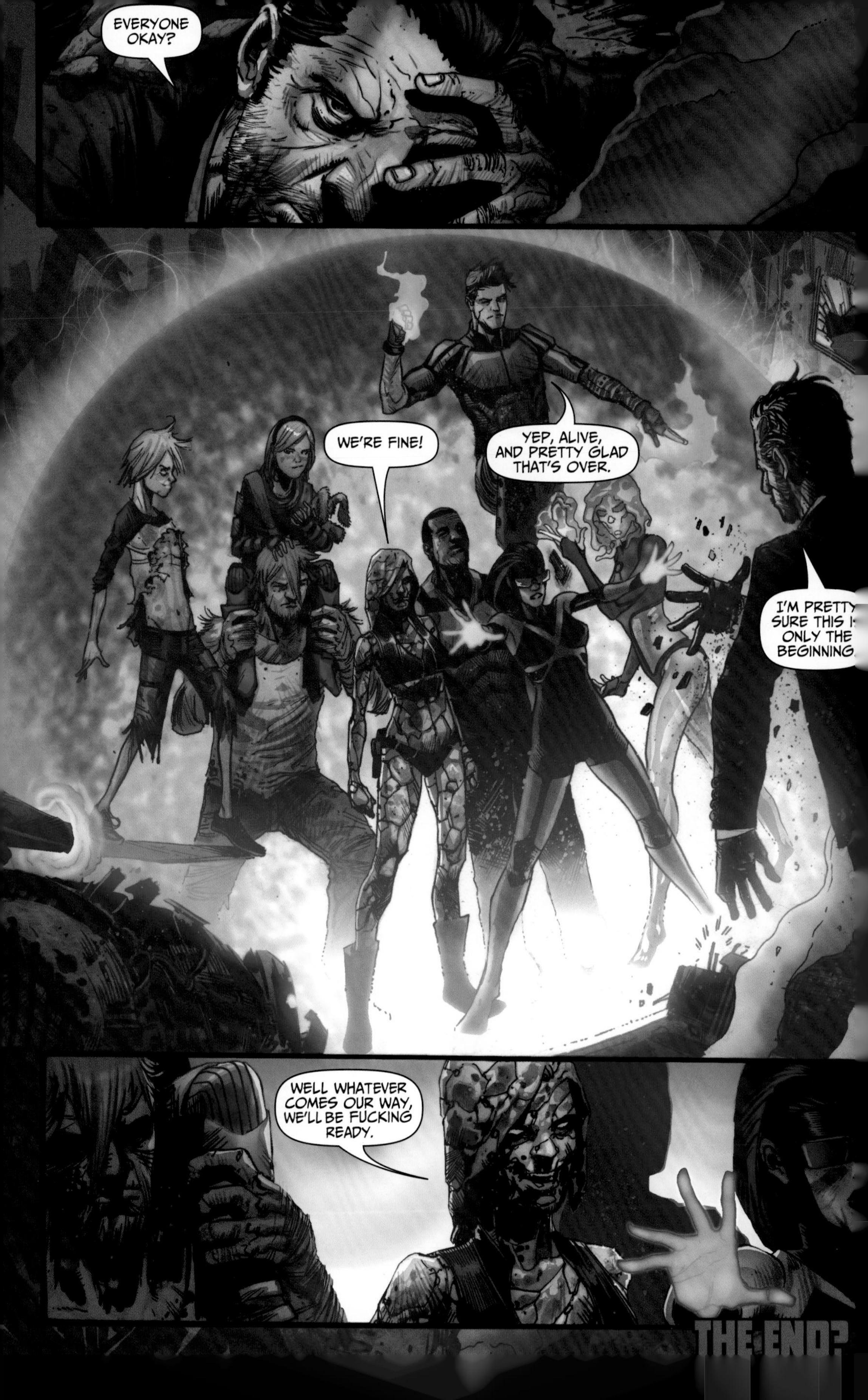
EVERYONE OKAY?
WE'RE FINE!
YEP, ALIVE, AND PRETTY GLAD THAT'S OVER.
I'M PRETTY SURE THIS I ONLY THE BEGINNING.
WELL WHATEVER COMES OUR WAY, WE'LL BE FUCKING READY.
THE END?

COVER GALLERY

COVER A
ART BY
JOSHUA CASSARA
COLORS BY
LUIS GUERRERO

COVER B
ART BY
ELENA
CASAGRANDE

COVER C
FP UK EXCLUSIVE
ART BY
JOSHUA CASSARA
& HI-FI

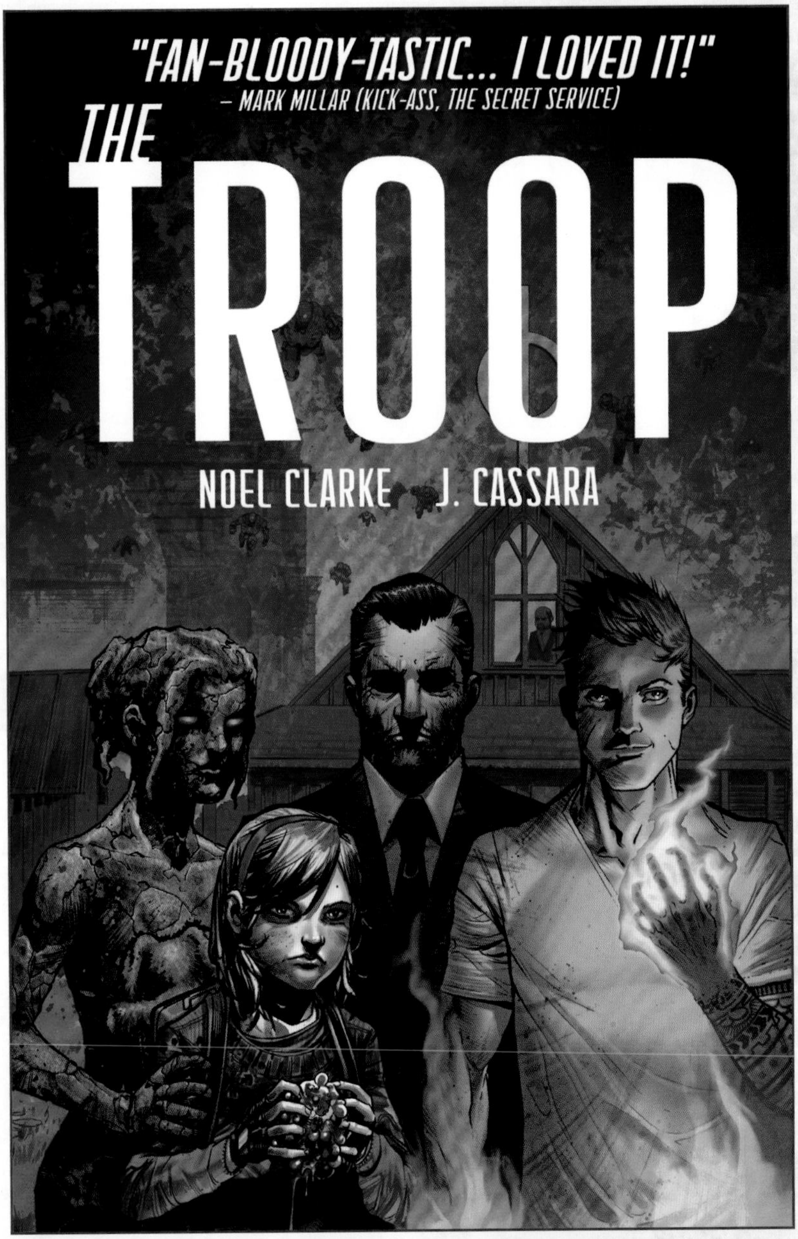
"FAN-BLOODY-TASTIC... I LOVED IT!"
– MARK MILLAR (KICK-ASS, THE SECRET SERVICE)
THE TROOP
NOEL CLARKE J. CASSARA

A

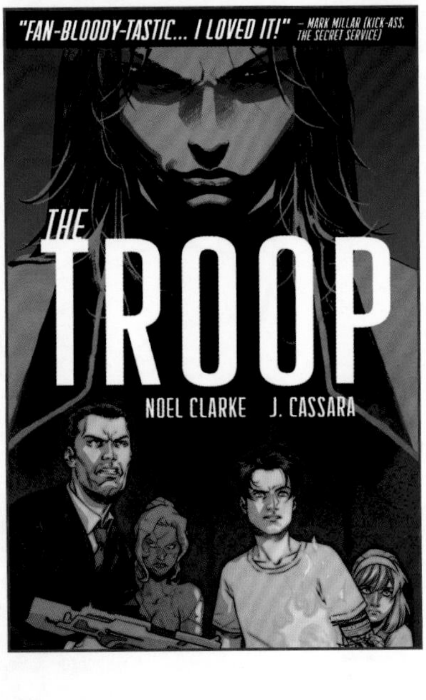
"FAN-BLOODY-TASTIC... I LOVED IT!" – MARK MILLAR (KICK-ASS, THE SECRET SERVICE)
THE TROOP
NOEL CLARKE J. CASSARA

B

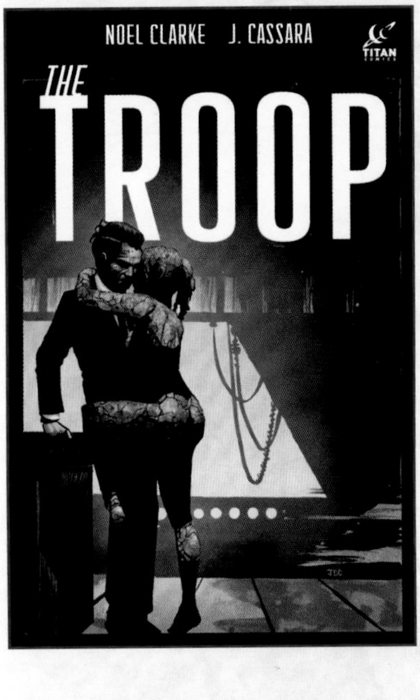
NOEL CLARKE J. CASSARA
TITAN
THE TROOP

C

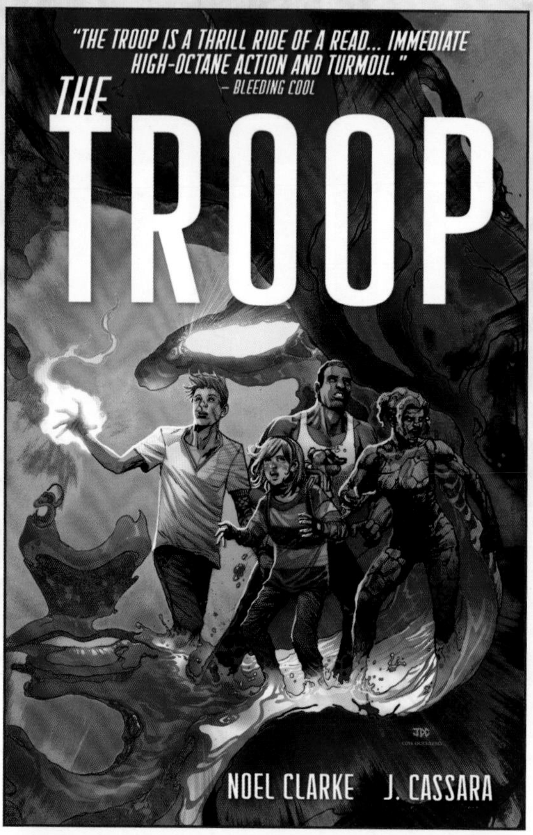
"THE TROOP IS A THRILL RIDE OF A READ... IMMEDIATE HIGH-OCTANE ACTION AND TURMOIL."
– BLEEDING COOL
THE TROOP
NOEL CLARKE J. CASSARA

A

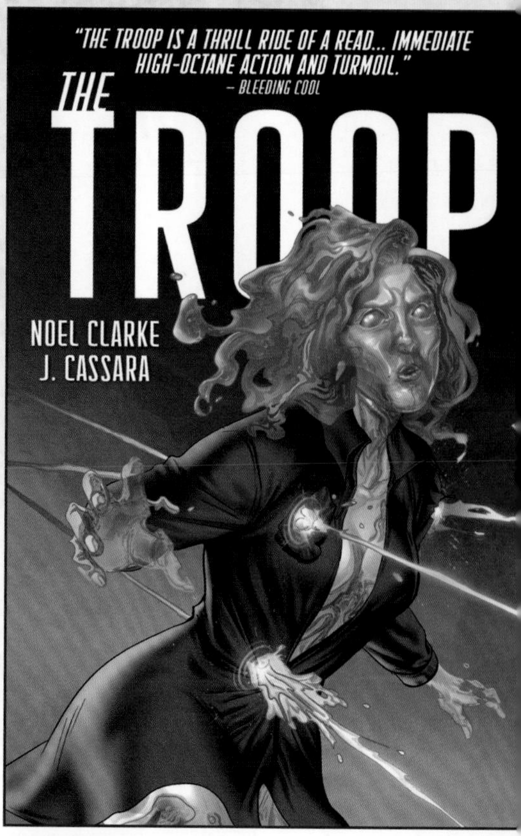
"THE TROOP IS A THRILL RIDE OF A READ... IMMEDIATE HIGH-OCTANE ACTION AND TURMOIL."
– BLEEDING COOL
THE TROOP
NOEL CLARKE
J. CASSARA

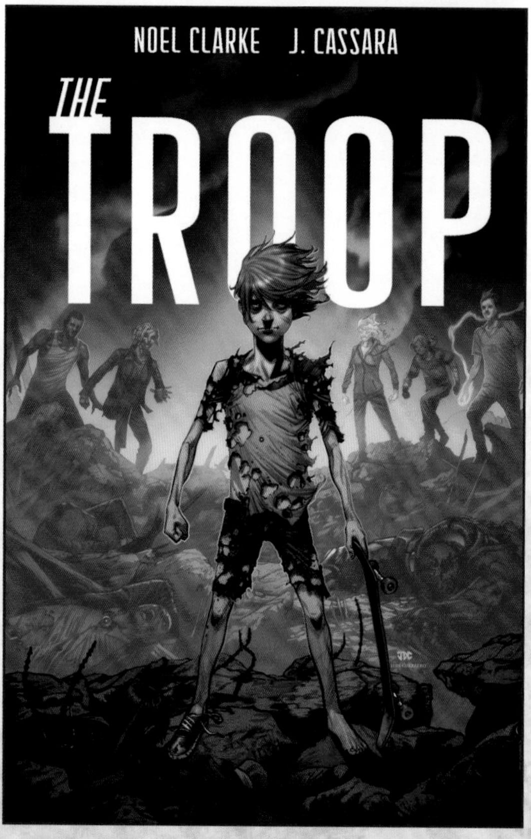
NOEL CLARKE J. CASSARA
THE TROOP

C

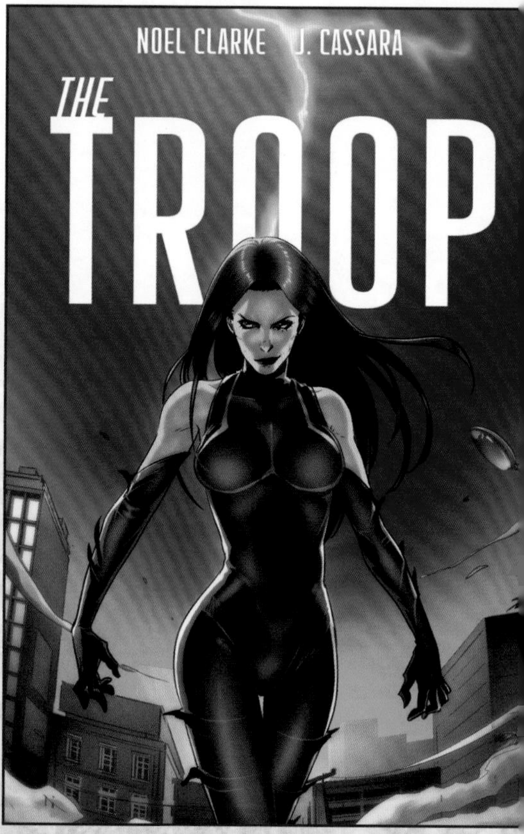
NOEL CLARKE J. CASSARA
THE TROOP

A - ISSUE 2
COVER A ART BY JOSHUA CASSARA
COLORS BY LUIS GUERRERO

B - ISSUE 2
COVER B ART BY YISHAN LI
COLORS BY LUIS GUERRERO

C - ISSUE 3
COVER A ART BY JOSHUA CASSARA
COLORS BY LUIS GUERRERO

D - ISSUE 3
COVER B ART BY YISHAN L
COLORS BY LUIS GUERRE

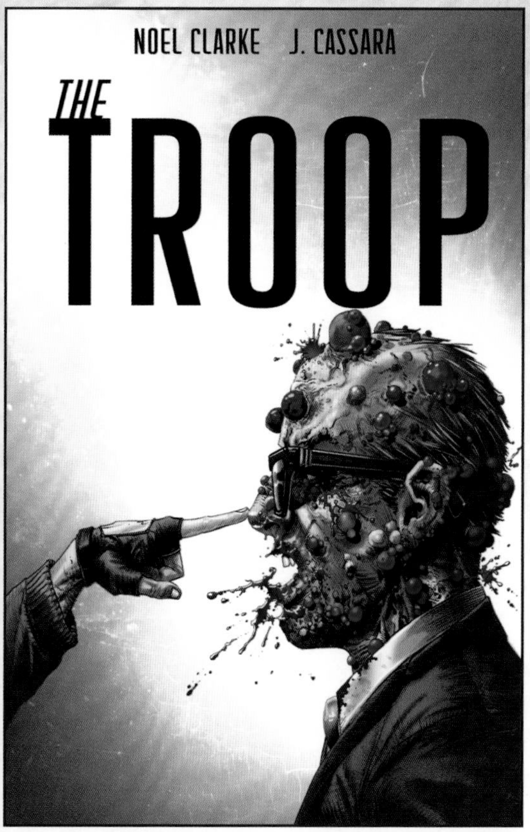
NOEL CLARKE J. CASSARA
THE
TROOP

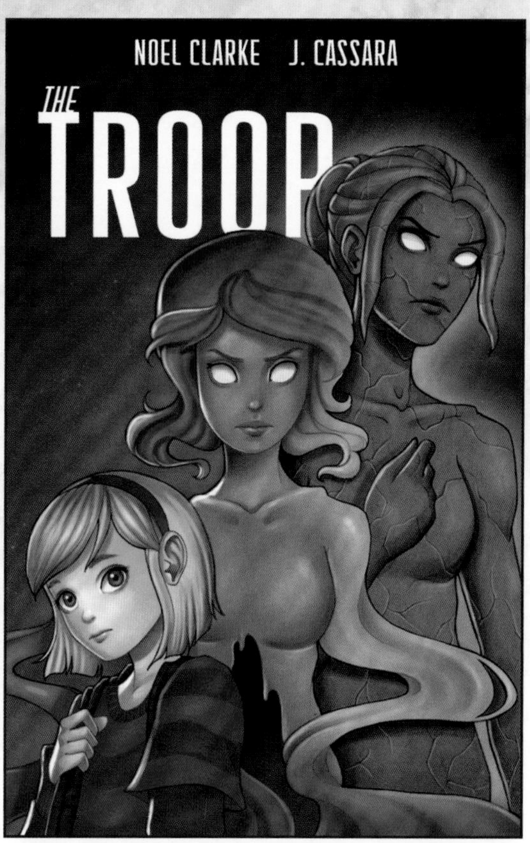
NOEL CLARKE J. CASSARA
THE
TROOP

F

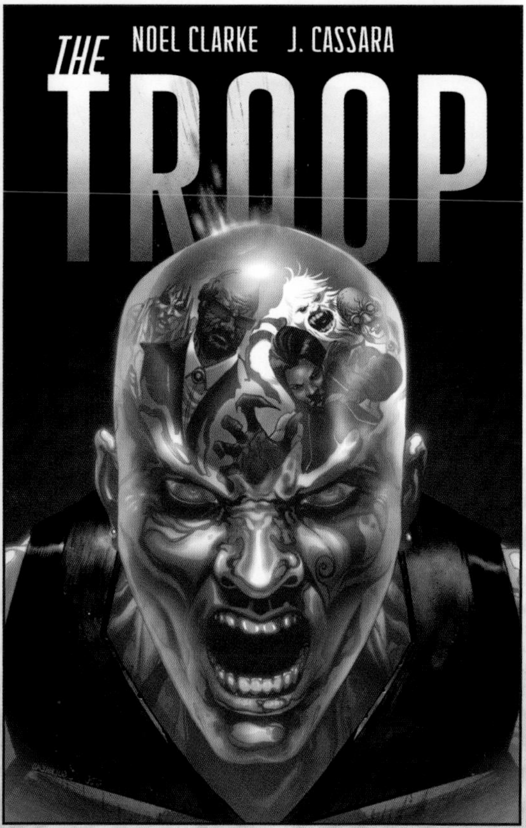
NOEL CLARKE J. CASSARA
THE
TROOP

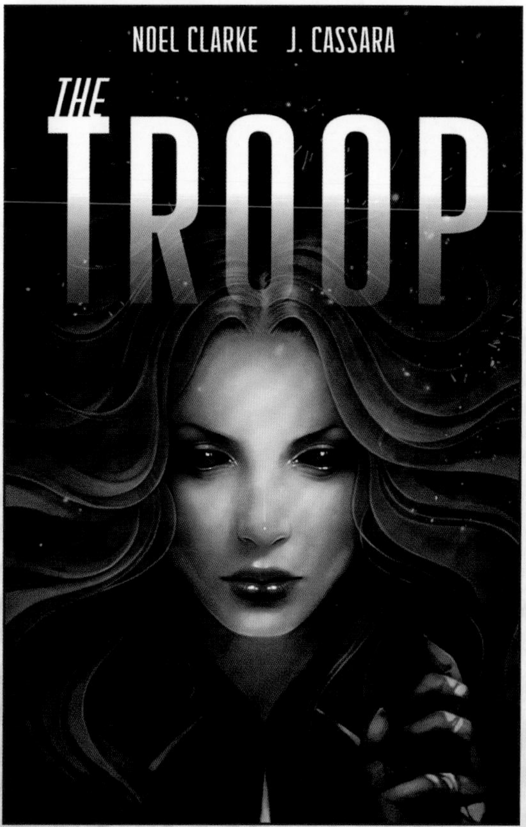
NOEL CLARKE J. CASSARA
THE
TROOP

H

E - ISSUE 4
COVER A ART BY JOSHUA CASSARA
COLORS BY LUIS GUERRERO

F - ISSUE 4
COVER B
ART BY CHRISSIE ZULLO

G - ISSUE 5
COVER A ART BY JOSHUA CASSARA
COLORS BY LUIS GUERRERO

H - ISSUE 5
COVER B
ART BY ANNA DITTMANN

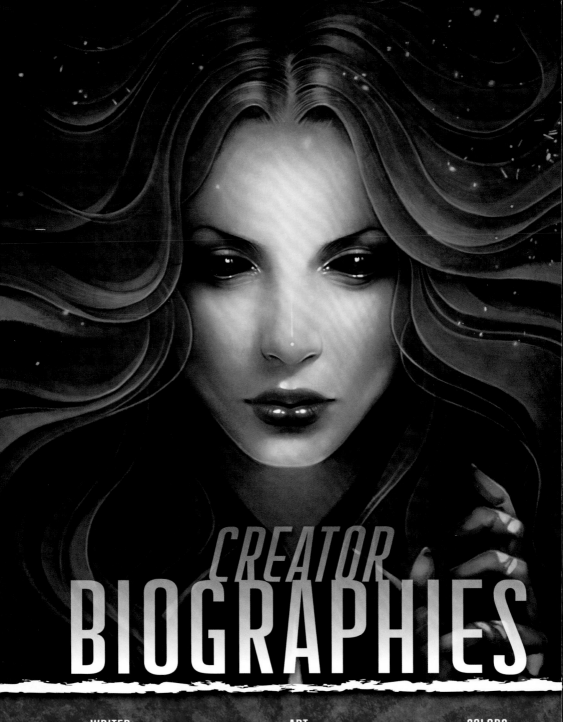

CREATOR BIOGRAPHIES

WRITER
NOEL CLARKE

Noel Clarke is an award-winning actor, screenwriter, director, and comic book writer from London. Best known for his roles in *Doctor Who* and *Star Trek Into Darkness*, Clarke also appeared in and wrote the screenplay for *Kidulthood*, and wrote, directed, and starred in its sequel, *Adulthood*. He continues to act, write, and direct!

ART
JOSHUA CASSARA

The Troop is Joshua's first longform comics work. He recently made his Marvel debut with Al Ewing on *New Avengers*, and has provided covers for *Doctor Who* and *Rivers of London*. His next comics series sees him teeming with basketballer and polymath Kareem Abdul-Jabbar for *Mycroft Holmes and the Apocalypse Handbook*.

COLORS
LUIS GUERRERO

A native of Mexico and a relatively newcomer to comics, Luis's earlier published work was for Big Dog Ink's 2012 series, *Ursa Minor*. Since then he has been a regular fixture at Titan Comics, coloring interiors and covers for a number of series – including *Rivers of London, Doctor Who, Mycroft Holmes,* and *Man Plus.*